IN THE NIGHT SEASON

IN THE NIGHT SEASON

A NOVEL

RICHARD BAUSCH

HarperPerennial

A Division of HarperCollins*Publishers*

The Library of Congress has catalogued the hardcover edition as follows:

Bausch, Richard, 1945–
    In the night season : a novel / by Richard Bausch. — 1st ed.
       p. cm.
    ISBN 0-06-018735-2
    I. Title.
  PS3552.A84615 1998
  813'.54—dc21   97-43690

ISBN 0-06-093030-6 (pbk.)

99 00 01 02 03 ❖ RRD 10 9 8 7 6 5 4 3 2

Again, for Karen

I am grateful to Harold Stusnick and Dave Brewer for important technical advice on the new wave of advancements regarding computer chips. William Kotzwinkle helped immensely, by sending me books. George Garrett provided the kind of bedrock advice one is seldom fortunate enough to get from any quarter. Cary and Karen Kimble provided light and laughter. And Nicola C. Neil, at Fauquier National Bank, was very helpful in showing me some of the ramifications of bulk storage in a bank. I am also the beneficiary, once again, of the kindness, graciousness, and wit of R. S. Jones. Finally, Karen printed out the manuscript and proofread it one rainy night in June, while I was miles away playing guitar, badly, in a bar. That is the sort of loving that ought to be reported in print.

R. B.

Terrors are turned upon me: they pursue my soul as the wind: and my welfare passeth away as a cloud. And now my soul is poured out upon me; the days of affliction have taken hold upon me, my bones are pierced in me in the night season: and my sinews take no rest.

Job 30: 15-17

PART ONE

THE HOUR OF
BRIGHTEST AFTERNOON

DURING THE FALL, A GROUP CALL-ing itself the Virginia Front began a hate campaign aimed at what might accurately, if with dismay, be called the traditional targets for such things at the end of the American century. The campaign took the form of letters and circulars, threats, mostly, the product of desktop publishing, with crude color graphics—doubtless the work, said the commonwealth attorney, of a coterie of nutcases with a computer, shaved heads, and a book. The book, predictably enough, was *Mein Kampf.* The circulars began arriving on the desks of various county officials and in the regular mail of some citizens, including several people the Front evidently considered worth addressing directly—people whose publicly stated opinions or whose behavior the group found wanting in terms of their very specific and obvious agenda.

One of these was Edward Bishop, a TV and VCR repairman who made house calls in the county and kept a small workshop in his home, an old farmhouse on five acres of grass and trees above Steel Run Creek. Mr. Bishop had made no public statements, and he was not a public figure, really, though almost everyone in Fauquier

County knew him. His family went all the way back to the eighteenth century in this part of Virginia, though their position, back then, and on into the middle of the nineteenth century, was understood in law and in the minds of almost everyone as being no more or less than property—chattel, salable goods, as Mr. Bishop would occasionally put it, when his long family history came up. "This is, after all," he would say, "a former slave state."

He described himself as a black American. He had served in Vietnam and been wounded—there was a piece of shrapnel still lodged in the bone of his left leg, just above the ankle—and he had a Purple Heart, a Bronze Star for valor. He was fifty-six years old, enjoyed a good business, and was trusted by a large clientele. Indeed, he was taken for granted by a lot of people: a quiet man, even a loner of sorts, who went his own way. A man with the self-sufficiency and the slightly eccentric attitude of someone used to falling back on his own resources.

He had recently formed a friendship with the young white woman who lived in a neighboring house, perhaps six hundred yards away down Steel Run Creek Road. He walked over there in the late afternoons, during the week, to spend time with her eleven-year-old son—actually, to provide adult supervision for the boy, who was unused to coming home to an empty house. When she arrived from her job teaching in town, Mr. Bishop sometimes stayed to dinner. It was often well after dark before he made his way back down the road to his own house. He had not spoken about this arrangement with many people, other than the clerk at the local Country Store, and his housekeeper, who happened also to be white.

But someone had seen him, or the boy had said something at his school, and word had got out to the Virginia Front.

And one morning in late November, Mr. Bishop found in his mailbox a message in boldface type, on the letterhead of the organization, written over an ugly graphic of a hanging black man with bugged-out eyes and a very red tongue:

Watch your step with the white woman. We are.

It was not signed, nor had it been mailed. Someone had come by and put it there, folded like a business letter. He stood gazing at it, in the chill of the morning, and then looked up and down the road. The innocent countryside seemed abruptly almost alien to him, as though it contained some element of the poison he held in his hand. He folded it back and put it in his pocket. He intended to ignore it. But it troubled him; it made him feel as though some border of his privacy had been violated, and later in the day he drove over to the county police headquarters. He spoke to a detective named Shaw, a thin, graying man, perhaps forty-five, with tired, sad eyes and a manner that seemed rather tentative. They sat in a warm, too-tidy office, while sunny wind shook the windows. People rushed around in the street below, collars turned up against the cold. Edward Bishop thought about all the comfortable assumptions of safety. A big bank of dark clouds was moving in from the west. It looked like the encroachment of trouble to him.

"Do you think this is a real threat?" Shaw said, rubbing the flesh on either side of his nose. Bishop noted that there were thin forking veins in the red cheeks. It was a rough, hard-living face which, in the circumstances, did nothing to reassure him. He wished for someone younger.

"Of course it's a real threat," he said. "I feel threatened. That makes it a threat. I think somebody must be watching me. I haven't been talking to anybody, or said anything. I watch the lady's kid for her in the afternoons. I'm her neighbor. She's run up on some bad luck, and I've been helping her out."

The detective folded his hands on the desk. "It wouldn't be anybody's business if there *was* more to it than that, Mr. Bishop."

"Yeah, but there isn't. Her husband died in February. He didn't leave any insurance and she had to go back to work. The kid's started messing up in school."

"I'm saying this isn't anybody's business but yours, sir."

"I know that. You don't need to tell me that. I'm just telling *you* what the situation is. Somebody thinks it's *their* business. And I can't figure out how in the hell these people know I'm spending any time over there unless they're watching me."

"Is the boy okay with you coming over?"

"I think so. He seems all right about it. If he isn't he's fooled me good."

"And there's nobody else—"

"My housekeeper. I've been carrying her, though. She knows I can't really use her, and I've been paying her anyway. She comes in twice a week. She needs the money—there's no motive for her. It has to be that somebody's watching me."

"You sure it's not her they're referring to in this?"

"I guess it could be."

"You go around to people's houses, right?"

Mr. Bishop felt a surge of impatient anger at the soft-spoken policeman. "I've lived here all my life. Whoever this is came to my house. I'd like to know what the hell is going on."

"I'm really sorry about it," Shaw said. "We're trying to track the thing down. To tell you the truth, I think it might be some high school kids playing ugly little games."

Another man entered the room—younger. Tall and long-faced and black. He offered his hand, and Detective Shaw introduced him as Officer Bell.

"Pleased," Bishop said to him.

"I was just telling Mr. Bishop that we think this Virginia Front stuff might be kids playing games."

"What're you basing that on?" Bishop looked from one to the other of them.

"Just a guess, really," Shaw said. "The intermittent nature of their communications. Some of the language."

"You think somebody the boy knows—he's in middle school."

"Could be."

"Well, now what do I do?"

"I'll have a car swing by your place a couple times a day for a few days. There's usually somebody out that way anyhow. Maybe we'll stumble onto something. But these kind of things—these types don't usually *act* on their threats."

"I'm going to tell you guys something," Edward Bishop said. "I mean to protect myself and my home. You understand what I'm saying?"

"Yes," Shaw said. "I understand you perfectly. Could be you'll never hear any more from this. But let me keep it, and we'll see what we can come up with."

"We'll get to the bottom of it eventually," Officer Bell said.

"Thank you," Bishop told them.

They shook hands, and Bishop made his way back home with a sense that an individual couldn't really hope for much from the authorities in a situation like this.

He watched through most of the following morning for a police car, and when one came by, slow, he felt a little better. Apparently, Shaw was a man you could depend on to keep his word. But that afternoon, walking across the field to the neighboring house, he had the feeling he was being watched by unfriendly eyes; the dark line of trees on the other end of the field was threatening now. He hated the change.

The boy was already home and had gone up in the attic. It took him a long time to make his way down to the door.

"You know your mama doesn't want you hanging out up in that attic," Bishop told him. "And you know I'm coming. How about meeting me at the door once?"

"A cop came to talk to me today, at school."

Bishop followed him into the kitchen. "What did he say?"

"He asked how many people I've talked to about you. Who I've talked to."

Bishop waited a moment. The boy had opened the refrigerator, got out a carton of milk, and was pouring it. His dark hair hung down over his eyes. "What did you say?" Bishop asked him.

"I told him the truth. I've told a lot of people about you."

"You want to tell *me* about it?"

The boy, whose name was Jason, looked up at him, pushed the hair back from his brow. "Well, I have. I've told a lot of people that you come over here to watch me so I don't get in trouble."

"And you've said I'm black?"

Now, the boy concentrated on the milk. "I guess so."

"How come?"

He was drinking the milk.

"How come, Jason?"

"Well, people said my mom would fall in love with you and you'd be my father. I just said you were older. And the—and the rest of it came out."

Bishop could imagine the conversation. It filled him with a sense of weariness. "I'm not trying to hide my color from anybody, son."

"Well, that's how it came out."

It occurred to Bishop that in fact he had never really been given any clear sign that Jason liked or disliked the arrangement; he seemed merely to accept it, as though it were weather, something he lived in and over which he had no control. "Do you not like it that I come over here to look in on you?"

"I didn't say I don't like it."

"But you don't." Bishop had an image of Jason walking over to his mailbox with the folded piece of paper in his coat pocket. No, this was not that kind of boy. This boy was suffering and had been sullen at times with that, but he was not mean, and Bishop remembered remarking to himself that Jason didn't seem afflicted with the usual failure to see through Bishop's color to Bishop himself. He had felt that they were nearly friends. "It's okay if you don't," he went on. "It is, after all, supervision. It's natural to resent it."

"I don't resent it," Jason said.

"I just meant I'd understand if you did."

"I don't." He appeared near crying now.

"All right, well—forget it," Bishop said.

"What happened?" Jason wanted to know.

"Nothing for you to worry about," Bishop told him. "Really."

But there were two more communications from the Virginia Front over the next week, and Bishop grew more worried; his work began to suffer. He kept hearing sounds. He was beginning to distrust his imagination. He kept going to the windows to look out.

Nights were long and troubled. He slept poorly.

A family of wild cats lived under the porch. Sometimes they chased each other and ran across the railing, and occasionally they knocked something over. He had tolerated their presence because they kept field mice away. But perhaps he would have to do something about them now. They kept waking him; they reminded him. The night after he'd got the last message he spent sitting in the wing chair downstairs in his living room, a deer rifle across his lap, waiting for light to come to the windows. *I know just about every soul here, black and white. And they know me.* The silence, the quiet of himself in the house alone, occupied his mind. It was absurd. This was his home. He tried going about his business, getting through the day's tasks. But there was the police car gliding by in the mornings, slowing to a near-stop, then going on. And he couldn't shake the sense of alarm that rose in him with each sound of the house, his own house. When he called Detective Shaw, he got the answering machine. He left messages, but Shaw never called back. And one morning, early the following week, there was another letter in the mailbox, this one with a drawing of a man lying in blood; the man looked like one of those minstrel-show blacks—a white man in blackface:

> *Keep it up. We will repay. The woman & her son will burn with you.*

He phoned Shaw and read the newest communication into the answering machine. "I know you don't believe this is serious, Mr. Shaw. But it's got me fixed good now. I am carrying my rifle with me when I leave this house for any reason."

That afternoon, Shaw called him back. "Bring the thing in, if you don't mind, Mr. Bishop. I'd like to have a look at it."

He drove to the station, keeping one eye on the faces in the windshields of the oncoming traffic.

Detective Shaw stared at the paper for a long time, saying nothing.

"Well?" Bishop said. They were sitting in the tidy office again.

Shaw put the paper on his desk. "People are getting this kind of thing all over the county. It's ongoing, I'm afraid. And we don't have much to go on. I wish there was something I could tell you about it. Three churches have received threats of arson, and somebody painted a swastika on the door of another one."

"You don't have a single lead?"

"Nothing that's panned out, no."

"You'll keep the cars coming by?"

Shaw nodded. "Like I said, we make the rounds out that way anyhow."

"Thank you."

He took to watching for the cars. He moved his worktable to the window facing out onto the road and the mailbox, and there he sat working. And at the end of that week, when he went over to the next-door house and waited for the boy's mother to come in, he determined to speak to her about the situation. He stayed for dinner, helping with the preparations, and he waited until Jason went to bed. She sat in the glare of the kitchen light, one strand of hair falling over her forehead, a perfectly lovely young woman with a faintly haggard look about the mouth, the look of grief and overwork, and the striving to keep afloat in a sea of troubles.

He almost refrained from telling her.

"What is it?" she said. "Come on, Edward—something's bothering you."

"I've been getting hate mail," he said. "About coming over here."

It was clear from her expression that the boy had said nothing to her about it. She looked puzzled, then frightened.

"I got the first one more than a week ago."

"I don't understand." Her name was Nora. She was young enough to be his daughter. He sat down with an arthritic slowness across from her, at the small kitchen table.

"Somebody's decided to warn me away from you," he said. "Some—group."

"Who?"

"The police don't know who they are, yet. They call themselves the Virginia Front."

She sat there, considering. It hadn't quite sunk in yet, he could see. Finally, she stood and went to the window in the door, then turned and began wringing her hands. "Are you going to stop, then?"

"If you want me to," he said.

"I don't want you to."

"You're sure."

She walked over and put one hand on his shoulder. "You've been my friend."

"I am that."

Bishop, who was often lonely, had admitted to himself that in fact he was a little in love with her. He would never act on it. He had felt this way about dozens of women in his life, black and white, to whom he had doubtless seemed only a quiet, honest, friendly ally. He might have sought excuses to be in their company, but he had always been a gentleman. In the present case, he had decided that it would've been monstrous to reach out and put his arms around her as he wanted to, desired to. It was often an impulse stemming from the perception that this was what *she* longed for—not a sexual embrace, but simply for someone to hold her, to help stop the shaking. Most of the time, he felt fatherly toward her. That was true. His natural gentleness played tricks on him. But he thought about her all the time, and he had wondered at times if his feelings were not evident.

He went home that evening and once again was sleepless, and the cats made their ruckus on the porch. At one point he went out in the cold, in his stocking feet, and threw stones at the wooden lat-ticework bordering the crawl space, in hopes of scaring them away for a time. And when he was back inside again, he felt the need for sound—music, or the television. He was awake into the early hours, and he left lights burning through the night.

He had developed a nearly compulsive passion for order.

By three o'clock every day, things must be straight: everything in its place, all surfaces dusted, papers put away. A plastic covering lying over whatever he was working on. His house immaculate. He waited until then to look into his mailbox. There were no more communications from the Front. He still saw the police car go by in the mornings, and once he stood outside and waved it down. A stooped, angular, boylike young woman got out of the car and walked over to him.

"Anything I can help you with?" she said.

"I wondered if there was any progress finding out who's responsible for all the hate mail."

"Hate mail?" she said.

Three o'clock. There was something about the hour itself now: middle afternoon, the ripened day, the hour when he used to feel the pull of something to do, his visit to the neighboring house, and the pleasurable anticipation of it. That was gone, and he dreaded going over there. Dreaded it because she was more and more uncomfortable, had grown nervous and watchful, worried for her son. She had already lost her husband. Twice he asked if she would rather he stay home; twice she had refused to hear of it. But she was clearly relieved whenever he decided not to stay for dinner. He could read the gladness in her hazel eyes when, politely refusing her offer of something to eat, he got up to leave.

It was ridiculous for anyone—even a social paranoid neo-Nazi—to suppose that he meant anything to her but exactly what he had been: a helpful neighbor. At least in his own estimation of himself, he was not a young fifty-six. It always struck him as odd when people told him he looked younger. He felt seventy, he would say. There was constant misery in his back; there were aches in his shoulders, sharp pains in his knees and in the place in his lower shinbone where the piece of metal had lodged all those years ago, in Vietnam. He had been perpetually worried about his health. One of the women he dated briefly, a couple of years ago, had said to him, "Eddie Bishop, you know your trouble? You think like a ol' man."

"I *am* an old man," he told her.

There was another communication in his mailbox on a Monday in late January. Someone had to have dropped it there in the middle of the night. The morning paper had crumpled it into the back of the mailbox, a single sheet of paper, folded as in a business letter, like the others; the drawing this time was a wolf's head, snarling white teeth, under a swastika dripping blood:

Stay away from her. This means you.

He lighted a match to it and stood with it burning in his hand, turning in a slow circle, holding it high. The wind put the flame out, and he worked to light it again. The wind bit at his face and stung his eyes. He got the flame going again and reached up with it, a man holding a torch, until it had almost reached his fingers. Then he dropped it, stamped the flame out, and walked back inside.

He had lived in this house all his life, a sharecropper's house. He owned it now. The sharecropper was his great-grandfather, whose own grandfather had been a freed slave. These acres of grassy hills once made up the central parcel of a large tobacco plantation. The plantation house itself, a restored, antebellum mansion, was now an inn and restaurant that the wealthy and famous drove out from Washington or up from Charlottesville to patronize. Most of the land around it had been bought up during the Great Depression by a retired army general, who wanted to raise cattle. The descendants of those cattle still grazed in the east pasture beyond Edward Bishop's fence, looking attached by their muzzles to the brown grass, though the general's cattle farm was long gone, sold piecemeal over the years of the general's decline.

The last, large, horseshoe-shaped section remained, still tended by the seventy-year-old son and his wife, people with whom one simply didn't form a friendship (they had come once to offer to buy the sharecropper's house and the surrounding five acres; Bishop graciously offered them coffee, showed them his collection of deer rifles, and then said no, he intended to live out his life here; they never spoke to him again).

The fact was that until his involvement with Nora and her son, he'd been keeping as much as possible to himself. There were blacks living in Point Royal, of course, and in the old town part of Steel Run, but he was the only one in this part of the county. He had never given this much thought, and he had never felt any particular need to seek anybody out merely because he or she was the same color. The men he hunted with every fall were mostly white. The older of the two sisters who lived up the hill from him had gone to school with him and once made love to him in the backseat of a '58

Plymouth. She had been wild and drunk—as wild and drunk then as she was sober and religious now—and she wanted to know, she had told him drunkenly, how it felt with a colored man. He was seventeen and reckless, and more than willing to oblige, even as he understood the insult in it. Afterward, she wept and blamed him, and until he came to understand that it was her racism that would keep her from telling the world what she had done, he'd lived in exactly the kind of dread that he was living in now.

He was old enough to remember that certain establishments in this very county had once sworn blood oaths to resist the inevitable and had fought tooth and nail to keep the degrading status quo; he had somehow managed to quell the passions in his blood and made it through all the changes in the same quiet, steady fashion, developing his business with televisions, and then later teaching himself the VCRs. It was the world, and he had made his way through it and even managed to prosper. In his own country he had gone from being a black boy to being a colored man, to being a black man, to insisting, at least most of the time, on being Edward Bishop, and he had decided to try stopping there. People seemed friendly enough when he went out in the area.

But he found that he couldn't quite believe in their friendliness now. He thought he saw something in their faces, and then wasn't sure, and finally he began to believe they were watching him, waiting for him to react. He couldn't trust anyone.

A man alone, if he kept at himself, could make all kinds of trouble. It was true that anyway he had always been rather morbid. His mother used to say to him, "You know, Edward, you could turn the brightest hour of the day into something to mourn about."

And he *had* mourned, all the time. The time itself, rushing past him. It was true, from the time he was a little boy. Yet he tried not to dwell on it, or let it stop him from moving through the days with some sense of gratitude. That was all ruined now.

One evening, two weeks later, Nora brought it up to him. She said, "You're feeling it, aren't you? What they want you to feel."

"You mean hunted?" he said.

She said, "Scared."

"Jumpy," he told her. "Yeah."

"That's no way to live."

"No."

She appeared to steel herself for something. She took a breath. "I understand if you want to stop coming over."

"You want me to stop coming over?"

"I don't want to cause you any more trouble."

"Wait a minute," he said. "Have *you* heard from them?"

She stood and walked to the counter, reached into her purse, and brought out a slip of paper. She opened it and held it out to him. He didn't have to take it to see what it said. He folded it and put it in his shirt pocket. "When?" he asked her.

"In the mailbox. Today, when I got home. I wasn't going to tell you about it."

His heart was beating in his face and neck. She walked into his arms and stood there. It was as though they were both standing in a freezing wind. When she stepped back from him, she was dry-eyed. "I'll do whatever you want me to," he told her.

"I'm just so tired of everything."

"You don't need this," he said.

She seemed at a loss for words. But then she sighed. "It's just some sick—" She halted.

"Do you want me to stay away for a while?"

"I don't want my son coming home by himself."

"But I can—I can leave as soon as you come in, if you'd like."

She said nothing for a moment. Then: "I don't know. Then—then they win, right? Besides, I don't think it'll matter. If you're here, you're here. I hate letting them win."

"They do sometimes," Bishop said. "Sometimes, hard as it is to admit, they do win."

This occasioned a long silence.

"No," she said. "I don't think we should pay the slightest attention to it."

"You won't hurt my feelings, Nora."

"I know." Her gaze was direct and apparently calm.

"Well," he said. "Guess I'll be leaving."

She let him out and stood at the door as he walked to the road and turned toward his own property. "You're fifty-six," he murmured to himself, waving at her as she shut the door. "Your back's killing you. She's a friend. Don't be a damn fool."

A car roared over the hill up the road, and its high beams came on, freezing him for an instant. It went speeding by, no one he recognized, a face looking at him out the back window, receding into the dark. He went home, reached into his own mailbox, and found another hate page, this one filled with close text, a frantic shriek of racist venom. He went into the house and took one of the deer rifles out of the cabinet, cleaned it, sitting in the firelight in the living room, trying not to think about anything at all. He stayed in the chair by the front window with the rifle across his lap, dozing fitfully, dreaming of running among oblivious people in a public place whose precise delineations he couldn't make out. He woke feeling sore, stiff, quietly enraged. There was nothing in the mailbox. He tried to work and couldn't. He called Detective Shaw, who, this time, did call him back. There was nothing to report, Shaw said. He was proceeding with the investigation. Others had brought in hate letters: the rabbi at the Temple Israel; a judge in the county, who happened to be female; the Catholic pastor at Saint Anthony's. Stylistically, the writing was similar in all cases; the same graphics were being used, the same printer.

"I guess I'm in good company, then," Edward Bishop said.

"Everybody's in good company," said Shaw.

Mr. Bishop thanked him and hung up, and then realized that he had not told Shaw about the latest messages, nor about the fact that Nora Michaelson was getting them, too, now. When he called back, the other had stepped out, so he left his name.

His one marriage had ended in divorce, eighteen years ago. Irreconcilable differences, but the truth was that Dorothy wanted to go home to Georgia, to live in the town where she wouldn't have to be alone all the time. She felt that way, she said, married to Bishop. "You were meant to live alone, Eddie," she told him. "You do anyway, even when you're with people. And I'm tired of trying to find you. You hate it, too. That's the weird thing about it."

He suspected it was true.

He slept badly, again. In the morning, he walked out to the mailbox and looked in. He remembered the face staring at him out the back window of the speeding car. It was a freezing morning. He went inside and tried to work. There were four VCRs in various stages of disassembly on the table by the living room window. He worked all morning, watching for the police car, but none came. There wasn't any traffic at all. At noon he made something to eat for himself and sat in the kitchen, in the quiet. Finally he went upstairs, to his office, and put some music on. Benny Goodman. Cheerful, unintellectual music, purely delightful, and sunny. He left the record brace up, so the arm would keep returning to the beginning of the recording, and he let it play into the afternoon.

Out on the porch, in the chill, he threw some scraps on the lawn, for the cats. He could hear the music out here. The sky was dotted with little tufts of cloud. He experienced a wave of loneliness, or depression.

The one was the other.

He went back into the house. Thinking had become so troublesome, these days: *This is how I've lived most of my life* He went to the living room and sat down.

His only remaining family connection, his sister, believed that her life and his had both been blighted by their parents, by the stern, quiet people who'd inhabited this Virginia property and then sold it to their eldest son as their interest in life and their health waned. Eugenia had washed her hands, she said, of every vestige of those two. She'd married a chiropractor named Crane and moved to Syracuse, New York. For years she led a rather adventurous life. The chiropractor made a lot of money, and she used it to travel; she had been in most of the world's capitals before she reached the age of forty. She gathered possessions from far-flung cultures and learned to speak several languages. And her manner toward her brother had become somewhat magisterial.

"Edward, do you know what your trouble is? You have no gumption. You don't like to make waves. You're just like Daddy in that respect. An old colored man with worries. I don't mean this in a bad way, particularly. It's just the truth. For instance, when is the last time you left the state of Virginia for anything? Even a vacation."

"I've gone places," he said. "Just because I haven't been around the world."

"Well, if you had been anywhere at all other than that—farm— you wouldn't be so painfully uncomfortable in social situations."

Bishop hadn't seen her in years and hadn't wanted to, for she had become a carbon copy of her mother—critical, painfully blunt, not to say cruel. A boxy-shaped, frowning, humorless woman with highly polished manners and a slight accent, an affectation of substantial wealth and influence, a heavy lady putting on airs. A snob, really, and Edward Bishop was evidently an embarrassment to her. She had been widowed more than ten years ago and was childless. Now she lived in a retirement village somewhere near Erie, Pennsylvania. Fifty-two and living there. Occasionally he would send flowers to her, for her birthday, or for one of the holidays. He rarely heard anything back. *Dear Edward. Thank you for the lovely arrangement. Please send no more, as I have very little room where I am presently living.*

Well, and now after years of a kind of growing acceptance about himself and his solitary existence, this young woman's trouble had drawn him into her life, and he could not get her out of his mind. Her need of him, even in the face of these veiled threats from thugs, had made him want all that much more to be helpful, to keep her from harm.

He had been sitting there daydreaming, watching the mailbox, and he heard something on the porch. He went to the side window and looked out again, but couldn't see enough. Entering the kitchen, he heard it again—and froze. The cats.

The wind kicked at the house. He ran the tap, washed his hands, as if to wash away the sense of his own ability to imagine things. Upstairs, the record player paused, and the music began again. There was the sound out on the porch. Quickly, not quite believing himself, he went to the cabinet and fetched one of the rifles. But then, with a small curse, he put it back in its place. This was broad daylight, and the cats were running under the porch. He would not make a fool of himself by walking out of the house with the rifle, a scared man in the middle of the afternoon. He strode to the front door, opened it, and stepped out. The sun had gone behind a wall of gray clouds. He walked around the house and on to the end of the side porch, where he could see into the back field. Upstairs the music was sounding, so quick and bright. He waited a moment, standing with his hands on the white-painted railing.

No, it was his damned imagination.

He walked around to the front door and heard the cats running before him, and how many alarms had they given him over the months? He headed toward the hallway, raised his eyes to the stairs leading up, and saw a man standing in the upper hallway, holding a pistol. The man was lean but powerful-looking.

"Who are you?" Bishop asked him out of pure startlement. He realized almost immediately the absurdity of the question, and he put his hands up, though he hadn't been told to.

"Come on up," the man said, almost friendly.

Bishop started out the door, but another man was waiting there. He saw the jowly, pale round face, the bulk and wideness of him, and emitted a cry. He had seen that face before. The back window of the car speeding past him in the night. The heavy man pushed the door open, and Bishop backed away from him.

"Up here," the other said. He held the pistol, barrel down. In his other hand was a bundle of cord. His demeanor was relaxed, nearly casual. "Come on."

CHIEF INVESTIGATOR SHAW HAD spoken to the computer lab teacher at the high school and had been given a list of names and addresses of youths who were known to be particularly adept at the use of the school's computers. That afternoon, he drove to Steel Run Creek to interview the family of one such youth—a starved-looking, pale boy with a strangely protruding breastbone and long, spidery fingers. The boy identified the type of program that could produce the graphics: it was common to every computer produced in the last five years, part of the software that came with them from the factory. Oh, yes, he said, they each came with it; IBMs, and all the clones, and Macs, too. Every one had a graphics program of one kind or another. And there were dozens of color printers that could have produced these pages.

No help.

Shaw went out to his car and sat there, looking over his notes. He felt sleepy, sitting in the warmth of the front seat. His own radio startled him. There was a call for him out at the Lombard farm, out near Darkness Falls. He picked up the handset and spoke into it.

"I'm in Steel Run now. Give me the address."

■ ■ ■

He had spent the morning sitting at his desk, papers open before him, bright sun washing into the window to his right, and, as had happened more often than he liked to admit to himself, he'd rested his chin in his hands and drifted off to sleep. He went through a fleeting dream about sitting in his office sleeping, and when he became aware that he *was* sleeping, he tried to move. The phone was ringing. But this sleep was so deeply, soul-nourishingly good, the only sleep that was ever any good at this time of the year. It was especially bad this year.

The phone kept on. He broke free of the stillness, opened his eyes. "What?" Had it indeed been ringing?

He picked it up. A female voice told him Edward Bishop was on the line. He spoke to the distraught Mr. Bishop, then got up and walked down the hall to the cafeteria, where he ordered a cup of coffee and sat drinking it, reflecting that if this was what he needed now, he would pay heavily for it later in the day, at the end of his day.

In the nights, he spent the hours reading, or sitting on a hassock in front of the television, channel-surfing. The avalanche of crap on television didn't even serve as an anodyne now; in fact, it sometimes kept him awake in recollection. Television was a depository of time past; you saw people doing and saying things they were doing and saying when you were elsewhere in your life. "Elsewhere" for Philip Shaw involved the loss of a son, through what he believed was his own neglect, a kind of neglect, anyway. And the memory of it had never come with any less force, or changed one element of the hard pure pressure under his breastbone, that the boy was gone—eleven years now, almost to the day. The anniversary coming around again, with its familiar force. Eleven years in which his marriage had deteriorated and gone to pieces, and his ability to do much of anything beyond the rote work of his daily grind had narrowed and narrowed. He had a daughter, the lost boy's younger sister, and his wife was taking her away, too, now.

The lost boy's name was Willy. Eleven years ago, while vacationing in Fort Lauderdale, Shaw, in the glow of too much alcohol, had taken the boy, nine years old, into the surf with him. The waves seemed moderate enough, deep swells, lifting and setting them both down, near shore. But the boy had disappeared at the base of one and not come up. It crashed and surged all the way to the beach line, and the foam of it washed back to reveal the shape of the boy on the sand, lying facedown, his head turned at a terrible angle.

A freak accident, the doctors said. It was just the way the water hit him, or moved him against the ground under the weight of it coming down. This type of thing was rare, but not impossible in such conditions. There were other people in the water, other boys Willy's age. No one was at fault, the doctors said. But Shaw thought of the beer he had had to drink—the careless, impervious sense of well-being with which he had plowed into the rough waves with his son.

There had followed a long spiral, an incremental sinking that both he and his wife, Carol, had not quite understood for what it was; they had both spent an awful amount of time drunk. Carol had come to see it first. "We have a daughter who isn't old enough to remember what got us started on this," she told him. "I'm so ashamed of myself."

When she stopped the drinking, she buried her longing for oblivion under a busy parade of fierce involvement in community service—the PTA at school, volunteer teaching, volunteer work in the nursing homes, day-care centers, hospitals, hospices, and shelters. For a month she had housed a pair of battered women and a homeless adolescent girl with a heroin addiction. Shaw came home late in the nights to the sprawl of human shapes on the living room floor and in the room that had been his son's. If he was not already drunk, he would get himself that way as quickly as possible. Mornings, he drove his daughter to school and ached for how little she was getting of what she had every practical right to expect. He would kiss her cheek and watch her walk into the low red-brick building that was her other life, the life with girls and boys who came from less confusing households, happy families.

It was after he managed to stop drinking that the sore places in his marriage began to be insupportable. The truth of the matter was that there had been trouble neither of them quite acknowledged before Willy's death, and perhaps it was so that without the duress of unendurable loss, such troubles exist in the silences of any marriage, without ever bringing the edifice to the point of collapse.

He had ended up feeling almost happy, at any rate, being out and away from Carol, and it had seemed, with the schedules the lawyers had set up through the court, that he spent more consecutive time with his daughter than he had ever been quite able to spend during the time he lived in the house. She came to him on weekends, and there were unexpected pleasures arising out of the fact that he had to think of things to do with her, to please her—to *interest* her.

But now Carol was moving to Richmond and taking Mary with her. It was all decided; she had invested in her cousin Betsy's beauty parlor, had drifted away from her various social work commitments. Her latest and most passionate involvement, other than making money, was the redress of political inequities. Carol had embraced a kind of ersatz radicalism that Shaw feared might poison his daughter against him, especially if she possessed the advantage of distance, and it seemed evident enough that, consciously or unconsciously, she was holding him accountable for Willy's death.

He did not blame her. But he wanted nothing to do with her anymore, either.

On some weekday evenings he spent time with a young woman, Eloise Lefler, thirteen years his junior, to whom he had been introduced at a gathering of people working on the Fall Festival in Point Royal. She liked television, and so he watched it with her, sitting in her small living room, with her father moving around in the next room. The old man, a former sheriff, had a hobby of carving wooden ducks, for decoys, and he liked to tell about the old days, chasing whiskey-runners on the narrow county roads of the valley. Shaw liked him and, in fact, felt slightly more comfortable with Eloise when her father was around. He was not quite ready to start things up with somebody else.

So he spent a lot of nights alone, in the light, reading. His nightstand was stacked high with books: history, biography, novels. He had been poring through *Anna Karenina* and a biography of

Churchill. At some point it had become part of his nightly routine to spend seven hours this way, not even expecting to grow heavy-eyed or sleepy. The nights wore on and became dawns, and at last he would drift off, the book lying on his chest, or, at times, the television playing, people talking and laughing as if they were trapped doing that, no matter who listened or slept. He would come out of these small dips into nonwaking, and he would have the day to get through. The slow hours of court, if there was court; the hours in his office, sitting in the sun from the windows, fighting sleep. He had been sober for almost a year now. But the sober life was presenting its own problems.

In one bad night, he dreamed that Willy came into the room where he slept; it was not any other room, none of the other rooms he had ever been in with the boy, but this room, with its clutter of books and its evidence of a desiccated spirit—the clothes strewn on the surfaces and the unwashed dishes on the counter, the general neglect of everything—the apparition walked in and stood there, in a glow. "Son?" Shaw said to him. "Can you stay a while?" He heard the casual note of pleasant conversation in his voice, even as the desperation raked through him to make the boy stay, to reach out and touch his hair, the thin carved-looking white neck and shoulders. "Stay?" Shaw said. And the boy responded almost jauntily, "No, gotta go." And he was gone.

There had been nights, in the past week, when he had come close to taking a drink.

The Lombard farm was the last farm that was completely intact in the county, having navigated the changes in population and development through the boom years of the sixties and seventies, when most of the larger farms had been parceled out for ready cash, the big money that came from selling to shopping malls and the builders of houses and apartment complexes. It was a ten-thousand-acre farm, ranged over foothills of the Blue Ridge Mountains, with at its southern edge the little town of Darkness Falls Courthouse: one green road sign, a few antiques stores, a white clapboard church, and a post office. There was no courthouse anymore, and for legal matters one had to travel five miles to Steel Run. The word *courthouse* in the town's title stemmed from an antebellum rule concerning county seats and the judicial map.

No one knew or could remember who had decided upon Darkness Falls as the name of the place. There was a lake called Darkness (Eloise lived at its southern edge), but no falls that anybody knew about. Lombard owned the land that skirted most of the circumference of the lake, and he had dumped several tons of sand along the north side of it. In the summer, families came to swim in the dark green water and sun themselves on the little artificial beach. Lombard was a community-minded man.

His farm had its own abattoir, its own processing and packaging plant, but much of the rolling countryside surrounding the Lombard house looked like uncultivated wild land. The house itself was a surprisingly small rambler, with shuttered windows and a gold eagle on the front door. It might have been brought forward untouched and unchanged from 1955. The only visible sign of the prosperity Lombard enjoyed was the Olympic-sized swimming pool in back. Lombard himself was a scrawny little man with fierce blue eyes and a sun-damaged face pocked with what appeared to be brown scales, over furrows and lines. He was standing at the gate as Shaw drove up.

"Wait till you see this," he said, already leading the detective along the fence toward what was apparently the property line. A creek wound along the curve of the road at that end—a runoff of Darkness Lake—it was thick with undergrowth, and it eventually coursed under the road in a cement culvert. A barbed wire fence ran across the culvert and up into the growth on the other bank. Lombard strode through the tall dry grass, which clicked and rattled with his tread; he skirted the bank and angled away from the road. His demeanor was furious. He said nothing, pushing through, leading the way. About fifty yards on, the tangle of undergrowth opened out, to the grass field on that side of the creek. Lombard stepped down the bank, over some stones and past the freezing little pools of collected water, up the other side, into the tall grass there. Shaw trailed along after him. They climbed into the field and along the undulating ground to a slight well of earth, a dip, like a crater that had filled after thousands of years, a circle of sunken ground, littered with stones and patches of dry red clay. In this space lay the carcasses of several beef cattle. Shaw saw calves, cows, and at least two bulls. Some of them were down in areas of wild grass, others lay on bare ground.

"Fourteen cows," Lombard said. "Three bulls and five calves." He was almost crying with it. He shook his head. He stood there with his hands in the back pockets of his jeans. "Who the hell would do such a thing?"

Shaw looked around them. The ground was hard; the grass showed no signs of movement through it. He looked down toward the road, the place where it crossed over the creek.

"Shot," Lombard said. "Like some kind of damn game—or something. Some son of a bitch taking potshots. Target practice on poor dumb animals."

The detective was visited with the unfriendly notion that a hundred years ago a man like Lombard, with his chewing tobacco and his jeans and cowboy boots, his hat emblazoned with the emblem of the National Rifle Association, might have well been one of those wild men who slaughtered whole herds of buffalo. Lombard spit. "Damned senseless destruction," he said. Shaw stepped close to the first dead animal, a cow. One eye was blown in—a bullet wound. There was a circular area of powder burn around it, indicating close range. Inches, probably.

"This was no target practice," he said.

The next animal, another cow, had multiple wounds in its side. Still another had been shot in the middle of the brow. There seemed no pattern, no discernible method: just someone shooting at random, walking among the startled animals, then running among them, firing. Several of them had been killed at distances from the first few. From the looks of it, the killings were recent—not more than a few hours.

"Jesus Christ," Lombard kept saying. "Look at this. Look at this."

Shaw said, "I've got to get some people out here, look all this over. You haven't touched anything, have you?"

"No." Lombard was crying now.

Shaw felt a stab of guilt for his earlier thoughts about him. On an impulse, he said, "Have you received any hate mail lately?"

Lombard held a handkerchief to his face, blew his nose, then seemed to study him. "What?"

"Hate mail."

"No."

After another swipe at his nose, Lombard regarded him. "Hate mail. What the hell're you talking about? Hate mail."

"It's nothing," Shaw told him. "There's been a few. You know, the usual racist, neo-Nazi crap."

"Racist." Lombard seemed offended.

"The mail—these letters some people have been getting. It's nothing for you to worry about," Shaw said.

"I ain't no racist," Lombard said, again wiping his nose.

"No, the people sending this—these hate letters. *They're* racists."

Lombard thought a moment. "Shit, I guess I am, too, if you get down to it. I can't help thinking this is some of those black punks from the high school. Gangs or some shit like that."

"You had any kind of a run-in with anybody?" Shaw asked him.

"Hell. I don't know what you're getting at. I wanna know who killed these cattle, that's what I wanna know."

The two men stood there looking at the scattered carcasses, and a little wind moved the fur along the neck of the closest one.

"Damn," Lombard said.

MONEY

BISHOP NOTICED ALMOST IMMEDI-
ately that there was a similarity about the two men—the same odd
dull green eyes, the same timbre in their voices when they spoke,
though one was tall and muscular, and the other was fat, round-
faced, with a wide, flabby neck and deeply sloping shoulders. This
one didn't look more than about twenty years old. He wore a red ear-
flapped hunter's cap, a lumber jacket, and overalls, on which there
were several dark stains near the bottom cuff of one leg. The tall one
wore jeans, a thick sleeveless denim jacket. He was thirty or so and
seemed to be the one in charge. A scar ran down the right side of his
face, from the corner of the mouth.

"I'm not afraid of you," Bishop managed to say, though he was
very much afraid.

The tall one smiled. "No need to be."

"What do you want?" Bishop asked.

"Move it," said the fat one. "Upstairs."

Bishop made the slow ascent, with the fat one behind him. The
one at the top of the stairs moved back as they came up and stood at
the doorway of the study where the music was playing. "In here."

"I don't know what you hope to accomplish," Bishop said.

"We just want to talk."

He entered the room, or was forced in, the fat man with his thick fingers wrapped around his upper arm. Bishop put his weight low and pushed suddenly against the heavy middle, at the belt, and the fat man fell against the wall, jarring the music all the way on the other side of the room.

"Don't touch me," Bishop heard himself say. His own bravado astonished him. He felt terror all along his spine; it was cutting off his breath, and yet he had done this, pushed this big, stupid boy away from himself.

The taller one put the pistol in his face. "No trouble. Okay?"

Bishop breathed the oil-metal odor of the gun; it almost choked him. "I don't have to be manhandled," he said.

"Be still."

The fat man rubbed one heavy wrist. "Son of a bitch hurt me, Travis."

"Go keep a lookout."

"Yeah. There's nothing out here to lookout."

"Just do it," the one named Travis said.

When they were alone, he moved Ed Bishop to a chair and pushed him down in it. Then he stepped back and regarded him, arms folded, the one hand still holding the pistol. "You a tough guy?"

Bishop was silent.

"Yeah, you're tough. You serve?"

"I don't understand you."

"The army navy marines coast guard—you know."

"What do you want with me?" Bishop asked him, still surprised at the strength of resistance he felt.

"Need to ask you some questions."

He waited.

"So, you served?"

"What has this got to do with anything?"

"You know these people in the next house. The woman and her son?"

"I help out with the boy," Bishop said. "It's—it's not what you think it is. You people have made a mistake."

"You people?"

"It just isn't what you think it is."

"What I—what?"

Bishop said nothing.

"No, no, no, no. I don't care what you do with the lady. You know the lady."

"I—yes, I know her. But not the way you think."

"Look," the man said. "Maybe you better let me do the talking."

Bishop glared at him.

"Did you know the lady's husband?"

"No. He died last—"

The other interrupted him. "Yeah, I know that. Do you know anything about him?"

"I just said I didn't."

"You don't know what he did for a living?"

"I know he was contractor. That's all. We never spoke. If you want to know the truth, he wasn't all that friendly as a neighbor."

"Kind of quiet and sneaky?"

Bishop said nothing to this.

"You've been going over there in the afternoons."

"What is this? Who are you people? There's nothing wrong with helping a lady who asked for help. Why don't you find someone else to spend your hate on."

"Hate."

"Do you think I'm an idiot?" Bishop said.

"You want to tell me what you're talking about?"

"You know," Bishop said.

"Hey, it's nothing to us—we don't mind you helping her," Travis said. "I don't even care if you're screwing her. Okay?"

Bishop felt a wave of exhaustion. "I don't understand you," he said.

"You've been going over there."

After a moment's hesitation, he said, "Yes. If you know that, why do you need to ask me?"

"Well, here's the deal. We're gonna need your help and cooperation. We're gonna need you to try and remember anything you can
about the husband. Anything she might've told you about him."

"What are you? Is this—are you an investigator or something?"

The other gave forth a small laugh. "That's right. FBI."

"FBI."

"A little joke."

"Well, who are you? Why're you doing this?"

The man stepped close and seemed for a moment nearly sorrowful. "We're leaving no stone unturned, you might say."

"I don't know what you're talking about. I go over there on
school nights to check on the boy. I don't know them. Haven't—
haven't really known them." The real truth of this seemed to dawn
on him as he spoke it. "I'm nothing to them. Understand? She—she
talks about the kid and her troubles on this—this job she had to
take. That's all. The husband used up everything—I don't know any
more than that."

"So she talked to you about her husband's business."

There was a loud series of thuds downstairs, the fat man running along the porch. Travis seemed momentarily distracted by this.

"Well, so—right?"

"I don't understand what you want."

The other was growing angry. "I want to know did she talk to
you about his business."

"No."

"You're sure."

"I wouldn't lie about it."

The fat man came lumbering back up the stairs. "I'm bored," he
said. "You should see the cats around this place. Loads of fun."

"Jesus, Bags. You're chasing cats?"

"Why not?"

"Will you get down there and keep watch?"

"There's nothing to watch. This ain't exactly Times Square."

"Shut up," said Travis.

"You feed all these cats?" the fat one asked Bishop.

"He don't know a damn thing."

"Well, then let's get on over there, if there's nothing here."

Travis leaned in close to Bishop. "She ever give you anything to bring back here for her? Anything at all?"

"No," Bishop said. "Nothing."

"You never brought anything with you out of that house."

"No."

"Never even baked cookies for you?" said the other one. "Gee, it looked like such a nice friendship."

Edward Bishop turned to him and felt his own dismissive expression.

"You see the face he gave me, Travis?"

"Well," Travis said. "She'll be home in a minute."

"No," Bishop corrected him. "She has meetings after school. She won't get out before six o'clock."

"I told you," said the fat man, lighting a cigarette. "Thursdays she comes home later."

"Shut up, Bags," Travis said.

"This is getting boring. It's all fucked up." The one named Bags opened the drawer of the desk and took out some of the papers. "Look at this." He held one out to Travis. It was the latest communication from the Virginia Front.

"Oh, okay—now I get it." He showed it to Bishop. "You think we had something to do with this."

Bishop kept silent.

"Shit." Travis dropped it on the floor. "That's funny."

"You screwing the lady?" Bags asked. "Huh?"

"Okay," Travis said. "I'm afraid we're gonna have to tie you up until we can figure out what to do. Unless there's something you can think of to tell us."

"I don't want to be tied up. I'm not gonna—what did you think I'd do?"

"It's just for a little while, pal."

They put him on the floor. He tried to resist, but the fat man hit him twice on the side of the head. He lay very still, the pain thundering under the bones of his skull. The fat man held his arms back while the other bound his hands and ran the cord to his ankles.

Bishop was on his side on the floor, and they had risen to their feet, were standing in the doorway of the room. There had been an interval. The music was still playing. It sounded weirdly out of place now. He kept still, eyes closed.

"Wait here," the tall one's voice.

"I'm bored," the heavy one said. "Come on. He's not going anywheres. He's out like a light. Look at him."

"Just do what I say, Bags, will you. For goddammit once?"

"What about her?"

"What *about* her?"

"One of us is supposed to be there when she comes out of the building."

"Look. Just wait here until I get back. We'll both go get her. We'll use his truck."

"You don't think I can be trusted?"

"Jeez, I wonder why. If the son of a bitch finds out about what went on today—"

"Shit. I think you're afraid of him."

"I'm not afraid of him, okay, Bags? Jesus Christ, you know what scares me? What a dumb fuck you are. You're gonna end up blowing the whole thing."

"Creating havoc," the fat man said. There was something chiding in his voice. "That's all. Imagine the laws trying to figure it out."

"You stupid son of a bitch—"

"Don't call me stupid, Travis."

"Just—shit—will you do what I say? Suppose we can't get everything today? Suppose we have to look for it?"

"You'll figure it out. You're the genius."

"Just quit fucking around."

"I don't like to be bored."

"Do what I tell you," the tall one said. "And don't hurt this guy, either. Understand? You leave him exactly like he is."

"I'll go get her and you go get the boy."

They went out into the hallway, then, and kept arguing, in whispers. Bishop struggled with the tightness of the cord around his wrists. He managed to get one hand almost out of the loop. One more pull might do it. He gathered himself for the next attempt, and then the fat man came back into the room, took the lumber jacket and hunter's cap off, and stood over him.

"Comfortable?"

Bishop heard the little dull-witted laugh, the sound of him blowing smoke. He didn't answer. He saw the wide, dirty fingers, wrapped with more cord, and now he was being turned over onto his stomach. His left hand came loose, and he tried to use it to hit at the other man, but the weight of the knee dropped down on him again, and the cord was being wound tight around the free hand. A band of it came against his face, chafing the soft flesh under his nose. The fat man worked on him, one knee down in the middle of his back. He thought his back might break. The pain brought him almost to unconsciousness. He couldn't get enough air to scream. He was spinning off somewhere else, the room losing definition, light fading. He tried to open his eyes wider to take in more light. He felt blind. But then he could see again, the room was as it had been, and the heavy man was still working to tie him.

"Oh, my God," said Bishop. "I won't say anything, please."

"Just hold still," the fat man said. When he was finished, he went to the other side of the room, leaned against the dresser there, and continued smoking the cigarette. "You know what you look like?" He didn't wait for an answer. "You look like somebody could pick you up and shoot a arrow with you." He laughed at this, pleased with himself, standing there smoking. The music played, stopped, repeated itself. "What is this anyway?"

Bishop didn't answer.

"I asked you a question, nigger."

"I don't know what you mean."

"You don't know what nigger means?"

Bishop said nothing.

The oddly self-satisfied little laugh came forth again. "I'm talking about this shit on the record player."

"It's—it's music."

"Don't be cute."

Bishop waited, feeling sick from the pain in his back.

"Kind of boring, id'n it?"

The muscles were beginning to cramp up, seizing. The pain was awful. He was aware that this man had orders not to harm him. But harm was coming, and he knew it. He remained silent.

"I said, 'Kind of boring, id'n it?'"

The agony he felt had begun to fill him with rage. It mixed in with everything—the whole of his life, with all its straining to be better, its striving for the smallest changes. It was all being taken from him, all being scorned, disrespected. He began to scream. It came out of him in a tearing. Some part of him understood, after the screaming, that screaming was useless. This heavy, nonchalantly brutal man could cause him more pain, and he was surprised to find in himself nothing but white-hot anger. An obstinate seething hatred.

Bags moved toward him. "I *said,* 'Kind of boring, id'n it?'"

Bishop could hardly speak. He said, "Fuck you."

"Pardon me?"

"You heard."

The fat man went over and crushed the cigarette out in the ashtray on the dresser and stepped slowly back to where the older man lay on the floor, stomach down, head and feet pulled up. "No shit, we could fire an arrow with you, man."

"Aren't you brave," Bishop managed. "Aren't you smart."

"Yeah, I'm not tied up."

"You poor sad dumb—" Bishop began. But once more the other's knee came down in the middle of his back. For a long time, there was just the terrible weight of the knee, pressing on the nerves of his spine. He screamed again. And then he had stopped it, was trying to draw air.

"Apologize," Bags said.

In his gasping for breath, he got the words out: "Go fuck yourself."

"You think I won't do it."

Bishop saw the other's hand, with something bright in it. But then Bags was behind him. Something had reflected light. The weight had lifted. He could breathe again.

"Well," said Bags. "I think it's time to get going."

Bishop closed his eyes, trying to remember the words of a prayer, any prayer. It had been so long since he had said anything like a prayer. The fat man moved somewhere in the room, out of sight. Something was being made ready. Faint sounds he couldn't interpret. "Our Father," he said, coughing. "Who—art—in heaven."

And then the hand came down across his forehead and pulled.

THE ATTIC

Fʀᴏᴍ ᴛʜᴇ ᴛᴏᴘ ᴡɪɴᴅᴏᴡ, ʟᴏᴏᴋɪɴɢ out over the brown field with its patches of snow and its sticklike, bare-branched saplings, Jason Michaelson saw the man coming. The field was frozen, but the man's boots looked dirty. He had come from the crest of the hill, beyond the little pond at that end of the property, moving slow, but with a sureness, too.

It was not Mr. Bishop. This was a white guy, bigger than Bishop and a lot younger and more solid. The man reached the wooden fence and put one hand on it, then used the hand to hop over. He was in the far end of the yard, turning to survey where he had come from, leaning on the top rail of the fence for a moment, almost as if waiting for someone. Jason watched him, curious—a stranger wandering by, walking across the farm fields alone. The man just stood there, but then he seemed a little impatient, turning and gazing at the house. He strode along the fence for a few feet, one gloved hand on it, still glancing back at where he had come from. Stopping, seeming to wait again, he leaned on the fence. His head drooped. Then he stood back and kicked at the lowest rail, broke it, and pulled a piece of it loose, with some effort.

Jason uttered a small surprised sound of alarm and ducked back from the square of the window. He waited, thinking about how he would tell his mother he had seen a man damage the fence, a grown man. A person walking in from the world and taking that liberty with something that didn't belong to him. In a way, the boy felt, it was only what he might've expected. The whole of life was upside down: his father dead; misfortune upon them and everything, everything wrong. Jason and his mother had joined the ranks of the unlucky, and he felt a surliness about it all the time.

A man had come walking out of the distance and broken the fence, and that was just part of the whole badness of things now. The world.

He looked out the window again. The man was facing away from the house, holding the piece of wood like a club; he turned, slowly, and faced the house again. One gloved hand went up to the face, the gloved index finger into the mouth; the hand came from the glove, and the glove still dangled in the mouth. The man wiped his nose with the flat of his bare hand, wiped the hand against his jeans, then took the glove from his mouth and put it back on.

The boy experienced a heightening of the sense of being hidden.

During the darker days of this winter, the attic was the only place he could stand—this hemmed-in area of boxes and old furniture at the very pinnacle of the old house. He had spent many recent afternoons up here, looking at the lawn and the adjoining fields below, and deriving an undefined sense of peace from the empty quiet spaces out there and the changes in the sky—Mr. Bishop coming to knock on the door and draw him down, talk to him about the weather and the thousand things he was behind on, trying to distract him from the thinking too much that all the adults were afraid he was doing. Or anyway that was what Jason had gleaned from their talk, the worry everyone had about what was going on in his mind now, with his grades falling and his teachers reporting on his general bad attitude and all the adjustments he and his mother had been forced to make—the job, these hours he spent alone in the house.

It had been a terrible year.

Mr. Bishop had come right out and asked him: "What's bothering you now, boy? What's on your mind?"

"Nothing," Jason said.

"What is it that you find so interesting up in that attic?"

"Nothing, sir."

Mr. Bishop shook his head, pouring coffee for himself. "It's none of my business, I know."

Usually, he'd take the cup of coffee and walk through the downstairs rooms of the house, quiet as a tourist in a museum. Jason would follow him.

"You get along in school today?"

"Fine," Jason said, though this was often a lie. It seemed to him that everything his teachers had to say was beside the point. The point was that you could work like hell and study hard and do everything they wanted you to do and then go out and die in a crash on the highway, and the whole thing would count for nothing.

This week, it had become so bad that he hadn't been able to bring himself to go. He had missed the last three days, using a forged signature from his mother, a request for absence to take care of pressing family matters. No one questioned it. He was a boy whose father had died, and everyone wanted to help.

Now, the man out on the lawn fidgeted and tapped the piece of wood against the top rail of the fence. He was quite big—someone who didn't care about private property. A man not just tall, but powerfully built. The heavy muscles of his chest stretched the denim of the sleeveless coat he wore. Jason thought of weights and weight lifting. He was still not much more than curious—the damage to the fence was an adult matter. But something about the casualness of the action had caused a part of him to tighten inside, a slowly increasing wariness.

The man made a pivoting motion from the hips, like someone limbering up, preparing for exercise. He started walking again, coming on a little more quickly, looking one way and then the other. There was something stealthy about him, a watchfulness, and abruptly the boy understood that an element of this had been there all along. The man headed straight for the house and now Jason's curiosity caved inward. He ducked back from the window, sitting down with a thud against the attic wall, not even breathing for a few seconds.

The house, the whole house below him, took on a living quality.

He remained perfectly still, listening, through the little creaks of the corners and joists and the small sighing of the radiator pipes, for some sound of the man entering. The doors, he knew, were locked. The man would have to break in. Jason remained still. Perhaps five minutes went by. The heat kicked on and whirred in the ducts, an interval of time in which he felt deaf to the rest of the house. It went off and revealed what felt like a listening silence. He waited, perfectly still, through the minutes.

And his fear began to leave him. It was like a game now.

Carefully, very slowly, he got himself below the window and rose to look over the sill. He saw the field, empty, the patches of snow, the trees, the gray distances of late afternoon in winter. He stood, keeping himself out of the frame of the window, and then he looked out again and down.

The man was standing in the yard, staring straight up at him, one hand up to block the light. Jason saw the grizzled face, the narrow muddy eyes, the long curve of the jaw. There was something white running down from one side of the mouth. He gasped, seeing it, but held still, and the man seemed to squint, tilting his head a little, peering at the window. The only thing to do was stay frozen, watching him tilt his head the other way, staring. When he looked out at the road, the boy moved quickly back, leaned against the wall, and waited. Silence. The wide world was wrapped in a quiet. There had to have been a reflection, or the glare of the gray sky in the window; it was possible the man hadn't seen him. He kept still, listening, and he didn't know how much time went by. The watery light at the window had begun to fade; it would be dark soon.

On all fours, moving as noiselessly as he could, and pausing now and again to listen, he made his way to the entrance of the attic. The wind had picked up outside and it roared in the eaves of the house. He couldn't hear any sound but that for a few seconds. He imagined the man walking on down the road, perhaps almost out of sight by now, and even so he descended the attic stairs very slowly. There were deep shadows in the hall and down the stairwell into the main foyer of the house. The pictures on the wall were all of the time before his father's death. He couldn't ever look at them anymore. He glided along the wall, to the entrance of what had once been his parents' bedroom, then peeked around the frame. The room was empty. The light on the bed was losing the outline of the window, which looked out on the same field where the man had stood. Jason eased himself across the open space of the doorway and started along the wall toward the stairs down.

The phone rang and brought a little gasp up out of the back of his throat. He braced himself against the wall, believing under the flow of his fear that he had created his own alarm, that this wasn't serious. The man was gone. He had damaged the fence in his careless passing and was elsewhere now, going on to whatever he would be going on to: a stranger, hitchhiking, with his life that was far from here. Mr. Bishop would knock on the door any second. Yet the boy couldn't bring himself to break the spell and move.

The phone rang three times and then paused, and the little mechanical clicking of the answering machine started, followed by his mother's recorded voice: "This is Nora. Jason and I can't come to the phone right now. Leave your name and number and we'll call you back." There was the beep and then his mother's voice again: "Jason? Edward? Where are you? Jason—honey, you're not in the attic again, are you? Hello. I know you're home, son. At least you better be. All right, I'll call Mr. Bishop. Bye." The machine beeped again, then was silent. The boy took a breath and stepped away from the wall.

"Oh, Jason." A man's voice, from below him, soft, almost affectionate. "Jason."

He backed soundlessly to the attic stairs, then froze again.

"Hey."

The house creaked. Some weight on the floorboards below, moving away, it seemed.

"On my way, Jason." The voice was coming from another part of the house, from the family room, beyond the kitchen, the enclosed porch on that side.

He backed soundlessly up the attic stairs and pulled the door up. It made a small squeak, and he held it a moment, then pulled it the rest of the way, in what seemed like far too much noise. He lay on the planks next to its pine-smelling, metal-braced stepboards and put his ear against the wood. His own heartbeat, which seemed louder than anything else now, pounded in his ears and face and neck. The heat pipes sighed and hissed, the furnace kicked on again, and for a long while there was the hum of it in the walls. When it stopped, the stillness was muffling, seemed to press down on him where he lay with his drumming heart.

"Hey, Jason." The voice was a whisper, close.

The boy stood, looked around himself for something to use as a weapon. He picked up a lamp, but it was thin glass—no real weight to it. The attic door was being pulled down, the springs stretching, and Jason set the lamp on the floor, moved quickly to the other end of the space, behind a stack of cardboard boxes, stuffed with old clothes his mother hadn't been able to part with. The smell of mothballs choked him. But he was motionless. He heard the heavy footsteps of the man, coming up.

"There's somebody here," the voice said. "Right? And his name is Jason. How old are you, Jason? I bet I know."

The boy remained where he was.

"Come on, kid. I know you're up here. I ain't gonna hurt you."

The heat came on again and whirred, and he edged himself deeper into the recesses of that space, under the angles of roof and ceiling, behind more boxes.

There was a cracking sound and then a thud, nearby. Something had broken through the ceiling. The heater stopped, and he heard the voice.

"Shit. My leg went through the goddam ceiling, Jason."

The boy held his breath, while the man struggled back to his feet.

"Gotta remember to keep to the studs and the planks, right?"

He couldn't see anything now, cringing behind the boxes, in the odor of the mothballs, and listening to the man moving around. The man pushed a chair aside.

"No, not there, Jason, old bud."

Something scraped across the planks.

"Come on, kid. I wanna make friends."

In the next instant, the boxes in front of him opened outward from him, and there the man was, leaning in, offering him a hand.

"Come on, pal. I ain't gonna hurt you. I need you."

"My mother called Mr. Bishop," the boy said. "He'll be here any minute."

The man smiled. "He'll be welcome."

"He'll call the police."

The smile broadened slightly; it stretched the scar. "*They'll* be welcome." The man was crouched down, with the one hand outstretched. "Come on. I ain't gonna hurt you. I swear."

"How did you get in?"

"I knocked, you know."

"The doors are locked."

"The side door wasn't. I saw you in the window, and I thought there might be something wrong. The side door was sitting open, Jason. I let myself in."

"Who are you—what do you want?"

"Come on out of there and we'll get to know each other. Here." He reached in as if to shake hands. "I'm Travis. Okay? Travis Buford Lawrence Baker. Nice to meet you."

"Go to the other end of the attic and I'll come out," Jason told him.

The head tilted slightly. "That's kind of silly, ain't it? Is that the way things are between men these days? Come on, shake hands."

"No," Jason said. "Go to the other side."

The man looked away for an instant and seemed about to comply, but then he reached back suddenly and caught the boy's wrist. His grip was paralyzingly strong; it seemed to send a weakening current through the boy. Jason felt himself being pulled out of the space and then lifted. He was big for his age, almost as tall as his mother's five-seven, and yet the man hauled him up as though he were a doll. They were face-to-face, and Jason thought he smelled decay, something foul from the scarred mouth.

"There we go," the man said, setting him down on his feet, holding him by the arms. "You're a big tall boy. Your voice ain't changed yet."

Jason was silent.

"Don't be scared. I ain't gonna hurt you, really."

"You're hurting me now."

The hands dropped away, and the man stood back a step. "See?" Then he held out his hand again. "I'm Travis. Like I said. And you're Jason. How old are you, Jason?"

"Why'd you come in here?" Jason said.

"Tell me how old you are, son."

"I don't have to tell you anything."

"Now, have I done one thing to hurt you?"

Jason stood there.

"Well, have I?"

"You don't belong here. You broke in."

"Hey, let's go downstairs and I'll tell you the whole thing. I ain't gonna hold nothing back. Okay?"

"Look," the boy said. "Why don't you just—take what you want and leave."

"Damn—" Travis laughed and ran one heavy-knuckled hand across his mouth. Jason saw a blood-mark on one knuckle. "You think I'm a burglar? Is that what you think? Me?"

"I want to stay here," the boy said and felt himself starting to cry.

"It's getting dark. Man—when I was your age there wasn't nothing in the world as scary as a dark attic. Ain't you afraid of a dark attic?"

"You go down," he said. "I'll follow you."

"Okay." Travis seemed to ponder this, then started down. He looked over his shoulder. "When's your mama getting home, anyway?"

"We don't have anything," Jason said, unable to control the tears now.

Travis turned there on the attic stairs and looked at him, and when he spoke it was with an exasperated urgency that reminded the boy painfully of his father. "Are you still harping on that burglar stuff? I ain't no burglar."

Jason followed him down, keeping back from him. They went into the kitchen, and the man searched for the light.

"It's above you," Jason told him.

"Thanks."

The kitchen was a long room, with a counter on one side and a small booth on the other. There was a window seat, and a pantry door beyond this; an island stood in the middle of the room, with pots and pans suspended from a rack in the ceiling above it. Travis sat in the window seat. "Nice house."

"What do you want?" the boy asked.

"Well, like I said. I ain't no damn burglar." Travis smiled.

Jason was on the other side of the room, near the entrance. Behind Travis, the windows in the door were darkening, but the boy saw that one of the panes was out.

Travis had seen him notice it. "Oh, that," he said. "I lied about the door being unlocked."

"We don't have anything," said the boy. "Please."

"Okay, look," Travis said, rising. "Turns out I ain't a burglar, okay? But I *am* a criminal. I'm being straight with you, kid. I'm telling you the truth." He reached into the back of his jeans, at the belt, and brought out a pistol. "There, see? Out in the open. I don't want nobody to get hurt. Promise. I'm being right up front with you, ain't I?"

Jason remained silent; his own legs felt like weights.

"Well, ain't I?"

He couldn't speak.

"Come on. Sit down. Really. I'll put this away." Travis stuck the gun back where he had got it, and moved to the door. There was some glass at his feet. He pushed this aside with the toe of his boot. "Look, I got accused of this crime I didn't commit. I mean I know they all say that—but this is the truth. They had all this circumstantial evidence on me, and there was bad feeling about me in the town anyway, and it all added up, and they sent me away. I swore I'd find the guy that actually did the crime. You see?"

Jason shook his head, wasn't even quite aware that he had done so. He was actually sitting here with this man, this armed someone, escaped from the penitentiary.

"Well, I couldn't very well prove my innocence behind bars, could I?"

"No, sir."

Travis smiled and shook his head. "Sir." He moved to the sink and leaned against the counter. Jason heard the small bump of the pistol against the Formica. "Sir. Wow."

"My mother called Mr. Bishop," Jason said.

The other seemed only faintly interested in this. "Yeah. That guy lives in the farmhouse over yonder?"

The boy nodded.

"He's not home."

"He comes over."

"Checking up on you, huh?"

Jason said nothing.

"They don't trust you."

"Yes they do."

"Well, Jason, it don't look like it. This old colored guy comes in to look you over. And your mother calling you like that. It don't look like there's much trust there. Course, you ain't done much to help them trust you. Been skipping out of things in the last couple days, right?"

"My mother knows about it."

"I bet she don't." Travis reached under his coat, into his shirt pocket, and brought out a cigarette. He turned the stove on and bent to the flame. The boy watched the side of his face, as the cigarette caught. Travis blew smoke at the ceiling and gave forth a small satisfied sound. He'd left the flame burning on the stove. He smiled, took another drag on the cigarette, then turned the flame off. "Guess you're wondering what we're waiting for."

"No," the boy said. "You're from those people that sent those ugly letters."

"Really." Travis seemed amused.

"Mr. Bishop has been kind to us. You're all a bunch of racists."

"Tell you the truth, son, I don't give a shit about that stuff, one way or the other. I'm an equal opportunity criminal."

"You picked the wrong people."

"Where's your daddy?"

Jason didn't answer.

"No daddy?"

"I don't see why I should tell you anything."

"No daddy."

He sat there under the flat green gaze. "Leave me alone."

After a pause, the other moved away from the sink and sat across from him. "Oh, hell. I'm really sorry, man."

"Stop it," Jason said. He was fighting tears again, and with this struggle to master himself, he discovered a slight lessening of his fear. The other sat there smoking, watching him.

"You feel like talking about it?"

The boy said nothing.

"I guess not."

They were quiet. Travis leaned back in the chair and watched the smoke rise from his face. Then he blew smoke rings. "You ever smoke?"

Jason kept silent.

"You want one?"

"No."

"What happened?"

He didn't understand the question.

"Your father."

"I don't want to talk about my father with you."

"I'm sorry." Travis sat forward. "Is the smoke bothering you?"

"No."

Again, there was an interval of quiet.

"He was killed in an accident," Jason said, feeling an inward shock. It was the first time he had spoken the phrase out loud.

"Jeez," said the other. "That's a lousy thing to happen."

The boy had the sense that this was some kind of game.

Travis smoked the cigarette, blew more smoke rings. "Were you close?"

Jason didn't answer him. It was a long silence.

"I bet you were close."

"What're you gonna do with us?"

"Come on, Jason. We were talking. We were making friends, weren't we?"

"I want to know what you're gonna do."

"Just answer the question for me. I ain't talking for the exercise. I'm interested in you, boy. I wanted to know were you and your daddy close. Did you talk to each other a lot. Did he tell you things, you know, man to man, and like that."

"I don't know. He was my father."

"Now that wasn't so painful, was it? Sometimes it helps to talk about these things. Even if it's with somebody you ain't all that happy to be talking to. So you were—you and him—you were close."

"I guess."

"He tell you things?" Travis smiled at him, blowing the smoke; it wavered out of his scarred mouth and made a stemlike trail upward, as he breathed. "Advice, stuff about life, all that?"

"I guess. I don't know."

"Nothing about his business, say?"

"What?"

"Man, it's so rough. See, I ain't close to my daddy. In fact, if I'd had my way, he might could've ended up like your daddy, and I wouldn't've minded at all, you know? I mean my old man ain't nothing but a sorry son of a bitch. Don't get me wrong, though. He's not quite to blame for me. I got off on the wrong foot down there, all on my own."

"Where—where does he live?" Jason asked. "Your daddy."

"Hey—see? We're getting along now. My daddy lives in Gainesville, Florida. But he raised me in Georgia, and I ain't seen him since he moved to Gainesville. You ever been to Georgia?"

"No, sir."

Travis laughed softly. "Sir." He cleared his throat, took a last drag on the cigarette, then got up and ran the tap over the coal. "Where's the trash?"

"Under the sink."

He looked there and put the cigarette away. The little click of the cabinet closing reminded Jason of the careful fastidious way his mother moved around in the kitchen. Travis turned to the door with its open pane and pulled the remaining pieces of glass from it.

"How did you escape?"

For a little space, the other seemed to be listening for something, head cocked to one side, standing stock-still. "Escape?"

"Were you in Lorton?"

It was clear that the question pleased him. "Place ain't fit for animals. Did you know DC sends all their criminals out there, too? From DC Jail, for Christ's sake. Pardon the language. Well, they were set to move me downstate. I mean I had my orders and everything and I was waiting to go. And the, ah, opportunity to go sooner— um, than planned, sort of presented itself. Easiest damn thing in the world. I jumped into a freaking laundry hamper. Me. Just like the movies. Rode out in the back of the truck. And when they stopped, I just let myself out and went on my merry way."

"Where'd you get the gun—and your clothes?"

Travis stared. "You're a smart boy, ain't you."

"No, sir."

"Well. I made a couple of other stops. Before I stopped here."

"What—what was the crime they said you did?"

"Agh." He waved this away. "Theft. You know. One thing and another."

"I thought you said you weren't a burglar."

"I'm not."

"Burglary is theft."

"Well, it's a particular kind of theft. This was a—a bank robbery."

"There's video cameras in banks. Wouldn't they know from the tape if you were innocent?"

"Boy, you watch too much TV. It ain't like TV everywhere, you know. There wasn't any tape this time. Just circumstantial. Some folks said they saw me. Well. Some said it was me and some said it wasn't." He took another cigarette out and moved to the stove again. "This is nice," he said, blowing more smoke. "Let's keep talking. What else do you want to know?"

"Nothing," the boy said. Something in the other's animation, his confidence, and that hollow little smile, had discouraged any response.

"Nothing else you want to ask me?"

"No."

"Course, I could be telling you a lot of lies here."

Now there was just the sound of the furnace running, and when it stopped, the grandfather clock in the hall was sounding.

"Five o'clock," Travis said.

"My mother won't get home till six."

"Hell, I don't know, man. That's a long time to wait for dinner. What do you usually do for dinner?"

"There's stuff in the refrigerator. I make my own."

Travis tilted his head to the side, regarding him. "She don't like the job much—right? The job is a bad necessity."

It was true. When the small contracting business Jack Michaelson had owned began to fail in the real estate slump, he had borrowed heavily on life insurance policies. Jason's father had spent nearly everything trying to save the business, and in the end there had been little more than the money necessary to bury him. The last months of the man's life had been so strange, requiring a kind of caution when with him that had never been necessary before, and he had spent many long hours looking through the account books, as if searching for the one mistake that had put him in the mess he was in. It had become almost impossible to talk to him, and his son imagined that when the bus had crossed the median strip, careening toward him, his mind was elsewhere.

But the boy had worked to unthink everything he knew about those last days, all of which seemed concentrated in the memory of a day they had planted maple saplings out in the back of the house; a freezing cold twilight, Jason standing with his father in the cold, the oncoming night having caught them before they could finish, Jason wishing he could be anywhere else, hating his father, and thinking about how good it would be to have him somewhere faraway for a while. . . .

It felt as though that were the last time he saw his father alive. But the tree planting had been more than a week before the accident. Jason spent so much of that week avoiding him, attempting as often as possible to evade notice, to be invisible. Trouble between them, and an anger in the boy's heart, a refusal, deep down, to forgive. He did not want to have his father to deal with, and he had succeeded too well. He could not remember the last thing he might have said to him, what had passed between them. It was buried in the blur and stress of avoidance, the enforced, moody quiet of those last days.

Now, Travis said, "Yeah. Your mom's left you for a career, I guess somebody's gotta make money—I figured that. And you're mad at her for it. I can see it. I can come up with stuff like that. I bet I'd make a good shrink."

"We don't even have much of a car. We had to sell the good one. There's nothing here for you."

Travis seemed to ponder this a moment, puffing on the cigarette and blowing the smoke rings. "Hell, I don't know. These farms— there's so much ground to cover out in the open."

"Mr. Bishop's gonna be here any minute," Jason said.

The other nodded, with that sarcastic smile. The boy was sure of it now: the whole thing was a show, a fake; Travis was playing, stringing him along. "Like I said." Travis kept the smile, breathing smoke. "The gentleman would be welcome."

A moment later, he went to the window in the door. "Well— nothing out there."

The phone rang again. They looked at each other. There was the small mechanical agitation and then the voice. "This is Nora . . ." The recorded message went on. The beep sounded. "Okay," came the now distressed sound of the same voice. "I'm getting scared. Where is everybody? Hello? Jason?"

"Pick it up," Travis said. "Come on. And son?" He took the pistol out of the back of his jeans. "You say anything about me, and I'll kill you both. I have no plans to kill anybody, but you fuck up and that's what'll happen."

"Jason?" came the voice. "Jason, please pick up."

They moved into the hall, and Travis took the receiver and held it between them. Jason took hold of it and said, "Hello?"

But the line had clicked. Travis took the receiver from him and held it to his ear, then slowly replaced it in its cradle. "Shit." He took the boy's arm and pulled gently; they were heading back into the kitchen.

"What're you gonna do now?" Jason asked.

"We're gonna wait."

In the kitchen, he made Jason sit at the table, then sat across from him. "How'd your neighbor get along with your daddy?"

"I don't know anything about it."

"He's a family friend, right?"

"Not before . . ." Jason halted.

"But he comes over to check on you."

"Yes. Every day. I don't know where he is today."

Travis folded his big hands on the surface, gazing at the boy with an expressionless calm, the scarred mouth an even line, the eyes almost lazily blinking at him and then simply staring. "How old are you?"

The boy told him.

Travis nodded. "That's a nice time in a kid's life. Just getting started on everything. Still a kid, and kind of figuring what's out there. You know what's out there, right?"

Jason said nothing.

"Yeah, a good time. I hope you appreciate what's ahead. When I was eleven, I was running around Atlanta looking for a place to sleep."

The boy shifted in the chair, staring at his own hands on the table before him.

"Hell, no need to feel bad for me. I was all right. I was up to it. My mother was a fancy lady. You know what a fancy lady is?"

Jason thought he knew, but he shook his head.

"Well, anyway. She didn't have much time to do the mother bit, and so I was pretty much on my own from about six years on. Rough time, let me tell you, boy. That was rough. But I got used to it."

"Where was your father?"

The slow dubious smile. "He was around."

Jason watched him begin to daydream or remember, leaning back in the seat and staring at the ceiling.

"Last time I saw my mother she was in a hospital bed, thirty-five years old and looking like she was sixty. Somebody'd shoved one of those little pencil sharpeners down her throat. Can you imagine such a thing? I mean it tore the hell out of her throat and esophagus. You know what that is—the esophagus?"

"Yes."

"Well, then you know what I mean. I had an aunt drink some kind of acid once. They had to sew part of her intestines to her stomach."

They were quiet. The boy watched him.

"You think I'm telling the truth?"

He nodded, believing he was expected to.

"Actually, all that stuff I just told you is kind of a lie. Matter of fact, my mother's a saint. And my daddy died before I knew him. The whole world lives on lies anymore, though. So I like to do my part. I'd say eighty percent of what I say is a lie of one kind or another."

"I have to go to the bathroom," Jason said.

The other frowned at him. "You ain't gonna play games with me, are you? I thought we were getting to be friends."

"I have to go," Jason said.

"Where's the bathroom? Maybe I got to go, too."

The boy led him down the hall, past the telephone, to the little cubicle under the stairs. It was windowless, but there was a square vent there, behind the hamper, which looked to be fastened with screws. The screws had long ago worn smooth the plaster of the wall surrounding it. This duct led around a sharp angle and through several sections of wall to a guest bedroom on the other end of the house. Jason had used this as a secret passageway when he was younger, playing his own games of spying; once he had crouched in the small metal- and dust-smelling space at the end of the duct and watched his own baby-sitter necking on the bed with her boyfriend, and there had been times, playing with school friends, when he had gone the other way, from the bedroom, and on into the bathroom to hide. His father had been intending for years to fix it, seal it off.

Now, Travis stood in the open door of the small bathroom and looked around. He stepped in and touched the wall, stared at himself in the mirror over the sink. "Man, I am one beautiful young dude."

"I don't feel good," Jason said.

The other studied him a moment. "You must have to go bad."

"My stomach hurts."

"Oh, you've got *that*." Travis looked at the room again. "Well, okay. But hurry. We've got to think about tonight. I promise you some excitement."

"Yes, sir."

He shook his head going out. "Sir. That is something. Sir." He turned, holding onto the door, and surveyed the room once more. He glanced at the hamper and pulled the revolver out. "You ain't got any hidden weapons or anything in here, right?"

"No, sir." Jason held his stomach and bent over slightly. "Ohh."

Travis walked over and opened the hamper, then upended it, pouring the dirty clothes out. He held the hamper up and moved the clothes with his boot. Then he looked at the vent for what seemed a terribly long time.

"Ohh," Jason said. "Come *on*, man."

Travis set the hamper back in its place. "All right, all right. Let her rip, kiddo." He made a little saluting motion, putting the barrel of the pistol to his forehead. Then he closed the door. Jason put the hook in its little slot.

"What was that?"

"It's just the hook."

"You don't think I'm gonna want to come in when you get going on your business, do you?"

"No, sir."

"Okay. So unlock the door."

He flicked the hook up. Then made another moaning sound.

"Sounds bad," Travis said, from the other side.

"It's bad," the boy said. He flushed the toilet and moved the hamper aside.

"Finished already?"

"No," he said and groaned. He waited a moment and then flushed the toilet once more and got himself down to the level of the vent. He was simply going to have to go ahead and take the chance that Travis would open the door on him. He pulled the metal screen off.

"You okay in there?"

"I'm okay." He groaned, and waited and then groaned again.

"Man, sounds bad."

"Come on," Jason said. "I can't do it with you listening in on me."

"I'm just standing here, kid."

Abruptly, he was sick. He got to the edge of the toilet and gagged, then spit.

"Oh, hell," came the voice from the other side of the door. "I hope you ain't got some damn bug or something."

"Leave me alone," Jason said. He reached up and flushed the toilet, then worked frantically to get his sneakers off, so many laces, so many useless laces for style, and how he hated them for it now. Finally, he was free and he crawled into the vent, feet first, pulling the sneakers after him. It had been a couple of years. His hips were tight in the opening. He turned his body slightly and slipped deeper in. Beyond the opening, the duct widened a little. He took a breath and pushed back, but there wasn't anything to use as leverage.

"Finished yet?"

"I'm gonna be a little while," Jason said, realizing that the straining in his voice was precisely what he needed. He was half in and half out of the vent now, and he heard something working at the door. The door was going to open. "I'm sick," he said and made another gagging sound.

"Tell you what," Travis said. "I just put a chair against the door. Let me know when you want out—or if you need anything."

"Yes—yes, sir."

"I hope you ain't got some virus. I can't afford to get no virus."

"No, sir."

"But then I didn't kiss you, right?"

Jason faked a cough, supporting himself on one hand and trying to push backward into the vent.

"Just bang on the door when you want me. I'm gonna take a look at the house."

"Yes, sir." He waited. And then he began furiously to scramble backward into the vent. He discovered that if he put his legs on top of one another, forcing his ankles together, and kept his body at the angle of the diagonal corners, he could use his outstretched free hand to push off the seams in the top of the duct and make himself slide along. When he got to the turn, he had enough room to bring that hand down to his side and scoot farther, until he had come into the wider space near the bedroom. Here, he could maneuver, so that he was on his back, and gradually he worked his way to the dim square of gray light, the vent in the guest bedroom, which was an L-connection, the vertical part of it running all the way to the top floor of the house. In that space, he would be able to get himself to a crouch. He inched along, holding his breath like a swimmer, and when the furnace kicked on, he tried to move faster, gulping the air that rushed through from the other side of the building. Here was the vent for the guest bedroom, and he had got himself out of the smaller duct and soundlessly into a crouch.

And he saw that Travis was there, sitting on the edge of the bed looking at a photograph in a frame. Travis was almost near enough to touch.

Somehow Jason kept back the gasp that rose in his throat.

Travis held the photograph to the light from the hall, then put it down on the bed and lay back, sighing. The light fell across the floor, to the bed, and his boots, the scuffed, scraped soles, one with a place wearing thin, showing the paper-thin layer of leather beneath. For a long time nothing moved. The furnace stopped; the house was terribly quiet now. Jason held his breath. A spasm had started in the muscles of his back, as though his body would make a commotion on its own. He suffered the pain along his shoulder blades, the searing strip of it across his hips. The other breathed slow, almost laboring, the first rattle of a nasal something, like snoring. Was he going to sleep? He might stay there an hour, two hours, until Jason's mother returned. The boy withheld a nearly overwhelming need to cry out, for the pain.

Everything hurt.

If Travis was asleep, it might be possible to push out of the vent and sneak away. But the vent would make a noise—some noise, anyhow. There was nothing to do but remain absolutely still, even as the muscles of his back tightened and quivered and sent a stabbing sensation up into his neck. It was dusty here, and when the furnace came on again, the dust stirred. He had not remembered that it had stirred so much dust before, and he realized dimly that it was his own passage through this metal space that had caused the motes to lift, where they could be pushed and agitated by the currents of warm air. He breathed, carefully, slowly, through his nose, beginning to worry about sneezing. Any second now, he would have to sneeze, or cough. Putting his hands over his mouth, he moved back into the vent, until his foot made a small thud. He froze. The sound seemed to travel out from where he was, an alarm, louder than he could bear. But Travis hadn't moved from the bed, an elongated shape extending from the two boot soles. Perhaps five minutes went by, and Jason remained still, his hands tight over his mouth.

Finally, Travis sat up, stretched, then stood. He looked at the vent screen, right through it, it seemed, the muddy eyes fixed on the hot, metal-smelling space behind it, at the crouched shape there. But then his gaze wandered to the window, and he took the two steps to reach it, moving the blinds aside. The furnace stopped again. Travis was whistling low, his tongue between his teeth. He opened a drawer, rooted in it, then closed it and opened another. He looked in the closet. The closet was mostly empty, but there were boxes of clothes on the shelf. He moved the boxes, as if wanting to see what they weighed. He went through everything; rooting, pulling clothes from the bureau, picking through the papers and envelopes in the drawers of the writing desk. At last, he walked out of the room. Jason moved to the screen and listened. The whistling sounded from the stairs. He pushed on the screen, and it came loose with a small hollow metal squeak. He was out, in the room, looking at the imprint of mussed blanket where the other had been on the bed. He heard the weight of him, moving around on the floor above: his mother's bedroom. With as much stealth as he could muster, he hurriedly pulled his sneakers on, tied them, his fingers refusing to function, bumbling everything. He could hear his own desperate effort, and Travis was everywhere now and nowhere. When the boy held his breath, he could hear nothing at all.

He stepped to the window, opened it soundlessly, slowly, and climbed out, dropping to the ground, crouching along the wall, edging out of the square of light from the windows. When he crossed into the line of darkness, he began to run, almost blindly, headlong into the frozen field, away from the tall, lighted house.

THE DARK

When he had some distance, he slowed, listened, looking around himself. There was a chilly breeze, a clicking in the branches of the pines that lined the far end of the field, toward the road. The air smelled of dead leaves, and, from somewhere, car exhaust. He headed across the back lawn, fearful of the sound of his passage through the tall grass: he wanted to hear everything, to be certain Travis wasn't chasing him. When he got to the fence he turned and looked at the house, waited a moment in the racket of his own hard breathing. He saw a shadow moving across the upstairs window. The shadow paused there, and the boy dropped to the base of the fence, lying flat along the dip in the cold ground. He could see the shape in the window moving, saw the hands go up to the face to blot out light. It was only a moment, and Jason lay absolutely still. The ground was damp here, beginning to solidify. He felt himself taking hold, thinking clearly about the dark, how any movement might make him visible. When the silhouette in the window went out of sight, he got to his feet, scrambled over the fence and ran on, to the edge of the creek, the little muddy branch of Steel Run, between his mother's property and Mr. Bishop's farm. The trickle of muddy water had crystallized. On the other side, up the small embankment, he turned to look at the house again. The lights were on. It looked like any other house, the warm, inviting windows and the porch. He would get Mr. Bishop to call the police.

The field rose to a crest and then dipped down into tall, skinny pines. Jason knew the path through. He ran now, and here was the Bishop farmhouse, a looming darker shape against the darkening sky, dotted with lighted windows and adorned by a bright, outward shining beam over the back porch. He bolted into the wide pool of the light and up the steps to the door. "Mr. Bishop," he said, banging on the glass. He peered in and could see the dining room and on through to the living room with its fireplace. The lights were on over the mantel—two electric candles. "Mr. Bishop," the boy called. He turned to look at the driveway; there was the truck. "Mr. Bishop?" He hit the door several times, and at last he tried the knob. It was locked. He waited a moment, hearing the wind move in the bare branches of the trees. Above him, the lights in the upper hall-way were burning. He stepped out into the yard and looked up.

Music was coming from somewhere. He went stumbling around to the side of the house. "Mr. Bishop," he shouted, coming up onto the porch. When he hit this door, it swung open; it had been sitting ajar.

"Mr. Bishop?"

Nothing.

In another room, some far part of the house, the music played. He stepped in and went along the downstairs hall. "Mr. Bishop." In the living room there was a half-glass of beer. He went through to the kitchen and up the stairs toward the sound of the music.

"Mr. Bishop?"

One room was empty—a bed, a nightstand; an open closet door; a cedar chest. He crept along the hall to the second doorway. Here was the music—horns and piano, the crackling sound of a needle on a record. The music stopped, the arm was lifted, and it made a little protesting noise, moving, then settling again, so that the music had started once more, through the same crackle and hiss.

"Mr. Bishop?" Jason said, not wanting to startle him, and wor-

ried, in spite of the feeling of urgency and panic, about having come
so far into his house. "Sir?"

He saw Mr. Bishop's bent knees before he saw the rest of him.

Edward Bishop lay on the floor, next to a small love seat or
couch; he was on his stomach with his hands tied behind his back,
then strapped to his ankles. Something else ran from under his nose
to the knots at his feet, thin rope, drawn tight, pulling his head back.
Jason saw something dark surrounding the dark figure there on the
wood floor, and an instant later, in the terrible quiet of knowing
that the eyes were not looking at anything—though they were
open—the boy understood, with a tremendous shock to his mind,
that the darkness surrounding Mr. Bishop in that wide shadow-out-
line of his body was blood.

He stepped back and then fell down in the frame of the door.
The music was playing, the needle crackling. For a second there
wasn't any other sound, save his own sobbing, and now he was up,
trying to run, stumbling and scrabbling toward the stairs. He had
gone halfway down when the thought occurred to him that Travis
might be in the house, would surely have discovered that he had
got out, and would know to come here. The part of him that had
been calculating things took hold again, and he stopped. He was
on the landing of the stairs, wiping his eyes, trying to be quiet, and
he backed against the wall, listening, not breathing, though his
lungs were stinging with the need for air. He looked back up the
stairs at the bright bulb burning in the hallway, then reached for
the telephone on the little antique table. The line was dead. Either
Travis had cut it before, or he was in the house now.

The boy pulled the phone from the wall and ran back up the
stairs and knocked the bulb out, bringing the dark down on himself.
He waited, listening. No sound except the song playing, and the low
sobs he couldn't control. He went to the lamp on the table and
reached in and quickly took that bulb, then stopped to listen again.
From some reserve of volition he did not know he possessed, he
found the presence of mind to do this through the whole upstairs of
the house, still pausing, breathless and crying. He had removed
every light, and Travis had not come.

There was still the downstairs—the kitchen. And his thinking had not been as clear as he'd felt it to be: there were knives in the kitchen; there were guns in the house, surely: Mr. Bishop talked about hunting. Hadn't he? It occurred to the boy that he had never come over here, never seen the inside of the man's house, never really listened to him. Hadn't he talked about hunting? There must be a rifle or shotgun somewhere. Jason stood crying, in the dark of the upstairs, trying to decide. Finally he drew the courage to go to the windows and look out at the lawn below, the near part of which was still bathed in light. Above the far roof of his mother's house, a full moon shone through a hole in the clouds. It limned the branches of the pines, which were like tall, watchful presences, and it shone on the fallow field that spanned the distance between. Nothing moved. He thought he saw a light go off in his mother's house. He couldn't be sure, couldn't trust it.

In the next instant, he heard movement downstairs.

Had the floor creaked? He was standing near the doorway of the third bedroom, in the dark, looking at the light at the head of the stairs. Something changed, the light altered, or it was his own eyes. In the next room, the music played over the dreadful quiet figure on the floor in its border of blood.

Jason moved into the room, certain that he was not alone, that Travis had followed him here. The clear part of his mind saw Travis moving carefully up the stairs, but there was nothing. Nothing came, and the music stopped, the record arm lifted and moved, dropped down on the beginning of the record. Travis would not expect him to remain with the body, would not think he would actually hide here.

He was certain now that he had heard movement on the stairs.

He worked his way under the love seat, next to the body. Mr. Bishop's face was only inches away, a darker blotch in the darkness, so awfully still. The eyes looked beyond everything; they were visible, terrifyingly inanimate in the form of the face. From where he was under the love seat, and because of the upper part of Mr. Bishop's body, he could see only the bottom part of the door frame. He watched it, hearing more sounds. Something was moving in the house, he was certain of it. He saw a shadow glide up from the base of the wall, and his heart jumped in its small space under the bones of his chest.

A cat strode into the room, tail up. A big gray Tom. One of the wild litter Mr. Bishop had talked about. It must have wandered into the open side door downstairs. The boy gasped at the sight of it, too startled to scream, then gave forth a sob of relief, and found himself having to suppress a wild laugh, like a part of his crying. The cat made a little leap onto the love seat, then leapt back down, to Mr. Bishop's back. It moved its head to his ear, as if to whisper something to the dead man. Jason crawled out of the space, and the cat turned to stare at him. In the doorway, he looked up and down the hall. The cat mewed behind him, and the rest of the house was quiet.

He went stealthily to the head of the stairs, taking hold inside, receiving again the sensation of thinking clearly, with a kind of icy calculation that surprised him: Travis could not afford to be patient about everything because the boy's mother was coming home. Travis would come here. Now. And the thing to do was get out of the house, get as far down the road as possible, toward help.

Except that there was his mother to think about.

He must head her off. He would have to get around to the other end of the field, across the area where Travis would be approaching. He would have to make his way out to the road, where he could try to stop her. Where he could flag someone, anyone, down.

At the bottom of the stairs, he made his way along the wall into the kitchen, keeping below the level of the windows. The only sound in the house was the insane brightness of the music, the record playing. In the kitchen he opened drawers in the counter, searching for a knife. Something to use as a weapon. The first drawer was filled with pornographic playing cards and pencils. The second had old bills and mail and a screwdriver. He gripped the screwdriver and edged to the other side of the room, hurrying, wanting to run, get out and disappear into the darkness. The drawer next to the sink was filled with knives, and he picked one, setting the screwdriver down. He stepped to the back door, breathed a moment, tightly gripped the knife, and moved the bordering curtain aside.

Travis was standing there with his back to the door, looking off toward the field.

The boy ducked back below the level of the window and saw the knob on the door begin to move. It turned one way and caught, then turned the other. The boy backed along the base of the wall, under the table and down a small stairwell, where a plywood door opened onto a dark, earth-smelling basement. He crouched against the door, trying not to scream, the scream rising under his heart. Somewhere and at some point he had dropped the knife. There was no thinking now—only the reaction, cringing against the thin plywood in that dim little cavelike enclosure and watching the pane break in the back door.

The big hand reached in and opened the door. And there was Travis, looking cool and calm and perfectly unemotional. He went on, into the living room, to the hallway and the stairs up. "Bags?" he said. "Goddammit. Bags."

The heavy, booted feet were just above Jason, creaking in the beams of the stairwell. He stepped up into the kitchen and out the open door, across the wooden stoop and down into the soft ground, where he fell. He was lying in the pool of light, and he rolled out of it, into the freezing, dead grass near the cellar window. There, in the dark, he came to his feet and hurled himself close to the house, toward the truck, then under the truck, and on, out into the gravel road, running.

AT MERCY

N<small>ORA</small> S<small>PENCER</small> M<small>ICHAELSON</small> <small>SAT</small>
in a meeting of other instructors of Sisters of Mercy School, trying to
be calm about the fact that there were no answers to her calls home.
She reminded herself of other evenings she hadn't been able to get
through—Edward sometimes took Jason to the store, or out in the
woods to mock hunt deer. It was not unusual for him to do something to keep the boy busy. Only last week there had been no answer,
and she came home to find them stacking firewood that Mr. Bishop
had bought; she had called four times that evening.

When she could hold this fact in her mind, she could breathe.

But she kept feeling the clammy sense of violation over what had
been in her mailbox two afternoons ago. It sent her spiraling toward
panic. She clasped her hands in front of her, like a student, and tried
to pay attention, tried not to think at all. If she could only attend to
things, she might be able to speed the meeting to a close. This, she
knew, was a hopeless fantasy. The meeting would drag on.

Lately it had come back to her, with a force, that she had quit teaching all those years ago for reasons more basic than her marriage to
Jack Michaelson. Something about the life had exhausted her and

made her feel obscurely angry a lot of the time. It was an element of her makeup, a severity that the inadequacies of her students seemed continually to aggravate. She suspected finally that she lacked the necessary patience, except that wasn't quite it, either; with students who were interested and working hard, she was more than forbearing; she suffered them almost to the point of indulgence. But so many of the students she encountered had already been ruined by other teachers, or by the culture they lived in, which seemed to value everything else over knowledge, and these students—ignorant, oddly cynical about life, often uncivil, and incredibly complacent about their ignorance—these students were so self-satisfied and aggressively obtuse that unvaryingly they made her feel a black desire to lash out, a smoldering rage.

It discouraged her. It made her long for some other task, some other way to spend her time. Though of course she was fairly certain there wasn't anything that would serve to get her mind off the living she was doing now, with its loneliness, its meagerness, its endless worry.

Today, the usual heavy workload, the hours of concentration that had been required of her, had served to deaden the sense of unease, of trespass on her privacy, which she now felt along with all the rest. Oh, how she had wanted to tell Ed Bishop not to come see her and Jason anymore. There was Jason's safety to think about. She had spent a bad long day yesterday, seeing images of her son receiving harm from strangers, men who were part of a sickness she was not up to fighting. She wasn't up to any of it. Unhappy as the realization had made her, she determined to accept the truth and to act accordingly. Mr. Bishop would understand; he had said as much, on more than one occasion. She was alone; she must think selfishly. She drove home with the conviction that she could do what she had decided must be done.

But the moment had come, and she looked into those kind, dark eyes and heard herself convincing him to keep on . . .

Her mother and father lived in Seattle now—one of her father's lifelong dreams; he had spent time there when he was first in the military, back in 1943. They were so far away. It seemed more than the simple miles. Nora's father was a man who kept all pacts with himself, and one of those pacts was that he would live on the edge of the Pacific after he retired from the air force.

Sometimes Nora thought of her parents as representing the luck people in love seemed to have, everywhere she looked.

Her last year with Jack had been so bad that she had contemplated a separation, since it had become nearly impossible to reach him, or find the way to talk to him, bring him around to being himself. She had come to suspect that it wasn't just the business failing, or the venture into computers, which had siphoned more money away. Everything had fallen into question.

Once, that last fall before the accident, she watched him from the window of their bedroom as, below on the sunny, leaf-littered lawn, he tossed a baseball back and forth with Jason. When Jason missed a throw and had to chase it, Jack stared off at the turning trees on the other end of the field and seemed to mutter aloud, shaking his head and facing away from the boy. She wondered what his thoughts were, what he could be saying to the air, waiting for his son to retrieve the ball.

When he came inside, an hour later, she said, "Who were you talking to?"

"What?" He seemed almost startled.

"I was watching you from the window—you and Jason. Jason went to get the ball out of the forsythia bushes and you were—I don't know. Disputing with—something. Who or what were you arguing with?"

"Nothing," he said. "Nobody. Are you spying on me now?"

"Spying on you."

"Just leave me alone a little, can't you? Give me some room to breathe, for Christ's sake. I'm tired of feeling supervised all the damn time."

"Jack, you'd tell me if there was something wrong, wouldn't you?"

"Wrong?" he said.

"Okay." She turned from him.

"No," he said. "Wait."

She faced him and said nothing for a space. Then: "Well?"

"Look, I wasn't—you—I don't know what you thought you saw."

"I love you," she said.

And he looked down. It was as if he did not want the subject of love broached at all. There had been times when—apart from her own growing doubt about her feeling for him—she had been ready to believe he was no longer in love with her. If it weren't for the lovemaking. Those nights, in the room, in the quiet, when he reached for her, and they were lovers again, and he would once more be like the boy she had married, a little nervous, and tremendously careful of her, almost worshipful.

But toward the end, even this had begun to feel detached, almost automatic.

"Jack," she said one night as they lay awake, not touching, "are you seeing someone else?"

"How can you ask that?" he'd said, apparently hurt.

"Something's different between us," she said. "You can't tell me you don't see it or feel it."

"I don't want to talk about this. Why do you have to pick at everything?"

"That's not fair," she told him. "I've gone along this whole year with you, not saying anything. Jack, what *is* it? What's happening to us?"

"Nothing's happening to us. Christ. I don't know what you mean. I'm trying to keep us afloat, and we're sinking. But it isn't *us*. Stop badgering me all the time."

"You feel badgered?"

"No," he told her, getting out of the bed, moving to the other side of the room. He put a light on and got into his robe. "I have some work on the books to do."

"What're you keeping from me, Jack?"

He had glared at her. She almost sank back from him.

"I can get money from my parents, Jack. We're not going to starve. We can start over. I can go back to teaching school. Jason is old enough so he doesn't need constant supervision and I've been thinking about going back anyway."

"No—look—that's not—I don't want to talk about this."

"But you're carrying the whole thing alone. Why?"

"Look, it's nothing—it'll work out. Trust me, okay?"

"I love you," she said again.

But he was already walking away, starting down the hall. "Don't wait up," he said.

"No," said Nora, to the empty doorway. "I won't."

There were other exchanges like this, and during those months she often caught herself wondering how life might change, how time and circumstance would take them away from this difficulty. She began imagining other troubles, actually dreaming them up to look upon them. She had an old school friend whose youngest daughter had recently declared herself to be pregnant; the woman who ran the country store had learned that she had diabetes, and the man who Jack usually engaged to do his plumbing work was going through an ugly divorce. She would be thinking of these troubles and then imagine herself with them, or some version of them—there was so much suffering in the world, so much pain out there beyond the windows of her house.

It was as if she were looking into a possible future in order to console herself for present complications—the tricks her mind would play: she would see herself years in the distance, with Jack restored to his old confident self, bankruptcy and the terrors of failure behind him. She had begun to see her life in terms of daylight and darkness. A pall had settled over everything, and she spent wakeful hours in the nights, thinking of morning, of a dawn that would again be more than a glare along the edges of the low hills outside the window. In these odd, idle dreams of worry it was always she who was carrying the burden of misfortune, and Jack who kept having to seek a way to get close enough to help carry them. And eventually she realized she could not tell him any of this.

Nothing could have prepared her for the shock of finding out how badly he had depleted the insurance: cancellations for lack of payments, borrowing on premiums. It was as if he had abandoned her and their son to whatever the world might do. She understood that he did not know he was going to be killed; he could not have supposed that anything would prevent him from restoring some of the borrowed money, fixing things, living past the difficulty. But the truth was that she had been grieving the loss of Jack for several months before he died—the man she had known and been passionate about once did not resemble the one who drove away from the house in the last afternoon of his life.

When these feelings washed through her, she tried reciting the Twenty-third Psalm to herself. *The Lord is my shepherd, I shall not want . . .*

The lines soothed her, and sometimes they helped her sleep. They made it so that she could be patient with her son, whose face was his father's, and whose reaction to the catastrophe had been so different from her own. She had sought some way to get down into his sorrow with him, to stop his withdrawal. It seemed to Nora that in her recent struggles with Jason, there were similarities to the arguments she'd had with Jack. Cause for sleepless nights and the sort of concentration which did not allow for the healing she needed, too. Just getting through the days required that she spend everything of herself. In the hours of the nights she lay restless, in a nervous kind of depletion, mind racing.

> *Surely goodness and mercy will follow me all the days of my life, and I shall dwell in the house. . . .*

"Ms. Michaelson."

At the opposite end of the long table, the headmistress eyed her with a vaguely curious half smile—Sister Agnes, whose round soft face was almost clownish, except that the blue eyes could turn to ice. As now. "Aren't you listening?"

"I'm sorry."

"I'd like to get this meeting over."

Sister Agnes was a woman whose demeanor was always humorous and rather friendly, even self-deprecating to an extent; yet she had a way of giving out little bitter doses of a capricious and cruel temper. Always with a jolly smile. "I asked who has been put in charge of the Easter pageant and what the plans were, if any. We only have a little more than a month to get ready. And you know how flustered I get about these organizational things. I just have no talent for them. You haven't asked anyone?"

"I'm sorry—I'm—I will—first thing in the morning."

"We have also got to do something about the SAT testing this weekend. We don't have a proctor." Sister Agnes kept the blue steel gaze on her.

"I can't," Nora said. "I have to take my son to the eye doctor on Saturday. It's the only time I can do it."

The others at the table, two laypeople and five nuns, went on talking about the proctoring of the exams, and again Nora's mind began to wander.

"Now," Sister Agnes said. "Let's see what else. We have to talk about the summer classes and registration for the spring athletics."

Nora stood. "I'm sorry. I've really got to go. My son is by himself. As you know. I haven't been able to get Mr. Bishop on the phone. I—I received that awful mail—" she trailed off. "It's got me worried."

Sister Agnes said, "Of course." But there was little understanding or forbearance in the features—a mannish, round-jawed, grandiosely ugly face, still smiling, but with the faintest edge of the sardonic: the face of a well-fed peasant who has just been proved right about something. Some of the younger nuns called her "Nikita," because she looked like the orotund former Soviet premier. The party chairman in a starched wimple and black veil. "I have received mail from the same group," she said proudly. "I think it's a badge of honor, and of course I know you do, too."

"I'd rather not have it," Nora said. The simple truth. It went through her with a chill that this statement, for all its honesty, could cost her the job.

"If you can't stay for the whole meeting, I wish you'd simply not attend it at all," Sister Agnes said. "We'd understand, I'm sure. We do understand, you know."

The others were silent. No one moved.

"Sister Agnes, if I'd have known it would last this long, I wouldn't have attended the meeting."

"Perhaps you want us all to accommodate our schedules to yours?" She pronounced the word the English way: shed-ule. It was a joke. She kept the small smile, as if to say this were all a form of banter, and no threats or ill feelings lurked behind it. But there were the cold eyes above the smile.

Nora held back what she wanted to say: *Sister Agnes, shove this job up your un-Christian ass sideways.*

She looked down at her hands on the back of her chair and said, "I'm very sorry, really."

"There's nothing these sick, unhappy people can do to anyone," Sister Agnes said, gently. "Remember, your church. Your God. 'My strength is as the strength of ten because my heart is pure.' And don't worry about this silly meeting for one second. We know how hard you work, and we all know how difficult it is to raise a child in these times."

Nora understood that the older woman, in her embarrassingly hortatory, vaguely ecclesiastical way, was trying to ease her fears.

Sister Agnes went on. "Someone will take notes for you."

Nora collected her things as quietly and unobtrusively as she could. Sister Agnes watched her go.

Out in the hall, she worked to shake off the feeling, which Sister Agnes always engendered in her, of being a child. She went to the central office, to deposit the pad of legal paper that she took to every meeting and never used. In her mailbox were the folders she had to take home, papers to grade; they always required work on into the night. At the main desk, Opal Stimson sat, paring her long fingernails. Small, dark, with the bulging eyes of thyroid-trouble, she appeared always to be about to break into conspiratorial laughter.

"Thy rod and thy staff, they comfort me," she said.

"You could hear that?"

"Hear what?"

"Opal, what're you talking about?"

"Just talking."

Nora looked at her. The flat nose, with a crooked place near the bridge where it had once been broken, and the crowded lower teeth, which when she smiled made the whole face seem rather oddly uneven and comical. Almost everything Opal said was in some way a non sequitur. "Did my son call?" Nora asked her.

"The school board called. The police want a list of all the kids who are computer literate. Can you imagine? They want to talk to all the hackers."

"Do you think it's some kids?"

"Somebody, coming or going."

"Coming or going." Nora was at a loss.

"Young or old."

"Thank you, anyway, Opal."

"Are you going home early?"

"It's too late for that," Nora told her.

Opal had been married four times, and two of the husbands had been from the same east Tennessee family, the Stimsons, and she'd kept the name. Her maiden name was Oiler, but she was from Wise, Virginia, and pronounced it "All-er." She had told Nora all this in the first few weeks Nora had been on the job, and when she found out that Nora was a widow, she had become so solicitous that Nora felt awkward. The subtle and circumspect expression of this awkwardness, which had really only been a gentle reluctance to accept the other woman's enthusiastic affection, had evidently hurt her feelings. Nora had been looking for a way back from this difficulty, but had not discovered it. Tonight, her weariness found expression in a wordless rush of deciding that she no longer cared what Opal's feelings were. The truth was that she lacked the will for any kind of social pressure or requirement, and if that bothered people, it was just too bad. And oh, how tired she was of this old concrete building with its fake Romanesque facade and its bad paintings and psychobabble sayings in frames on the walls. Above the main doorway, carved in the lacquered wooden block letters of the shop class, were the words: *Today is the first day of the rest of your life.*

Nora stood in the harsh, institutional light and realized that she had reached this impasse concerning her work: she no longer believed it was of any value at all. Out there, in the darkness beyond the doorway, the ignorant and the bigoted were gathering; it felt that way, something awful spreading in the dark.

A student approached her from the doorway off the left hall. One of the good ones, she thought. Her heart went out to him—a thin, usually disheveled boy with bad skin, whose clothes never seemed to fit. A child whom the system was badly failing, all the time. He was seventeen and had had to repeat a grade. She had been one of the teachers he came to for help, or solace, since at home he was mostly left to his own devices—his parents concentrating on their respective careers. Nora never saw him without thinking of Jason, and this had colored her behavior toward him. Not long ago, he started showing signs of having a crush on her. She had very gingerly discouraged it, while trying to maintain his confidence. He only appeared to grow more tentative, more painfully timid, and she had the feeling that something relentless was weighing him down.

He walked over to her now, with his hands in the pockets of his jeans. His blond hair stood straight up on his head, like a fright wig. She could see through it to the shine of his scalp under the lights. She possessed neither the time nor the energy to offer reassurance to him at this moment, and her mood was standoffish. She knew her expression had already communicated this to him, and it made her feel sorry again. Still, she spoke in an even, professional tone. "What is it, Greg?"

"Is the meeting over?"

"What're you doing here this late?"

"Yearbook." In the past month, he had taken on extracurricular activities, to keep from going home. The other students were already complaining about his slovenly habits, his bad breath, and body odor. He never seemed to get anything done.

"Is it going well?" she asked him.

"I guess not. They asked me to take a break out here."

"I see," Nora said. "Well, gotta go."

"The meeting's not over."

"No."

"I have to speak to Sister Agnes."

"Well, she'll be a while."

"One hopes so," Opal Stimson said in a singsong voice. Then: "Good night, Mrs. Michaelson."

Nora shouldered her purse and gathered the folders under her arm.

"Sister Agnes wants to see me about being late all the time," the boy said.

"Well," Nora told him. "I'm sure it'll be all right."

"You helped me before," he said, trying for something. Clearly, he had taken her demeanor toward him as a rejection. "Will you talk to Sister Agnes?"

"Oh, Greg," she told him. "It'll be just fine, okay? Now, I really have to run."

"You won't talk to her?"

Nora sighed. "Well—sure."

"Thank you," Greg said and then just stood there.

"I have to go now," Nora said.

"Okay."

"You gotta do what you gotta do," Opal Stimson said. She opened her desk drawer, then closed it. "If that door opens, and the meeting's over, and she finds you standing here, *then* you'll be in trouble."

The boy, Greg, thanked her and hurried back down the hall.

Nora smiled. "Were you talking to me, or him?"

"You."

"Thanks." She turned and started out and felt abruptly like crying. She was alone; and her loneliness was like a failing.

That was what she had been fighting all these weeks and months, a pervasive feeling of her own culpability in the circumscribed life she was leading. And there had been no one to talk to about it—not really, not with things as they were. No family lived near enough to be of any consolation to her, even if she could have found the time for them. Her days were too crowded with work—six classes a day, each with twenty to twenty-five students, a total of more than one hundred thirty, all told. The grueling daily round of teaching classes, grading papers, proctoring exams, working on the holiday functions, the dances and the programs—religion classes, chapel hour, the student newspaper and the yearbook committee—everything requiring her best attention, all of this while grappling with her own grief and the grief of her son. . . . Everything had become this dizzy, dispirited rush through the days. She couldn't find time for herself, to be alone, to replenish anything of her spirit, her once-humorous way with the world; there wasn't enough time to decide much beyond what to eat in a given day, what to make for her son, what to do, or undo, or leave undone concerning the house, the bills—which kept piling up—or the future, which seemed to be collapsing. There hadn't even been time for friends. (It seemed that *they* were also falling away from her: the couple she and Jack had been most comfortable with, and closest to, had moved to Arizona over the summer, promising to keep in close touch. Nora had stood in the shady lawn out in front of their house, thinking of the hours of summer evenings relaxing with them, when she and Jack had been happy, and there was time and hope was easy.)

During the weeks just after Jack's death, she had spent some days with an elderly friend from Charlottesville—Elaine Tyler, who had been the principal of the first school Nora had taught in after college. Elaine had come to the house to stay for a time, and Nora had gone to Charlottesville to stay with her, too, though Jason was restless and obviously unhappy to be away from his own circle of people—those skinny inarticulate boys with their video games and their science fiction, who seemed always to be harboring some grievance against the adult world. Elaine had lost her own husband thirty years ago and remembered it quite well, and she knew how to talk to Nora about everything, even when it began to be clear that Jack had left nothing behind.

"You're angry with him," she said at one point, as Nora sat crying at the table in the small kitchen of the house in Charlottesville.

"I can't understand what he could've been thinking."

"And you're angry."

"Okay," Nora had said. "Yes. I am angry at him." And she felt suddenly as though she were able to breathe out, after a long holding-in of air. "Yes. I'm so damn mad."

"You see?" Elaine said. "Perfectly fine."

"God *damn* it."

"I'm mad, too, honey."

She hadn't seen Elaine since early in the fall. She hadn't had the chance to get away, or to do more than speak to her briefly over the phone. The school consumed everything. Edward Bishop had become the one person she could talk to about all of this.

Outside the heavy stone walls of the entrance, in the chilly dark, she paused and composed herself, kept back the rising urge to stand there crying. If the Virginia Front was just high school children, and there were no real repercussions to worry about, would she be able to come back from her already expressed hesitation? Why had she shown it to him if she hadn't hoped he would volunteer to stay away for a time? Surely he must have perceived this. She felt the necessity of seeking to make Edward trust that she would not again, at the first indication of trouble, make this kind of capitulation to her own fear. No, she wouldn't let herself think about it anymore.

She gathered her will and walked to the car, aware of the large, many-paned window to her left, the room where the meeting was still going on. It perplexed and troubled her that she could be made to feel guilty, even now, for walking away from there.

Somehow she plucked her keys from the confusion of her purse and managed to open the car door without dropping the folders. She leaned in and unlocked the back door, got it open, and put the folders on the backseat. Three of them dropped to the floor.

"Fuck," she said, low, glancing up at the lighted window as though she expected to find Sister Agnes standing there staring at her, reading her lips. She said again, "Fuck," pronouncing it exactly and clearly, then reached down and retrieved the folders, stuffing the papers back into them.

She got behind the wheel, settled into the seat as if she had collapsed there. She had left the keys in the door. She opened it, leaned out, and couldn't get them from the slot. It was necessary to get out of the car. She did this, then turned to the night and bowed from the waist. "Thank you, ladies and gentlemen of the fucking jury."

She had the usual fight with the ignition, and the car took an age to warm up, while she sat breathing into her hands, trying not to cry. The street was mostly a picture of decay and neglect: empty glass facades where stores had failed, a pawnshop with an iron gate in front of it, and a little all-night diner that no one ever seemed to enter or leave. Someone crossed from there now, going behind her car and away, a heavyset man in a lumber jacket, and a hat with furry earflaps. He headed toward the end of the block, twice glancing at her over his shoulder. Then he stopped and came back toward her, walked up to the window on her side, and knocked. The directness of it alarmed and momentarily paralyzed her. She had locked the doors when he started back, and now she cracked the window slightly.

"Yes?"

The man stood there with his hands in the pockets of his coat. He looked up the street and then down. "I was gonna follow you," he said. "But let's take your car."

She quickly rolled the window up and put the car in gear. It stalled. He watched her, chewing something, the ample flesh of his jaw shaking. He seemed completely sure of himself. In the next instant, he brought his left hand out of the coat pocket, and she saw that he was holding a gun.

"Oh, God," she said. "Oh, Christ. Great. Just fucking great."

He put the gun back in the coat pocket and signaled for her to open the window again.

She yelled at him through the glass. "I don't have any money, and I'm HIV-positive." A phrase she had decided upon as a protective lie, because she had to drive alone into the city each morning; she had never thought she would actually have to use it. And in any case it was lost on the man, who with all the casual officiousness of a police officer stood back a step and said, "Come on. Out."

"Are you—is this—am I under arrest?"

"Right," he said.

"You're a policeman?" She felt herself grasping at this.

"Uh, no," the man said, with a little exhaling laugh. He went around the back of the car and pulled at the passenger side door, and once more she tried to start it and get it going.

"Open it," he said.

"Please leave me alone," she said.

"Open the door."

She didn't move.

"Open it. If you don't, I'll hurt you. And your son'll die, too."

"Oh, God," she said. "Oh, no." It might only have been a breath.

When the man brought the gun from his coat pocket, she reached over and pulled the lock. He was in the car with a heavy bouncing of the shocks, looking back through the rear window and then leaning into the windshield and squinting, as if trying to read one of the neon signs down the street. "Be a good girl," he said with that respiratory laugh. "And you won't get yourself hurt."

"All right," she said.

He was too big for the seat. He looked at her over the roundness of his folded arms and said, "Can you get it started?"

"Where's my son?" she said, hearing the words and disbelieving them.

His heavy, bloated face gave no indication that he'd heard.

"Please," she said. "What is this? Are you with those people?"

The laugh came forth. "What people?"

"I don't have any money," she said. "You're wrong about me. I came to work—we're the wrong people. Please."

His face registered nothing at all. "Come on, get it started."

"Where—" she began.

"Let's go to your house," he said.

The lighted windows of the school building looked gold in the increasing dark. They were safety. Without quite realizing that she would do so, she opened her door and tried to get out. He was startlingly quick for his size. He had her by the upper arm and pulled roughly, hurting her. She screamed, her head still outside the frame of the open door of the car. But now he gripped her by her hair and forced her back, reached beyond her with one bearlike hugging motion and shut the door.

"Don't scream again. If we don't get to your house, your boy'll die. We already got your boy. You understand me? I mean I thought you understood me."

"Oh, God," Nora said. "Oh, please—no."

"Calm down," he said and smiled. "You've got the power." He laughed—the small unpleasant sound—apparently pleased with his own expression. She was silent. "Start the car." He looked out again and back down the road. She commenced struggling with the ignition.

"I got a vehicle over there," he said. "We could take it, I guess. But it's hot and I'd like to leave it behind, if you know what I mean."

The engine caught.

"What do you want?" Nora asked him, through tears.

"Hell." He smiled. "I'm not the one with the ideas."

"Oh, come *on*," she said. "You put that filth in my mailbox."

The smile changed slightly. "Drive," he told her.

In the lunar light, the trees looked as though they were reaching helplessly skyward. Their shadows on the uneven ground made a cross-stitch of lines intersecting other lines. Jason had made it to the other side of the house, keeping to the trees, and he had reached the hill overlooking the road. He was winded, shaking from the chill and from his own terror. The trees confused and frightened him; the moon was so bright. Even the stars seemed brighter.

On nights like this, nights of the amazing country sky, where you felt you could see all the way to the end of the galaxy, and you understood why they called it the Milky Way, he and his father used to take long walks, keeping to the county road, away from the new developments on the other end of Steel Run Creek, where the highway was. His father would talk about the way farmers used to predict the weather by looking at the night sky. This was the same kind of night sky, with a bright, wide halo around the moon. To the boy it was a sick pallor, that brightness all around. The moon was the color of bones.

He came down the embankment to the road, then looked back at the trees, the thousand stitches of shadow. On the other side, beyond the wild-grass field there, he could see the dark shape of the LaCombe house—Mr. LaCombe had once been brother-in-law to some army general who had owned much of the land surrounding Mr. Bishop's farm. Because of the housing developments starting up out near the highway, old Mr. LaCombe had sold his house and land and moved to Wyoming, where there was more space. The house had been empty, like so many others in the county, and his land had been divided into five-acre parcels, for sale, but the real estate slump had stopped all that, and there were now three other empty houses on what had once been the LaCombe farm. The boy knew all this from listening to his father's talk in the months before he died.

The nearest house where there would be people was halfway up Cider Mountain, almost a mile away; it was the next stop the school bus made in the mornings after Jason got on. Missy James lived there with her mother and her aunt. Jason thought of trying to make it up the long, packed, earth-and-gravel road to them, and abruptly he had an image of himself finding them dead. He shook this off, deciding not to chance missing his mother.

Skirting the edge of the road toward where it descended, he tried to hear—over the soughing of the wind in the high tree branches and the clicking of dry wood—the sound of a car. He thought he could hear the low, far-off hum of trucks on the highway, two miles to the north. But it might have been the wind. He stood in the middle of the road. The night was almost day brilliant, except for the trees and the thick dry undergrowth, which was ink-black, impenetrable, a wall of dark, out of which Travis might leap at any moment. The boy was exposed here, and he took himself to the edge of the asphalt surface, at the crest of the long hill leading down toward the highway. He could not stay still, could not simply wait, but kept moving along the road, cold, half-crying, frightened so deeply that his senses had become excruciatingly sharper. He could smell the woods, the several odors of damp and death and the decay of leaves, the larvae of millions of dormant insects, everything. He heard breathing in the interstices of darkness behind him, and he crept away from the edge of the road, still following it, looking back.

He fell—stepped in a hole, or an unevenness in the ground—and pitched forward, facedown in the mulchy leaves and grass. Immediately he rolled to his back and tried to come to his feet. Something moved inside the black wall of the woods, a few feet away. He got to a crouch, then limped over to the other side, aware of the stark definition of his own shadow on the blue surface, and dropped into the declension there, which was almost as deep as a trench. The wind had picked up; it was so cold. He put his hands to his face and shivered, crying. A moment later, he looked back at where he had been and saw movement out of the corner of his eye. Travis emerged from the woods a few yards farther down, came bursting out, almost stumbling. He had been running. He slid down the embankment and then stood, hands open as if to claw the air, looking up and down the road. "If you can hear me, boy, I'm gonna tell you the truth. I'm scared bad. I don't know what happened. I don't have a goddam clue. But it wasn't me. I didn't do it, kid. I'm telling you. And I respect you for outsmarting me. Okay? You hear me? But we got your mother." He looked around, slow. And then he shouted. "You hear me?"

Jason felt himself about to gag on the cold; it was like that: he was shivering so severely that he had become nauseous. His sides hurt; his teeth were chattering. It amazed him that the other hadn't heard. But the wind swept across the moon-white sky, as though it might drag the stars down with it. Travis turned and walked in the very center of the road, back in the direction of the house. He stopped and turned around and appeared to be listening. "Goddammit."

The wait for him to continue was horrible.

"Don't do this."

The boy sobbed, put his hands tight over his mouth.

And now Travis was running, coming fast down the center of the road, not looking to either side, but sprinting, and Jason felt himself rising, unable to keep still with that rushing shadow nearing him, the violent, crazy blast of the other, coming like wind. The shadow veered at the last second, Travis having seen him move, and Jason scrambled up out of the trench, his ankle hurting, his hands grasping at the grass and dirt and stones. Travis jumped on him, his boots landing on either side of his shoulders, and the boy found a stone with his left hand, turning in the closing darkness to swing it. He hit the side of the knee and heard Travis yell. He swung again, still trying to push with his legs to get away, and Travis reached down to catch the wrist of the hand that held the stone. His grip felt strong enough to break the bone.

Jason used his other hand to grab the lower leg and, with all his desperate strength, bit the flesh of the calf. He was biting through the heavy denim of the jeans, but he heard Travis yell again, and then he was loose, he had got out from his grasp and scrambled up onto the road surface, running. Travis had fallen, and from the trench he yelled, "I'm gonna make you pay for that you little son of a bitch!"

The boy ran, or attempted to run. There was a piercing stab of pain in his ankle with each stride, but he was managing it now, running, staggering, and the chilly air went through his chest, stinging his lungs. Light shone from behind him, the whir of a car. He got to the edge of the asphalt and up a small embankment there, toward a wooden fence. The car came on. He saw no sign of Travis. He hauled himself back to the road and waved with both arms at the brightness. The car slowed, then stopped. The driver's side door opened. "Jason? Honey?"

His mother. He heard the note of fear in her voice and relief, too. He went toward her, and then the passenger door opened, and he saw, over the headlights, an enormous man getting out, a red and black wideness, like a wall.

"Mom?" the boy said.

"Oh, honey." His mother put her arms around him. "Don't be afraid."

There was a surge of warmth and relief inside him, as though everything would be all right now. But then he understood that it was just beginning, and he heard himself whimper.

Travis came limping up from the dark beyond the fan of the lights. He looked at the heavy man. "Jesus Christ, Billy." Then he took Jason's mother by her arms and pulled her away into the blinding space of the headlights. "Go on and park the fucking car in the driveway of the house," he said to the fat man.

They were big shadows moving in the glare. The fat man went out of the light, got in, and the car moved forward with a whine of the little engine; it took the light on up the road. Travis held the boy's mother by the arms. "A short walk," he said. "Just the three of us. Right, Jason, buddy?" He had started walking her toward the house. "Course, you can stay here, if you want, and I'll just put a bullet in her eye when we get inside. What do you think?"

"You better leave us alone," Jason shouted, following him.

The fat man stood by the idling car in the driveway, waiting. His big loose coat hung on him, and he was chewing something. In the shadows, his jowls looked rubbery and thin. The eyes were small, way up in the mass of flesh. Travis went on into the house with Nora, and Jason ran to catch up. By the time he got to the back door, his mother was already blindfolded, her hands tied behind her back. And now the fat man grabbed Jason, lifting him by his arms, pulling them back.

"Get him good and tight," Travis said. "He's a slippery little son of a bitch."

"What do you want with us?" the boy's mother said. "What're you going to do?" He heard it as the fat man trussed his hands, hurting him, and then Travis walked over and put a pillowcase over his head. Nora said, "Please don't hurt us."

They were led outside again and forced into the back of the car; Jason hit his head on the door, and one of the men put a hand to the back of his cheek, pushing him down. He was on the backseat, and his mother was there, lying over on him. He could feel her shoulders, and the line of her jaw along the top of his head. He breathed her perfume.

"Ow," she said. "Don't."

The door closed on them.

"Mom?" he said.

She was crying. The car rocked to one side and then to the other with the weight of the men getting in.

"Okay," Travis said. "Now I think we're all gonna get to know each other."

They were moving, the car moved with slow jerking motions, the engine whining.

"Should've kept the other car," the fat man said. Jason could tell his voice from Travis's. "This thing's a piece of shit."

"Yeah, well, shut up about it," Travis said. "Everybody comfortable back there? Let me know if it gets too warm or anything."

The fat man laughed. "You're meaner than I am." It was the fat man's voice.

"I told you I wanted you to shut up, Bags. So shut up."

"Don't talk to me like that."

"Yeah, well, just do it. Shut the fuck up. You stupid, fat-assed, murdering ape."

"What're you gonna do, Travis. You gonna beat me up? The man kept talking at me, yapping at me, okay? Yap-yap. Running his mouth."

"Shut up. Stop running *your* mouth."

The fat man muttered something the boy couldn't make out, and then there was only the sensation of motion, the road winding, and the turns, and more turns. One of the men put the radio on— Jason heard disconnected talk, voices, parts of songs. It stopped, and there was a jazzy something, piano and guitar, drums and bass. It sounded to the boy like something his father had listened to. The kind of music you couldn't hum.

The smell of the pillowcase made him cough, and he thought he might suffocate. They were jostled and shaken as the road dipped and wound through the hills—and time went on and on. He heard other music, and a newsman talking, advertisements about skin cream, new cars, the Door Store, banks, restaurants. The weight of his mother's body on him, her tearful breathing, and his own struggle for air seemed to take on a force and reality all their own, separate from the sound of the engine, or the lunacy coming from the radio. And it was lunacy; it rattled through its bright messages in voices that sang or crowed, as if there were no harm in the world. It was so terribly separate and distant now, this radio banter among the safe, the nice. It sounded insane. He hated them for their very insulation from the terror he felt, though he could not have put this into words. The terror had become a numbing force in his limbs, like something cold dripping down the inside surfaces of his skin.

When the car stopped, he simply waited for what would follow. He had lost the will to resist. His mother was pulled from the car, and then the rough hands took hold of him, and he was jerked out of the space, his legs flailing. He fell, he was on the ground briefly, something barking his knee—a stone in the hard surface. Then he was lifted and half-carried across some span of uneven ground.

There was a doorway. His mother had started screaming. The rough hands pulled him through an opening, into a room, and his mother's cries echoed in the walls. He was pulled forward, then turned and pushed down into a chair.

"You leave my mother alone," he said.

She was in another part of the building. Jason kicked with his feet and hit only air.

"Stop it!" he shrieked. "Let her alone!"

The fat man pulled the pillowcase from his head. He saw a bare room—finished walls, with crown molding and chair railing, a dining room, with new windows that had crosses of masking tape in them. A kitchen with a refrigerator, a stove, a place carved out for a pantry. The fat man, who stood out of reach, arms folded, simply stared at him. He walked around the chair, took off his lumber jacket, and let it drop to the floor.

Then Travis came in, from an opening in the wall. Jason saw stairs going up into the dark. Travis walked over and bent down to look into his eyes. "So," he said.

"What did you do to my mother?" Jason demanded.

In the next instant he heard her calling from what sounded like another floor. "Jason!" she yelled. "Jason!"

Travis reached over and put a hand on the boy's neck. It stopped his breath. "Go up there and take care of that," Travis said to the fat man. "And if you hurt her I'll break your fat neck."

"Shut up, Travis."

"Just do what I say."

The fat man went up the stairs.

"Jason!"

The fingers were tight on the boy's throat. The room wavered and seemed to darken, then was gone for a space. He coughed, choked, drew breath and the light came back. The fat man had come down the stairs. He had Nora's dress.

"What did you—" He couldn't get the words out. The words ran together into a scream. Travis took hold of his throat again and stopped everything. Once more, there was a blank space. The boy seemed to clamor upward inside his own skin, so that he was looking out again. He saw Travis standing on the other side of the room. Travis now held the dress. "This is just to keep her from getting loose and running, okay? Like you did."

The boy tried to glare at him.

"We were talking about you and your daddy," Travis said. "Remember?"

"My—mother—" The boy coughed again, attempted to draw air in.

"Mom's safe."

He sobbed, fighting it with everything in himself.

"Tell me about your daddy and you," said Travis.

"I'm not talking to you."

"You and your daddy were close. You told me that."

The boy said nothing, still fighting back tears. The tears rolled down his cheeks. He felt them and closed his eyes.

Travis walked over and wiped the tears away with one rough index finger. "Sure. And you miss him. Tell me some of the stuff you used to do with him."

Jason looked at him defiantly.

The fat man stepped closer and seemed to squint. "Come on, kid."

"Just stay out of it, Bags," said Travis.

"I could get it out of him."

"Stand over there and shut up. You've got enough to answer for."

"Yeah, well, I didn't let the kid get away from me. Talk about queering things."

"Just shut up."

Bags moved to the other side of the room, hands shoved down in the pockets of his overalls.

"Did you and your daddy go fishing a lot?" Travis asked.

"What's it to you?" Jason said.

"Believe it or not, kid, I'd like to get through this without hurting you or your pretty mama."

"He ain't the one to talk to," the other said, from across the room.

"Billy, shut the fuck up."

"I don't know anything," the boy said. "I don't know what the fuck you think you're doing. And I know you killed Mr. Bishop."

Travis straightened a little. "This is a tough-talking kid. Your mama know you talk like that?"

Jason said nothing.

"Your daddy ever talk to you about secrets?"

"What're you bothering with him for, anyway," Bags said. "She's the one."

Travis turned on him, but said nothing.

"Shit-fire, Travis—it's true. Besides—we're supposed to wait."

"I'm gonna hurt you," Travis said.

"Well, we are."

When he faced the boy again, his lips were pulled back over his teeth. He shook his head, then reached up and rubbed the back of his neck. "Okay, you little smart ass," he said. "Upstairs with the lady."

BLINDNESS

THE FAT ONE CAME UP, PULLED THE blindfold off, and put a rag in her mouth. He removed her dress, pulling it roughly down over her legs, and then he put his crushing weight on her, licked her ear and cheek. He grasped her chin, turned her face to his, and she thought she might vomit into the rag and drown. She coughed, closed her eyes tight. His hands moved down her body and under her slip. She squirmed, tried to kick, tried to scream. His finger pushed in, and that horrible doltish laugh came forth, with the awful decay-smelling puff of air from his mouth. The finger moved, then stopped, then moved again. It hurt, deep. She kept her eyes closed tight, gagging, crying, and finally he stopped, tied her feet, and ran the cord up to where her hands were already tied. He made a noose and ran it from her neck to her ankles, so that when she moved, the noose tightened. She lay there, gagging on the mildew-and-dust taste of the rag, feeling the trickle of blood between her legs, filled with such a mixture of wrath and fear that her heart faltered, lost rhythm. Any second now, it would stop, from sheer rage. But it went on beating, thrumming against the hard floor where she lay, a creature, more aware of the sinews and bulk and bone of her own body than she had ever been in her life. When she could gather something of her strength and her ability to calculate, she attempted to pull her hands out of the knots, choking from the noose. She kept pulling at the knots, and trying to expel the rag. The effort caused her to grow faint, and she lost consciousness for a time.

She came to as Travis carried Jason up—Jason fighting him all the way—and tied him, too.

Travis walked over and took the rag from her mouth. "Sorry," he said. "You okay now?"

She coughed and spit and then retched emptily for a bad few seconds. He simply watched her.

"What did you do to my boy?" she said.

"Everybody's fine, okay?"

"No, everybody's *not* fine," she said. "Oh, God. That—that animal."

"Did Bags—" Travis seemed genuinely concerned.

She couldn't put the words together. Jason was lying there staring, sniffling.

"Look, if you'd help us out, we'll go away and you'll never see either one of us again," Travis said.

"I don't know what the fuck you want!" she shrieked at him.

There were the heavy footsteps on the stairs. She screamed again. "Keep him away from me!"

Travis walked to the entrance of the room and spoke in a fierce whisper to the other man, who then waited there, leaning on the frame, an expression of stupid gratification on his face.

Travis came back. "Okay," he said. "Business. Tell me what your husband left you."

"My husband is dead," she told him, crying.

"I know," Travis said. "Tell me what he left you."

She didn't answer. Jason lay there whimpering. She saw the fear in his eyes and the pain.

"Well?" Travis said.

"I don't understand," she told him. "We don't have anything."

"Your husband spent every penny."

She waited for him to go on.

"Right?"

"Who are you?" she said. "What is this?"

"She don't know shit," the fat one said from the doorway.

"Shut up, Bags. Go downstairs like I told you."

The other made a lot of thumping noise, going down. He whistled above the clatter.

Travis put his face up close to Nora's. "Your husband tell you about his troubles?"

"Please," she said. "What is this about?"

"Answer the question."

"He was my husband. What do you think?"

"You had money trouble."

"My arms and my back hurt," she said. "My son's hurting. Please."

He got to his knees and undid his belt.

"No!" Jason screamed.

Nora, at the same time, shouted, "If this is what it's about, goddam you, let my son go!"

"Calm down," Travis said, "Christ. Calm down." He pulled his jeans to his knees, then sat and scooted around to hold his leg toward Nora's face. "See that? That's a bite mark. And this, this is where the little son of a bitch hit me with a rock." He stood and pulled the jeans back up. "I ain't likely to worry about any discomfort he might be feeling now."

"Just say what you want and leave us alone," Nora said with an exhausted sob.

He leaned close again. "I want you to talk to me about your husband."

"I don't understand." She gasped, then tried to look right at him. "He's been dead almost a year."

"Did he give you anything to keep for him?"

"I don't know what you're talking about."

"It's a simple question," Travis said. "Don't make me mad. You don't want me to get mad. We ain't got a lot of time here."

"He spent money we didn't have and borrowed from our insurance and then he got himself killed in an accident and left us with nothing." She glanced over at Jason, whose face didn't change—it was all pain and fright, watching everything.

"But before he got killed. Did he give you anything—something to keep for him, or hide for him?"

"Hide?"

The other took hold of her arm and pulled her a few feet across the floor, causing her to choke on the noose.

"Leave her alone!" Jason shrieked.

When she could get any air, she said, "I'm okay, son. I'm all right."

Travis got down and put his face close to hers once more; she smelled stale tobacco. It made her gag again. Travis's lips were touching her ear now, and he murmured: "Where are they?"

She sobbed. Caught her breath.

"Come on. Tell me where they are."

"Who?" she managed.

"You and I can go in together on it," he said. "I can help you."

"What," she said. "Oh, God—I don't understand. I don't understand you."

"You can't do anything alone," he said. "You're gonna need somebody."

"I don't know what you're talking about. Can you understand what I'm saying?"

He stood. "All right. If that's the way you want to play it."

"I'm not playing anything. For God's sake!"

"You understand what I'm telling you," he said, low, with an urgency. "You tell me about it and you won't have to deal with anybody else."

"Please don't hurt us anymore. Please let my son go. You've made a mistake."

"I'll let him go right now. Right now. Lady, all you got to do is help me out a little and you can walk free."

"What do you want me to do?" She couldn't stop sobbing.

"Tell me," he said.

"Oh, Christ. Tell you what?"

He stood and went over to where Jason lay writhing. Then he turned to look back at her.

"Please," she said.

He reached down and struck the boy on the side of the face. "That's for biting me," he said. "You little fucker." Then he strode to the doorway and was gone.

Nora tried to move toward her son, but the noose tightened and stopped her. He moaned, still trying to get free. "Don't," she sobbed. "Son, don't."

"I'm scared," Jason said.

"I know."

"Mom—they killed Ed Bishop. I saw him, Mom. Mr. Bishop's dead." His voice rose on the last words, and his sobs were at the pitch of a scream.

She said, murmured, "Quiet. Jason—you have to be still."

Perhaps he had heard her. He kept crying, sniffling. But he wasn't trying to struggle free anymore.

"Jason," she whispered.

His response was another sob.

"Honey, please."

"I'm sorry," he said.

She made another effort to get herself closer to him. It wasn't possible to move more than a foot or so before the tightening of the noose choked her. She felt herself falling into the dark. Everything went away and came back. Jason was a dim shape on the floor, a few feet away.

"They killed Mr. Bishop," he said, low.

"I heard you." Now, again, she was having to fight tears.

"They're gonna kill us, too, aren't they?"

"I don't know," she said. Then: "No, of course not."

"Yes they are," Jason said.

"They would've done it already, wouldn't they?"

"They're going to." His voice shook.

There were heavy footfalls on the stairs, coming closer. Nora felt her own heart jump in her chest, felt the shiver go through her of this terror, hearing the ragged, fright-stricken breathing of her son. The fat man stood in the dim light of the doorway, chewing something.

"I suggest you both shut the fuck up," he said. He waited a moment—evidently he was enjoying the sound in the room of panic in the shaken exhalations of the two people on the floor. Nora saw the round shape of his face there in the dimness, and then he had turned and left them, laughing the small stupid huffing laugh. "All hell's breaking loose," he said, going away, apparently delighted with himself.

Jason sobbed softly in the darkness.

Again, she tried to edge closer, and once more the noose choked her to the point of losing consciousness. She came to, coughing. The cough hurt her lungs, her throat. She lay still. Jason appeared to be all right—there were no wounds that she could see. "What did they do to you?" she whispered.

"Nothing. They—asked me stuff." He whimpered.

"Shhh."

"Mom?"

"What did they ask you?" she got out.

"The same kind of stuff about Dad."

She saw blood on the bottom of his pant legs and the sides of his shoes. "Are you hurt? Where are you hurt?"

"It's Mr. Bishop's—" the boy began, then went on weeping.

"Oh, baby," she said. "My baby." She pulled at the rope which held her, and the noose tightened.

"Did—did he hurt you?" Jason asked.

She husbanded all her strength, fought back the painful swelling in her throat. "No."

He sniffled and wept for a long while, and a few times he struggled with the rope they'd tied him with. At last he was still.

"Jason?" she murmured. "Honey?"

Nothing but his slow, stertorous breathing. Below, she heard voices. Talk. It went on for a long time, but she couldn't make out any of it. An argument was going on, though, and now she could distinguish some words: "How the fuck do we go back there, huh? You tell me just how in the fuck we're supposed to go back."

This was followed by a low, guttural something, a protest or growl. Other words, unintelligible. She put her ear to the floor, seeking to hear better, but the noose was too tight, and anyway the roar of her own eardrums and her heartbeat stopped her.

But then the other voice—Travis's?—came clear again. "Answer me that. What the fuck do we tell him?"

She strained for the other voice. But the furnace came on, and she heard only the rumble and wind of it in the vents. The house settled into silence. Now and again there was a laugh, or what might have been a laugh. Oddly, she remembered that when Jack was alive, she nearly always went to bed before he did and liked the feeling of him awake elsewhere in the house.

The furnace stopped.

"What happens . . . "

She heard a mumble which ended in "Shut up." It could have been "Both of you shut up."

Was a third man there now? Someone else?

She strove to hear. The floor was so hard on the bones of her hips and shoulders. A low sob rose from her throat; she was unable to help herself. Below, the talk went on. And once again there was the voice shouting.

"Why the fuck we have to . . ." The voice trailed off. Then a moment later, it rose again. ". . . want to mess up your fucking hobby . . ." She filled her lungs with air, then held perfectly still again. ". . . Christ's sake."

But there was just the quiet, the furnace kicking on again, sighing, with its mutter of a fan turning. She remained awake. She thought she heard snoring. It struck her as the most bizarre and horrible thing, these men on the floor below, helpless as babies in their sleep—one of them even saying something and groaning. She was certain she'd heard it. And Jason, on the other side of the room, emitting a small guttural, liquid sound in the back of his throat. This went on, and it seemed that none of it had ever been, and she was far away, in a crowded room with very high ceilings, and a train was coming.

This was a train station. A dream. She was aware that it was a dream, and she could watch herself having the dream. Still, according to the dream, she was in a desperate hurry, late, and she couldn't locate Jason or Jack. She moved through the crowd of others, while a hollow voice harangued her from the walls, and when she saw Jack she felt her heart leap in her chest, as though this clear moment, seeing her husband in a confusion of faces, were something she could grasp, this could save her, save everything. She did not know what it meant and had no memory of what it was that needed saving, but all of life was in question, and she was moving through the packed room, approaching him. He stood only a few feet away, holding a handful of tickets. She took a step toward him and then she took another. *Oh, Jack.* Everything that had happened was gone. It was elsewhere, like a story about someone in another town. He was here—turning to see her, recognizing her. He smiled, *Baby*—

—As he had been when she first knew him: brash, always on the edge of one kind of excitement or another, a clutch of enthusiasms, wide-eyed with curiosity about everything, still a boy: twenty-three years old, just out of the army, with an idea that maybe he would go to college and learn how to write music. He had hooked up with a bluegrass band, was playing bass for them and singing. "I think I might actually get good at it," he told her. "There's a thing that happens when we're playing—I feel like—like nothing can go wrong. This is all going to add up to something good and nothing can ruin it. It's got a life of its own." She enjoyed the passion that came to his eyes when he talked about it, liked the feeling that all their choices lay in front of them. She had always been the kind of person who could step outside herself and look at the life she was leading. She possessed what he had called powers of appreciation, of savoring the time. He, on the other hand, always felt its rush, the sense that life was speeding past him. And there was the fact, all those years ago at the beginning, that his father expected him to perform the part of the only son: the contracting business needed his help, and Jack was always a soft touch for the old man. You had to love the devotion in him, the hope of raising a family of his own, the wanting to be the father his own father had been, though Nora secretly believed the old man acted too certain of things all the time, was often unbending and demanding. When he died, two years after Jason was born, she thought Jack might break down with the loss. But she was glad. She'd had to admit that a part of her was, well, relieved, anyway: there would be an end now to Jack's commitment to the business; he could sell it and go back to something he really wanted.

Except that Jack had decided differently: "He worked all his life so I'd have this—so we'd have this."

"This isn't what you wanted, Jack."

"Do people ever get exactly what they want?"

"What about the music?"

"Oh, come on, Nora."

"So that's it—you're just going to stop here?"

"This is a pretty good place, isn't it? Why do you want to upset everything?"

This was when she began to know—even as her whole heart resisted the knowledge—that she was stronger than he was and had always been stronger. . . .

Had she been asleep? The squares of the windows had grown pale. The house was deep in silence.

"Jason?" she murmured.

He sighed, groaned. He was asleep. She waited, sniffling softly. Time had ended, stretched out and died; hours, years went by. It seemed to her that she counted minutes, hours, days, weeks, months; it all ran together, years and decades. Generations. She had been dreaming again. She clung to consciousness, looking into the endless night, searching her mind for some indication or hint of what Jack might have left her that these men could want. The hours passed, slow as the stages of evolution. She slept, then woke again. Jason was still, quiet. The world had stopped in its tracks. Her life would end here. The knowledge came to her in an instant of panic. She inhaled, exhaled, and she could feel her heartbeat on the hard boards of the floor, which creaked now and creaked again. The house settling slowly, passing through its stages of completion. A moment later, half-conscious, she heard movement. She was wide awake, striving for the sound: someone was walking back and forth downstairs.

PART TWO

Nora's mother wore a wrist-watch set to eastern time, so she could know at a glance, without having to think, what time it was where her daughter and grandson lived. This was a mildly superstitious indulgence, actually—some small part of her believed that the connection was stronger if she could at least maintain this much of her life in the other time zone. The odd thing was that it had affected her life here: she often felt three hours ahead of everything. Making a quiet dinner for Henry, who liked to eat precisely at six o'clock, she imagined it was later, no matter what the light outside her windows said. For Gwendolyn Spencer, it was nine o'clock.

In the evenings, before she went to bed, she watched the news and paid close attention to the weather on the other side of the country. She was more attuned to that than the weather here, which was rainy less often than she'd been led to expect. She liked Seattle, in fact. And Henry seemed very happy, doing his consulting work with computers, keeping his own hours, really, and spending weekends puttering around the place, fixing the room where Nora and Jason would stay whenever she got around to bringing the boy out for a visit. He had been after Nora to sell that old house in Virginia, with all its bad associations, and make a clean break with the past (his phrase). He was of the opinion that Nora's resolve was growing weaker. She would relent and come to Seattle.

Her mother wasn't so sure.

Tonight, it was raining, a steady gray downpour, and she stood at the window in the kitchen, thinking about the thousands of miles that lay between them. She did like it here and yet—and yet. It seemed so far, such a long way away from her only grandchild. She was sixty-four; it seemed somehow perversely selfish, not to say idiotic, to be spending her retirement at such a distance from them. When she tried to speak of this to Henry, he grew restive, as if he were afraid she would ruin his good time by hinting that she was less than satisfied with the arrangements. Well, she was. For all her enjoyment of the cloud-capped mountain out her bedroom window, and the fine country, and the friendly neighbors, she wanted to be nearer her daughter.

Henry was a man blessed with a talent for seeing whatever he wanted to see in a given situation; this was not a quality she found particularly distressing, either. It meant that he considered, almost always, the positive side of matters. He would try to find something to work with in the worst situations because he believed in making the best of whatever was given or thrust upon him. He was seventy-four now and still enjoyed the energy and the interest in the world that he'd had when he was a young army air corps pilot with a record of heroism in Europe. He could still wear the uniform he'd worn then and still stood as erect. He had long-fingered, expressive, freckled hands that she loved watching him gesture with. His straight-ahead vision was still as good as it had always been, too, though there had been some erosion of his peripheral field, and he might have to stop driving a car in the next couple of years if it grew worse. He didn't think it would. He seldom thought anything would have a negative outcome, and this was a man who had looked upon destruction and suffering. It just wasn't in him to dwell on the harsh facts of existence. He was interested in the sports on television, and in the history he was always reading, and in what there was good to eat and drink, especially the huge variety of delicacies that came from the ocean, on the edge of which they now lived.

Summer evenings, he often drove down to the shore and took long walks. He'd stop and pick up shells that interested him. There were two big buckets of them in the garage—every shape and color and size, every texture, from scalloped edges to polished smoothness, some of them blemished with tiny holes of erosion, all of them beautiful and delicate as ancient artifacts. He intended to make something with them one day, a kind of wall, he said. A whole wall of shells, so he could gaze upon it and think of his walks along the edge of the coast, the last mile of land, of his country. How he liked to watch the sun go down over the sea. He wanted Gwendolyn with him for these passes of course. But the sunset always filled her with sadness. She would go with him, would sit with him while the light failed and think how Nora and Jason were already in the dark, already in bed, probably. The thought unnerved her, their helpless sleep, so far away, and she sometimes caught herself thinking of death, too, watching the sky turn dark purple, the haze of the far-off redness, the rim of the last light, like embers sinking into the sea.

There would be no embers tonight.

The rain came straight down, in a windless calm—lazy, somnolent. Henry was asleep on the couch in the living room, having drifted off while watching a movie. She had sat for a time in the lamplight, reading the paper, listening to him snore. No one on earth slept as deeply or as innocently as Henry.

Now he stirred, sat up, ran his hands through the sparse, wiry brown hair on his head. She had once teased him by saying that he didn't have the decency to go gray. She herself had been dyeing her hair for years, since just after her fortieth birthday.

"Lost track of the movie," he said.

"Wonder why."

"Must not've been very good." He liked mysteries, suspense movies, and adventure-thrillers. Long ago the two of them had decided that their taste in books and movies was never going to coincide. They compromised, mostly, if they wanted to be together. But in the last few years she had noticed that they spent more time in different parts of the house. She supposed it was normal.

"You decide what you want for dinner?" he said.

"No." She sometimes attributed the success of their marriage to the rather unromantic fact that they were temperamentally suited to each other: they had remained affectionate, and generally interested, because their moods were often the same.

"I don't much feel like going out. Do you?"

"I guess not. I hadn't thought the rain would keep up."

"No." He stood, padded to the window in the door, and looked out. "There's a car in front of the house."

"Must be for the neighbors."

"Looks like there's somebody in it."

"Probably waiting for the rain to let up."

"It's not going to let up anytime soon." He crossed to the entrance of the kitchen. "Maybe I'll make some spaghetti."

"Oh, honey," she said. "I've had heartburn the last couple days. I don't feel like anything too spicy."

He stood there thinking. Then he went on into the kitchen. She heard him bringing out dishes, rattling pots and pans.

"What're you doing?"

He was quiet. She got up and went in to him. He had put his hands down on the counter. His head drooped between his arms.

"What?" she said.

"Let's go out and see a movie or something."

"You just woke up from a nap. You're always restless when you sleep in the middle of the day. Why don't you make yourself a drink and relax a little."

"The last few days," he said. "I can't explain it—but I've had the odd sense that somebody was following me. I keep seeing this guy. A young guy." He shrugged. "Seems to be watching me. I saw him outside the post office last week, and I thought he was behind me in traffic a couple of days ago. Then at the grocery store, as I was going out. I almost said hello."

She waited for him to go on.

"The strangest thing. Can't put my finger on it. I see other faces, you know. People who go to the store the same time I do. But I— this feeling of being watched. There's something about the way this guy looks at me. And just now it upset me to see that car out there, exactly as if—hell, I don't know."

"Was that the same car you saw in traffic the other day?"

"I can't remember. I didn't really look at the car. Maybe I'm losing my mind."

She said, "A feeling isn't always to be explained one way or the other, is it?"

He put his arms around her. "I suppose I can never be one of those men who says his wife doesn't understand him."

"You sound almost regretful about it."

"No," he said. "I'm quite happy." He opened the refrigerator and stood gazing at the confusion there.

"I've been thinking of going back for another visit," she told him.

He closed the refrigerator. "There's nothing holding her in Virginia, is there? She can teach here just as well as she can teach there, can't she? And she'd have us to help out."

"Would you mind if I went to stay with her a few days?"

He considered. "Yes, frankly. I would mind."

She turned from him.

"It's been almost a year," he said. "The guy left her with nothing. I think a certain period of mourning is fine—but the guy did leave her with nothing."

"It was an accident, Henry. He didn't do it to her. It happened. They loved each other."

"I'm going to make myself a sandwich, and then I'm going to go out and see a movie," he said. "You're welcome to come along."

Lately he had assumed this abruptness, this way of closing off discussion by means of an announcement of plans. It was his way of saying he would not speak about it further, and it never failed to make her cross with him. She suppressed the feeling now, though she wanted to say that sometimes his positive nature was little more than that of the spoiled child used to having his way in everything. And in fact she had mostly given him just that.

"I'm going to see about going back to spend a week with Nora and Jason," she said. "And *you're* welcome to come along."

He said nothing, reaching into the bread basket for slices of rye bread, which he set out on the counter.

She went back into the living room and was startled to find a man's shape, head and shoulders, in the window of the door. "Henry?" she said.

The man knocked lightly on the glass.

Henry came up behind her. "Who's that?" He stepped around her, walked over, and spoke through the glass. "Yeah?"

Gwendolyn couldn't make out the words the other said.

Henry opened the door a crack. "What is it?"

"Could I use your phone, sir? I'm stranded."

Henry looked beyond him and held the door tight.

"I'm sorry, I'll go to the next house."

"Hell," Henry said, low. Then he opened the door. "Come on in, son."

The man was big. Tall and blocky, with wide shoulders dripping with the rain. He wore a dark blue baseball cap, which he took off now, and held in front of his body. He had long dark hair that was thinning at the crown of his head. He nodded at Gwendolyn, then followed as Henry led him through to the kitchen and the telephone on the wall. Thanking Henry, he picked up the handset, punching the numbers with a kind of emphasis. He cleared his throat and waited. Henry stood by and then seemed to think better of it. He came toward Gwendolyn a little. "I started thinking about how it would be if I followed every damn paranoiac impulse," he murmured.

"Yeah," the stranger said into the phone. "This is Robby. Let me talk to John."

Henry walked over to the door and looked out at the street.

"John. I'm broke down. Yeah. Wait a minute." He looked at Gwendolyn. "What street is this, ma'am?"

"Jonquil Street," she said.

He repeated this into the phone and waited again. He looked around himself, at the kitchen, the walls. When his eyes settled on Gwendolyn, he smiled at her, revealing a space between his front teeth, right at the center. "Okay. Thanks," he said into the phone.

Then he put the handset back and nodded at Gwendolyn, starting back through the living room. "I'm very grateful, thank you."

"Miserable day out there," Henry said to him.

"Yes, sir." His movements, the rustle of his coat, the air of the outside that was on him, all seemed to have set something loose in the room, an energy that disturbed Gwendolyn. She had a moment of realizing how much she had come to depend on the closed door, the insulation between her and the rough life outside. She felt oddly threatened by this very large and very polite young man. He pulled his hat from the coat pocket, put it on, and nodded at Henry, even bowed slightly toward Gwendolyn. "Sorry to bother you."

"No bother," Henry said.

The other bowed again and was gone. Henry closed the door and looked out the window for a moment.

"I swear," Gwendolyn said to him. "That scared me."

"What scared you?"

"This strange big man coming to the door, after you talked about being followed."

"I'm sorry," he said.

She walked to him and put her arms around his middle. "Henry, let's go back east."

He took her elbows and stepped back. "What?"

"Just for a visit."

"Look, is it the place you miss, or Nora and Jason?"

"Don't be ridiculous. You *know* what it is. But Nora and Jason won't come out here. And you know that, too."

He returned to the kitchen, and she went down the thin hallway to their bedroom. She lay down, without putting the room light on, though it was dim here, the windows running with the steady drumming of the rain.

In a while, she heard the television. He had started watching the same movie again. She heard the gunfire; the shouts, but they grew far away; she was drowsing. How wonderful it felt to let go—the sweetest pause, with the soft tattoo of the rain on the windows. She woke to the television: explosions. The windows were dark. For a few seconds she couldn't remember where she was. "Henry," she called out. "Please turn it down."

Nothing.

In all the movies he had ever brought home, there was a scene where people were running or diving to get away from exploding fire. The scene was obligatory, she decided, like those absurdly religious-seeming sexual passages in the movies of the sixties and seventies, as though that small biological act between complete strangers were somehow more mystical and freighted with the spiritual than it could ever be in such barren circumstances. She got out of the bed and moved to the doorway of the room to look down the hall into the space of the living room where his chair was. He was sitting there, but he wasn't looking in the direction of the television. His face was white; he looked aghast at something.

"Henry?" she said.

And a man leaned into the open space to look back at her. He had a ruddy, round face, with very thin lips, and small flat ears. He was holding a pistol. "Could you come here please?" he said in a shaking voice.

"Henry?" Gwendolyn said.

"Please do what I told you, lady," the man said.

She came toward him, slow, watching Henry. She thought of the young man who had asked to use the phone.

"Your friend is out there somewhere," she said to him.

"No," Henry said. "You don't understand, Gwen."

"I don't have any friends out this way, ma'am."

"This is the—the follower," Henry said.

The man gestured with the pistol for her to move into the room, to Henry's chair. She did so and put her hand on her husband's shoulder. "What do you want?" she said.

"Well," he said. "I need to stay here a little while. Might need to look through some of your things. We'll see."

"Are we hostages?" Henry asked.

"I wouldn't say that. I'm not all that sure myself."

"Excuse me?"

He wiped his mouth with one hand. There was something almost childlike about it. "I got these friends—uh, associates. They're in

Virginia with your daughter—" He paused, looking like someone trying to remember a name. "It's eight-thirty in Virginia. So they've got her and the boy."

"What is this?" Henry said.

"Uh—listen—listen and I'll tell you. They assigned me to come out this way and keep an eye on you all. In case she causes them any trouble. There's some business."

"What in the world?" Henry said. He stood.

The other man aimed the pistol at him. "Could you please sit down, sir."

"I will not."

"I don't want to hurt anybody, but I will if I have to."

"You tell me what this is about," Henry Spencer said. "Now."

"Sir, if you don't sit down, I'm going to have to shoot you."

"Henry, for God's sake sit down," Gwendolyn said.

He did so. It was almost a collapse into the chair. She put her hand on his shoulder, felt the tremble there of what she knew was fury. She patted the shoulder twice and stepped forward. The man retreated a step. It was almost a faltering.

"What, exactly, do you want from us?" she said.

He gave forth a small laugh and seemed relieved. "I almost didn't do it—when that big kid came to your door. He was scary. I thought he was something I hadn't counted on. Well, he was, of course. You try to cover all the bases, you know."

"What do you want?" Gwendolyn said. "Please."

He took a breath. "I don't want to hurt anybody. Okay? There's no need for anybody to get hurt."

"Do you want money?"

"You bet," he said, almost laughing. "Tons of it. All there is."

"We don't have money."

Henry stood suddenly. "You punk. If you do anything to hurt my daughter I'll kill you—"

The stranger held the pistol toward Henry, shaking slightly, but talking: "I don't want to, I swear, but if I have to I'm gonna blow your brains all over that wall."

"Henry, please," Gwendolyn said.

Henry was still standing, half-crouched, as though he might make a rush at the other.

"I mean it. Lady, you tell him I mean it."

"Henry." She took his arm and pulled him toward her. "Let's just use our heads here."

"You tell me what's going on—"

"You just better be quiet, man. I mean it."

Henry straightened. "How much do you want? How much?"

"I don't want your money. I want you to sit still and I won't touch a thing of yours if I don't have to, or hurt you in any way. And nobody you know will get hurt either. Okay? I just need you to sit down, sir. For now. Please sit down."

"Henry."

He sat back down slowly.

"That's better."

"Now," Gwendolyn said. "Will you please explain?"

"Well, no," he said. "We just have to wait a while."

"You said friends of yours are with our daughter?"

"It's only until they get something she has. Or find out where it is."

"Where what is?"

"Has she sent you all any packages in the last year?"

"Of course she has," Gwendolyn said. "This is a family."

"What was in the packages?" He looked from one to the other of them, brandishing the gun. Something had excited him.

"What is it that they want from her?" Henry said.

"Tell me what she sent you."

"A shirt for Henry," Gwendolyn told him. "Some music for me. A few books."

"Look, what is this about?" Henry asked him.

The stranger seemed incredulous. "Money," he said.

A GRAY SLOW STILLNESS HAD SETTLED over everything.

Nora lay on her side in the pile of newspapers and rags. Her hands tingled badly from lack of circulation, and her back felt as if the bones had come loose in her spine. She looked at what she could see of the room—empty walls, curtainless windows with the manufacturer's stamp still on them. This was a new building. One of Jack's unfinished sites? She was fairly certain that they had driven only a few miles from the house. There was something about the number of turns they had taken, as if the men were driving around to confuse her. The room smelled of plaster and, oddly, of garlic. She remained silent, watching the incremental arrival of light at the window. Across from her, Jason's face was twisted into a grimace of pain. Finally he opened his eyes. He seemed startled to find himself tied and then the clarity of his memory came back to him; she saw it in his eyes. "Mom?"

"Shhh."

Below them, there was movement. A car pulled up outside, a small-sounding motor. She heard the door and then slow footsteps.

"Help!" she yelled. "Up here!"

Someone started up the stairs. A head became visible at the level of the floor. Neither Travis nor the fat man, but someone else. She saw dark, arched brows, a heavy sensual mouth, flaring nostrils. The hair was parted in the middle and combed carefully back on either side of the head. It was an oddly familiar face. She had a moment of feeling as though she knew it, had seen it before.

"Help us," she said. "Please!"

"Morning, lady and gentleman. It's almost five o'clock A.M. Do you know where your abductors are?" He laughed at his own joke.

Nora said, "What do you want with us?" Then: "Let my son go."

"Can't do that, I'm afraid." He smiled. He had an accent that Nora couldn't quite place. "No one is up here with you?"

She said, "What do you people want from me?"

"You were alone here for a while. Did you know that? You might've escaped, and then where would we be?"

"Are you the Virginia Front?" she said.

"Perhaps when Travis and his amazingly stupid brother return, they'll be able to tell me what you're talking about."

She thought about the brothers. Something must have shown in her features.

"That's correct," the stranger said. "Brothers."

She was silent. German? Swedish? She had seen him before.

"Well, this will all be over before very long."

"Look," she said. "We don't have anything. We don't have any money. You understand? My husband died and left us with nothing."

He smiled, then dipped slowly below the level of the floor.

"Untie us," Nora shouted. "You goddam fucking son of a bitch!"

Silence.

She looked over at Jason. "I'm sorry, honey."

He said nothing. The muscles of his face pulled down.

Perhaps an hour later—it could have been less, or more, they had no way of knowing; it felt like a long time—they heard another car, her car, she could tell by the tapping of the rocker arms, the sound it made when it needed oil. Again there were the voices downstairs, another argument, this time in much quieter tones. After another wait (fifteen minutes?), she heard them coming up. First was the one who called himself Travis. He walked over and stooped down to look into her face. "That's got to be uncomfortable," he said to her.

"Please," she said. "Can't you understand? You've got the wrong people."

"I'm gonna untie you now," Travis said. "Okay?" He did so. She came to a sitting position painfully, slowly, almost crying out from the stiffness in her arms and back and the cramps in her legs. Travis had moved to untie Jason's ankles, but he left the hands tied. Nora saw this, and she and the boy exchanged a look. Jason had come to his knees and remained there.

"Okay," the man with the accent said. "Let's introduce ourselves, hmm? I'll go first, since I'm the teacher."

Nora noticed that the fat one stood in a corner of the room, looking at the others with a sulking frown, chewing the fingernails of one stubby hand.

"Untie my son," she said.

"Don't interrupt," said the one with the accent. "It's time for our little lecture."

"If you don't untie my son you'll get no cooperation from me."

"Cooperation." He walked to the other side of the room and turned. "What a wonderful word." He paused and stared at the fat man, then shook his head, coming back a little.

Nora stood and held her hands across her body.

"We're going to be very disciplined from now on, hmm?" His face was impassive. "Let's be calm, please."

She tried to think where she had seen the face.

"Our friend Travis here has explained to me the significance of the so-called Virginia Front. I'm afraid we can't take credit for such a fine organization; perhaps we'll be able to use them to our advantage." He paused. Apparently, he was pleased with himself. "Now. A little history. If you'll pay attention, perhaps you'll learn the answer to all your questions."

"You've made a mistake," Nora told him.

He seemed to consider this, then nodded, moving to one side a step and then coming back. He had a slight smile at the corners of his mouth. "It seems that once there was a man who ran his own business for himself and his family, hmm? A contracting business, with a little computer wholesaling on the side."

She felt the chill rising at the back of her neck.

"Well, for one reason or another, this man ran into some financial difficulty. He couldn't pay his bills. So, like a lot of people in similar circumstances he borrowed money to pay them, hoping things would get better. But things got worse, and there were more bills to pay, and he couldn't borrow any more money. No one would lend him any more money. Do you see the situation he was in?"

"Will you please untie my son and let him go?"

The man with the accent walked toward her. He paused a few seconds, then said, "You're trying to decide where you've seen me."

She waited.

"You've seen me—" he paused. "On a street corner."

"I don't understand," she said. She was speaking to all of them.

"You've seen me when you walked from your little car into the nuns, or perhaps in the grocery store, or crossing the parking lot where your son goes to school." He held his arms out, as if he expected her to walk into them. "It's me," he said, with a scary kind of glee. "The devil." Then he reached into his pocket and brought out a small snuffbox, opened it, took some of the powder there and licked it from his finger. He put the snuffbox back. "It was me walking by you in the street."

"Please," she said.

"I've been watching you for some time now."

She could only repeat, in an exhausted murmur, "If my husband borrowed something from you, I'm sorry."

"He didn't borrow from us."

She waited.

"There's another matter."

"I don't know what you're talking about," Nora said.

He put one finger to his lips. "Shhh."

She heard the fat man's ugly laugh.

The one with the accent continued, addressing her in that soft voice. "Shall I tell you what will happen if I don't get cooperation? Hmm? Shall I?"

She said nothing, but held her ground, looking straight back at him. In an absurd little turn of her mind she noted that he was almost exactly her height. She had a brief image of herself trying to describe this to someone else. A policeman.

"Yes, I'll tell you," he said. "Let's see, what was it? Oh, yes." He walked casually across the room and stood over Jason, smiling back at her. Then he reached into his coat pocket and brought out a revolver and held the barrel of it against the boy's temple.

Nora screamed.

He stood back, then put the gun in his coat again.

"Oh, Christ," Nora said, crying. "Please, no. Please."

"Shall I finish with the little history lecture?"

She stood there.

"Travis, give the woman her dress."

Travis went out and was on the stairs.

"Shall I continue?"

She nodded, crying. She was only faintly aware that she had responded at all.

"Well, this—as I was saying—this businessman was in a lot of trouble, and as luck would have it, he happened to run into an old acquaintance—someone he knew in the army, you see. All those years ago. And this friend is—shall we say this acquaintance—this acquaintance was in business for himself, of a slightly less than legal nature. Are you listening?"

"I don't understand what that has to do with my son and me."

"Ah—but, now, let me finish."

"No," she said. "You let *me* finish. My husband never arranged with anybody to harm my son or me. That pig over there—" She shuddered. "Your pig—that slab of—filth—" She couldn't finish.

The man turned and observed Bags for a moment. "Yes, Billy— or Bags, as we call him. Well, Bags is just a picture of human possibility, isn't he? I confiscated his weapon this morning, because of a little matter of some cows he felt like slaughtering. Did he rape you?"

A sound came from Jason's throat.

"No," Nora said. "He—he put his hands on me."

"Sorry for the bluntness of the question."

"Just keep him away from us."

Travis had come back up the stairs, and he handed the dress to her. She stepped into it and then couldn't reach the zipper. Yesterday morning, putting it on, she had called to Jason, who had come from his room to zip her up. As he did so, she'd had an unwelcome memory of Jack, pausing as he performed this small courtesy, to kiss the nape of her neck.

"Let me," Travis said.

"Get away from me," she said. She got it halfway, reached over her shoulder and finished the job, then stood with her back to the wall again.

"So," the man with the accent said. "As I was saying. It just so happens that these two old acquaintances agree to take part in a little scheme. A scheme that promises to bring them both a great deal of money. Almost two million dollars, hmm? They agree, they establish contact with other parties, you see. And they make a deal. They take possession of some—well, let us call it merchandise. It's portable, this kind of merchandise, it's small. Valuable—oh, very valuable—and it's untraceable. As yet. Which, of course should make it relatively easy to—well, shall we say, resell?"

"I don't understand any of this."

"Maybe she's not in on it, Reuther."

The one called Reuther spoke calmly. "Please refrain from speaking, Travis."

"I don't think they know a fucking thing," said the fat man.

Reuther crossed the room again, stood before the fat man, then came back, shaking his head. The fat man's eyes were full of hatred, staring from his corner. Nora saw this and felt herself marking it inwardly as something she might use later. Reuther turned and indicated him. "It seems I hurt poor Bags's feelings this morning. Poor boy doesn't like being disciplined." He looked back at him. "Stay there until I tell you to come out."

"You don't tell me," Bags said, stepping out of the corner.

"Bags," said Travis. "Cool it."

The fat man moved back to the other side of the room, sulking. Reuther moved to the boy's side. "Everyone calm down," he said. He leaned down to gaze at Jason, then straightened and paced the room again. "What's next in this little lecture is really quite inspiring. It seems that the businessman, the one in all the financial trouble—let us call him Mr. Citizen—it seems that Mr. Citizen starts feeling bad about his new business partners, and as the merchandise comes to him, he puts it in a safe place. His business partners— some of them—are a little stupid and disorganized, and they get in trouble for something else. All of this happens while the man responsible for bringing the—the merchandise—the one who arranged to have it brought into the country . . . let us say this person is in Europe, working to provide ways of shipping even more of the merchandise. And let us say that things are somewhat in flux— because interested parties have begun to bid for this particular merchandise. Two different groups with lots of money. But the fact is that the people who manufacture the merchandise are already making even newer and different merchandise, merchandise that will become available for sale very soon now and will seriously devalue the merchandise in hand, shall we say. And they're also finding ways to increase security—it's a matter of time before they develop a way of labeling the newer merchandise, which will make it identifiable and traceable. And so what does he have to do? This person? He has to stop everything and make plans to come to the States and straighten things out, because the merchandise is changing, hmm? And because the companies that make the merchandise are acting to make it harder to resell, this creates a situation where the merchandise already stolen—er, procured—is even now almost a third less valuable than it was at the beginning. But just as the details might be worked out for a quick sale in the United States, the one who is in possession of the merchandise meets with an unfortunate accident." Reuther stopped in front of Nora and put his hands on his hips, waiting.

"You're talking about my husband."

"What do they say here in the States? Bingo."

"There's some mistake."

He kept smiling at her.

"I mean it. I don't. We—Jack and I—" She glanced at Jason. "We—we weren't very close the—the last year." Jason's face showed nothing.

Reuther turned to Travis with a pleased expression, as if he had accomplished something. "She is a very smart lady." He waited a moment, studying her. "Well, everything's been complicated a little by our stupid friend in the corner."

"Travis, are you gonna let him talk to me like that—"

"Shut up, Billy," Travis said.

Reuther had not taken his eyes from Nora. "There is one slight advantage gained by what's happened," he said. "Fatso there made a problem for us with your neighbor. I'm sure there will be police all over that house very soon. The business, shall we say, of the neighbor is a problem we'll have to contend with. But the fact of it can be useful, hmm? Because now you know what we're capable of. So perhaps you can save us some trouble by telling us right now where they are."

"Where what is?" she said.

"You're asking us to believe your husband never spoke to you about it?"

"If you'd tell me what it is, maybe I'd know."

"You don't know, even with what I've told you?"

"No."

"I'm sure I saw recognition in your eyes. Maybe *you've* sold them to someone."

"Sold what?" Nora said. "Tell me what I'm supposed to have sold."

"I wonder if you're not hiding them, as your husband was, for your own use later on. You know the value is going down, even as we speak."

She waited for him to go on.

"Well? *Are* you?"

"You've been watching me. What do you think?" she said. She was surprised at the aggressive sound of it.

"I think, from talking with you, that you might be a very smart lady."

"Is it jewels?"

Reuther smiled. "Perhaps you sent the merchandise somewhere else?"

"How could I do that if I don't know what it is. *Is* it jewels?"

He shook his head, regarding her with a disappointed expression.

"Well, then what—drugs?" She looked from one to the other of them. "I don't understand."

"You're sure." Reuther walked over to Jason again and took out the revolver. He aimed it at the boy's head and pulled the hammer back.

"No!" Nora said and tried to run at him. Travis had caught her and held her, kicking and flailing, and now the fat man was holding her, too.

"I'll count to three," Reuther said. "And maybe you'll tell us then."

"Oh, God! I don't know!" She was screaming now. "Please, I don't know! I don't know!"

"One," Reuther said. He gazed at the boy, who was crying, his eyes closed tight. "Two."

She opened her mouth on a long shriek.

Reuther eased the hammer down and put the gun in his coat. He nodded at the others, who let Nora go. She rushed to the boy's side, kneeling, sobbing, trying to cover him with her body. "Please," she was saying. "Please leave us alone."

"Listen," Reuther said.

She sniffled, holding tight to the boy.

"Are you listening?"

She looked at him.

"I think I'm satisfied that you don't know what we're here for. It's now necessary to proceed with other plans."

"Please, no."

"We're going to keep your boy here, hmm? And you are going to go back to your house, with Travis, to make a little search of your husband's—effects, shall we say. A search of the house."

"I don't know what I'm looking for," she said.

"That will become more clear, perhaps."

Travis pulled her to her feet.

"None of this makes any sense," she told them through tears. "Please."

Reuther walked close again, suffocating her with the sharp peppermint odor of his breath. "Was my husband selling—drugs?" she said.

He said, "Drugs. You mean this."

She was silent.

"Not drugs. No, this merchandise is not at all like that. This is something that one can get rid of much more efficiently than drugs."

"Can't you please just tell me what it is?"

"What you're looking for will be in four Styrofoam cartons, about the size of a suitcase. And square, like that. Does this ring a bell?"

"No."

"Yes, well. Perhaps when you've had some time to think about it."

"What's in the cartons?"

"It's not important that you know that, hmm? And if you're able to find them, or remember where you put them, we can disappear from your life, and you'll never have to worry about us again."

"It's ten minutes to six," Travis said.

Reuther touched her hair, smiling. "You and Travis will go in your car."

"Please let me have my son," she said. "I'll help you find whatever it is you're looking for."

"Of course you will. But we'll just let him remain here for safe-keeping."

"Jason," she said.

"He'll be quite safe."

She moved around him and knelt at the boy's side. His wrists were red and rope-burned, and she saw that his ankle had swollen to nearly twice its size. "He's hurt," she said.

"The more quickly you get this done, the more quickly you can get him to a doctor."

She stood.

Jason said, "Go on. I'll be okay." But he had gasped out a spray of saliva, and she thought of him as she walked out to the car. He was still suffering through the death of his father. She began to weep again. "It's not fair," she muttered, following Travis, who was limping slightly.

He got in behind the wheel. "We'll find what we're after and then we'll get out of your way, you'll see."

Had she heard a note of something like kindness in the voice— at least of concern? "How can you do a thing like this?" she said.

"Well," he said, holding back a laugh. "It sort of goes with the territory."

"Were you the one—my husband—"

"I knew him in the army, yeah. A couple centuries ago. We did some hanging out. He was a funny guy, your husband. Fun to be around."

She saw the fat man standing in the window. The grayish sky beyond the line of the roof hurt her eyes.

Travis had started the car and put it in gear, but it stalled.

"You have to wait for it," she told him.

He started it again. It caught and stayed on. He put it in gear and slowly began to pull out. Then he stopped. "Shit."

"What?" she said.

"There's blood on the backseat." He turned the engine off, got out, and walked back to the house. The sun had come up through the trees—burning through the cloud cover, a blinding radiance beyond the shadows of pine branches. She sat waiting for him, her stomach churning, and when he came back, she stepped from the car. He carried a towel—one end of it sopping, dripping suds. She had a moment of a kind of wonder at the ordinariness of it. Soap. He opened the back door and began scrubbing the seat back. She watched. It was cold, and she shivered, turning to look at the house and the surroundings—woods all around, the pines growing thickly as grass, the dense undergrowth. She thought she saw water through an opening in the green boughs as the wind lifted and then died. She couldn't be certain. When she faced the house again, she saw that in the near upstairs window Reuther stood, with a displeased cast to his features.

"I have the feeling your boss doesn't think much of you," she said.

Travis looked back over his shoulder. "Boss?"

"The foreigner."

He went on working, scrubbing, then taking a dry part of the towel and sopping up the moisture. Finally he stood back. "Guess that'll have to do." He opened one of her folders and spread the papers on the seat. "Okay," he said. "That ought to be okay." Then he waved at the house, strode around to the driver's side and got in. She saw Reuther step away from the window.

"Come on," Travis said.

She got in and closed the door. The smell of the soap was strong; the window had fogged over.

"How do you work this?" he said, pushing the defrost button.

She set it, and they waited for the car to warm up again. "He's not your boss?" she said.

"Who, Reuther?"

The engine made a whining noise when he pressed on the accelerator.

"You're gonna call in sick today," he said.

"Jack never talked about you," she told him.

"He should've. You know how many crimes are committed in this country every day? You have any idea how many crimes I already got away with?" Something almost gleeful shone in his face.

"You can't—" she began. She had been about to say, *You can't kill us*, as though she would be describing the rules of some game to him. She thought about how careless the three men had been about saying their names. The only interpretation of this fact was that they planned to kill her and Jason. The logic of it was inescapable.

"Can't what?" he said.

It took all her strength to speak at all. "Nothing."

He put the car in gear and backed out of the space, then turned. She sought to place the surrounding woods, to recall anything about them. But the sun blazed like the wide bloom of a far-off explosion through the branches now, and it was difficult to see anything very clearly. This was somewhere near one of her husband's unfinished sites—an unsold mansion he had been building for a man who lost everything in the stock market crash of 1987. The site was in this area. She felt almost certain of it.

"Okay," he said. "Get down."

"Down—"

"Put your head down."

She folded her arms on the dash and rested her forehead against them.

"Jack never talked about his buddy Travis, huh?"

"No."

"I guess we weren't all that close in the service. We knew each other. If you want to know the truth, I think I irritated him, pretty much. I was always after him to tell me jokes."

It occurred to her in an obscurely detached way that this man with whom she had been speaking was an accomplice in the murder of her friend. She couldn't stop shaking.

"More heat?" he said.

"No."

"You gotta think about it like a game," he said.

This sent a deeper chill through her and gave her the awful sensation that somehow he had access to her thoughts.

He went on: "A big game with a lot of interlocking pieces. Where we all fit into the thing. The country'd fall apart if it weren't for a little criminal activity."

"What happens after we find whatever it is you're looking for?" She hadn't known she would ask this. Her breath caught.

He appeared to be deciding to ignore the question—she was near to doubting that she had actually said the words out loud—but then he seemed definite, almost casual. "We'll let you go, of course. And you'll never see us again. I start my new life south of the border, and your life will go back to being dull."

She recalled that they had been watching her.

"Admit it," he said. "It was pretty dull before."

No, it hadn't been anything of the kind! She saw what it had been—a kind of puzzled dreaming-through, a haze of worrying and striving and being glad of moments or passages that were happy. Oh, it had been gloriously ordinary, ridiculously carefree!

And all of it was over there now, on the other side of Jack's death and this trouble.

The last time she saw Jack, he was in a hurry. She brought groceries into the house, and he helped, wearing his coat. He was on his way out to a meeting in town—with a group of builders who gathered each week to discuss the loss of momentum in the market. "A lot of houses sitting empty," Jack said. "And they want to talk about what we're all gonna do. There's nothing *to* do, of course. We've got ten million homeless people in this country and I can't put anybody into three fucking houses. These meetings won't help that."

"Go to the meeting," she'd said. "You'll feel better afterward."

"I'm sorry," he said—something he had formed the habit of saying almost automatically.

"Don't be sorry," she told him. "Go."

He kissed her on the cheek, waved at Jason in the other room, turned, and was gone, pulling the back door closed behind him. She didn't go to the window to wave good-bye.

That was the last time she saw him alive.

Often enough, since then, she had wondered what she must have been thinking or doing the instant that Jack stopped being Jack in that burning mass of tangled metal. She lifted her eyes to the window. The road descended, around slow steep curves through bare trees. It was Virginia, somewhere near the Blue Ridge Mountains—or perhaps somewhere in them. She peered out, through the interstices of branches and tree trunks, at the rolling hills beyond the declivity to her right. He took the curves slowly, carefully. She saw the side of his face and thought of poor Ed Bishop, and she understood, without words, that she needed to know more—that her survival and the survival of her son depended on what she could find out. The first thing she must know was where Ed Bishop had made his mistake.

"What did—why—" she began.

"Yeah." His voice was impatient. "Put your head down."

"I don't know where we are," she said. "It hardly matters."

"Just do it."

She did so. "Mr. Bishop—" She stopped. She could feel her heart beating in her neck.

"Who?" he said.

"Nothing."

"No—you wanted to ask me something."

"Never mind," she said.

"You know how many times people have begged me for things?" he said in that strange casual tone. "I mean kneeling down begging, too. The real thing."

She held still.

"You really think Reuther's my boss?"

"No."

"Well, what were you gonna ask me?"

"I don't remember."

She heard other cars go by them—fortunate people, and once more she was fighting to hold back tears. This would end in violence and death, and there was nothing she could do about it, nothing she could think of to try doing.

"We'll get these cartons, and you'll never see us again," he said. Again, it was as though he had been reading her thoughts. She remembered that she must learn from him, work toward knowing him well enough to increase her chances of extricating the boy and herself. . . .

"What's in the cartons?" she said. "If I knew what was in them, it might ring a bell. For all I know, Jack might've said something about it."

"You really ain't holding back?"

"Jesus Christ." Her own anger amazed her. "Just tell me what's in the goddam cartons."

"I hate to hear a woman cuss," Travis said.

"Yeah, well, fuck you." Almost immediately, she wanted to call the words back. He reached over and took hold of her hair, and she cried out.

"You gonna behave?"

"Yes," she said.

He let go.

She was fighting tears, squeezing her eyes shut. She thought of Jason.

He said, "That's a girl."

Perhaps a minute went by.

"I just hate to hear a woman talk that way," he said.

She turned to him. "Would it hurt to tell me?"

He stared out at the road, half-smiling. "Jack was all over it when I brought it up to him. I mean it was picture-perfect."

"What was? What was picture-perfect?"

He shook his head, watching the road. He was evidently going over it in his mind, some aspect of his own part in it that pleased him. There was something almost innocent about his face now, a boy's excited face, relishing the memory of something good.

She waited.

"Reuther's a very big-time guy, okay? Used to work for Interpol, and like that. A once cop—you know? And—well, what the hell. Why not? It was like this: I was stationed in Germany, working computers for this company based in LA. And—and I'm sitting on this assembly line, talking to this guy about these—you know what a microchip is?"

"No."

He shook his head, this time with a small, snickering laugh. He was the type of man who enjoyed having the advantage of superior knowledge. "It's these little things that computers run on. They *are* the computer, okay? And—and so this company's making them— expensive, top-of-the-line technology: high-end workstation stuff, and video-compression chips, these new graphics-rendering engines for virtual reality. There's this revolution in immersive virtual reality. You know anything about computers?"

"No."

"Virtual reality? Ever heard that? Your son must've mentioned that to you—it's the coming thing in video games."

"No," she said.

"Well," Travis went on. "This is state-of-the-art stuff, hot off the line. Hell, they hadn't even put it out on the market yet. And they had all this quality control, you know, and security badges, and stuff. Because new-wave microchips are always worth a lot of money. More than twenty-five hundred dollars apiece on the legal market. Well, I was pretty good at getting around security. I'd been trained in the army. So one night I break into the place and take some of the chips. A whole lot of them—more than twelve hundred—no bigger than a saltine cracker. Unmarked, untraceable. Real easy to move around and hide, once you pack them right. And each one's worth twenty-five hundred bucks—well, a little more than half that on the black market. But we had a couple of parties interested, you see? We were gonna get near-market value, because these—types—didn't have the technology and wanted to use them to make a bunch more of their own. So it was perfect. We'd got ourselves the best thing to steal. Except getting it to where we could settle with our—we'll call them bidders— turns out to be a little more complicated. These are Pakistanis and Japanese, with no love of us, or of each other. So it was a matter of getting Reuther's help bringing them over, and your hubby's help keeping them safe."

She looked at him.

He nodded. "Jack was the guy we sent them to over here. There was this guy we knew in the army. Bobby Rickerts. Jack knew him pretty good. Rickerts was supposed to be arranging things with the other parties. The bidders."

"I never saw or got an inkling of any of this," she said. "You'll just have to believe me."

"You know how much money we're talking about?"

"I don't care," she told him.

He said nothing for a time, humming low to himself.

She observed the countryside, which she did not yet recognize specifically. She searched for a landmark, something to place herself.

"Put your head down, goddammit."

She did so. "My husband wouldn't be a part of something like what you've just described," she said.

"He didn't even hesitate. His cut was going to be a hundred-seventy thousand dollars, and he didn't even hesitate."

"Well then—" she paused, stifled a sob, swallowed.

"Well then, what?"

"What did Mr. Bishop—what was his—how did he—"

"Oh, Mr. Bishop. He dead." Travis laughed. "You ever read *Heart of Darkness*?"

She said nothing.

"Mr. Bishop. He dead." The laugh came again.

"Oh, God," she said. "Please."

"It's literature, you know. I've done a little reading."

"I wasn't asking you about literature, you—" She was trying to stop crying. "You—"

"Hey," he said. "Don't call names."

To her own astonishment, she held on.

"That business was all Bags. Billy boy. My excitable younger brother. What happened with the—the black guy. That got me, too, when I found it. Bags is a little high-strung, and he's been getting worse. The guy must've got on his nerves."

"Why did you wait until now to come here?" she said.

"We had this nice bidding situation. Even had some Indians and Russians interested for a little while. But it would've been sooner. I mean there's time pressure now, because the technology is changing all the time, and the value's sort of sinking. Billy and I messed around and got ourselves arrested and sent to the farm for a few months. And then we thought we'd have plenty more of the damn things, too. Didn't see no sense in taking any unnecessary risks. But then the authorities were starting to get wise, and we started seeing the value of what we'd already brought over. But then we got put away and that was a complication, too. Bags ain't fit for the life of a thief. If he was, I never would've had to think of approaching old Jack. But we just couldn't trust Bags alone here. And Jack knew Rickerts."

"I never heard of him. Or you. We were married for almost thirteen years—"

"You think I'm making all this up?"

She let the tears come now.

"Okay, that's all the crying," he said.

She couldn't stop it.

"Come on," he said. "Cut it out. It's annoying."

She felt the car slow to a stop, and when she tried to sit up his hand closed, hard, on the back of her neck.

"Okay?" he was saying. "You gonna stop now?"

"I'll stop, I'll stop," she said, rasping.

After a time he let go, and the car started moving again. The quiet seemed to lengthen. The muscles of her back contracted in a spasm. She straightened a little, breathed out, then drew herself down, attempting to be absolutely still.

A moment later, wanting to keep him talking, she said, "What did you do to—to—" She couldn't get it out.

"What?" he said impatiently.

"Get arrested?"

He said, "Oh, that. Well, it's true I can't control Billy like I used to. He got into it with this guy in a bar in Annapolis and ended up knocking a cop around, too, and I had to step in and help him out. We got a year apiece. A year apiece, and when I think what they could've got us for, it's funny. But we were on best behavior and after five months we got assigned to this halfway house in Montgomery County." He laughed. "We just walked away from it. And Reuther—fucking Reuther was waiting for us, of course."

"I don't get it. My husband was a contractor. He built houses and sold them."

"He did computers in the army, right. I worked in the same section with him. And he got to know Rickerts. Rickerts has the resources to get rid of everything at top dollar."

"I don't believe this," Nora said. "I don't."

After a period of time, she sat up again.

They had come down out of the hills and had entered Route 66. She glanced furtively back to see what the road had been. It looked like the Grand Meadows exit. She couldn't be certain. They went along Route 240, heading into the little town with its shops and its road sign with all the distances painted on—the mileage to cities in Florida and Maine and California and so on, the thousands of miles to the Far East. They turned right and went on through the central cluster of streets and up the incline, the low hill, which then slowly

descended, along Steel Run Creek. Soon they were circling the big
end of Bishop's farm, coming around to the turnoff to her house.
She saw the house off in the distance as they made the turn. The
road was stitched with shade, and the morning had become still
brighter, the sun showing the rich white, billowing folds of the tall
clouds that were drifting off to the west. The house looked like itself.
As they pulled into the drive she saw what was visible of Ed Bishop's
place—the curve of the roof—and her stomach turned over under
her heart. It was so quiet. She got out of the car, and Travis did, too.
He seemed the slightest bit wary. He looked up and down the road.
"Okay, what we do—we play this very calm and straight." He
stepped close. "We got lots of time to look around. Anybody sees us,
I'm an old friend of your husband's, visiting from out of town. Helping you go through his things. That's the truth, so it'll be easy to say.
And let's see—anybody wants to know where your boy is, he's on the
road south with his grandfather. They're—visiting Civil War battle-
fields. And they haven't got in touch. They left two days ago. Got it?
He didn't go to school the last couple days anyway."

She stopped. "His grandfather? What have you—what are you—"

"Got it?" he said, squeezing her arm.

"Yes."

"Repeat it."

She did so. She could tell by the small tremor in his voice that
he was nervous. She saw the big slope of his shoulders, the power-
ful arms, the cords of muscle in the neck, and felt damp under her
skin.

"You didn't know the boy hadn't been going to school, did you?"

She glanced at him, but gave no answer, attempting to remove
all expression from her face.

"Forging notes from teachers and faking homework. Right?
Probably forging your signature, too. I think he's on his way to a life
of crime."

Still, she kept silent.

"Okay, look," he said. "We play it nice and cool. And when we
find what we're after, we get out. That simple. Anybody calls, you
handle it exactly the way I said."

Inside the house, there was a chair sitting out in the hallway—the only thing out of place. "I have to change," she said. "I have to wash my face."

He smiled. "You look like hell, it's true."

"Please," she said.

"I ain't gonna do anything. When the time comes, I won't have to."

She walked through to her bedroom and he followed. She brought a pair of jeans out and put them on under the dress, then pulled it over her shoulders, and quickly got into a blouse. She put socks on and tennis shoes.

"Love to watch a lady go about keeping herself covered," he said.

She edged past him and hurried through to the bathroom, where she ran water over her face and buried it for a few protected-feeling instants in a clean terry cloth towel. In the kitchen, she indicated the broken pane in the back door. "What about this?"

"Yeah. I'll have to do something about it."

"I don't even know where to start looking," she said. She hoped to keep him focused on the task at hand.

He said, "Where did Jack keep things?"

"He wasn't like that," she told him. "We didn't have any secret—" She stopped. "I didn't think there were any—"

"Where'd he work?"

"In the basement."

"Come on."

She led him down—remembering with a painful sick twinge what had happened with the fat man last night. The sound of Travis behind her on the stairs, in that closed-in space, the proximity of him, made her woozy. There was all his talk about crimes he hadn't been caught or punished for. It was as if these acts, whatever they might be, should be grafted to him somehow, on his skin. In the slovenly features of his gross brother. And the terrifying thing was how ordinary they both looked: men obviously fixed in one social strata—the kind whose very appearance announced what sort of music they listened to, and what kind of car they might want to drive, what their attitudes would be on problems involving politics, or sociology; or the relations between women and men—except that these two had dull, flat green eyes and the demeanor, really, of big, headlong schoolboys. Young men who were easily entertained and liked to laugh. And Travis was evidently a man who had some education, too.

"What a mess," he said, standing in the center of the basement.

She took part of a plastic cover off an old typewriter. Dust flew. He lifted a box of books and began emptying it on the dusty cement floor.

"I don't know what I'm looking for," she said. "There's no cartons down here."

"Look for a piece of paper with a number on it—phone number, box number, bank, anything like that."

Together they went through the desk, a big antique rolltop, with a hundred little drawers and compartments—old bills, old letters, plans to houses, some sketches, a pad of legal paper with a series of numbers written across the top. "Is that a combination?" he said.

"I don't know what it is."

"Let me have it."

She gave it to him.

He held it close in the dimness. "Looks like a combination."

"I don't know."

"Anything padlocked, that you know of?"

"No."

He tore the page from the pad and put it in his shirt pocket. "Might find something later, you never know." He paged through the rest of the pad, then put it back on the desk. "Nothing else."

She had brought some ledger pages out of one of the drawers. "What're those?"

"Account pages," she said. She handed them to him. It was all columns of numbers. He only glanced at them. She went back to rifling the drawers, pulling out old checkbooks, out-of-date magazines, cut-out pages of newspapers—Jack had saved everything on the Gulf War.

In a corner of the room, stacked against the wall, Travis found some panes of glass. "Look at these," he said.

"My husband—broke—broke the door once in a fight with me," she said and felt as though she had given away a part of herself. She sat in the chair at the desk and put her head in her hands. "I don't know."

"You guys fight a lot?"

The anger came rushing back; there was something almost hopeless about it, a giving in. "Fuck off," she heard herself say.

"Hey, I'm a friend of the family. I told you how I feel about a woman talking that way."

"I won't talk about my marriage," she said.

"Okay. So he broke a window. And he bought some panes of glass for the next time? He had plans to break it again?"

"He was a builder. He bought things in lots. I don't know."

"Well, this is a happy thing," Travis said. "This makes me think we're gonna get through all this. You keep looking, and I'll go replace the pane in the door."

She didn't move from the desk. Perhaps five minutes passed. She heard him walking around up there, overhead. Finally she started sifting through the papers on the desktop. She stood and opened all the smaller compartments, most of which were empty. She felt as if she were prying. In the years of their life together there had been a mutual respect between them concerning some personal matters: their intimacy had never extended so far as to include, for instance, opening each other's mail, or intruding on the other's area of responsibility regarding the house, the business, and Jason. Jack had kept the accounts and managed the money.

He had left everything in such a ruin.

She rifled the drawers of the desk. In one drawer there was a key on a little circular chain. She held it in the palm of her hand, trying to recall ever having seen it before. Then she put it in her coat pocket. There was a rustle behind one of the smaller drawers, something caught. She pulled it all the way out and looked into the hole. Something had creased there, attached with tape. She reached in and pulled it out, and part of it tore. She worked to get that, too, and stood piecing the thing together—a sheet of paper with writing on it.

No guilt and no regrets, either. We don't have that, at least. We stopped in time. We'll both say that, I know. But I know it cost you, saying no to me, Jack. No one will ever know what it cost me. We did the right thing. We did do that.

                                        Love, Ruth

Nora stood crying in the basement, alone. The letter was written on the business stationery letterhead of a real estate agency Jack had done some work for a year and a half ago. Eighteen months. A woman she hadn't known about and now perhaps would never know about. Ruth. Ruth. He had never mentioned anyone named Ruth.

She crushed the pieces of paper and put them in the woodstove, lifting the iron lid carefully, slowly, and setting it back.

But she was abruptly assailed by the sense that the woman, Ruth, might hold the answer, the information these men wanted. When she tried to lift the lid again, she heard him on the stairs. She hurried to the desk and began looking through the other letters and papers, and he came partway down.

"Anything?"

"No."

"Keep looking."

When he had gone, she moved to the woodstove and retrieved the crumpled pieces. She put them in the pocket of her coat and went back to searching. She looked in the metal cabinet where Jack kept most of his tools and found a tin full of assorted nails and screws, the blades of a hacksaw. She put one blade in her coat pocket with the key and the crumpled pieces of paper and another in the bottom of her tennis shoe, hurrying, frantic, while Travis's footsteps grew louder, nearer.

He came back down the stairs, still holding the pane of glass. "It's too big for the door. I can't fix it." He put the glass pane back in its place, exercising care not to break it or chip it. There was a strange fastidiousness about him, she decided. Now he appeared momentarily troubled. "Shoot," he said. "I thought it was working out so nice."

CHIEF INVESTIGATOR SHAW STOOD in the strips of shadow from the blinds at his office window, hands in his pockets, surveying the street below. A sunny winter day, men and women hurrying past, bundled up against the wind. Their shadows on the walk looked darker, more sharply defined by the clear cold air. Across the way was the county jail, the new building with its heavy, dark glass windows. He would have to go over there soon to report to the county attorney what he had been able to ascertain from the evidence concerning the slaughter, by gunfire, of some cattle near Darkness Falls Courthouse. A canvas of the area had turned up a few boot prints and several empty shell casings from a .38-caliber revolver. People in the vicinity were spread wide apart by the open pasture and woods, and apparently nobody had heard anything. Nobody could think of why someone would do a thing like this, either.

He had been working on the report, sitting there in the sunlight from the window, and the warm light had done to him what it had been doing to him for weeks now, except that his brief dip into unconsciousness had been colored by the appalling scene of apparently recreational slaughter that he had been trying to describe in his report. He saw it again in his sleep and came awake with a start.

The fact of it was unnerving in some elemental way. It weakened him. He wished fervently that he was elsewhere on this particular morning.

The night had been terrible. He had lain awake, restless, a pervasive, clammy sense of horror in his bones, unable to keep his mind on what he was reading. This was the day, the eleventh anniversary of the boy's death, and Carol's plans to leave Steel Run with Mary made it all that much worse; it brought everything back, a desolation. The scene at Lombard's pasture, the inert shapes bulging in the grass, kept dissolving into the image of what he had struggled toward out of the tossing surf with such deepening horror, all those years ago.

He would lose his daughter, too, now. She would grow away from him, in her mother's house.

Near dawn he dozed off and had a vivid dream that he had drunk three glasses of whiskey, swallowing it greedily, thinking of forgetfulness and waiting for it to begin. He woke in the quiet dark. Pure fright. No chance of sleep. He was vaguely dizzy and lightheaded; but nothing happened. The numbers changed on the digital clock by his bedside. At first light, he arose, made his way into the kitchen, prepared some dry toast and poured himself a glass of milk, then sat at the table.

"Lord," he said, low. "Please help me today."

Now, he turned from the window and sat down again to his report. How does one describe the creepy nature of such a crime, its weirdness?

He couldn't think. He put his head in his hands and felt the whole thing drift off again.

His partner, Frank Bell, talked about depression. There were the relentless facts: the lost years of alcoholism, of a kind of functioning pathology, a marriage soaked in grief and recrimination, the recent divorce, his wife's decision to leave and take Mary with her. Frank said it was plain as daylight.

Shaw didn't think so. People spoke of depression as an *interruption* of normal patterns of life, whereas Shaw's pattern had been

unchanging for years now. It wasn't any interruption, no shift in the
status quo. It was just harder on the anniversaries, and this particular anniversary was especially difficult because of the coming
change, Mary's departure for Richmond. He felt no great longing to
keep Carol near.

She was making a statement with her life.

Shaw considered that her grief had brought out of her something of an almost freakish turbulence and agitation, a need to
involve herself, a willingness to embrace causes that were far from
her old life. The latest was an oddly rote rejection of what she called
the male-dominated idea of herself as a wife and mother. She could
be a mother without a patriarch in the house.

It felt, to Shaw, like blame. It *was* blame.

He understood, and he could even forgive it. It was all part of
the waste their relationship had mostly been since Willy's death. The
truth was, he had spent a lot of time away, over the years, a lot of
time under the influence of one substance or another. It had almost
cost him his job. Carol would say it had ruined his marriage. Lately,
she had taken to putting it in terms of her newfound political
awareness: he had demonstrated the essential bankruptcy of the
male-centered culture. This was her particular battiness now,
another of her ways of pocketing her grief, and the fact was that he
felt quite willing to have her practice her newfound political beliefs
away from him. He was a little sick of her—even as he felt pangs of
sorrow for her—with her insistence on putting a political spin on
everything, including the ways he had wrecked her life, with alcohol
and overindulgence and dread. The alcohol was a form of seduc-
tion, a way of depriving her of her freedom. She had even put the
political hex on their lovemaking—particularly their lovemaking. It
was all power to her. And the phrase was *gender issues.* She used it in
every context, even about the boy's death, and without the slightest
hint of self-examination or the least discernment as to the sense of
the language as it was perverted by such jargon: *gender issues* was
the overall rubric. It was gender that had killed their son—the boy
following his macho father into the waves, never suspecting for a
moment that his father's willingness to plow into such a dangerous

surf had been produced by the alcohol coursing through his veins. There were a few phrases borrowed from Marx and the Soviets, too: every single human action or inaction was one kind of political gesture or another to her, and it was as though this belief *spared* her, in some incalculable way, from the terrible, remorseless fact of the child's death; at least, it explained that death for her.

And Shaw was further culpable for continuing to drink after the tragedy. Yes. He had failed miserably in the years of Mary's infancy.

This was true.

Sometimes, listening to her, though, he had thought he might go out of his mind. Carol could take her dull, humorless, frozen, narrow attitudes, her bromides, and her pain, and go.

Yet he hurt so, as the reality of it approached.

The fact was that because he was the chief investigating officer for Fauquier County, and spent more time away from home than most men, the court had deemed it in the interest of the child that Carol keep custody. But Shaw hadn't been quite ready for her to pick up and move back to Richmond. He hadn't thought of this as part of the deal, no matter how forcefully his lawyer went over it, showing him where it said that she could relocate with Mary, up to three hundred miles from Steel Run Creek and Fauquier County without having to seek the permission of the court, or of Philip Shaw.

So they were leaving. All that remained of his family. And Shaw suffered from bad insomnia and increasing thirst.

"It's depression," Frank Bell told him. "Classic case. I've seen it. My sister once got this way, after the birth of her second child." He shook his head and snapped his fingers. "Like that. Went down into herself—got into bed and stayed there for six weeks. Six weeks."

"Did she sleep during that time?"

"Almost the whole time."

"Well, I *can't* sleep. So I guess I don't have what she had."

"It manifests itself in different ways, Phil."

"You just said I was a classic case."

"All right. I'm just saying . . ." Bell was a rangy, stoop-shouldered man with a deeply lined, dark face and large, deep-socketed eyes. He had come to Shaw from the traffic division two years ago, and Shaw sometimes thought of him as being a man with tidal patience and calm. Having never taken a drink in his life, having in fact kept such charge of his own affairs that it was hard to imagine him in any kind of extremity, he sometimes took a faintly parental attitude toward Shaw. He was inclined to offer advice. Shaw liked him, even when he found the advice annoying, because Bell obviously meant to help, and because you got the feeling, talking to him, that he was thinking about you at odd hours of the day.

"How're things going with Eloise?" Frank said.

"What's Eloise got to do with anything?"

"Just asking. I think she's a nice lady. I think she'd be good for you."

"I don't think I'm depressed," Shaw said. "This is grief, not depression."

"I have some sleeping pills my doctor gave me when I tore my knee up last year."

"I'm fine, really," Shaw said. "Everybody's fine. Really."

But there were these petit mal episodes in his office, when the warm air and the quiet made him feel as though his head were stuffed with buzzing cotton, his eyelids made of melting sand. He would feel the whole of himself begin to pause, to sink, and he would have to struggle back to the surface, worried that anyone might find him like this, sitting in a city office, drowsing.

What he had on the books for today, beside the slaughter of Lombard's cattle, were two cases of check fraud, two break-ins, a car theft, vandalism—someone had sawed the head off a parking meter—and Shaw had already put in a call to the local video store asking for a list naming everyone who in the last week or so had rented *Cool Hand Luke*.

Concerning the cattle kills, Mr. Lombard had stated unequivocally that there were no ongoing conflicts or feuds of any kind between him and anyone else. He ran an honest business, he said. He had no enemies he could think of. This was a case of random destruction. Shaw believed that whoever was responsible had probably left the area. Lombard wanted to call the FBI. Shaw had assured him that the problem did not warrant involving the federal government.

Now he stretched and yawned and wondered how he would make it through the rest of the day. He had to make a court appearance at noon, a grand jury appearance in the hour after noon, and he knew all this would involve sitting and waiting to testify. Otherwise he would be out on the county roads, looking for cattle killers.

On his desk was a large paper cup with cold tea in it. He took a long drink of it. When the phone rang he almost doubted it. It rang twice. He picked up the handset. "What?"

"Daddy?" Mary's voice.

He leaned back in the chair and experienced a rushing sensation in the exact middle of his chest. "Hi, sweetness."

"Mommy said I should call you about this. I won the spelling bee."

"Aw, honey," he said. "That's great."

"I get to go to Wordsworth High School next month and compete for the whole school district." She was almost twelve years old, in sixth grade.

"I'm so proud of you," he said into the phone.

Frank Bell walked in, carrying a notepad. He sat on the edge of the desk, looking rushed and aggravated. "Phil," he began.

Shaw held up his hand. "Tell me all about it. Will I get to see you compete?"

"If you want to."

"I wouldn't miss it for the world."

"Are you picking me up today?"

"You know I am."

"Okay—I've got to go now. Bye."

"Bye, darling." Shaw started to hang up, then had a thought. "Honey, does your mother want to talk to me—"

She had broken the connection.

"Lombard is waiting out in the hall," Frank Bell said. "About his beef cattle."

"I can't see him now. I don't have anything for him."

"He says he's not leaving until you talk to him."

"You know what I think?" Shaw said. "I think we're not gonna find whoever did this."

"I dare you to say that to him."

Shaw smiled. "Maybe I'll just get you to tell him."

"Not me."

The two men moved to the door of the office and out into the hallway, at the end of which Lombard sat reading a pamphlet. He wore a red baseball cap. A wooden rack of pamphlets hung on the wall: instructions for witnesses, household security hints, advice for setting up a neighborhood watch program. When Shaw approached, Lombard stood and put the pamphlet back in among the others. "It's about time you came out here and earned some of what my taxes pay you," he said.

"I'm sorry to have kept you waiting," Shaw said. "Truth is, I have to be in court in a couple minutes. An arrest I made for breaking and entering a few weeks back. If you'll just write out what you want me to know, I'll be glad to go over it and get back in touch with you, sir. And I do have people working on it."

Lombard backed down a little. "You know it's just one guy?"

"We're not sure yet it *is* a guy, are we?"

"I just get worried that nothing's being done."

"I promise if it's at all possible to do we'll get to the bottom of it, sir. It's only been one day, after all."

"I just can't imagine," Lombard said, starting out the door. "Shooting cattle. At the end of the goddam twentieth century. A damn mean thing like that."

"It's one for the books, sir."

As Lombard opened the door to leave, he nearly walked into David Ross, the deputy state's attorney. Shaw was surprised to see him. Ross, looking grim, stepped aside for Lombard to pass. Lombard went on, shaking his head. The door closed on him.

"David," Shaw said.

Ross walked into the first office, a small room with two cluttered desks facing each other. Shaw and Bell followed him. "Boys," he said, turning at the first desk. "There's been a homicide out on Rural Route Six."

"The housing development?" Shaw said. A tremor of alarm ran through him. He had just spoken with Mary.

"Back in the meadows," Ross said. "The Bishop Farm. Bishop's the victim."

"Bishop?" Frank Bell said. "Isn't that the guy—"

"He was in here a while back," said Shaw. "That Virginia Front outfit threatened him." He walked back down the corridor to his own office, and from the top of his desk he took the folder with Bishop's name on it. Inside was one of the sheets of folded paper, the printed threat, the crude graphics. The others had followed him, and he held it out to them.

"Aw, Christ," Ross said.

Frank Bell walked to the window, put his hands high on the frame, and stared out.

"Christ," Ross said again. "I hope not."

Shaw folded the paper and put it in his shirt pocket.

"Looks like they broke in," Ross said. "Bishop's tied up."

There hadn't been a homicide in this county of Virginia for almost five years, and that had been the result of a fistfight in the old Beverly Tavern, something arising out of the passions of the moment.

"Who's at the scene?" Shaw asked.

"A state trooper called it in. I don't know any more than that. I've already called the officer of the court for you."

"Hell," Frank Bell said. "What in God's name is happening?"

"I think I'm going to try to file it as a violation of Bishop's civil rights."

"You want the FBI?" Shaw said.

"I think so, yeah."

"Okay." He turned to Frank Bell. "Let's go."

Most of the land beyond the south fork of Steel Run Creek had been farm country for generations—wide green fields with soft slopes leading into the foothills of the Blue Ridge. Family farms, mostly, some of them going back to the eighteenth century. The sale of the land north of the creek to developers had begun when the pressures of the expanding city began—and there were many people, like Philip Shaw and his wife, who were neither farmers nor commuters to the city. In the years since Vietnam, the county's most important—its only—industry was house building and construction.

Riding along in the patrol car with Bell, Shaw looked at the hills, brown with widely separated patches of dirty snow on them and bordered by stands of naked trees; there was a dry-brush look to the trees, through which houses were visible now and then. All this country was up for sale. The farmers were leaving the land. But there were no takers. Near Steel Run Creek, they saw several half-finished houses and a few finished ones, empty, no one working on them. They belonged to the banks now. Kids used them for games and for hiding from their parents. There had been incidents: in the summer a girl had been cornered in one of the houses and harassed by two boys from the high school, one of whom was a state all-star in football and the stepson of a prominent doctor. No sexual assault had occurred, but her clothes were torn, and she pressed charges, then—perhaps not inexplicably, though she offered no reasons for doing so—dropped them. Last month, several boys had ignited a fire in the basement of the same unoccupied house; they had put the fire out, or so they thought, but smoldering ashes had set the thing going again, and in the subsequent blaze the house and several old trees surrounding it burned.

"I've only had two homicides in the sixteen years I've been here," Shaw said. "Both were pretty straightforward. Involuntary manslaughter, one of them. And voluntary the other. Both of them the results of altercations. And the guys responsible stood around and waited to be arrested. Never had a cold-blooded one yet."

"Neither me," said Bell, who had grown up in Louisiana, had Cajun relatives on his mother's side, and still occasionally slipped into the patois. "That's why I didn't want city work."

"I guess it was only a matter of time."

"Law of averages," said Bell. "Been a pretty strange couple days. Those cattle yesterday and now this. Pretty screwy."

The Steel Run Creek housing development took up much of what had once been Shaw's grandfather's farm. The grandfather had sold it before Shaw was born. Now the son of an army general had sold much of it to Argosy Development Corporation. By arrangement with the general's son, Shaw used to hunt here, in these woods and hills; up into the deep greenery around Darkness Lake. And when he had lived in one of the houses of the development—the one on the corner as they turned, in fact—he had spent a lot of time walking back in among the trees. Now they took the road up, winding to the steepest part of the hill and on past the open field on one side and the heavy woods on the other. The road climbed again, and they were well past the houses, out of the shadows of the trees, surrounded by the wide field of one end of the Bishop Farm. There was a house in the middle of this field, three acres carved out of the property—a white clapboard house, the old place once lived in and owned by Shaw's grandfather.

"Id'n that—" Frank Bell began.

"Yep," Shaw said.

"They fixed it up real nice—looks like."

"That's that contractor who died last year in that bus crash on twenty-nine."

"I remember." Bell looked at the house as they went by.

"Young guy, too. With a wife and kid."

"Lord."

The Bishop farmhouse was only another field away, partially obscured by the rising ground between the two tracts of land and bordered by tall, skinny pines. They pulled into the driveway behind the two state cars and the truck with Bishop's name on the door.

"Did you know this guy was pretty well-thought-of around here?" Bell said as they got out of the car.

"Never heard his name until he came to see me about the obscene flyers somebody put in his mailbox."

A state trooper emerged from the front door and stepped to the edge of the porch to meet them. He was ghost-pale. "I seen accidents," he said. "Bad ones. And a beating or two, you know?" He shook his head.

He had put the call in for help, and two other officers were securing the scene. The county medical examiner was on his way. Frank Bell, putting in the call, had been told that the examiner had already been notified.

"You touch anything?" Shaw asked the trooper, who kept shaking his head.

"Looks like the son of a bitch wanted to play some kind of game with him. The bulb's broken out of the hall light upstairs, and all of them are out of the lamps up there—in every room. The record player's on. I left it all exactly the way I found it."

Shaw went on into the house, the living room. He saw through to the kitchen, the broken pane in the back door.

"What's your name?" Shaw asked the trooper at his side.

"Bryan."

"No, your last name."

"That's it, sir. Bo Bryan."

Shaw followed him up the stairs, noting that there were bloodstains on the floor, that the phone was there, as if thrown, and there were broken pieces of lightbulb strewn down the hallway. The music was still playing. Shaw put latex gloves on, then lifted the record arm and set it down. On the table was a piece of paper, one of the Virginia Front's hate messages. He pointed at it. "See this, Frank?"

Bell said. "Yeah."

The room seemed almost supernaturally quiet now. The others were waiting for him to begin. He stepped carefully over to the body, scrunched down, and looked at the face. Something heavy dropped down into him, and for an instant he couldn't get his bearings, almost toppled over. The cord running from the head to the ankles was thin, the kind that people used to string clotheslines. It looked as though a sharp blade had simply been drawn across the throat. One motion. An execution. "Do we have the weapon?"

"Not so far, no."

"Look like anything's missing?"

"House seems fairly undisturbed—except for the kitchen door and the lightbulb in the hall, and like I said all the lamps have the bulbs out of them. There's a half-glass of beer on the end table in the living room."

Shaw took a breath and tried not to shiver. He felt the others watching him, and for a bad few seconds his mind went blank. The quiet was like a substance pressing against his face. Leaning in, he traced without touching it the line of the cut. "Looks like a knife blade. Serrated. The flesh is torn." He took a breath and gingerly put his gloved hands under the body, at the chest. "Fairly advanced lividity." He moved the fingers of the hand.

"Twelve hours?" Bell said.

"Maybe more. Hell, maybe less."

Bell sighed. "Lord, lord."

Shaw pushed one eyelid farther back, exposing the blackening sclera, then closed it slightly.

"Jesus Christ," the trooper said, putting a hand on the frame of the door.

"As you know, we don't want to touch anything," Shaw said, without turning to look at him.

"God, I'm sorry."

He moved back a little and observed the pattern of bloodstains. "Arterial spray on the floor and the wall," he said. He was gaining control of himself now, burying his horror in the intricacies of procedure. Beyond the body, near the love seat, he saw streaks in the blood, and there were odd tracks of it along the baseboard. "Look here," he said to Bell, pointing at one of the brownish-black smears on the baseboard.

"What do you make of it?"

"Looks like part of a footprint. Tread from a tennis shoe, maybe?" With his hand held in the air, he traced a line from this mark to an imprint in the blood. "And this looks like it could be the fold of a shirt."

"Somebody—"

"There's another mark over here." He pointed to the left of the first mark—perhaps two feet away. Then he stood and went out in the hall and bent down to look at those splotches. "It's the same. I'd bet on it." He went back into the room, Bell and Bryan following.

"He hid here?" Bell said.

"Why?" Shaw wanted to know. "I mean it's blood—so the killing's done. Somebody come in on him, maybe?"

The others were silent.

"Well, I guess we'll find out, soon enough." He pointed to a place next to the body. "Cat print?"

Bell leaned down to look at it. "Cat or maybe a little dog."

"There's a bunch of cats around the place," Bryan said. "I saw them when I pulled in."

"They keep the rodents at bay," said Shaw.

"Speechless witnesses," Bryan said.

Shaw glanced at him, then walked to the bureau. An ashtray with cigarettes in it was there, along with a butane lighter. "Could be they did some talking or waiting before things got drastic. Or this could be the victim's. They walked in on him while he was listening to music, smoking a cigarette."

Bell was writing everything down in his pad.

"No, hell. Two brands of cigarettes in the ashtray."

"Maybe there was two of them," said Bell.

"I don't understand the situation downstairs," Bryan said. "The drawers being open like that and the broken window in the kitchen door." He pointed at the stain on the baseboard. "Blood tracks just like those, down in the kitchen and the hallway and on the stairs, too."

"Any full prints?"

"Smears. It looks like a—well, like a kid's shoe."

"Show me."

Bryan led him out into the hall, to the stairs. There was one smear that looked to be the whole left part of a shoe print.

"That's a small shoe. What—an eight, say?" Shaw put his own shoe next to it, an inch away. "I wear a ten."

"I'd say that's at least three sizes smaller," Bell said.

"Who discovered the body?"

"Come with me." Bryan started down the stairs.

"Wait a minute," Shaw said. He walked over to the telephone answering machine on the hall table and pressed the playback button. A soft baritone voice came: "I'm not here. Please leave a message. Good-bye." There was a hang-up and then another. And then a female voice, faintly distressed or irritated, tinged with exasperation and weariness. "Ed? Oh, where is everyone? Is Jason with you? I can't get home before six-thirty or seven." The line clicked; the little tape ran back to the beginning.

He opened the machine, took the tape out, and put it in a small plastic bag he had drawn from his pocket. He set this down next to the phone. "Okay," he said. "Let's go."

Bryan led him down the stairs and through an arched doorway, past the outside door, on into the little den where the TV was. A woman sat on the sofa there, her hands resting on her thighs, her face a perfect expressionless mask—lovely features, lovely blond hair, a bluish cast to the skin, eyes dark blue as a clear winter sky. Shaw discerned that she was scarcely holding on.

"Hello," she said. He heard a jittery energy in the voice. She was fixed, with her panic, looking from one to the other of the men and seeing only what she had stumbled onto less than an hour ago. For her, life would now be colored by this—her perceptions would continually give off the sense of the proximity of harm, and it would go on that way for months or years, and even if time dulled the edges of it, she would never really find the self she had been before. He felt a kinship with her, and he thought of all those who had suffered the world's unrecoverable shocks, including the ones who had walked into the scenes of violence and mayhem, as a group of initiated people, a growing army of the psychologically scarred. Perhaps the country's fascination with violence was explicable in terms other than its famous appetite for it—perhaps people so wounded and marked by it wanted to see it cosmeticized on their TV screens as a way of exorcising the ghost. His own daughter stood in his mind for an instant, that scared and scarred girl, going through the years of her father's grief and now the separation of her parents—having already spent unhappily long periods of her babyhood in the company of aunts and uncles, or family friends, while one or the other or both of her parents foundered in an alcoholic haze—overly worried about herself and how she appeared to them, how she seemed in their eyes, inwardly convinced that she had done something to cause all the trouble and believing that the world was breaking down. His heart hurt. For a second it was as if this woman were that girl in some future circumstance.

He sat down near her, almost reached over and touched her arm. Then he looked at Bell and the trooper. "Could we get some coffee or milk or something—some tea maybe?"

"There's stuff moved around in the kitchen," Bryan said. "Drawers open."

"Yeah," Bell said to him. "We weren't talking about touching anything in the kitchen. There's a Seven-Eleven nearby, isn't there?"

"A Country Store," Bryan said.

Shaw turned to the woman. "Would you like something?"

"No, thank you."

"A Danish, or a glass of milk?"

"A glass of milk," she said. "Thank you."

Shaw signaled to Bryan.

"I'll go with him," Frank said.

Shaw nodded. When he turned to the woman again, he saw that she had begun to shake. Someone had put an afghan over her shoulders, and she pulled it around herself.

"My name's Philip," he said. "I'm sorry you have to go through this."

"It's fine," she said, though he could see that it was not fine at all.

"You've probably already answered some questions. I wish it didn't have to be this way."

"Yes."

"Do you feel up to it?"

She indicated with a look that she was.

"May I have your name?"

"I told the other one," she said. "I'm Marjorie Powers."

"Ms. Powers, I'm so sorry to have to put you through this."

"I cleaned for him," she said. "I do it in several houses around here. Every week. I have two children in school, and it's extra money. My husband's a carpenter." She shook again, pulled the woolen cloth tight around herself. "Oh, God."

"I've got a little girl," he told her. "I—I had a son." The level of this confidence briefly shook him; he had not known that he would say it.

The woman's gaze only brushed by him. "You have a little girl—" Evidently she had decided not to address it.

"We started late," he said, relieved. "She lives with her mother."

"You're—divorced."

"Right," he said.

"I'm so sorry." Now she seemed to mean she was sorry about everything. Her eyes took him in, and in.

"Well," he managed. It was becoming clear to him that he was not fit for this work now; his mind was a fog of old sorrow and this young woman's pitying gaze.

"Oh, God," she said.

"I know." Shaw reached for his handkerchief. But she sat forward and pulled one out of her small purse, which lay on the coffee table. He took the purse and set it carefully on the floor. "I'm gonna need to talk to you," he got out. "I know it's hard. Do you—would you want to wait a little?"

"I'm shaking."

"It's a terrifying thing," he said to her. "An awful thing."

And she started to cry. "I was—I would never just walk in. Never. But the door—" She pointed. "That door was ajar. Sitting open. I—I knocked on it several times. Then I—I stepped in and called him. Calling him, you know. And I heard the music. So I—I went out to the car and waited for him to see me. I waited ten minutes—fifteen. A long time. A long time. And then I went back, and knocked again, and called him. Nothing. So I—I went in there, into the kitchen, and saw the drawers open and the glass on the floor. And then the blood." She sobbed. "I thought he might've cut himself or something. And there was the music going on, and then it stopped and I yelled his name. And then the music started again, I heard it—heard the needle drop down—and I—I think I knew. I ran outside, but—but it seemed so—I thought I was crazy. You know, you think there's some reasonable explanation. So I went back in, calling him, and I went up there. Oh, God."

"It's all right," Shaw said. "You're all right."

"I called the police on my car phone. I didn't know which ones to call."

"You did fine."

"Oh," she said, sniffling. "I'm so terrified. What kind of world is this anyway? What's happening to us? I didn't know what I was doing or anything. I just ran."

He put his hand on her shoulder and patted softly. "You did all the right things."

"I cleaned house for him. Oh, what kind of people are out there?"

"Mrs. Powers, I need to ask—have you received any kind of sign that somebody might find your coming here to be—that someone looked upon it in any way that might be construed as—"

"I just cleaned his house—"

"I'm asking if you got any sign of an objection—a nasty letter, say, or even somebody saying something to you."

"I didn't even know him all that well. I've worked for him five years. He was a nice man, a good man."

Shaw took the page from his pocket and opened it, so she could see what was printed there.

"Oh," she said, rocking slightly and sobbing.

"Have you seen anything like this?"

"It's not me, is it? They don't mean me, do they? How could they mean me? It has to be the one—oh, God, I don't know what I'm saying. He was—he was friendly with the lady who lives in that old house over the way. In the horseshoe, he called it."

"I know the place," Shaw said. "I think she's on the answering machine. Actually, that house was in my family before I was born. My grandfather used to own part of this land."

This held of course no interest for her. "Well—he—Mr. Bishop used to go over there in the afternoons—" She began to sob, the tears rolling down her lovely cheeks.

"I knew something about that," Shaw told her. He waited a beat. "Did—did Mr. Bishop ever say anything about this?"

She looked at him. "No."

"Any—tensions or conflicts that you know of? You know—regarding his, um, color. With anybody?"

"He never talked about anything like that. We never talked about it."

"Do you happen to know who his next of kin was? Anybody in the area that we ought to notify, you know."

"He had a sister, I think. But I don't know where she lived. I don't even know if she's alive—he talked about her a little."

"He didn't have any kids living here with him, or visiting him, right?"

"He lived alone. Nobody ever came here that I know of. Except me."

"Did you ever talk to him about his—the people he knew. Anything like that?"

"The Jameses—up the hill. He talked about them now and then. I think he was friendly with them maybe, years ago. They went to school together—I don't know. Now and then he'd do things for them. Help them out. I said I don't think he had any family here."

"Okay," Shaw told her. "You've been really helpful. Would you—how do you feel? Would you like us to have a doctor look at you?"

"No."

"He could prescribe something to calm you."

"Well," she said, sniffling. "Maybe."

He said, "I'll get right on it."

Out in the kitchen, two troopers were standing over an open drawer. They stepped back with a little startled motion when he entered the room. One of them was older—the lined, pale, yellowish look of someone with bad drinking habits. Shaw knew the look well enough.

"What do we have?" he said.

"Pictures," said the older one.

The younger one still held a few playing cards. He looked like a teenager—his cheeks were pocked with acne, and obviously he was not shaving on a regular basis yet.

"You boys get those out of the drawer?" Shaw asked him.

"Well, yeah. Take a look—"

"Put them the fuck down, please."

The trooper started to put them back in the drawer.

"Not there. On the counter."

He did so.

"Okay," Shaw said. "Now one of you go out to your car and radio that we want a doctor here, with some sedatives for the lady."

"I'll go," the younger of the two said.

When he was gone, his partner stood staring at Shaw, who stared back. "Think we'll ever find the doers?" the trooper said.

"Not if we keep fucking with the evidence," said Shaw.

THE COUNTY MEDICAL EXAMINER
and the trace evidence team arrived in front of several cars full of
newspaper reporters and two vans from the local television station.
Soon, two more television vans pulled up, both from Washington.
They emptied out, and technicians began laying wires and setting up
cameras. It looked to Shaw like a movie set. He went out to meet the
gathered media and to make sure that Marjorie Powers was safely on
her way home. She moved inconspicuously through them all as they
rushed to speak to Shaw. They thrust microphones at him, all talking
at the same time.

"It's a homicide," he said in answer to the general run of the
shouted questions. "We don't know much else right now."

"What was the method," asked one reporter in the tone of a com-
mand.

"There'll be more to say later. Now, if you'll excuse me."

"Is this a serial killing?"

Shaw looked at the face—a handsome, bony, dark female face,
dark hair perfectly arranged around the sharp features; thin lips, very
white teeth. "Not unless there's another one that I don't know about
yet."

"Is that a no?"

"Yes, that's a no."

"How can you be sure?"

"I just said how. Are you listening?"

"What is your feeling about the fact that it happened here, so far from the city?"

"You know," Shaw said to her. "You folks never come out here. Hell, we don't even get into your weather reports. Please excuse me, I have work to do. If you have any other questions, please put them to the commonwealth attorney." He started to walk through them.

"This killing is racially motivated, isn't that right?" A blocky, broad-shouldered blond woman had reached with a microphone, almost hitting his face. He recoiled from it. She repeated the question.

"We don't know that for certain," he said.

"The victim received hate mail and threats from a group calling itself the Virginia Front. Isn't that so?"

"I don't want to get into any of that yet."

Another leaned in—a skinny, bald man with strands of very black hair pushed across the bald place. "Do you deny that there is any racial overtone to this killing?"

"The victim received some hate mail," Shaw said. "We're taking it into account."

A black woman wearing a blue pinstriped suit said, "This is a hate crime, then."

"I'd rather not jump to any conclusions."

"Weren't the communications from this group in the form of threats?"

Shaw looked at her. "They were."

"Then isn't it logical to suppose this is the work of the same people?"

"The logic doesn't always add up. When we know more, we'll be able to say. It's too early to say."

"Do you have experience investigating homicides?"

"Some," Shaw said.

"You're not ruling out the Virginia Front?"

"I'm not, at present, ruling anything or anyone out."

The other was persistent. "You're not ruling out the possibility that what we have here is a hate crime."

"I'm saying it's one of the possibilities," Shaw said. "Now, if you'll excuse me." He walked through them and their shouted other questions and protests, to the car, and got in. Frank Bell was already sitting behind the wheel.

"Where to?" he said.

Shaw sat back and rubbed his hurting eyes. "Any idea how they got all that so fast?"

"Troopers, maybe. They've been talking to everybody."

Shaw sat there.

"Bad news gets around fast, doesn't it," Bell said.

"Well, they'd have known about it soon enough."

"Where to?"

"Let's canvas a little."

Bell pulled out and started up the mountain. The road wound through dry dead branches, and the sunlight pouring through had a strobelike effect—brightness pulsing too fast for vision to fix on. Shaw closed his eyes. "I'm so damn tired, Frank. And I've got a headache."

"Me too."

They rode on in silence, reached the top of the rise, and came to a narrowing of the road. It was gravel and packed dirt here, with big holes and the edges of what might well be glacier-sized stones pushing through. The car bounced over these uneven places, and twice the undercarriage scraped against the rocky surface. Beyond the first rough curve there was a clearing and a small dirt drive which led between two red-clay banks. The clearing became a wide grass field bordered by barbed wire. Frank Bell took the turn and pulled them up into another clear space, surrounded by thick underbrush and trees. In the middle of this was a small white house with a side porch and a barn. There was a car on cinder blocks in the side yard. Chickens ran in front of them and fluttered toward the porch. A woman came out, wiping her hands on a towel. She was solid-looking, with heavy, ruddy features and iron-gray hair.

"Hi," Shaw said, getting out of the car. He introduced himself, offering his hand. She looked at it, then clasped it with a surprisingly strong grip and let go. She said, "I'm Agnes James."

Behind her, a younger woman emerged, thinner, with darker hair, but with the same florid complexion and the same heavy features. Shaw introduced himself again. Then he turned and introduced Bell. Agnes James said, "This is my younger sister, Marsha."

Marsha looked faintly suspicious.

As if in some sort of intuitive response to the look, the older sister emitted a small throat-clearing sound and stood straighter. "What do you want with us?" she said.

"We wondered if you knew Mr. Bishop."

"Of course we—what's happened to Mr. Bishop?"

Frank Bell told them.

Agnes James put the towel up to her face and seemed about to fall. The younger woman took hold of her.

"Oh, Lord," Agnes said. "Who would do such a thing?"

Shaw said, "It looks like someone broke in. There's a—there's something more too."

Shaw took the folded piece of paper out of his shirt pocket and held it toward them, open. Agnes James seemed to sink again, and her younger sister took hold of her under the arms.

"Agnes? It's okay. You're okay."

"I'm really sorry," Shaw told them, putting the paper back.

The younger woman peered out at the borders of her property.

"If you—if anything seemed at all unusual yesterday, we'd like to know. I mean if you saw anything, or anybody—you have to go right by his place in order to go out to the highway."

"We haven't been out for days," Marsha James said. "My sister's been feeling ill. My daughter, Missy, rides the school bus by there every morning and afternoon. But she's gone already this morning. She didn't say anything."

"I went to school with him," Agnes James said, not really addressing anyone. "So long ago. Nobody remembers—nobody could ever—" She halted. Her sister was holding her up.

For a small space both men waited. Agnes James sat down on the top step of the porch, watching the line of woods, as her sister had. Marsha stood over her and frowned.

"I'd appreciate it if you could tell us about the people Mr. Bishop knew," Shaw said, as gently as he could. "Anybody he might've been having trouble with in that way, you know, anything like that."

"I knew him a long time ago," the older woman said. "We—we were never close."

"We didn't really know him that well," said Marsha. "We'd wave to him when we went by."

"Oh, Lord, Marsha," the older woman muttered, standing, turning. "I'm terrified."

"It's prob'ly gonna be all right, ma'am," Frank Bell said. "We'll catch whoever did this, you can rest assured."

For a moment, no one spoke. There was just the sound of Agnes James's breathlessness.

"Well," said Shaw. "If you think of anything, don't hesitate to give us a call."

"Murder," said Agnes James. "All the way out here, after all these—" She stopped herself.

Shaw drove on the way back down the mountain. The car rocked with the deep crevices in the road, and each jarring sent a throb up into the reaches of his skull. They came back past the Bishop house, with its crowd of reporters and onlookers, and drove on, down the slow decline, winding around to the Michaelson place—the house he had never entered, that his father had spent a good part of his boyhood in. Because his father was a good storyteller and liked to talk about those times, Shaw had a pretty vivid idea of some of the details of the place: the walk-up attic that ran across the whole length of the upstairs; the oak-paneled sliding doors of the dining room; and the basement, where a boy could play undisturbed for hours on end, and where Shaw's grandmother had hung her laundry to dry during the winter months.

"This feels so strange, coming here," he said, pulling into the driveway and stopping. "What time do you have?"

"It's after eleven."

There was a small Datsun in the drive. Shaw walked up onto the porch and rang the doorbell. He waited, looking at the reflection of himself in the glass of the window.

Frank Bell stood out in the yard, looking toward the Bishop house. "You can just see the top of the roof from here."

Shaw pushed the button again.

"Maybe nobody's home."

The door opened a crack, and a shadowed face looked out, the eyes red-rimmed and dark—a bottomless brown. There was something taut and held-in about the expression. "Yes?" she said.

Shaw introduced himself and asked if he could come in.

She said, "I've been ill."

"I wondered if you—if you could spare me a minute of your time," Shaw said.

She waited there, without speaking.

"You—ah. This is hard. You're a friend of Mr. Bishop's?"

She nodded.

When he told her about Mr. Bishop, she closed her eyes, the head drooped slightly. Then she straightened, as if expecting to have to resist something beyond him.

"I'm awful sorry to have to tell you a thing like this," he said.

She stepped back a little space. She wore a bathrobe, wrapped tightly about her. Shaw stepped into the frame of the door, but she didn't give any ground.

"I just have to ask a couple of things of you, Mrs. Michaelson—" He halted.

The dark eyes were brimming. "Ed Bishop was my friend."

"Has there been any kind of trouble—from any quarter, even hints of disapproval—about the fact that you and Mr. Bishop were friendly?"

"No."

"Nothing in the mail? No phone calls, anything at all?"

"No. Nothing."

He brought the paper out and showed it to her. "You never got anything from these people?"

"Oh."

He waited.

"No," she said.

"Did Mr. Bishop ever mention this to you?"

She shook her head.

"Have you or your son—"

"My son—"

"Yes."

The dark eyes gave him nothing.

"The lady who found the—who found Mr. Bishop. She says he used to come over and check on your son. Mrs. Michaelson, your son's name is Jason, isn't it?"

"Yes."

Shaw nodded, folding the paper and putting it back. "I listened to a message you left on Mr. Bishop's phone, I guess yesterday?"

"No."

"Well—recently."

"A couple—a few days ago. Last week, maybe."

"He didn't play his messages every day?"

"He forgot sometimes. I don't know. I didn't call there yesterday."

"Mr. Bishop used to come look in on the boy in the afternoons, is that right?"

"Sometimes."

"Have you seen anything unusual—anybody you didn't recognize, or anything at all out of the ordinary, Mrs. Michaelson?"

She considered this, then shook her head slowly. "I've had this virus. I've been sick since yesterday when I got home from school."

"You sounded a little—well, bothered, I guess, in the phone message."

"I don't recall. I didn't call him yesterday, I told you. I've been going through my husband's things."

"Pardon?"

She stared back.

"Is your son at home today?"

"No."

"Would it be all right if I spoke to him at some point?"

"Why?"

"Well—"

"I'm sorry, I—this is such a terrible shock. I don't feel well."

"I understand. I could stop by the school—"

"No," she said. "I don't want Jason bothered at school. He's not doing well as it is. My husband—you see, my husband—"

Very gingerly, Shaw interrupted her. "I—uh, I know about it. The—the lady who cleans for Mr. Bishop—"

"Yes, I know about her."

He left a pause. The fact that he had known of her trouble before today made him feel oddly as if he'd lied to her. Behind him, Frank Bell made a throat-clearing sound.

"You can talk to my son," she offered. "But I mean—he's out. With—he's—with his grandfather."

"He's been with his grandfather how long? If you don't mind my asking."

"Two days ago. They went in the car. They were going south together."

"You took him out of school?"

"It's a week. He hasn't been doing well. Why do you want to speak with my son?" Her features appeared about to collapse.

"I'm sorry," Shaw told her. "If they've been gone two days, it doesn't matter. We found some—there seems to have been someone else in the house around the time—or I mean just after it. It appears that it could've been someone—younger. How old is your son, Mrs. Michaelson?"

"Eleven." She looked beyond him—just a glance, but it made him turn, too. When he faced around again, she had put her hands to her face.

"Mrs. Michaelson, any of your boy's friends—anybody his age or maybe a little older, that might've been in the area yesterday evening?"

"I don't know. I haven't seen anything, no. I'm sorry."

"And there was nobody Mr. Bishop was having problems with, that you know of?"

"No." She seemed momentarily irritated, but then she got hold of herself. "I didn't really know him that well. Not well enough for someone to—" She seemed to catch herself. "Some types of people will think whatever they choose to think."

"But you're not talking about anyone in particular?"

"No."

"And you never got the sense—any kind of sense—of trouble about him coming here in the afternoons."

"No," she said. Then she sobbed again. "I'm really—I'm not feeling well at all. I wish I could be more helpful."

"I just have a couple more questions," Shaw said. "I'm sorry. What time do you usually get home from work?"

"Six."

"And last evening, what time did you get home?"

"I don't know—I didn't really look. Sometime after. Not long after." She wiped her eyes with trembling fingers.

"And you don't recall seeing anything out of the ordinary—a car you're not used to seeing in the neighborhood, or somebody walking along the road. Anything like that?"

"No."

"And Mr. Bishop never mentioned anything to you."

"No, that's right. I can't imagine why anyone would want to—" She appeared about to sob again.

Shaw pressed on. "Jason left with his grandfather on—what, Wednesday?"

She said, "Yes. Mr. Shawn, please."

He said, "Forgive me—it's Shaw."

"Mr. Shaw—I'm—I'm sick—I'm upset—I don't have any idea."

"I apologize. I wish I didn't have to be this much trouble. Do you mind if I come back? Say, in a few days? I'd really like to ask Jason a few questions—just about his friends, other boys he knows who might've had reason to be over there last night. I promise I'll be careful about it. Do you mind?"

"That would be fine. I—I hope you—I've got so much to do." She stopped herself.

"Yes?"

"Nothing," she said.

"Well, again, I'm sorry for troubling you," Shaw told her.

"I'll call you?" she said.

Shaw gave her a card. "If you think of anything, don't hesitate. Anytime, okay?"

"Yes—anytime."

"I'm sorry again," he said. "I'll check back with you in a day or two, see how you're doing. Would that be all right?"

"Yes," she said. And then she repeated it. "Yes."

"I wish I didn't have to be the one bringing you this news," he told her, as the door closed. He turned and walked back to the car, where Bell had gone. Bell had already started it and was sitting behind the wheel, waiting for him.

"Did you hear all that?" he asked, arranging himself in the passenger seat.

"Most of it."

Bell had backed to the end of the driveway and then pulled them away from the house in the direction of Steel Run Creek.

"I don't think she's telling the whole truth."

"Neither me," Bell said.

"Why the hell would she lie?"

"Think her boy's involved?"

Shaw said, "The boy's off with his grandfather. Left two days ago. According to her."

"I'd bet it'll check out, too. She did register fear, to me, Phil. I don't think she's telling the truth about the circulars. I bet she's heard from the Virginia Front, and she's scared quiet."

"Let's check the wires—see what's out there. If there's been anything—"

"She did look pretty sick," Bell said.

"Well," said Shaw. "I would be, too."

THE WATCH

SHE CLOSED THE DOOR AND FELT that she might pass out. Leaning against it, the cold wood on her cheek, she heard Travis Buford Lawrence Baker sigh behind her, a sound of frustration. "I thought you were going to ask him in, for Christ's sake."

She said nothing.

"Think he believed you about the grandfather?"

"I don't know. How would I know that?"

"Yeah, well. It doesn't matter." He took her by the upper arm and walked her into the hall, where the phone was. "Call your folks."

"What?"

"Do it." He held the handset toward her.

She punched the number, or tried to. Twice she got it wrong and had to start over. She pushed the buttons, heard the tones change. It rang for a long time on the other end. Her mother answered. There was something in her voice. "Nora, honey—oh, baby. Are you all right?"

"Mama?"

"There's a man here, Nora."

She said, "Oh, no."

"Honey, are you all right?"

She looked at Travis, who took the handset from her and spoke into it. "Please put your new friend on the line."

Nora sank against the wall, while he talked to the man on the other end. "Make sure she's the one that answers any calls. And she says the old man's out here—he took the kid on a road trip south. Make sure she keeps to that. You got it? Repeat it back to me. Just do it, Bozo."

Nora put her hands to her face and shivered.

"Okay." Travis went on speaking into the phone. "There's been a little complication. No. Nope. Just take my word for it. Maybe Reuther'll be calling you. Stay put. Just stay put. Well, it's gonna be a little longer. Just make sure the old man doesn't answer the phone." He hung up. He was standing over her. "I gotta give it to Reuther, you know. Reuther's thorough. And it's a good thing, too."

"You're not going to let us go," she said into her hands.

"Hell, we might fall in love and get married. I'd take better care of you than Jack did."

"Stop it," she said, through the swollen pain in her throat.

"Come on," he said. "Up." He took hold of her arm.

She pulled loose, then got to her feet, facing him.

"You know how long it's gonna take them to decide to come back here?" he said.

"Look," she said. Jack didn't tell me anything." She moved from the door, taking the robe off and dropping it over the back of a chair. The robe had been Travis's idea. He had decided that faking friendship was too risky, would only be a last resort.

"Maybe something'll come back to you," he said.

"How many of you—" She halted.

He smiled. "The faster we find it, the faster everybody gets their life back."

"I don't believe you."

"You ain't got any choice about it."

She walked away from him toward the living room, where the paintings on the wall depicted people in silent civilized relation to each other, talking in a sunny garden, or walking on a bridge over a shimmering blue river, or negotiating the colorful crowds of others in a city street. The trappings of an orderly life.

"What about Jack's office?" Travis said.

"That's what we were looking through down in the basement."

"That was his office?"

She went to the little space between the dining room and the living room and began rifling through the drawers of the bureau there. For a time Jack had kept his computer on top of it; there had been a tray with disks in it and a box full of computer paper routed into the printer.

"I bet they're here somewhere," Travis said.

"Well, if I had some fucking idea what they looked like—"

"Boxes—big ones, wrapped with tape. Suitcase-sized, you know? You remember, like people lug to the airport. About that size. Bigger, actually. Like a—like a trunk. And light. You'd almost think they were empty."

"He never brought anything like that into the house. I was a housewife. I was here, and I'd have known it."

"Then he's got a storage slip, or a contract for bulk storage, or a ticket with numbers on it. Something."

She looked through the drawers. There was a small plastic bag with Jack's old army insignia in it, his name tag. She hadn't really had the strength to go through some of his things, had left much of it essentially in place, including the clothes on the other side of her closet in the bedroom. Travis remarked on this as they pulled all of it out and looked for papers in the pockets of trousers and suit coats. They searched all the closets in all the rooms; they went up into the attic and pushed the boxes around, opening them one by one. Nora combed through the debris of her twelve-plus years of marriage. There were old clothes, old photographs, old letters—all of the ones Jack had written when he was stationed in Japan, all of hers to him. She had been someone else entirely back then: so much a child, still clinging to the world her parents had given her to believe in. The world they had once inhabited, all so distant now. She felt something like pity for the girl who had written these letters and then sprayed them with her perfume to send to her young man

across the sea. Absurdly, she had a brief vivid memory of a light
blue checked dress she had worn in those day. Jack had said it made
her look like a Victorian doll.

Across the attic, Travis held up a picture. "I'm in this picture."
Delighted, he held it toward her. It was a group photo, perhaps fifty
men in three long rows. "I'm the third one from the right in the second row," he said. He flipped it toward her. She picked it up and
glanced at it. Jack was circled on the far left, in the third row. She
looked at his young face.

"Handsome devil, ain't I?"

She put the picture down.

"The first row, third guy over from the right—that's Rickerts."

She looked at the picture again. A boy's face, blond hair, an
uneven, ironic smile, small ears flat against the sides of the head,
which gave the whole face an oddly Asian cast.

"Young studs," Travis said.

"Is he the one you talked to—"

"Our man in Seattle." He smiled.

She looked at the face. It looked so ordinary.

"Sexy guys, huh."

She didn't respond to this. "We're running out of time," she told
him.

"You're a handsome woman." He had paused. His face gleamed
with sweat, and there was a slackness to his scarred mouth that
caused her middle to clench. She thought of the brutal groping of
his brother the night before and almost gagged.

"You know it?"

She said, "They're going to come back."

"That'd be too bad," he said. But he made no move toward her.

They worked silently for a time, emptying boxes of clothing and
old papers—tax returns from ten years ago, canceled checks going
back to the first year of her marriage.

"Look at the checks—the dates on them. You have to pay for
bulk storage. Look for receipts, too, or a safety deposit key."

"They wouldn't fit in a safety deposit box."

"The contract for bulk storage would."

"That's ridiculous," she said. "Why would he do that? And besides, if that's the case, no one can get into it but Jack. You can't get them if he put them in storage."

"Wanna bet?" He smiled, but it was an automatic expression, involving only his mouth. "Why'd you keep all this shit?" he went on. "Jesus. I thought we'd get the damn things and be out of here."

She looked at him. "Doesn't it ever—"

"What?"

"Never mind."

"No," he said. "Talk."

"Your brother killed a man. There's police all over the county. They're bound to be on the lookout for strangers."

"Hey, I ain't no stranger." He winked. "I'm your husband's old army buddy, and I got the picture to prove it. I'm helping you through the bad time. I'm somebody for you to lean on."

She could not return his look. The air had gone bad here; it was harder to breathe. The dust rose into the dimness. The smell of mildew and naphtha choked her. She pulled another box out and opened it, bringing out old toys of Jason's—airplane models and paint sets, a small clay sculpture he did in the first grade.

"We got to keep moving," Travis said.

She caught herself thinking what sort of trap this was: talking to him created a familiarity she needed in order to seek deliverance from him, but it was also the thing that encouraged him.

And how he repelled her, with his barrel chest and heavy arms, his dirty fingernails—that dull green gaze.

"Like I said before, you know how many unsolved crimes they have in this country?"

She chose to ignore this, too.

"Hey," he said. "I'm talking to you."

"There's nothing here," she said.

"A key. A receipt. Something that he might've written on that tells where he put the damn cartons. Or the cartons themselves. We have to comb the place. Answer the question."

"I don't know how many unsolved crimes there are."

"A lot." He laughed.

She opened another box. Manila folders. Papers that belonged to Jack, from his days in high school. There were photographs, too, of Jack and his father standing in the sun and shade at the edge of a calm green lake or river, and of Jack in a basketball uniform.

"What's that?" he said.

"Nothing."

"Let me see it."

She hesitated, then reached over and let him have the basketball one.

He stared at it. "I played ball."

She moved the box aside and reached into the cobwebbed space of the angle of the roof for another.

"I did. I was good, too. I haven't always been a bad guy."

"I don't know what you expect me to say."

"Once," he said, "in Chicago, I saved a man's life. He keeled over at the table next to mine in a restaurant, and I did that maneuver—can't remember the name—and a piece of steak as big as a pack of cigarettes came out of his mouth."

She waited for him to go on.

"You believe that?"

She sighed. "I don't know."

"I did. I come from good people, really. We went to church every Sunday. Ate together and prayed together. Mom and Dad, and Sis, and Nathaniel, and Mary Sue and John-boy. Dad was a radiologist. We lived up on a mountain. It was the Depression and I was lonely."

She opened the box. Clothes.

"You believe that about the guy in Chicago?"

"I guess," she said.

"Actually, the guy had a heart attack and died. But the steak did come out of his mouth. You believe that?"

"Please," she said.

"What happened was we all thought he was having a heart attack. It was my father. I was fifteen years old and I tried to pick him up and the piece of steak came out. I did the whole thing by accident. Didn't even know about the maneuver thing. You believe that?" he said.

"Okay," she told him.

"You believe it about my family?"

"I believe you," she said.

"It's all a lie. Mom hated us. Dad was a durn little club-footed gap-toothed murderer."

She reached for a cedar chest in among the other boxes.

"You believe that?"

She said. "We're supposed to be looking for something."

"You can't talk while you look?"

"I don't even know what I'm looking for."

"There," he said, indicating the cedar chest. "Like that. That size, with a lot of masking tape around it."

For a few moments there was just the sound of their hurrying to open the chest. She said under her breath, "This isn't it." But she so hoped it was; a part of her mind convinced her it might be.

The chest was full of clothes from Jack's army days.

They spent another hour rummaging among the boxes.

"Hey," he said. "I shouldn't have said that about my dad, earlier. He was an air force guy. Colonel. We traveled a lot. Went to a lot of different schools. That's why I joined the army. Bags wasn't even in high school yet."

"Why're you telling me this?" she said, hoping that he might reveal something useful, yet fearing that he would take it the wrong way.

"Telling you how it was," he said.

She did not reply.

"The trick is to guess how much of it—or if any of it—is true."

She had opened a cardboard box and found some of Jason's baby clothes and toys, and a tied stack of cards—his birth announcements. She felt a tearing, deep down. "There's nothing up here," she told him. "What you're after just isn't here."

He pulled another box out of the space between the eaves and the boards he was kneeling on and tore at its taped flaps. "Hey."

She saw him lift out a tin canister. He pulled at the lid. It came off and spilled tobacco all over the front of him.

"Shit."

"My husband smoked a pipe the first year we were married," she said.

"He must have got a contract or a ticket of some kind. Goddam, what did he do with them?"

"They're not here," she told him. "And if he put them in a bank, there's not going to be a way to get them out because I didn't know about it and I won't be on the contract."

He went at the search in a kind of furious panic now, tearing at boxes and dumping them out. Then he lifted the boards up and pulled at the insulation. She did so at her end, too, pulling it up along the whole length of the attic. They found nothing. "Jesus Christ," he said. "What the hell."

When they had torn the insulation up, they stood and ripped it out of the sides of the wall, along the curve of the roof.

"We're wasting our time," she said.

He snapped his fingers. "Your boy slipped away from me last night in this damn passageway from the bathroom. Come on." He reached for her wrist, but she pulled back.

"I'm right behind you."

He said angrily: "You first."

She descended the attic steps and went down to the little bathroom under the stairs. Here was the hamper moved aside, the vent pulled out. She thought of Jason climbing in there to escape and wanted to turn and strike at Travis. She managed to resist the impulse, understanding that while she had no control over him or this situation, she must try to exercise the most rigid control over herself.

"Can you get in there?" he asked.

His closeness worried her. She steeled herself, then stepped into the room and knelt to look into the vent. "No way. I don't know how *he* got in here."

"Well," Travis said. "He did."

She surveyed it again. "It's just metal duct—as far as I can see. There's seams in the side of it."

He reached down and took hold of her upper arm. "Let's go look where he came out."

She stood. He had not taken his hand from her, nor had he moved. His face was perfectly expressionless. She received its blankness as an indication of his confidence in the advantage he possessed over her. She said, "Well—let's go."

"If I was a certain kind of man," he said.

"Well, you're not," she told him. It had come out of her before she could stop it. Once more, she had the thought that she must be far more vigilant and cautious.

"I meant the kind that forces himself on pretty ladies," he said, with an energy that harrowed her soul.

"Like your ape of a brother?" she said. She could not believe herself.

"Want to tell me about it?" He waited a few seconds, still holding her arm, then he undid part of his shirt and wiped her cheeks with it. She cried out, but stopped herself from saying anything. Finally he buttoned the shirt and moved out into the hall, turning to wait. He followed her into the small bedroom, the room she had slept in more and more often as what she believed was the stress of failing business made her husband so remote. On the floor next to the small desk and chair was the vent. She knelt again and looked in.

"Well?" he said.

"It's all metal duct. It's like an L. And it runs to the top floor, but all metal."

He was silent.

She got to her feet and bumped into him; he had stepped close.

"You know what I think sometimes?" he said. "I think 'Take your pleasure while you can.' You know? The words go through my mind, like that. It's from Henry Miller. I read Henry Miller when I was in the army. You know who that is?"

She heard her own breathing and made an effort to slow it, control it.

"Well?"

"Yes, I know who that is."

"What do you think?" he said.

"You said you were not that kind of man."

"Tell the truth," he said. "Ain't you drawn to me just a little?"

She stared into the muddy green of the eyes. "You and two other men are holding my son. You've got somebody else holding my parents. You've killed my neighbor, my only friend. Your pig of a brother brutalized me. How can you ask me that?"

"Because I can see it." He reached for her.

"No," she yelled. And she swung at him. Her fist glanced across his stubbled jaw—it felt as though it had barked her skin.

He took her by the wrists. "Wait," he said.

She kicked at his groin, but missed and hit his thigh. And then she had the sensation of having been thrown a great distance, wheeling, the walls caving toward her. Wobbly inside, light cascading over light, roiling, she arrived at the understanding that she lay on the floor, had fallen or been pushed. Her head hurt. He was somewhere behind and above her. Something grabbed her ankles. She thought of the hacksaw blade in her shoe and tried to kick, was pulled along the floor. And then her feet came crashing to the hard wood surface. He was bending to pull her up, reaching along her shoulders. She saw something under the bed, something lying on the dusty shine of the hard wood, thin as a cracker but with a tiny metal gleam along its side. "There," she said.

He sounded as though he were winded, having fallen back from her, leaning against the closet door, cussing low.

"Look." She felt the word come almost dreamily from her. Something coppery dripped on her tongue, and she realized it was blood. "Something—" she said, reaching for it under the bed.

His foot came down on her arm. "Hold it."

She looked back up at him, at the great swaying height of him, and said, "Under the bed."

He took his foot away, and knelt, his right hand in the middle of her back, pressing her down. She couldn't breathe in. She saw his left hand reach and pull the object, whatever it was, out. He stood and held it up to his face. He had to hold it close. He squinted at it, and she realized that he was nearsighted—something she might be able to use.

"Shit," he said. He looked at the bed. "Get up."

She struggled slowly to her feet, still tasting the blood, while he began pulling the bed apart, pushing the mattress and the box springs over against the wall, and searching through the frame. There wasn't anything. He stepped into the frame and brought a switchblade knife out of the pocket of his jeans. The metallic click of it as he opened the blade brought another small shout up out of her throat. He cut into the box springs, tearing the cloth away carefully, slowly.

"Help me here."

"He wouldn't put them there," she said. "How would he do it without my knowing about it?"

"Yeah, well, you found a chip. He might've repacked them somehow."

"I'd've known it."

"You didn't even know he had them," Travis said. "Come on."

"He couldn't have done this without me knowing about it," she said.

"Bet me."

She stepped to his side and started to pull the rest of the cloth away from the springs.

"Wait," he said. "There can't be any static charge. You understand? Do it slow." He began cutting into the mattress.

She stepped up again and pulled gingerly at the stuffing, dropping it behind her, reaching in and getting more, and fighting with it when it caught on the interior springs. Gradually it came to her that the phone was ringing. He seemed to realize this in the same instant. They stopped and stared at each other.

"Answer it," he said.

She hesitated.

He raised his hands as if to grip her by the neck. "Come on."

She went out into the hall and along it to the phone. She picked up the receiver, held it to her ear, and found that she couldn't speak.

"Hello?" It was the slightly wavering voice of Elaine Tyler, her elderly friend from Charlottesville.

"Oh," Nora said. "Yes. Elaine."

Travis leaned close. She felt his hair on her cheek.

"Are you all right? You sound funny—is this a bad time?"

"I—I can't talk right now, Elaine."

"What is it?"

"I'll try to call you back." Her voice shook.

"Poor baby," Elaine said. "What is it?"

"I'll call back," Nora said. "Everything's fine." She hung up.

Travis glared at her. "You didn't handle that too good."

"Okay," she said, controlling herself. "I didn't handle it too good. The lady lives in Charlottesville. It's seventy-five fucking miles away."

"Don't cuss," he said. "Christ."

She remained straight, and silent.

He crept to the end of the hallway and looked into the living room. Then he came back. "Thought I heard something." He entered the little bedroom, with the torn mattress and cotton stuffing all over the floor, and began taking the books out of the shelves on the wall there. He opened each book, flapped the pages, then dropped it.

"What're you doing?" she said, standing in the doorway. "He wouldn't have hid anything in his books."

"A contract on a folded piece of paper," Travis said. "He could've put it anywhere. When we shipped them to him he was putting them in bulk storage in the First National Bank in Point Royal. He's put them somewhere else. Maybe he hid a key, or a combination or a fucking treasure map. The shit was worth more than two million dollars, and he knew that. It's losing value every day now. Come *on*. Help me."

"I'll look in the ones in the living room," she said. "And upstairs."

"Don't make a mess out there. Somebody might come back. And remember where your son is."

In the living room were the objects of her previous life. She hadn't quite noticed them in the steady terror of the minutes. Jason had left things out—books he meant to read or return at school, papers and magazines he'd stacked on the coffee table, a bowl with a dried spot of milk at the bottom of it next to a small statue Jack had brought back from a trip to New York early in the marriage: a cherub, lounging on a small square of marble, set in the middle of a polished wooden base. Beside this was a stack of art books. It all seemed rather pathetic now. The possessions and effects of someone woefully out of touch with the relentless facts of existence. She hated them, standing there gazing at them.

"Well?" Travis called from the other room.

"Nothing," she said. She opened each of the art books and put them back. At the bookcase, she pulled a big volume off the shelf and thumbed through it—a history of the Second World War. Jack had belonged for a few years to a history book club. Scribbled on the title page was a note: *Nora's birthday present . . .* No year, and no inscription; the note was evidently something Jack had written to remind himself. The pages were intact. She put it back on the shelf and was reaching for another, when a shadow crossed the window to her left. She gasped, turned, and shrunk back. Someone was at the door. There were voices outside.

She stood. Travis kept making noise, pulling books out, opening them, and throwing them. Whoever was out there now rang the bell. Travis came quickly out into the hall and toward her. "Shit," he murmured. "Get it."

She looked out through the side curtain in the door. Agnes and Marsha James. Nora had rarely seen them in the twelve years she lived here. She had waved at them as they passed by in their ratty old Ford Fairlane with its unsteady left rear wheel and its serrated, rusted-out undercarriage, and had stopped to exchange pleasantries when she met them in the aisles of the Giant Food Store in Steel Run Creek. The little girl, Missy—timid, overly skinny, nervous, and perpetually downcast—was in Jason's classes at school. Jason had in fact been protective of her on occasion, though he seldom spent much time with her outside of school. The two women had come to pay their respects when Jack was killed. They had spoken of finding other reasons to see Nora—the distance was so small between their two houses. They were anxious to have her call on them for anything at all. And, as had been the case with others, this did not materialize. The two had come by once, when Missy was selling Girl Scout cookies, and another time they prevailed upon a nephew to clear Nora's driveway after a snowstorm, and Nora asked them all in for coffee. The conversation had been warm and friendly, but wore thin rather quickly, and soon the two women were asking about Jack's death. Nora wanted to run from them.

Now she opened the door a crack.

The two sisters wore outlandish, multicolored serapes or ponchos and had brushed back their hair in exactly the same way. Their faces shone, as if they had been running.

"Such a terrible thing," Agnes said. "You heard about Ed Bishop?" They swept toward her.

"I'm—I've been sick," Nora said.

"So has Agnes," said Marsha. "Can we come in?"

Nora felt the door move and sought to resist it, but the pressure was surprisingly strong, and she realized with a shock that Travis had taken hold of it from behind her. "Come on in, ladies," he said.

They hesitated. Their gaze went from him to Nora and back again.

"I'm a friend of Jack's, from the army," Travis said. "Please." He stepped aside, and he had Nora by the wrist, pulling her with him. "Nora's got a little bit of a cold and fever. You know how it is in the winter."

"Yes we do," said Marsha, with a faintly puzzled air, moving Agnes forward. She walked in and surveyed the room.

Travis closed the door. He offered them seats on the living room sofa. As they settled themselves, he put his arm around Nora's middle.

Agnes murmured, "Such a terrible thing."

"Times are scary," said Travis. "One thing and another."

"Tell you the truth—we're glad to see a man here," Agnes said. "There are killers on the loose." Then she addressed Nora. "I'm surprised you're even here, given the nature of the—the situation."

"We heard something about it, didn't we, Nora?" He squeezed her again, then let go, crossing the room to stand in the entrance of the hall. He relaxed, resting his shoulder on the frame. He pulled a cigarette out of his shirt pocket and lighted it. "Oh, where's my manners. Would you two ladies like a cigarette?"

"No," Agnes said. "We don't smoke."

"Honey?" he said to Nora.

She said, "No." It had come out too loud.

"Oh, that's right," Travis said. "You quit."

"I never knew you smoked," Agnes said.

"Oh, she used to," said Travis. "Something awful. Now where'd I put that ashtray?"

"We don't have any," Nora said.

"That wasn't an ashtray I was using?" The green eyes fixed her and appeared to brighten.

She went into the kitchen and brought out one of the lids from the jars she had used for canning.

"There it is," he said. He put it on the coffee table, flicked ashes into it, stood back, took a long pull of the cigarette, and blew smoke rings at the ceiling.

No one said anything for a few seconds. Travis smiled and blew more smoke.

The two women showed sudden concern, looking at Nora, and abruptly she realized that her nose had begun bleeding. Travis had the same realization and offered her a handkerchief. "My Lord," he said. "Look at yourself, honey."

She held the handkerchief to her face.

"How'd you do that?" He turned to the others. "She was up in the attic. Honey, you think being up there might've got you going— you know, the dust and all?"

"It's nothing," she said. She felt the nausea come. "It's just a little nosebleed. I get them all the time in the winter."

"It's the dry heat," Agnes said.

"Guess what happened," Travis said. "Nora was up in the attic and stepped between the beams, you know, and her foot came right through the ceiling. I thought she was going to drop right through. Come here." He started a little way down the hall. "If you stand here you can see where she came right through the plasterboard."

Agnes did so. "Oh, dear."

"I thought she'd fall right through. And you know she was stuck for a little while. We just got her sprung loose." He waved to Marsha. "You want to see this?"

Marsha said she could imagine. But then she got up and joined them in the passageway, her hand on Agnes's shoulder.

Travis said, "It scared us when it happened, but of course it's kind of funny now."

Both women agreed that it was indeed funny, but they were very solicitous of Nora. "You might've really hurt yourself."

"I'll bet all that dust got to your sinuses," Travis said.

"Please," Nora said. "It's fine."

They were all quiet again. She excused herself and hurried into the kitchen to tend to her bloody nose, running water into the sink, and daubing at herself with the wet handkerchief. When she returned to the living room, the others were as they had been—Agnes and Marsha on the sofa, Travis leaning on the frame of the entrance into the hallway.

"All better?" Marsha said.

Nora said, "It's fine."

"I used to get them all the time when I was a kid," Travis said. "I'd look like a crime scene or something."

Again there was a silence.

Agnes cleared her throat. "Well, as I was saying, we got so scared after the policemen came by and told us about Ed—about Mr. Bishop." She leaned toward Nora. "You—you must be so frightened. They—did anyone—you know about the hate letter?"

"I know about it," Nora said.

"It meant—they mean you, don't they?"

"I don't know who they mean," Nora got out.

"We just couldn't stay there alone in those woods," Marsha said. "I've never seen my sister so upset. We decided to get out. We're going to pick Missy up at the school and then we're heading into town to stay with my friend Ruth Morrisey. Nora, do you know Ruth?"

"She wouldn't have any way of knowing her," Agnes said.

"Well, I don't know. I'm so out of touch. She's in real estate. And Jack worked with real estate people sometimes, didn't he? Didn't she say Jack did some things for them?"

"I don't think I know her," Nora said. The sisters had averted their eyes from her. She thought briefly that they might know something about this Ruth—the one who had written the note, Nora was sure—and Jack. But then she understood that they were reacting to the fact that Jack's name had been mentioned. She said, "Jack might've known her."

"I'm sorry, honey," Marsha said.

"You haven't done anything to be sorry for," Nora told her.

Travis smoked his cigarette and again Agnes said how good she felt to know a man was on the place. "Are you staying a while?" she asked.

"A little while," Travis told her. "Few days."

"Too bad you can't stay longer."

"I would if I could."

"Everybody's in such a rush these days."

"Yes, ma'am. I agree. That's the truth." He drew on the cigarette, raised his chin, and blew more smoke rings. Once more, they were all quiet. "I've got a picture of me and Nora's husband back when we were in the army—want to see it?"

"They don't want to see that," Nora said nervously. She saw Agnes glance at her and was aware that she had begun to tremble, still daubing her nose with the damp, red-stained handkerchief.

"I'm so glad you're getting on with life," Agnes said to Nora. "Forgive me. But I'm a plain person and I just say what I mean."

"No one could ever stop you," said her sister.

"So, how was Mr. Bishop killed?" Travis asked. His voice was soft, a pitch higher than Nora had heard it before, and his eyes were scarily innocent, wide with interest.

"We don't know, really," Agnes said. "Do we, Marsha?" She turned to Travis and continued: "We went by the scene of the crime, and there were a lot of people there, cars and vans and police people combing the scene. A lot of newspeople. I saw two television trucks. It's so frightening."

Travis lighted another cigarette, using the coal of the one he'd been smoking. He said, "You know what I'll bet? I'll bet it was, like, a serial killer. Something like that."

"It was racial," Marsha said.

"Oh, that's right. But hey—that doesn't mean it's not a serial killer."

"No, I guess not."

Travis crushed the first cigarette out in the lid, and when he spoke his voice was even softer. "I think I read somewhere that they tend to kill people who *irritate* them. You know? Like a kind of acting out."

"I never heard that," Agnes said. She cleared her throat and turned to her sister. "Have you?"

"No," said Marsha. "But I don't know anything about it."

Travis said, "I read somewhere about this guy who killed people by making them swallow things—bottle caps, and pencils, and lye. Things like that. Can you imagine?"

"God."

"Yeah. People who *irritated* him. Imagine. Guy'd meet a woman at a lunch counter, and if he didn't like her voice or her accent, he'd just decide on her. So—think of it—you go into some place and talk to a person, and you don't realize it but you're talking to a criminal. Somebody making a decision about you, just because you're irritating him. I find that really frightening, don't you? I mean—it's like there's no rules of safety you can follow and be safe. Except staying inside all the time. But this guy, he was as likely to hurt you at random—come in your house, and all, so even that wasn't enough."

"I wish we could talk about something else," Agnes said.

"Well, you know what—I read that he went around to houses claiming to be a deacon in some religious group. He'd ask if a person wanted to hear a true message about Jesus Christ, and then when people let him in—well—"

"Oh, Lord," Agnes said. "I don't feel good."

"It's got so you can't trust anybody."

"I had the most wonderful afternoon once with two young men who were witnesses for Christ," Marsha said.

"Well, you took a risk," Travis told her, blowing the smoke rings. "You shouldn't've let those men in. Because you can never tell when a person'll use the good graces of the community against you. The devil can assume a pleasing shape, as the Bible tells us."

"That's true," said Agnes. "Oh, Lord." She was growing more agitated with each passing second. "But this hate letter. This group—they call themselves the—what is it, Marsha?"

"The Front," said Marsha. "Something."

"My God, what is that? Front. What do they mean by it, anyway?"

"You know what I think it is?" Travis said. "I think it's a sign that people are losing all their sense of compassion."

"I think the media just don't tell us the right stories," Marsha put in. "Look at it—they're all over there photographing that awful scene, and talking about hate groups and cults on the news, and here you are helping a friend, having traveled here all these miles to help. I don't know why they don't put that in the news."

"There you go," Travis said. "There you go."

Nora felt herself starting to lose control. It occurred to her that she hadn't eaten anything since yesterday afternoon. Yet her abdomen felt bloated, stuffed, queasy.

"I certainly had a wonderful afternoon talking to those two boys about the Bible," Marsha said.

The phone rang.

Nora looked at Travis, who simply stared back. The ringing repeated.

"Isn't anyone going to get that?" Marsha asked.

Nora got to the phone and picked up the handset. Travis had stepped into the living room and was not in sight now. She saw the two women giving their attention to him and knew he was talking to them, snowing them in a low, reassuring murmur. "Hello?" she said into the phone.

"Mrs. Michaelson, this is Phil Shaw."

There was an icy feeling at the back of her neck. "Yes?"

"Would you be able to come in here and talk to me this afternoon? There's just some minor things I'd like to talk to you about."

"No, I told you—I'm—I'm not feeling well." As she spoke these words, their truth gave her a moment's panic; she was so close to being sick. She swallowed, tried to breathe, fighting the sensation. She made a coughing noise, holding one hand over her mouth.

"Well, Mrs. Michaelson, can I come out there and see you, then? I need to establish some things regarding the time elements involved."

"What are you talking about?"

"Mrs. Michaelson, when exactly did your son leave with his grandfather?"

"I thought I told you that. It was the day before yesterday."

"And, if you don't mind. Could I just have your father's name?"

"Henry Spencer," she said, feeling abruptly furious at the sensation that she was acting as an accomplice of Travis's. "1645 Jonquil Street. Seattle, Washington. Do you want the phone number there?"

"Is it a listed number, Mrs. Michaelson?"

"Yes."

"I'm awful sorry to bother you about all this."

"You said that, Mr. Shaw. I heard you the first time."

"Oh, of course. I understand. Well, thank you."

"Thank you," she said and hung up. She put both hands down on the phone table, then forced herself to straighten and to assume a calm expression.

Travis looked around from the living room. "Was that the police?"

She nodded. "Mr. Shaw."

He addressed the two women on the sofa, who were sitting in identical stiff poses, hands on their knees. "They stopped by here a little while ago, asking questions about Nora's boy. Imagine." He lighted still another cigarette. "I think it upset her a little. Poor kid's not even here and the cops want to talk to him about a murder."

Agnes looked aghast. She put one hand over her heart.

"Something," Travis said.

"Why would they—"

"They said they found a small shoe print in the blood."

"Oh," Agnes said. "Please. We ought to go."

There was an interval where Nora supposed bitterly to herself that she was expected to step in and ask them to stay. She refrained from allowing even her gaze to betray her, staring down into the folds of the stained handkerchief.

"We're sorry," Marsha said, preparing to rise. "We shouldn't have imposed."

"Well, it's a bad time for everybody," Travis said. "Right, hon?"

Nora said, "Yes—right."

Marsha settled back. The two women sat there, waiting for

someone else to speak. Agnes sighed heavily and held tightly in her leathery, mannish fist a handkerchief she had brought from somewhere inside the poncho she wore.

"Well," said Travis, crossing the room in front of them—it was almost as though he meant to parade himself. "What were we talking about? Oh, yes—the serial killer posing as a religious guy. Now that's really the worst."

"It's terrifying," Marsha said. "I wish we could talk about anything else."

They seemed to be waiting, then, for the new subject, whatever it would be, to emerge. Nora could not get the tension out of her face, and for an instant she felt the horror that they might have asked her a question. "Pardon?" she said.

Travis went on. "The thing is, you don't want to turn yourself into a suspicious type of person, either." He was still pacing. There was something fitful about him now.

"I think we should go," said Agnes to Nora. "We know you're not feeling well."

"Oh, she's better, though," Travis said. "Right?"

Nora sought to indicate that she was, but the revulsion was rising in her. He had walked over and put his arm around her. "So nice of you two lovely ladies to stop by."

Agnes got to her feet and tottered toward him. "My back, you know. I've got arthritis."

"My mother had that," Travis said. "So I will, too. And I ain't looking forward to it."

"No, I guess not."

He pulled Nora with him to the door and waved them off the front porch. "Bye now," he said. He squeezed her at the waist. Under his breath, he said, "Wave to the nice ladies."

She lifted her hand and tried to smile.

Marsha had stopped, turned, and labored back along the walk. Travis straightened and murmured, "Well, okay. Here we go, then."

"No," Nora murmured. "Please."

"I'm sorry," Marsha said, struggling up on the porch. "But I do need to use the bathroom."

"Bathroom, of course," Travis said. He turned to Nora. "Did we clean up in there after the mouse?"

"Mouse?" Marsha said.

"Afraid so. I had to put a broom into the air vent to chase him. I've been chasing them all over the damn house."

"Oh." Marsha stood there.

"Excuse my language."

"That's okay," she said.

"You know how going through things in a house can stir things up."

"I—yes."

"They're as persistent as rats."

"Oh, yes—well." She turned. "Maybe I'll—I'll just go on down the road—"

"You're welcome to use it here," Travis said. "Really."

"No, that's quite all right."

"I don't blame you," he said. "I went down the road twice today myself."

"Yes, well—"

"Bye."

She had started off along the walk. The sun had dipped behind a drifting cloud, and the light was gray-bright, the sky beyond the tops of the trees a deep cerulean blue. Out in the driveway, Marsha's sister waited for her, hands held up to shield her eyes. Marsha made her way to the car and got in. They backed away, waved, and were gone.

"That was close," Travis said. "I thought it just might get ugly. Though I have to say it certainly was fun, too." He left her there, returning to the little room. She stood at the bookcase, pulling books out—all Jack's volumes on the wars. No, she decided. He would not put important papers in a book. She went to the entrance of the room where Travis was working. "Jack wouldn't hide anything in a book," she said. "He just wouldn't."

Travis stopped, leaned against the bookshelf. He was out of breath. "Shit."

"Whatever the answer is, he took it with him."

"What about this?" He held a small thin notepad out to her, and she saw, in Jack's hand, the scribbled words *Fauquier County Savings Bank* and a number: *706877–9.*

"Where did you find that?"

"In the middle of this book." He held it up. "And this, too." He brought out of the pages a single sheet of paper, a contract for bulk storage at the same bank. "Well?"

"I don't know," she said.

"You bank there?"

"No."

"Did he?"

"I don't think so."

"You don't think so."

"That contract isn't filled out, or signed, or executed. Maybe he was thinking of using that bank."

"Yeah. And maybe he went ahead, too. What else would this number mean?"

"I told you he didn't tell me anything. He didn't confide in me. I don't *know.*"

He tore the page out of the pad. "All you have to do is prove you're his wife, and he's dead. And you can get into whatever he's got there. Right?"

"I worked at a bank when I was in college," she said. "The answer to that is no."

He stared.

"You better hope that's not where he stored the cartons. Because if it is, nobody can get to them." Her own voice sounded exhausted to her. It made her feel all the more depleted and discouraged.

"Shit." He folded the page and put it in his shirt pocket. "He didn't put them in no *bank*. He put them somewhere so he could get at them in a hurry and not during any damn banking hours. Hell, when we first started shipping them he was keeping them in a motel room. I saw them there. He had them in a big blue trunk next to the bed. He was paying for the room by the week. Reuther was sending him money."

For what felt like too long a time, they were quiet.

"They're somewhere obvious, you wait. Right in front of our noses."

"Reuther sent him money?"

"Couple hundred a month, yeah. Sure. Good-faith money."

Again, they were silent. The extent of her husband's involvement in this scheme began to take on its true proportions; she cast about in her memory for any sign of it and could find nothing, save his odd estrangement from her. She had a sorrowful few seconds of realizing that this was sign enough.

Travis stood there, watching her. She thought she saw something of the cold-blooded killer in his expression; there was an element of the predator in it, almost hungry.

"You would've hurt those two women," she said.

"Like playing mumblety-peg," he said calmly. "You know what that is?"

"No."

"It's a little game you play with a knife." He nodded at her, smiling.

"Just because they irritated you."

He gave a sardonic little laugh. "Now don't put me with *that* guy. That wasn't me. Did you think that was me?"

She didn't answer. He was entertaining himself with her, the same way he had entertained himself with Agnes and Marsha James.

"You must see that it's possible we're never going to find what you're looking for," she said.

"Oh, we'll find them, all right. I'm planning on being rich."

She said nothing.

He stepped away from the bookshelf and folded his arms. "Okay. Listen up. I'm not a former abused child, and I ain't got any body parts stashed away in no meat lockers. I have two years of college, on the GI Bill, I've held down steady jobs before, and I don't normally do a lot of drugs. I got a baby brother who's a little slow and easily *irritated*, and I've spent some time and trouble trying to keep him in line. I'd like to get what we came for and fly as far away from here as it's possible to get, and to tell you the truth, things're pretty desperate. But there's no use crying about it. And this ain't about Bags, anyway. This and poor Mr. Bishop and Bags and his stupid animal ways are separate things, and not about this problem in the least. This is about an enormous—a stupendous amount of money—okay? A mountain of money, and you gotta understand that I'll do anything to get my hands on it. The whole fucking world is falling apart and this money can fix it right up, you know what I mean? Fix it right up."

"We don't have the chips," she told him.

"Yeah," he said. "Well." He moved past her, out into the hallway. "Come on, let's get to the other rooms."

"They're not here," she said. "And I think we know where they are."

He paused. "Okay." His expression was blank.

She went to her coat and brought the key out of it. "I think this is a key to a bulk-storage cage."

He had followed her, was standing too close. "At Fauquier."

"I don't know that. But there must be something among the papers."

"No—he was thinking of it, but he didn't put them in no bank."

"Why wouldn't he?"

"Why didn't you give me this key earlier?"

"I—" She couldn't find the lie to tell him.

He took the coat and held it out for her to step into it. Then he closed his arms around her. "You're getting to like me, just a little, admit it."

She said, "Travis, please."

"I like the way you say my name."

Her heart flailed in her chest, pure terror and loathing, as his hands trailed along her arms, down to her hips, near the pocket with the hacksaw blade in it. He had interpreted her silence, her stillness, as acquiescence. She said, "Please leave me alone." The words dropped from her lips in the plaintive tone of a beaten child.

"Come on," he said irritably. "Back down to the basement."

They went down. They commenced picking through the papers in the desk, looking over the bank slips again. None of them were from Fauquier Savings. He pulled out the tin of old nails and screwdrivers, opened it, and stared at the contents for a long time. Then he closed it and crossed to the other side of the basement, running his hands through his hair, thinking. She watched him. There was a toolbox on the shelf on that side of the room. He walked over and lifted the lid. "Bring me the key."

She did so. He put the key into the slot on the lid and turned it.

"Shit," he said. "This ain't no storage key."

She said nothing.

He took hold of her wrists and held them tightly. The bruises on them hurt. He reached into the pocket of her coat and brought out the hacksaw blade. He held it up in front of her face, pulling her toward him. She could feel the other blade in her shoe, the pressure of it bending against the ball of her foot. "What were you gonna do with this?" he said. "What were you thinking you might do, hiding the goddam key?"

She couldn't speak. Couldn't push the air through her larynx to make the words, or any sound at all.

He tilted his head slightly. "This ain't some—movie," he said. "This is real life. You know what happens in real life? In real life, I cut your throat with this thing and leave you here for the citizens to find."

She said, "You're—hurting me."

He stepped behind her, still holding on to her wrists, and now he let go of them, one hand gripping the hair at the back of her head and yanking downward, so that her throat was exposed, and the other hand bringing the blade of the hacksaw to her neck. She felt the cold, minutely serried metal. When he spoke, his voice was at the level of a soft, almost tender murmuring. "You know how it works, don't you? The blade cuts through the arteries on each side and you bleed to death in a couple minutes. Are you appreciating the severity of the situation now?"

She forced out a thin whimper of assent.

He threw the blade across the room. It made a small dinging sound on the concrete floor. Then he released her and bent down to pick up something at her feet. It was half of the note from the woman, Ruth. He opened it and read, then grabbed for her and forced the other one from her. He pieced them together and stood there reading, one side of his mouth curling up. "This must've hurt. You just found this, huh?"

She said nothing.

"Where'd you find it?"

"I've had it for weeks," she told him.

He didn't believe her. It was in his face. "What were you gonna do with it?"

"I don't know."

"This is the friend, ain't it? Morrisey, wasn't it?"

"I don't *know*," she said.

"Shit." He folded it carefully and put it in his shirt pocket. "Looks like you need somebody?"

She waited, afraid to breathe or move. He was a shape to her left.

"You ever cheat on hubby?"

She started to step around him, and he shifted to stand in front of her.

"Answer the question. It's just a friendly question."

"No," she said. Something moved in her stomach. The nausea had started again.

"You feel, like, you—you missed chances?"

She kept still.

He put his hand on her arm, and she let a small sound of alarm escape her. "If you would—please, please stop," she heard herself say.

He hesitated a moment, not moving, then let go and stepped to one side. "After you."

THE WAIT

Henry Spencer sat next to his wife on the sofa of his violated house and watched the man wolf down a sandwich. They had spent the long night in almost unbearable silence. The intruder had told them he didn't really feel like talking. His voice cracked. His hands shook. He might do anything. Sometimes he seemed on the verge of panic. The hours passed. Spencer cared for his wife, under the wide-eyed gaze of the man with the gun. They knew Nora was in trouble, and they knew little else. The tension felt like a thickness in the air. Sometime after midnight, the young man had insisted that they lie down side by side on the bed, where he wrapped them in the blanket, then placed himself on its edge, so he could doze off. He never let go of the gun. Spencer fell asleep for fleeting, tortured periods and woke feeling the restriction of the blanket. His stirring always brought the intruder to his feet, and once the man pointed the gun and cocked the hammer.

"Don't," Henry Spencer said.

Gwendolyn cried, holding on, her arm thrown over her husband's chest.

"Keep still," the young man said. "Christ. You realize I almost shot you. I almost shot you, man."

Later, Spencer asked if they could get up.

"Be still," the man said.

They lay there, awake—Spencer and his wife—listening to the intruder's heavy sleep-breathing, afraid to stir.

When the phone rang, the stranger jumped up, waving the gun. Spencer managed to pull the blanket toward him, and Gwendolyn screamed.

"Hold it!" the gunman said. "Don't move, man, I mean it."

"I'm not doing anything," Spencer said.

Then the other seemed to come to himself. "Here," he said. "Answer the phone. Quick."

Gwendolyn had got out of the bed, was already moving to get it, and the man backed away from her, pointing the pistol. She answered the phone. It was Nora. She was alive and safe for the time being.

Tears dropped from Gwendolyn's eyes, though she made no sound at first. A little later, the gunman took the phone. Henry tended to his wife, trying to hear what was said. She buried her face in his chest. The man was arguing with whoever was on the other end.

"You said a few hours. This has been all night."

Henry paid close attention to the color of the skin around the gunman's mouth; it was flushed and red.

"Well, come on. Tell me what's happened. I don't understand. Why does she have to be the one to answer?"

Finally, he hung the phone up. He sighed and appeared frustrated. As he told them what Gwendolyn was supposed to do when the next call came in, the phone rang again. It was a friend of hers from the church who wanted to come see her about plans for Easter. Gwendolyn put her off. After she hung up, the man made her write down what her script was for anyone else.

"Why?" Gwendolyn said. "What are they going to do?"

"I'm just following orders. Something's come up, and they're dealing with it."

"I don't understand." She commenced crying again.

"Look, it's gonna be a long day. Let's just make the best of it."

"Something's happened," Gwendolyn said. "I know it."

"You gotta stop talking like that," said the other. "It's gonna be okay."

For a time she worked to get hold of herself. Spencer held her, without taking his eyes from the stranger, who said, "Everybody just has to stay calm. Everybody just be cool, really."

"You're the one with the gun," said Gwendolyn.

The other seemed not to have heard this. "I think we should just go on about the business of the day," he said. "Who's gonna make me something to eat?"

"You have to tell us what this is," Spencer said. "Please."

"I don't have to do anything. You have to fix me a sandwich or something."

"Please," said Gwendolyn.

"I'll talk after I eat, how's that?"

Now he sat across from them on the piano stool, with his pistol lying on one thigh. The pistol was a Glock 9mm, ten-shot. Spencer had entertained an intellectual interest in small arms, from his days in the military.

"Where'd you get the gun?" he asked.

"I've had it a while."

The rain kept rolling down the windows; the same slow falling of yesterday, and all night, without the slightest breeze; the sky looked like dawn, though it was past ten o'clock. At his side, Gwendolyn sniffled and took her hand from his. She was, he knew, mostly frightened for Nora and Jason. "What's your name?" he asked.

The stranger, chewing, held up one hand.

Spencer waited. It was not the first time he had asked the question.

"Okay. You can call me—" There was a pause. "Um—Ricky."

"Ricky."

"Sure."

"Why're you doing this, Ricky?"

"I told you, I think. Money."

"We don't have a lot of money."

"It's not *your* money."

"My daughter doesn't have any money," Gwendolyn said.

"Maybe she doesn't know where to look for it."

Gwendolyn's hands made fists in her thin lap.

"Don't worry," Ricky said. "It'll probably be okay." But a note of doubt sounded in his voice. Spencer was certain he'd heard it.

"You want to tell us what this is about?" he said.

"I just did."

"I'd like to understand it better," Spencer told him. "I might be able to help you."

The other man took another large bite of the sandwich. He had stood in the kitchen with the gun on them, while Gwendolyn made it, and he had thanked her for it when it was done. Now, his cheeks bulging while he chewed, he held one hand up again. "Best case," he said. "I get a call, and I take off out of here, and you never see or hear from me again."

After a long pause, Spencer said, "Is this—some kind of ransom?"

The other pondered this. "Naw."

"Didn't you hear my wife? Our son-in-law didn't leave them with anything."

"Yeah," Ricky said. "Well."

"This is *his* trouble, isn't it."

"It's our trouble right now. And yours."

"How long?" Spencer asked.

Ricky shrugged and put the last of the sandwich in his mouth.

Gwendolyn murmured something about having to use the bathroom. Spencer helped her to her feet and escorted her, under the wary gaze of the stranger, to the entrance of the bathroom. She went in and closed the door, the small click of the latch sounding in the quiet. Ricky stood at the end of the hallway, with the Glock aimed at the floor. Spencer had the thought that if he could some-how get into a position to surprise the other man, he might strike him, might be able to surprise him enough to get the gun from him. There was something obscurely reluctant and jittery about him, for all his pretended casualness. Spencer believed that he had probably never used the gun, that he was involved in this particular scheme—whatever it was—for the money and would not want to compound his troubles with violence.

He said, "I don't have the feeling you're a criminal."

"No." Ricky smiled. "I been in some trouble."

"I wouldn't say you struck me as the criminal type."

"Yeah. Well, I want a lot of money and I don't want to work for it. I guess that qualifies me for something."

"You ever fired that gun?" Spencer asked him.

"This?" He held it up. "Sure."

The older man kept very still. Perhaps he had miscalculated.

"Want to see me fire it?"

"No."

"You know what? I liked it better when we didn't talk."

The door opened, and Gwendolyn emerged. She walked with a rickety slowness, toward the living room. Henry followed. They went past Ricky, who stepped back and leveled the gun at them. When they were seated, he let the gun hand drop to his side. "Aren't you all hungry?"

"No," Gwendolyn said.

"It might be a while. You ought to go on about your usual stuff, you know. I'll try not to be in the way. As long as you understand that I can't have you mess with me, or try anything. And she answers the phone and says what she's supposed to. I don't want to hurt you but I will."

No one said anything for a time. They sat there. The clock made its small, orderly sound on the wall and chimed the quarter hours. Ricky put the television on and they all watched it. Quiz shows, reruns. *The Andy Griffith Show*, *I Love Lucy*. Now and then he laughed, but as the time dragged by he grew nervous again. It was possible that he had been nervous all along, Spencer thought, observing him. The skinny legs were all jittery motion, and he kept biting the cuticles of his fingers, holding the pistol.

There was a long span of quiet—just the chatter and frantic light of the television.

"Shit," Ricky said, finally. "I'm gonna have to tie you both up for a while."

"Why is that?" Spencer said.

"I gotta use the bathroom."

"We're not going anywhere. You have our daughter and grandson, for Christ's sake."

Ricky stood. "Come on. Into the kitchen." He waved the gun.

In the kitchen, he said, "Where's the duct tape?"

"Duct tape?" Spencer said.

"Come on, man. I've been watching you. Where do you keep it? I really don't want to shoot you."

"Here," Gwendolyn said, opening the utility closet. "Here's the duct tape."

"That's right," Ricky told her. "That's doing the right thing."

He got her to tape her husband's hands to the back of a kitchen chair, then made her sit in another chair with her back to him and taped her hands to her husband's. Spencer felt her lean her head on his upper back, and he asked in a whisper if she was all right. Ricky said, "Sure she's all right. We're all okay." Then he said how sorry he was about everything.

"I wish I could believe you," Spencer said.

"I don't think it matters," said Ricky, sounding sad. He left them there, and he was gone in the bathroom for a long time. Gwendolyn wondered aloud, sobbing softly, if he might be sick.

"I can't catch my breath," she said.

Spencer lightly pressed her hands with his own, under the duct tape. Ricky came out of the bathroom, but did not come into the kitchen right away. He remained in the living room, watching the midday news. There were the nearly identical voices, male and female, the asinine disconnected and unrelated tones of television news.

"Hey," Spencer called out. "My wife needs help."

"Don't," Gwendolyn said.

Ricky entered the room. "Sorry." He took the tape off in a ripping motion that stung their wrists. "You okay?" he said to Gwendolyn.

"No, I am *not* okay. How can you ask me that?"

"Hey, it's gonna be fine. If you can just please not get out of control here."

"You ought to be ashamed of yourself," Gwendolyn said.

"Look, you don't want to know me, and I don't want to know you. Let's just leave it there."

They returned to the living room and sat facing each other.

When the telephone rang, Ricky came to his feet, holding the gun on them. "Okay," he said to Gwendolyn. "You know what to do."

She picked up the handset. Spencer reached over and held her hand. She said, "Hello," then looked at them both and nodded. "Is something the matter?" she said into the phone. Ricky held the pistol to her head. She faltered, couldn't speak, and it was evident that the person on the other end had started repeating her name, might even think the connection was broken. "I'm—I—" The words caught in her throat.

Spencer signaled for Ricky to remove the gun, to step back. He did so.

"I'm—yes—I'm sorry," Gwendolyn said into the line. "I'm—I dropped something." Her gaze traveled to Spencer's face, sought him, as if for something on which to anchor itself.

But she controlled her voice and spoke into the phone. "No, he went east—to spend time with his grandson. Is something wrong?"

They waited.

She was trying to keep her fear quiet, holding one fist to her mouth. Then she took it away to speak again. "Yes, yes, that's—that's right. Thank you. Good—good-bye then." She put the handset down with a suddenness and almost collapsed. Spencer hurried to her side, held her by the elbow, supporting her.

Ricky had relaxed a little. "Well?"

"That was someone named Shaw," Gwendolyn said. She looked at Spencer. "Henry, they've—they've already killed somebody."

"What?" Ricky said. "*What?*"

Gwendolyn glared at him. "Don't look so innocent. My daughter's neighbor. They murdered him." And now she broke down.

The other seemed to waver. Henry Spencer was certain he'd seen it. "You didn't plan on anybody getting hurt, did you?"

Ricky shook his head. "It must be some kind of fucked coincidence."

"It was already done when they called you this morning," Gwendolyn said. "And my girl—oh, God," she sobbed. "If they hurt my girl, or that little boy—"

"Nobody was supposed to get hurt," Ricky said.

"Why don't you let me have that," Spencer said to him, indicating the Glock.

The other seemed startled by the suggestion. "Both of you be quiet. I have to figure this out."

Gwendolyn kept weeping into her hands. She was off in her own suffering now, far from both of them. Spencer put his arm around her, and she pulled away. "No," she said. "No, no, no, no."

"Please make her stop that," Ricky said.

"What are you going to do," Gwendolyn said. "Shoot us?"

Ricky got up and went to the other side of the room. "Jesus," he muttered. "Jesus, Jesus."

"What do we do now?" Spencer asked him.

"Jesus."

"You don't want to be an accessory to murder."

"Shut up."

Spencer took a step toward him. "Think clearly, son."

"Shut up, goddammit. And stay there. And don't call me that. I'm almost forty fucking years old."

Gwendolyn lay with her head on the arm of the sofa, her hands over her eyes, moaning to herself.

"You can't tell me you want to be a part of murder," Spencer told him. "You didn't know what they'd do in Virginia. I'll testify to that. We'll both testify to it."

Ricky said, "I don't know, man. I don't know."

"We understand," Spencer told him.

"Jesus."

"We'll help you. We can help you, can't we?"

"What?"

"Maybe we can help you."

"I swear Travis never said anything about anybody getting hurt. It was just to keep Reuther happy. Just his German clockwork mind. We joked about it. Just in case anything went wrong."

"Well," Henry Spencer told him. "Something went wrong."

PART THREE

HOURS

Jason lay on his side in the upstairs room. It was overly warm now. Sunlight poured through the window glass; the crossed tape made a shadow cross on the floor. Below him, the fat man and the foreigner were keeping up a low muttering that he could not make sense of. His wrists hurt. A pins-and-needles feeling crept up and down the bones of his fingers. Whenever he moved, the noose around his neck tightened. He would have to urinate soon; his lower abdomen ached terribly. Below, the two men had apparently broken into an argument. One of them took a car away and came back.

"Hey!" Jason yelled. "I have to go to the bathroom!"

Silence.

He tried it again. "Hey!"

Footsteps on the stairs. Bags. He did not want anything to do with Bags. The little muddy eyes in their folds of heavy flesh gazed at him with an impervious flatness, as though he were something small and dumb, a cat, or a mouse. "What's the deal?"

"I have to go to the bathroom."

The fat man went back down the stairs, and there was another discussion—Jason couldn't make out the words. Finally Reuther came up, walking briskly. "Nature calls," he said.

"Hurry," Jason told him.

Reuther untied his feet, then pulled on the rope, lifting him by pulling his arms backward.

"Ow!"

"Sorry."

Reuther stood behind him, got him to his feet, then walked with him out of the room, down the hall to a bathroom. There wasn't any toilet here—just the open pipe. "Can't I go downstairs?"

"Piss in the hole," Reuther said. He did not seem the slightest bit nervous, or worried.

Jason stood over the hole and then sighed. "I need my hands."

Reuther said, "Of course you do. What's the matter with me?" He untied the boy's hands and held him by the shoulders. Jason let the stream come, thinking about all the movies and television shows he'd seen where the prisoner whirls around and surprises the one standing behind him. But the grip on his shoulders was strong. He finished and put himself back and Reuther pulled his hands around and tied them again.

"Can I please not be on the floor?" Jason asked him. "Please?"

"What do you want to do—stand?"

"Can't I walk around a little? I'm not going anywhere. Just up there in the room."

"No," Reuther said. "Travis told me about you." He walked the boy back into the room and forced him down onto the floor, where he began to tie his feet.

"Can't you please tie it in front, so I can sit up?"

Reuther smiled. "The point is to make you helpless."

"You've got my mother. Where would I go?"

"Good point. Not good enough."

"Come on, mister."

The other took a moment to study him. "Life's been bad to you lately, hmm?"

Jason gave no answer.

"Tell me—you like computers?"

He nodded.

"You have one, yes?"

He kept his head down.

"You have a computer, yes?" Reuther simply waited.

"Yes."

"You and your father ever talk about them?"

"My father showed me how to use mine."

"Did you know your father was a hacker? Back in the beginning, when they were big and clunky."

"No," the boy said.

"You're lying, aren't you?"

"I'm not lying."

"Your father trained you on this wonderful machine and never mentioned that he worked on them years ago when they were all getting started?"

"I don't remember."

"I actually talked with your father, you know. Several times, long distance. I sent him money. I remember that he sounded intelligent. My great misfortune is that I got myself tied up with the bozo brothers, hmm? But I couldn't really be choosy. Travis had the means of procuring my merchandise, and your father had the means of arranging a sale. I'm the one who could get everything out of one country and into another. And then it was so good, and so easy, I got greedy. Just as your father was getting a conscience."

"I don't want to talk about my father."

"I suppose he was a disappointment to you."

"He was not."

Reuther took out his little shiny box, opened it, put a little of the powder on his tongue, then put it back. "Well, to find out that he's got himself mixed up with shady dealings—"

"Shut up," Jason said.

"It's perfectly understandable—"

"You don't understand anything," he said under his breath.

"Okay," said Reuther. "On your stomach." He pushed the boy over, and pulled his feet up. "I feel like an American cowboy when I do this."

"Can I not have the noose around my neck?"

There was a pause. "Well, okay—no noose. But if I hear you moving around, I'll have to come up and fix it."

"How long am I going to be here?" Jason asked, but the other didn't answer.

A little later, he lay half-dreaming, in dull pain. His whole body felt like an exposed nerve. The house had grown quiet. Sweat ran down his sides and gave him the unpleasant sensation of crawling things, insects. Were the men dozing, too, or had they gone somewhere? He hadn't heard a car. He could move slightly. It was just possible to make himself slither along the floor, though it made the pain in his wrists worse and caused awful stabbing spasms in his lower back. He had no sense of the time of day, or how long he had been here. When he closed his eyes, a rush of sound rose in his ears. He had been seeing his father on one of the last days, when they had spent a cold early twilight planting the two maple saplings in the backyard. The boy had stood by while his father worked, digging the holes, and the wind came on across the open field, all ice, the north itself flying down the continent, carrying snow and freezing rain.

"I'm cold," Jason had said to him.

"For Christ's sake," said his father. "Quit complaining."

"But I'm freezing."

"Move around a little. Here, dig the other hole."

"I can't."

His father mimicked him. "I can't. Jesus—you should hear how you sound."

"Well, my hands are too cold. Why do we have to plant trees now?"

"Because I said so, okay? Now shut up and quit complaining."

Jason had watched him work, hating him. It was as though some spell had got hold of him. The boy was old enough to understand that his parents had run into some trouble involving money. He had seen his mother sitting on the sofa in the living room, with notebooks open on her lap, frowning, figuring the numbers, while his father sat next to her chewing his fingernails, looking worried and angry. He had watched his father walking alone out on the lawn, hands in his pockets, muttering to himself and shaking his head. Now he was flailing away at the ground, and the boy touched his arm. "Dad?"

"Can't you see I'm busy?" he said. "Stand there and shut up."

It seemed that the cold was coming from the frigid spaces beyond the stars, but finally the trees were planted, and father and son walked back to the house in the dark, the deepening chill.

"For God's sake," Jason's mother had said. "Look at him. He's freezing."

"Maybe I should've waited till it was warmer," said his father.

"Yeah, maybe."

"I couldn't feel it as much. I was working so hard. Forgive me." His father knelt before him. "You okay, son?"

The boy was too cold to speak. And he was furious. He pulled away from the other's grasp and started toward the stairs. He listened with a sense of vindication to his mother's displeasure at the whole affair. And later, when Jack Michaelson went out and got into the pickup truck and pulled away, the boy hoped that something would keep him gone for a time. He was tired of the complication of his father's presence in the house, and he lay on his bed, imagining the freedom of having him somewhere else, some great distance away.

China.

He fell asleep dreaming of his father moving among exotic buildings, in a crowd of foreigners, happy, finding some answer to the trouble that had made him so hard to be with. This was more than a week before Jack Michaelson died, and yet in Jason's memory, he was having this same dream when his mother came into the room and woke him to say that there was trouble, an accident. He had never heard that note of almost childlike fear and grief in her voice. "Honey, a terrible accident—your father," she said.

His memory was playing tricks on him.

She had waked him to tell him, but it was not the night of the dream, not the night of wanting him far away. Jason had thought of it in those first moments of knowing his father was gone, had remembered thinking about his father in distance.

He woke now. It was all fresh. He even looked around for her and discovered again that his hands and feet were bound. His cheekbone was sore, and he had a pressure headache on that side. To move was anguish.

"Hello?" he said.

The house was still. He made another slithering movement toward the wall, wanting to squirm out of the square of hot light from the sunny window. He got to the baseboard and put his heels against it. The pain in his shoulder and hip felt like fire.

"Come on," he said.

Still no other sound in the house. He waited a few seconds, listening, and then began working to get one hand free of the knot that held his wrists. He couldn't see it, but felt it pressing the nerve there, too tight, cutting off circulation. When he attempted to turn his head, the pressure was too much, the pain made him stop and lie still—exhausted, dizzy. He thought he might pass out. Then he thought he might die. This made him struggle more, pulling with one arm and then the other. It was no use. Maybe they had gone for good, and he would starve here.

He wriggled and pulled and struggled desperately to extricate himself, every muscle of his arms and shoulders and back burning. His own effort blotted out all other sound, and so it startled him to find that Reuther had come upstairs again and was watching him from the doorway.

"I think if you had enough time, you'd get out of that," Reuther said.

He lay in the noose again, all his nerves jumping with pain, and every movement choked him. After what seemed an hour, Reuther returned. The light had changed at the windows. It had to be afternoon by now.

"I'm going out for a little food. Remember how Bags can be, and keep very, very still, hmm?" He went away.

The boy heard the car engine, the tires on gravel or stones. He couldn't remember if he had heard this earlier, when the car had gone away and come back. Maybe there were more than two cars now. There was the whine of the car, pulling away. It sounded the same. In the silence that followed, he listened for Bags. The house itself seemed suspended in a terrorized pause of expectation. Outside, a gust of wind moaned in the angle of the roof. The light had begun to change once more, and he was sure this was the brightness before sunset; it had to be. And now there were the heavy footsteps on the stairs. He couldn't look right at the doorway, could only see it out of the corner of his eye.

Bags stood there, a swollen, vacant look about his features, a look almost of docility. "You don't look too comfortable," he said.

"Please untie me," the boy said. "At least take the noose off."

Bags made a murmurous dismissive sound and walked into the room. He crossed to the window, hands in his pockets. His shoes scraped the floor. Looking out the window, he brought a package of chewing gum out of his shirt pocket, unwrapped a piece, and stuck it in his mouth.

"Untie me," Jason said. "Come on, man. I'm not going anywhere."

Without turning from the window, Bags said, "I know."

"Then untie me."

"Shut up."

"You're afraid to."

Bags turned, put his arms across his big chest, and shivered. "Oooo," he said.

"You are. You're afraid."

"I'm in a panic. Shaking in my boots."

"You're afraid Reuther'll get mad at you."

"Want to see my knife?"

"Reuther took your gun. You're afraid of him."

"Keep talking."

"You won't take the noose off because Reuther'll be upset with you."

Bags smiled. "You must think I'm stupid."

"Can't you at least take the noose off? I'm choking."

"Aw."

"I won't run, man. You've got my mother."

The smile changed. "I'd like to have her. In fact, I got a little something of her last night."

"You fat piece of shit," Jason said.

"I did get a little jolly yesterday, you know."

"You fucking—*stain*," Jason said.

"You know how all that stuff works yet, old son?"

Jason watched him.

"Yeah. You know."

"If you touch her again I'll kill you, you—goddam tub of shit."

Bags walked over to him and picked him up by the small length of rope between his ankles and his hands. The noose tightened on his neck; his arms were pulled painfully back at the shoulder. He couldn't scream for the lack of air. Everything spun in the periphery of his vision, and then it all grew cloudy. It was going far off. But then he was jolted by the surface of the floor, thudding pain in his chest and knees, his abdomen. The son of a bitch had dropped him. He struggled for air, coughing and gagging, and Bags stuck a finger into the noose and pulled at it, loosened it. Jason sucked in air, the pain traveling along the front of his body and through his shoulders and wrists, his lower back. Everything, every nerve, throbbed.

Bags had knelt by him and taken out a knife—a switchblade. He opened it and held it to the boy's throat. "See this? See how easy it is?"

"No," Jason said, choking. "Please. I'm sorry."

"Guess what I'm gonna do," Bags said.

The boy tried to see him, the wide wall of him, blocking out light.

"When it's all over, I'm gonna stick you like a pig and watch you bleed out."

Coughing, still choking, his throat burning inside and the skin stinging with the cold blade held against it, Jason was appalled to hear himself say, "Put the knife away, man, or Reuther's going to give you all kinds of hell when he gets back."

Bags leaned in. His breath smelled sickeningly like peppermint. "You think I'm afraid of the Kraut?" He folded the knife and stood, putting it back in his pants pocket. Rocking slightly on the heels of his shoes, he turned toward the window again. "Shit," he said, then lifted one leg and, in a clownish pantomime of stress, farted, loud and long. It sounded to Jason like a motor. In school, he would have laughed at the sound. "That's for the Kraut," Bags said.

The boy watched him shamble to the window, where he looked out, hands in his pockets, and belched deep. The stupid, vulgar sound of him in the room called up a deeper vein of terror.

A sound came up out of Jason's throat.

"Cut it out."

"I can't help it."

"You shit your pants yet? People get scared enough, that's what happens, you know. I seen it before."

"Reuther thinks you're stupid," Jason told him. "He calls you and Travis the bozo brothers."

Bags turned. "I think I'll haul your little ass down to the basement. That way I can come up here and keep watch without the irritation of listening to you."

Jason tried not to breathe.

The fat man stood at the window, hands still in his pockets, rocking on his heels. He lifted one heavy leg, the same antic motion, and farted again. "For the Kraut." He laughed to himself, that moronic little windy sound, and came back, stooped down, working the knot at the boy's feet. When it came loose, Jason's feet dropped to the floor, and the shock in his calves and behind his knees made him yell. Bags lifted him by the back of his collar and pulled the noose from around his neck. He brought the knife out, clicked the blade open, and stepped to one side. "Down we go," he said.

THE STAIRS

Jason had descended, past the empty kitchen where he saw brightness in a quadrant of the sky out one window—and knew that it wasn't much past midday: the gray changing light at the window of the upstairs room had deceived him. At the realization of this, something in him gave way, a discouragement so profound that for a heartbeat he lacked the strength to keep moving. Bags pushed him in the upper back. "Get the lead out." They went around to the stairwell and down, toward the basement. A dirt cellar. Jason saw exposed earth and received a sensation of its chilly dampness. Behind him, the fat man pressed forward, with the knife. The cellar was dark, and the mineral, wet-clay smell came over the boy. He stopped. At his back, a looming heavy shadow, Bags stopped too.

"There's nothing down there," Jason said.

"It's dirt," said Bags. "Id'n it?" He emitted his weird idiot's laugh. "You could bury people here, and they'd finish the basement, and nobody'd ever find them."

"Bags," said the boy. "Please don't make me stay here."

"All you need is a shovel."

"Please," Jason said. "You're not supposed to do this."

"Oh, that's right." Bags widened his eyes and mocked being afraid. "The Kraut."

"Come on, please," Jason said.

Bags leaned down, gazing into the dimness. "Hey, mud, too." The laugh came again. "Fucking place leaks." With his free hand he pushed the boy between the shoulder blades, a nudge. "Go on."

"Please. I'm not gonna try anything."

The hand shoved him now, and he fell a step, grabbing onto the railing. He righted himself and tried to hold on, looking back at the massiveness of the other, one step up from him.

"Come on, Bags—please!"

The fat man made another pushing motion, and Jason, out of reflex, ducked away. The motion caused the big hand to miss him, and Bags pitched forward. He grabbed at the railing and missed that, losing balance. Jason was under him, then above him, and then, once more out of reflex, he kicked at the big shape. Utter desperation, a nightmarish flailing. He felt the knife cut his wrist, then his sore ankle, but he had made contact with his foot—he had hit bone or cartilage with it—and he kicked again, and still again, and it felt like the fights he had in dreams, when his body wouldn't move fast enough, or with enough power. His legs felt heavy, slow, yet insubstantial as air, and there was no force behind any of his motions. He swung his arms wildly, trying to kick, hearing his own crying, and the thick gasping of the fat man, and then through this he heard the clatter of the knife dropping on the steps. He kicked one last time, with everything he could gather of his small weight, hitting something, feeling it move, a soft pushing-through, and the fat man went tumbling to the bottom of the stairs, yelling. It sounded like a scream of pain. But Jason knew it was rage. Bags was scrabbling, knife in hand, face bleeding, up the stairs. The boy slammed the door on him, pressed the little button in the center of the doorknob, then backed away, looking around for something to fight with. His hand was bleeding. At some point he had grabbed at the knife blade or hit it; his shoe was filled with blood. He limped to the doorway and saw trees, sun falling through bare branches, a brown patch of dead grass. There was the tremendous slamming of the other against the door. The hinge cracked away from the thin wood of the frame.

The fat man was coming.

Jason got the back door open and staggered, crying, across the small space of grass and into the trees. There wasn't enough growth here. He kept on, struggling up an incline, among rocks and packed pine needles, to a row of hedgelike bushes, where he fell, sobbing, dizzy, feeling that he might pass out. For what seemed a long time there hadn't been any sound but his own striving. He tried to hold his breath, to clear his mind. When he looked through the interstices of pine needles and branches, he saw Bags standing in the yard, looking down. Bags was going to trail him, using the blood. There was blood on the knife. The boy backed away from the bush and went down a small dip in the ground. A creek. He washed his hand in the stinging partly solidified cold of it, crystals of ice clinging to his wrist, then crossed and went along the bank.

Bags yelled something.

Jason ran a few paces, or tried to, then stopped again. The other's voice was coming to him through the woods, like an echo; it was not close.

"Hear me?"

He got down on all fours and moved through a wall of dry brush that clicked at his face and neck. Then he came to his feet and, crouching low, made his way along a dirt path and up into more trees.

"I'm going to slice your mother up real good when she gets back," Bags yelled.

He knelt down, looked at his own bleeding wrist and hand, struggling not to make the slightest sound.

"You think they can stop me?"

He lay still on the cold floor of the woods, exhausted, confused, growing weaker by the second.

"I know you can hear me, you little fucker. I'm gonna hurt her good. I'm gonna make the old man look like a picnic."

He tried to rise and couldn't. The world went off into nothingness for an increment of slow time, sight and sound—the cold earth, the odor of dead leaves. He'd thought the fat man had come closer, but there was just the quiet, the cold, the shivering. He had curled into himself, where it was a degree warmer, but something stirred in him, an urgency. He couldn't make himself get up. He thought he had rolled over on his back and looked at his wounds, and then he thought someone was standing over him. He seemed to ascend into light, and sense, and it was true that someone, not Bags, was there, ranged above him. His father. He was sure now that it was his father. He looked into the white shape of the face in the failing light.

"Dad?" he said.

FEAR OF DARKNESS

Nights when he was younger, he would wake to the sounds of his parents in the house with friends, would hear the laughter, the voices rising, people trying to talk over each other, and he lay back in the warmth of the bed, content in the half-light from the doorway, the light that led along the upstairs hallway to the spacious area over the foyer and the living room. He would listen to the voices, choosing among them for those of his parents; it felt that way, as though he were making a choice, picking through an abundance of good sounds for the familiar, best ones. Time ended. Aware of his own safety and warmth, and the darkness all around like a living thing that had been pushed back and defeated, the boy wanted to keep awake, to hold on, but gradually a kind of hollowness would come to him, a blankness, and then he would come awake, startled, opening his eyes to darkness and silence, as if the house had emptied out in a terrible instant. The dark had covered everything, was all around. He would lie there, afraid—even as he understood that he had fallen asleep and this was merely home after the hours of being asleep. The fear gathered in him, and finally he would not be able to support it anymore, would feel the need to call his father in to him.

It was always his father he wanted to see, because his father was big and strong and could do things with his hands. It was always his father who came.

Sometimes with impatience. "What's the matter now, Jason?"

The boy would feel compelled to make something up. "I had a bad dream."

His father was a sighing shadow in the dimness. "Want to tell me about it?"

"I don't think so."

"Tell me about it," his father would say, sitting on the edge of the bed and rubbing his eyes.

And so the boy would make it up. His father never gave a sign that he had seen through this ruse, but would let the boy talk—a patient stillness, elbows resting on knees, waiting for him to wind down. It never took him long to come to the end of whatever it was he had made up. Something about the other's silence always distracted him. "And—and," he would stammer. "That's all I remember."

"Do you feel better, having talked about it?"

"No."

"It's supposed to make it go away, Jason, if you talk about it."

"I don't feel any better."

"You want me to sit here with you until you go to sleep?"

"Yes, sir."

His father would sigh and wait. And the boy fought sleep with everything he had, wanting to keep him there. "You sleepy?"

"Not yet."

The big hand would come down on his chest and pat it softly, then become very still there, a protecting soft weight. Jason felt sleep coming on, struggled to stay above it, hearing his father sigh in the dark, perhaps even nodding off himself. Finally, with what felt like another kind of suddenness, it would be morning, light at the windows, and Jason's father would not be there. Even in the light, he felt oddly bereft, angry with himself for falling asleep.

He had confided this to his mother, some time shortly after his father's death. She surprised him by confessing to a fear of her own, also involving darkness. "Morning is the best time," she told him. "My favorite time. And I never liked the nights, not when I was a little girl, and not now. Especially not now."

Once—it was sometime before the planting of the trees—Jason had a dream that his father had died and was back, had been to the bottom of the vast dark that was the reason for all those wakeful nights when he had been smaller. His father was dead in the dream, as the people in movies and on television were dead, with an unreal, cosmetic, facile staginess, but walking and talking, teasing his mother as he used to do in the lighthearted days, when there wasn't any tension—his parents obviously grateful for what they had together, amusing each other, and everybody having fun. That phrase was always an important one in the house: everybody having fun. It had been his father's question. He'd walk into the house after working at one of the building sites and say, "Everybody having fun?" And the boy would run to him, throw his thin arms around his middle. In this dream, his father was a ghost, but exactly as he had been when things were happy. The dream poured horror into the boy's bones, woke him in a cold sweat, and he cried out, twice, then waited in the stillness of the sleeping house for the sound of his father moving around. Silence. So he sat up in the bed and yelled, and yelled again, and finally his father came to the doorway of the room.

"You awake?" he said.

"I had a bad dream," the boy told him.

"Go back to sleep." The shape turned in the doorway.

"Dad?"

A small throat-clearing sound—irritation. "What?"

"Sit with me?"

"You're a little old for that, son."

"I'm scared."

"Well, don't be. There's nothing to be afraid of."

"I can't help it."

His father moved into the room, but this was almost a threatening motion. "Look, I'm trying to get some sleep. You're too old for this. Now be a man and stop it."

The boy, who was a long way from being a man and knew it, simply lay there waiting for his father to say or do whatever he would say or do now.

His father sighed deeply and sat down on the edge of the bed. "You had a bad dream."

"Yes."

"Want to tell me about it?"

"I dreamed you were here, but you were dead."

Silence.

"We were—like we used to be but you were—" The boy couldn't say it again.

"What do you mean, 'like we used to be'?"

Jason couldn't imagine how to explain. He said, "I don't know."

"Of course you do."

"No, sir."

"You said, 'we were like we used to be.' Well, what did you mean?"

"It's hard to explain," he said.

His father ran his hands through his hair. "I guess I know what you mean."

Jason recognized, without words, the note of resignation in the murmuring voice. He waited, understanding through the nerves along the back of his neck that his father was far away from him, sitting quietly with whatever was troubling him.

"Look," came the voice, and the big hand settled with wonderful soft weight on his chest. "I know it's been rough around here lately. But it's gonna be all right again. I promise."

"Yes, sir."

"We just have to—" He stopped. The hand moved, caressed. "Well."

The boy was shaking.

His father lifted him, put his arms around him. "It's gonna be all right, son. I'll find a way to make it all right."

"Yes, sir."

"Listen—whatever you ever hear, or come to hear—whatever anyone ever tells you, I love you and your mother. You know that."

"Yes, sir."

"We've just hit a little hard place in the road." The big hands were patting him in the middle of the back. "It's gonna be all right."

He cried into the hollow of his father's shoulder, breathing the faint talcum and shaving lotion odor of him.

"Dad?"

"Try to go to sleep," his father said.

They were quiet a moment. It was almost as if they were listening for something.

"I need you to be a brave young man now."

"Yes, sir." He lay back down.

"I know you will." The hand came down on his chest again. "What is it that you have lots of to face the big bad world with?"

This was a question the answer to which his father and mother had taught him before he was old enough to understand what it meant. "Resources," he said. For most of his growing out of babyhood this exchange had been as automatic as a wish good night. It had only been recently that the boy thought about what it signified. And, recently, almost as if understanding broke the spell, his father stopped asking it. But he had asked it now, and Jason answered it, and for a long time his father held him, the two of them sitting there in the dark, as the house made its night noises. Finally, his mother came to the doorway, a slender shape with the palest shimmer surrounding the outline of her body—light from the moon, shining through the hallway window. She said, sleepily, "What's the matter?"

Jason spoke up. "I had a bad dream."

She yawned. "Didn't we all."

"Meaning?" said his father.

She came into the room and sat on the boy's bed and put her arms around her husband's neck. "I had a nightmare, Jack. Can't I have them, too?" There was something forlorn in her voice. The boy knew there was trouble between them, but even so this astonished him. His father held her—he held them both.

"I'm sorry," he said. "Honey, can you forgive me?"

She must have nodded into his shoulder, for he held her tighter.

"Sometimes I wonder why the hell you're still here," he said.

"Because I love you," she told him.

They were quiet then, but no one moved. To Jason, it seemed as if they were huddled against something enormous and threatening, staggering toward them from the night, the darkness outside the windows of the house. He wanted them to crawl into the bed with him. But they stood; they were thinking only of each other now. His mother, almost as an afterthought, turned to make sure he was tucked in.

"Okay now?" she said.

"No."

The two of them paused, as if waiting for him to say more. But then his father walked over and sat down on the edge of the bed again. "Hey," he said. "Come on, now. You told me about the dream. It should be gone now."

"Yes, sir."

"If you're scared, sometimes you have to just weather it. Go through it."

"Yes."

"Good man." His father stood. "And what is it you have lots of to face the big bad—"

Jason broke in, saying the word at the shadow looming above him. "Resources."

"There you go."

But after they were gone he lay very still in the dark, with its shades and shapes of deeper blackness, and felt that he had no resources at all, nothing inside him but expanding fear, the sense that it filled him up, made it hard for him to expel the air he gasped in with each small spasm of his chest. And finally, when he couldn't stand the stillness anymore, he sat up, gulping the close room air, sitting against the headboard with the blankets pulled high up to his chin, watching the subtle changes in the dark, waiting for morning. It seemed that morning would never come.

Of course, it did. It took him by surprise; it was almost impossible to imagine that it had actually happened. He opened his eyes in light, and his heart leapt at the fact of it: daylight. His back was sore, and his arms, from the near crouch he had fallen asleep in; and he

heard the sounds of his parents in the house, his mother's voice calling him down to breakfast.

There was less than a year left in his father's life.

In the nights after the accident, he lay awake in the dreadful
knowledge of it and thought of all those times he had lain here with
the comfort of knowing his father was sleeping in the next room.
Now his mother slept alone there. The thought was so strange and
so freighted with pain that he couldn't quite get his mind to accept
it. He stared into the dark as if into the badness itself of what had
happened. And when he dozed off, the lapse frightened and
depressed him—as though he had let go of his father, betrayed him
somehow, drifting away into dreams, into not-knowing.

Later, on some of the endless nights, his mother would come in
and lie down at the foot of his bed. "Don't mind me, honey," she
would murmur. "It's just so miserably uncomfortable in the other
room."

"No," he told her, relieved.

It was all such a confusing mixture of emotions: that first couple
of months she came to the room several nights a week, and a part of
him felt happy about it, a separate floating part of him inside, which
rejoiced all on its own that he was no longer alone in the dark so
much.

"What is it we have lots of to face the big bad world with?" his
mother would say sadly, emptily, sometimes almost sarcastically.

He would nod.

And she would answer herself. "Resources."

It had been, after all, her expression—an exchange she and her
mother used to have that Jason's father had picked up, as family
members do. But it never seemed quite the time to say the word
back at her in those instances when she used it, during the hard,
cruel days of trying to adjust to the new job and to the house being
empty when he came home each day from school. He had preferred
the silence, hadn't wanted to talk about any of it. He had wanted the
quiet and hidden feeling of the attic.

He was being carried, head down, by the waist. He saw the ground moving below, only inches from his eyes. This was Bags carrying him, and he would die soon. It would be death. He would find out what it was, and he had the thought as if the dying were simply the next thing in his life. It raked through him that this was the thing itself, happening, and there wouldn't be any time, no person to look back on it and call it a name. His mind sped. Everything throbbed. He tried to look up, but his neck and shoulders cramped, and then he seemed to drift again, all the blood having rushed to his head. It pounded in his ears, and something lifted him so that he could see that his bleeding hand dangled before him, that it had struck the ground and was hurting again. He held it in front of his eyes and looked at it—a bad slash across the palm, and another bleeding cut on the back of the wrist. His head hurt. He was sick to his stomach.

And then he remembered, with a surge of hopeless excitement, that he had seen his father. He tried again to look up. "Dad?" he said.

He couldn't see. The ground went by his face and then became concrete. He saw drops of blood there. He was being let down, his feet came in contact with the ground. He tried to stand, but his legs

gave way—the sprained ankle, and the cut, too, now. Whoever it
was held him up and carried him through a doorway into the
kitchen of the unfinished house. He was pulled to a chair and seated
in it, and when he looked up again into the light from the windows
he saw his father. "Dad?" he said. The face rearranged itself.

Reuther.

Jason started to let down inside, and sound issued from him
that sounded like a combination of crying and laughing, a hysterical
nerve-tic, which he sought to control and couldn't. He simply let it
go, staring at Reuther there, who had put his hands on his hips and
tilted his head to one side, curious, frowning.

"I don't think you quite understand the situation," Reuther said.

He couldn't answer.

The other took him by the shoulder and shook him. "Listen
to me."

It went on. He saw, out of the corner of one eye, the fat man
move past the space of the open door.

Reuther clapped a hand brutally over the boy's mouth. It
closed off his air. He sucked in, receiving the odor of the hand, a
sick, dirty human smell of sweat and skin and something like wet
paper bags. He coughed. Something hot rose in his throat, to his
mouth; he leaned forward, out of Reuther's grasp, and spit onto
the floor.

Reuther cursed, turning from him. He ran water in the sink,
then came back and put a cold rag across the boy's mouth, over his
eyes. He held the boy's head in a tight, painful grip, roughly abrad-
ing his skin with the rag. Then he stepped back, using the cloth to
wipe his own hands. "Now," he said.

"He was going to throw me in the basement," Jason said.

"Was he."

"He would've murdered me."

"Shit." Reuther threw the rag into the sink and crossed the
room, working his hands in front of him. "I'm so lucky in my choice
of fucking partners, aren't I?"

"I didn't mean to run away," Jason said. "Please don't let him
hurt my mother."

"You're a pretty brave fellow," Reuther said. He had the light from the window behind him; you couldn't quite distinguish the features of his face.

The boy tried to see the room, and it spun with the motion of his head. Reuther reached for him, supported him in the chair.

"You're a little weak."

"Yes." He heard the note of gratitude in his own voice. The fat man was outside somewhere, and Jason groped for some sense of hope from this fact.

"You've lost a little blood."

"I was afraid of the basement," Jason said, fighting tears. "I didn't mean anything."

Reuther knelt down and tore a piece of the boy's shirttail. The sudden sound made him yell.

"Take it easy. Nobody's hurting you now."

Reuther applied the torn piece of cloth to the wounds on Jason's hand. Jason saw the smooth flesh of his face, the little pores where whiskers grew, the mark just under the right eye, like a small chicken pox scar. The eyes were such a cold, watery blue. "It's stopped mostly," Reuther said.

"He tried to kill me."

"Yes. Of course. Mr. Bags is a very brutal, bad man. And the thing that compounds it of course is that he's also quite stupid." There was the smallest grain of sympathy in the soft, German-accented voice; it brought all the boy's grief flooding toward the surface again. He couldn't stop sniffling. "I was only defending myself."

"You're a brave fellow, as I said." Reuther smiled. "Now, I'm afraid I have to tie you up again." He brought the rope out of his coat and tied the boy's hands to the back of the chair. He tightened the knots, working swiftly, and here was Bags, coming in from the outside, carrying a leather backpack by the loop handle at the top.

"Put it on the counter," Reuther said, still working.

Bags did so, never taking his eyes from the boy, a grin of satisfaction and triumph on his face. His eyes were murderous. A bruise had risen in the slack flesh of the left cheek. He reached into the bag and brought out two wrapped sandwiches. Opening one, he began to eat, making a lot of noise, still staring at the boy.

Reuther took the other sandwich for himself. He faced Jason. "Hungry?"

The boy couldn't speak.

"Guess not."

"I'm gonna have some fun when this is all over," Bags said, chewing, nodding at Jason. He wiped his mouth with the back of one hand. "Yessir."

Reuther spoke. "Try to comprehend what's at stake here, hmm?"

Jason couldn't tell who this was addressed to. Reuther strolled to the other side of the room and leaned against the wall, eating his sandwich.

"I'm just saying," said Bags. He took part of the knife handle out of his belt as if to show it to the boy. "Some fun."

"Go outside, please," Reuther told him.

"There ain't nothing to watch for."

"Your brother is not much brighter than you are, and therefore anything might happen. But mostly I'd rather not have you here."

For a long time, Bags didn't move. He stood there eating the last of his sandwich. The two men seemed to be waiting for whatever might happen next. Bags reached into the backpack and brought out a can of V–8 juice. He opened it and drank it down, then crushed the can and tossed it across the room, so that it clattered against the baseboard and rolled back a few feet. The noise of it made the boy jump.

Bags smiled, regarding him with the cold passive sureness of a killer. "The little hero's feeling kind of jumpy."

"Go outside," Reuther told him. "Now."

Again, Bags waited.

The other gazed passively at him.

"This ain't no Third Reich, you know."

"Just do as I say," Reuther told him. "And maybe you'll get to be a rich man."

Bags turned to the boy. "Some fun," he said and went out, closing the door, slowly, behind him.

Reuther cleared his throat and took another bite of the sandwich. Jason kept his eyes on him, though he was aware of the door, with the fat man standing in the window, hands on hips.

"Sure you don't want something to eat?"

He shook his head.

"You should keep your strength up."

"I'm not hungry."

Reuther pulled another chair up and turned it around, straddling it to face him. For a few moments, he just sat there, as if waiting for his captor to speak. "What is the strangest thing that happened between you and your father?"

Jason was silent.

"Can you think of anything?"

"No."

"There has to be something—some inexplicable thing. He punished you once, say, and you didn't deserve it."

The boy shook his head.

"You feel you always deserved it."

Again, he was silent.

"You were close?"

"Travis already asked me all this," he said.

Reuther reached over and cuffed him on the side of the face; it stung. The ends of his long fingers were hard and rough. "Did that shake loose any thoughts?"

The boy glared. He was dizzy. It had been a small slap, with only the weight of the hand coming across his cheek; yet he couldn't seem to get his breath. His throat hurt. But his mind was made up: he would not speak now, no matter what Reuther did or said.

"Did he ever hit you?"

Jason blinked, waiting for the blow.

"Did he ever hit you?"

He commenced crying once more. He put his head down and fought it and was aware that the other had stood. Reuther moved the chair to the other side of the room, then came back.

"I wish life were not so hard for all of us," he said.

IN FRONT OF HIS DAUGHTER'S SCHOOL,
Shaw waited behind a blue van, into which several black children
were climbing. A big woman stood holding the door for them. She
had dreadlocks and looked to be pregnant. One of the children, a little girl, reached up to her face and offered a kiss. The woman smiled
and bent down to take the kiss. Then she glanced at Shaw sitting in
his idling car behind the van. He tried to signal that he was in no
hurry, but she took it wrong, lifted the little girl in and closed the
door, then walked around to the driver's side with an expression of
tolerant dislike on her face. He smiled at her, held one hand up to
wave. She shook her head, not quite seeing his friendly wave, got into
the van, and slammed the door. Shaw watched the van pull away.

Every day had its portion of misunderstandings. And everybody
seemed to be spoiling for a fight. He suppressed the urge to think
about the first peaceful feeling after a drink. It kept coming at him
now, an increasing pressure.

Mary waited for him on a little wooden bench outside the door,
and when she saw him she fumbled with her book bag, putting it
over her shoulder while trying to arrange a large piece of poster
board under one arm. She had other books too, and she dropped

one, attempting to cradle everything in the arm that held the poster board. He left the car and hurried over.

"Here," he said. "Let me help."

"I've got it," she said. And she did. He walked with her to the car and opened the door for her. She wore a dark blue dress, which hung below the level of her winter coat, and her wool cap appeared about to slide off the side of her head. Her movements were very sure and graceful, for all the difficulty she was having. She dropped everything in a clattering heap in back, then settled on the front seat and folded her hands in her lap, reaching up to straighten her cap. He fastened the seat belt over her and closed the door. Someone waited behind him—a young woman in an idling Volkswagen Beetle, looking very impatient. He nodded at her and she gave no response. "All right," he muttered under his breath, as he edged in behind the wheel.

"What?" Mary said.

"You say, 'Pardon,'" he told her.

"Mom says that's for company," she said.

He decided to change the subject. "So, how's it feel to be a champion?"

This pleased her. "Oh, Daddy."

"Must be nice," he said. "I've never been the champion of anything."

She stared out at the countryside. He thought of being that age and having the house you live in come apart. She was a bright, good-natured girl, with pretty brown eyes and light brown hair, the healthy shine of which caused subtle changes in his heartbeat. He had always been shy with her, always felt the ways he had failed her, and it had been all the more difficult now that he was living in other rooms, away.

"What're you thinking about, darling?"

"Oh, nothing."

"Are you okay?"

"You mean am I happy that I won?"

"Well, all right."

"I'm happy I won," she said. "But that isn't what you meant."

"No?"

"It isn't, is it?"

"No."

"So tell me."

"I meant—just—generally. Are you okay?"

"I'm okay," she said simply. "My horoscope for today said I would meet a new friend and that I would succeed at something I wanted to do."

"Since when are you a person who thinks about horoscopes?"

"Since always."

"Really."

"Mom and I have been reading them every morning. And you know they're true a lot of the time. It's amazing."

"They're general. So they *seem* true."

"No, really," she said. "The one yesterday said we were going to move. It was right there in black and white."

"But it only *seems* that way, Mary, because it's written to sound like it. It's written in such a way that you can—interpret it any way you want to. It's like an optical illusion."

"It is not." Her voice was definite. He heard the voice of his wife. "I saw it. A move is imminent. That's what it said. And I can spell the word. I know what it means."

He attempted to change the subject: "Listen—honey—about the move—"

"What?"

"You're not afraid or anything—I mean it's not making you worry—"

Her smile was tolerant. "I don't know what you mean."

"Well," he said. "I guess it's a silly question."

She reached into her book bag and moved things around. "I have my medal in here somewhere."

"Are you all set for the move?"

She stopped, but left her hands inside the bag. "I guess."

"It'll be all right," he told her.

"I don't know what you mean," she said. "What will be all right?"

"Everything."

"Of course it will."

"Well, that's all I meant."

She gave a little nod, then sat forward and looked out at the road. He attended to her out of the corner of his eye, taking the turn down Highway 29, toward Steel Run Creek. A little girl with a looming change on her mind, trying to keep from thinking about it too much. Believing horoscopes. And he had not been able to keep from hectoring her about it. He knew from her mother that she was afraid of the move.

"I'm gonna come see you so often you'll get tired of me," he said.

"No you won't," she said simply.

It occurred to him that children don't like being lied to any more than adults do. He said, "We'll spend whole weekends together."

She didn't answer.

"Don't you believe me?"

"I believe you."

There seemed nothing else to say. He watched the road. Not two hours ago he had been in a room where a murdered man lay. He worked to put this far from his thoughts. He saw an image of the bloody shoe print along the baseboard of the Bishop house and glanced over at his daughter, as if there were some possibility that the image might've got out of him and found its way into the flow of her mind. It struck him with a different kind of force that in all likelihood there was a child out there carrying that image, too. Whose child?

"Daddy," she said, without looking at him.

"Yes?"

"I've been thinking how old Willy would be now."

This sent a pulse through him, fright and sorrow in the same shivering instant. He kept his eyes on the road. "Honey, what made you think about Willy?"

"I don't know," she said. "I've been trying to think what he might look like grown up into a teenager. Mom was looking at his pictures when we were packing some things. I don't remember him."

"No," he said, through the constriction of his throat. "But you would've liked him. You would've liked him fine."

They had reached the house. Carol was out on the lawn, her coat pulled tight at the collar, talking to a man who stood out of the open door of a panel truck. The man had a ponytail down his back and a scraggly, long, pointed beard. The side of the panel truck was emblazoned with a white horse in midgallop. The red letters below this read WHITE STALLION MOVERS.

Mary got out of the car and marched toward the front door, head down. Carol said something to the man and then stepped over to greet her. The man looked at Shaw, who could see that his arrival was troubling him—it was as if Shaw could read the other man's natural inclination to be wary around police. He was probably a nice character, though he looked like the sort who was still trying to live out the sixties: all those young men dressed in the style of 1968, as if time had stood still. The man waved at him, and he returned the gesture.

"Thank you," Carol said.

The man got into the van and backed out. Carol put her hand on Mary's shoulder—what was it about all her gestures now that seemed protective, as though she might have to shield the child from her own father?—and waited there as Shaw got out of the car and approached.

"That was a mover," she said.

"I saw. You don't have to explain anything."

"What's wrong?"

"Nothing. I'm sorry, Carol."

"You look a little the worse for the wear," she said.

"Can I talk to you for a minute?"

"Does it have to be now, Phil?"

He turned to Mary. "Honey, go on inside a minute. Mommy'll be right in."

Mary kissed the side of his face—just the sort of unbidden, thoughtless affection from her that could haunt him through the sleepless hours—and went on to the house. At the door, she smiled at him, then turned and was gone.

"Okay," Carol said, all business.

"Carol, what're you doing reading horoscopes to her?"

She glowered. "Is that what this is about?"

"I just want to know. She thinks they're true. You know she takes them seriously?"

"So do I take them seriously."

"Are you drinking, Carol?"

"No. You?" Her gaze was a challenge.

"No."

"I didn't know reading horoscopes qualified a person for AA," she said. "I've always taken them seriously."

"Since when?"

"Since none of your business. Okay? You never noticed it because you never noticed anything."

"I noticed plenty. For Christ's sake, Carol. Horoscopes."

"Is there anything else you'd like to say?"

"If you weren't causing damage, you know, you'd be funny."

"Damage?" she said. "Really?"

"All right. That's enough."

"No—you said damage. How am I doing damage?"

"Maybe that's not the word," he said.

"Good afternoon, Phil."

"Wait."

"Do you just want to make trouble? Is that it?"

"All right," he said. "This isn't what I wanted to talk to you about—"

"You got it in, though, didn't you?"

"I can't help it. I can't help feeling a little bad about the fact that you're teaching her that crap. That's my daughter, too, and there ought to be some agreements between us about this kind of thing. What the hell's going to be next, Carol? Spaceships behind the fucking celestial bodies?"

"Watch your language, please. I think she's heard enough aggression for one day."

"Aggression. Everything's aggression with you. Disagreeing with you is aggression. Tell me, what *isn't* aggression?"

"I'm going inside. I don't need this shit."

"This *is* your shit, Carol. I'm just repeating it back to you."

She said, "You don't call this aggression?"

He glanced at the house and saw Mary watching them from an upstairs window. He said, "Look, I don't want a fight."

"Oh, really." She started to move away from him.

"No—Christ—wait a minute," he said. "Carol. I'm sorry. Jesus. I really don't want a fight. I didn't come here to argue with you."

"You could've fooled me." She crossed her arms and turned partly away from him.

"Carol, can't we agree on some of the so-called curriculum?"

"So, okay—and what do we do? We agree that she learns only what *you* want her to learn? We read horoscopes together in the mornings. For fun. Is there something *else* you wanted to tell me?"

He shifted a little. The anger moved through him. "Yes," he said. She waited.

"Mary said she's been thinking about Willy a lot."

"We both have. We're leaving here. I had some of the pictures out—" She halted. For a time neither of them could speak.

Shaw felt, as he had so many times over the past month, the bitter strangeness of being here with this woman, so removed from him now, though she was close enough to touch. She wrapped her arms tightly around herself, and there was a chilly wind blowing, but this motion was not, he knew, quite exactly connected to the cold. She seemed to be remembering everything, all the hurtful, sad, hard ways in which her own life was so painfully bound to his. It was in her brimming eyes, and the way she edged away, putting the smallest distance between them. He almost embraced her.

"Carol."

"No," she said. "What did you want to tell me about it?"

"Nothing," he got out. "Just wanted to be sure you knew."

"Well, I know."

There was a pause, during which she did not look at him. The wind pulled the hair across her face, and she faced into it.

"Don't let Mary out of your sight over the next few days, okay? And keep the doors locked and the alarm on."

She drew in a breath to speak, then evidently realized the import of the first part of his speech. Her whole expression changed. "Is this that Virginia Front business? I heard it on the radio. It's a hate crime. We don't fit the bill, you know?"

"Yeah, well—it's not so sure it was a hate crime. There's something weird going on, so keep a close watch on her, that's all." He pointed. "The Bishop house is *right* over that hill."

"I know that." She had drawn up slightly, her arms still folded.

"Okay," he said.

"I don't let her wander around unsupervised, Phil."

He chose to ignore this; it was probably, he decided, unintentional. "I didn't say you do."

"And I didn't mean anything by that," she told him.

"Okay," he said.

"But I *don't* leave her unattended."

The emphasized word grated on him. He started to move off.

"I'm glad we're leaving Steel Run."

He spoke over his shoulder. "Lock the doors. I'll try and check in later if you want."

"Could you?" There was actually a note of pleading in her voice.

It struck him as ironic. He nearly said so. It took all his self-possession to remain silent. He got to the car and turned to face her. She was standing there clutching the collar of her coat. "Of course I will," he said.

The night Carol announced that she wanted him out of her life, he went into a bar in Steel Run and nearly got himself into a fight with a pair of marines on their way to Quantico. The marines carried him forcibly out to the parking lot and left him sitting in the back-seat of a '78 Mercury convertible. They told him they understood his anger; he seemed to recall the sound of their laughter as they walked away. He came to in sunlight, wondering why the owner of the Mercury hadn't come out of the bar. No one was around to answer this for him. It was a blazing hot July day, and he walked around the establishment, in weeds and scattered piles of litter, seeking to know. He was in a daze; the sun blinded him and seemed to be cooking the oxygen out of the air. Finally, he went to his own car and drove home. Carol had taken Mary to a summer program at the community college and was packing Shaw's clothes into a suitcase. She wanted him to move out right away, and she wanted him to know that her decision to end the marriage was not necessarily for any specific reason having to do with the past, or with his nature—after all, she understood the alcohol problem, having suffered with that herself. She desired freedom from him.

"Freedom from me?" he said.

The terms of her response were general: self-expression, fulfillment.

"How about vaginal aggrandizement, Carol? I think that's an excellent purpose."

"Talking to you is like talking to a child."

"You know what you need to do, Carol? You need to manually bring yourself off in front of a picture of Karl Marx. I think that might be just the thing."

"Fuck you," she said.

"Oh, now we're getting into the meat of the discussion."

"I want you out. Okay? How's that for vocabulary. I want you as far away from me as you can get, as soon as you can get there. Okay? Oh, how badly I want for you to have never happened to me!"

He struck her. He hadn't known he would do it. And having done it, he was immediately contrite, following her through the rooms of the house, apologizing, agreeing to everything. Yes, it was best that he leave. He would give her a divorce, whatever she wanted. But he couldn't have it be other than what he knew it was: the loss of the boy had broken them. "That's what it is, Carol. That's what happened to us."

"No," she said. "I felt this way before. I never admitted it to myself. I endured everything because I thought I was supposed to and I felt sorry for you, and when we lost Willy I stayed to nurse you through it. That's what happened."

All right.

Driving away from the house, he had again the sense of having failed to control himself in all the important ways. He recalled that when the two of them were drinking together, there had been a hazy kind of solace that made everything seem bearable.

Before going back to the station, he drove up to Darkness Falls and Eloise's house. The dark water of the lake shimmered with a million flecks of reflected light in the distance. Her father was out in front of the house, bundled in a hunting jacket, digging in the dirt next to the stoop. He stopped and leaned on the shovel as Shaw got out of the car and came along the sidewalk. The windows behind him were bright, giving back the cold sun. The grass was brown, the shapes of shade lengthening in it from the naked trees. Bordering this acre of cut grass and bare, rutted clay, beyond the wide circumference of the lake with its diminutive white sand beach, there were steep hills, covered with tall pines, and you could see the sunny windows of several unfinished houses, more casualties of the real estate slump. The far edge of the lake was partly frozen. Shaw looked at the color of the grass, like broom straw. The old man kept digging.

"What's up, Aaron?" Shaw said.

"She's inside," said the old man.

"What're you doing?"

"Digging."

"I can see that."

"Go on inside," the old man said. "Door's open."

The house smelled of something scorched. In the living room there were piles of laundry on one chair and stacked newspapers on another. The decor here was in the style of the midsixties. Eloise's father had kept it very much as it had been thirty years ago, when he was a young man and lived here with his wife and daughter, supposing that he would live in other houses, on other streets. But he liked the place too much to move, finally, and so he had changed his mind. Eloise left for college and stayed away for almost a decade. She was home to stay now, having weathered a long, useless (her word) live-in relationship with a jazz musician in Chicago. The musician was gone; she didn't know where. And she was home. The wall above the mantel was adorned with several framed photographs of her in the stages of growing up. She harbored no unhappiness about coming home to live: her father needed her. He was slipping, just a little. At heart, she told Shaw, he had always been a child.

She was in the kitchen, head into the oven, scraping at the inside.

"Eloise," Shaw said.

She bumped her head, backing out. "Oh, God—you scared me."

He picked up one of the entertainment magazines on the table and paged through it, then let it drop. She had risen and now regarded him.

"What's wrong?"

"Got any iced tea?"

"It's cold as hell out. What's going on, Phil?"

"I was just—I'd like something cold to drink."

"What're you doing here now? You're not supposed to be here till six. The place is a wreck."

"It's been a bad day, Eloise."

"Tell me about it. We started off this morning with an oven fire."

"Sorry."

She moved to the sink, reached into the cabinet above it, and brought out two coffee cups. She filled them both with water and brought them back. There was a languidness about her, a slow fluidity that made her seem almost somnolent.

"What's he doing out there?" Shaw asked her.

"He buried a bird out back. I don't know what he's doing now. Probably trying to dig one up. Last night he went out for a walk and didn't come back for two hours. I almost called you."

They heard the door, the sound he made kicking his boots against the jamb to get the dirt off them.

Shaw sipped the water and felt her eyes on him.

"You're wanting something a little stronger, aren't you?"

"I'll be all right," he said.

"Poor Phil."

"Listen," he said to her. "I've got something bad going on—"

"I know," she interrupted. "You don't have to tell me."

"You know about it?"

She frowned. "Your girl moving away—"

"No," he said. "This is something I'm—it's work. The job. I'm gonna be working tonight. I'm on my way back there now."

The old man had come to the entrance of the kitchen. "That murder," he said. "Am I right?"

Shaw nodded.

Eloise drank her water. It was as though she had decided not to respond. Her father came into the room, poured himself some coffee from the machine on the counter, then shambled to the table and sat down, chuffing through his nose and clearing his throat. He lifted his cup of coffee and blew across the surface and sipped, making a loud slurping noise. "Any ideas?"

"Not much," Shaw said. "Some folks called to take the credit."

"Heard that, too. Yeah."

"I think somebody's finally gonna buy one of those houses over on the other side of the lake," Eloise said. "I saw some cars pulling in and out over there."

"Never had a murder while I was sheriff," the old man said. He had the look of someone who had just suffered an insult.

Shaw was silent.

"Just lucky, I guess."

"Daddy," Eloise said. "Could you leave us alone for a minute?"

He took a long time getting up—but it wasn't intentional. His bones creaked, and he was clearly sore from the digging he had done. When he was gone, she moved into Shaw's arms and kissed him on the mouth. They had not been intimate; he was not prepared for the kiss. He took a small step back, and her full weight came against him. Then she broke away.

"All right?" she said.

"Eloise."

"Do you believe somebody can feel the future?" she demanded, turning from him.

"I don't know," he said.

"I had a dream last night. It woke me up. I was standing at the edge of a cliff and you were down at the bottom."

"I've got to go," he said. "It's a dream, Eloise."

"Don't you want to hear the rest of it?"

"I never liked listening to people's dreams, Eloise."

She faced him. A young woman with a strange, angular loveliness—fine skin, slightly crossed eyes, thin lips, high cheekbones—all her features combining to give a troubling sense of crisis, as though her emotions had worn through all the paths in the flesh and brought her countenance to the point of dissolution; there was something so sad in the eyes, an expectation of complexity, or trouble. It made her seem more vulnerable than she probably was. At any rate, he supposed she had the strength to handle living alone with her father, essentially serving as his nurse and housekeeper, while the decade of her thirties began. "You were pretending to be dead," she told Shaw. "It was like you wanted to get away from me."

He pulled her into his arms and held her. In the other room, the old man coughed deeply.

"I hate winter," she said. "I've always hated it."

THE RAIN HAD STOPPED. RICKY walked back and forth, holding the gun with both nervous hands. He had said nothing for almost an hour, had demanded that they keep still, pacing back and forth and going over everything in his mind. Gwendolyn watched him and worried about what Henry might do. The wait was driving Henry toward something desperate; she could feel it. Henry stood by the passage into the hallway, his hands at his sides. She knew it was getting to him, though he seemed patient, even calm, compared to the younger man, who stopped now and brought one hand up to his hair, pushing through, fingers spread, so that he appeared to be grasping at something painful right at the crown of his scalp.

"It's not too late," Henry said abruptly.

"I told you to shut up. The call's gonna come."

Gwendolyn, sitting near the telephone, tried with her facial expression to make Henry see that he should say nothing more. To her it was clear that Ricky's own fervid mind had presented him with all he needed to consider. She feared that he might start shooting out of panic alone.

Henry went on talking low, soft. "They lied to you. They told you no one would get hurt. You don't want to hurt anybody."

"You better just—shut up, man."

"Henry, please," said Gwendolyn. She reached for him. Henry crossed slowly to where she was and sat next to her.

"Don't keep walking around like that," Ricky said.

He paced. The windows were black now, the sky clear, a moonlit night, almost eight o'clock. Gwendolyn thought of Nora and Jason, in the dark of Virginia, three thousand miles away, with murderers.

"Okay, look," Ricky said. "Here's the thing. The guy that's running things, he'll kill me if I back out now. He would've capped your son-in-law. I talked him out of it. Me. And then Jack goes and gets himself killed in that accident. We don't get those chips, I'm dead."

"He can't kill you if he's in prison," Henry said.

Gwendolyn wanted him to be quiet. Ricky was reasoning with himself. Then he raised the pistol to Henry's face. "Shut up!"

Henry blinked, but stood his ground.

"Shit," Ricky said, pacing again. He went to the window and surveyed the dimly lit street, ticking off something to himself—reasons, chances, excuses—counting fearfully. Then he faced them again. "Your daughter's husband had to get upright all of a sudden." He appeared close to tears. "Goddammit, all your daughter has to do is give them what they want."

"What is it they want?" Gwendolyn asked, squeezing Henry's wrist.

"They want microchips. Okay? A couple million dollars. Fuck." Ricky waved the gun at them, white-faced. He went back to the window, then turned and came toward them. "I'm not gonna die over this. And I'm not going to prison, either."

Gwendolyn realized with a start that he was beginning to think he would have to kill them both to keep from being caught. In the next instant, it occurred to her that no matter what happened, he would believe that he must leave no one alive in this house.

"We don't know your real name," she said. "We won't tell anyone."

At the same time, Henry had spoken. He glanced at her, then turned to Ricky and said, "You hear me? I think we might have what you're looking for."

"Shut up, I'm telling you."

"No, but you said microchips. Listen, there's a safe in the basement."

Gwendolyn understood that her husband had come to the same realization about Ricky, and she knew he was playing for time now, for an opportunity to use the younger man's jitteriness against him. In the basement, there was a safe built into the cement floor. It had been one of the curiosities of the place when they bought it: a safe the original builder of the house had planted in the concrete, and then misplaced the combination which could open it. He had never bothered to write to the maker of the safe to get the combination, and the company had subsequently gone out of business. The safe contained nothing. The Spencers were using it as a table and as a conversation piece; it could not be opened, short of a small dynamite charge, or the skill of a safecracker.

Ricky stood with the black pistol aimed at Henry's middle, staring.

"Do you understand me?" Henry said.

"*You* have them?" Ricky said. "Jack gave them to *you*?"

"I have a couple of packages he sent me. I put them in the safe. He said they were important, so I put them in the safe."

Ricky shifted slightly. "Wait a minute, just a minute, here. You were—you must've—you've been pretending you didn't know what this was about?"

"How would I have known?" Henry said. "You come in here waving that thing and I think you're holding my daughter for some kind of ransom. How am I supposed to connect that to packages my son-in-law sent me last year? He didn't say what was in them. He wanted me to store them for him in a safe place. For all I know, it's records from his business."

Ricky studied him, thinking. "No," he said. "You work with computer people. I've been following you, man. You'd know if he sent you these chips."

"How would I know? I'm not saying it *is* the chips, but it might be. Or there might be something in the packages that will tell you where to find them."

Gwendolyn thought he'd gone too far. The story sounded too made up to her. She sought for something to say, something to distract the other from zeroing in on what Henry had decided to attempt.

But Ricky had bought the idea. "Jesus Christ," he said. He put one hand to the side of his head—someone trying to blot out a rush of thoughts. "I gotta concentrate."

"Let's go down in the basement and see," Henry told him.

"Wait a minute. Just wait a minute."

Gwendolyn touched her husband's shoulder, wanting him to slow down, to wait. As soon as Ricky knew the truth about the safe, he would kill them both. She was certain. It was only moments away. Whatever Henry was up to, it would have to break upon the gunman very soon now, and she wanted to be ready for it. She reached down and squeezed Henry's wrist again, and he patted hers with his other hand. He kept talking. "It might be that you can do what you said you were going to do, Ricky. You can disappear, with what you wanted. Isn't that what you wanted?"

Ricky approached him, arm extended, the black pistol barrel only inches from Henry's nose. "You better be telling me the truth, man. Or I swear. Because I'm in a trap here. They already killed somebody."

"They're three thousand miles away," Gwendolyn said.

"Nobody can hurt you," Henry told him.

Ricky backed up a step. "All right," he said. "Let's go."

RESOURCES

Nora and Travis had gone through the garage, the shed, the closets, even the kitchen, the pantry with its dozens of cans and glass jars and tins of cookie forms and decorations. And they had found nothing. For her, it was all the more painful that these personal things—these things which came from her life before her husband's death, the months of grief and worry, and now the invasion of these bad men—that it all looked so meager, so awfully beside the point.

The point, of course, was survival. The point was to make sure somehow that her son escaped unharmed, that her parents stayed alive.

The searching had turned up nothing but a single book page with the name of a bank written on it and a letter from someone who might have been her husband's lover, or one of them, Travis said, with a wily kind of angry relish. He was getting more and more agitated.

"Shit," he said at last. He took hold of her, above the elbows. "Okay, look. Here's the deal. Jack must've said something to you."

"Don't you get it?" she said. "We were barely talking at the end."

"This is *before* the end." He shook her. Then he let go and walked away from her, swinging his arms as if to knock away invisible impediments. He reached into his pocket, brought out a cigarette, and lighted it; his face shone. She saw the little tail of a scar running from his mouth. They were in the kitchen. It had been dark for a long time.

"I know he was thinking of getting out," Travis said. "He was looking for a way out. He wanted out." He drew on the cigarette and sighed the smoke. "We had them in a nice safe place—and it wasn't any bank, either—" He reached into his pocket again and brought out the folded page. "No. He might've been thinking about it, but he didn't do it. They were in that motel room for weeks, and we were delivering them to him." He took another draw on the cigarette, thinking. He put the page back in his pocket. "*I* was delivering them."

"Well, if you know where they are—" she began. His look stopped her.

"The son of a bitch checked out. Put them somewhere and was trying to use them to get out free and clear. He was bargaining with Reuther over the telephone."

He smoked the cigarette.

She waited for whatever was next. The little hacksaw blade had made a blister on the instep of her foot; it stung every time she moved. Perhaps she was bleeding. During the long hours of their search there had been moments when she experienced an unnerving feeling of cooperation with him in the process of her own destruction, as if they were accomplices.

Now he said, "Reuther." There was something in his tone, a note of regret, or fear; she couldn't tell which.

"Jack was backing out," she said.

"He was *chickening* out." He turned and ran water on the coal of his cigarette, then put it in the trash bag under the sink. "Come on. Let's clean this mess up. Make it look natural in here."

She did not question him. They worked together putting away all the signs of the ransacking they had been engaged in. In the bedroom, he turned the bed over and put the torn parts of the mattress on the floor of the closet. She was setting the books back into the bookcases.

"That woman—that Ruth," he said abruptly, breathing with the effort of his work.

Nora said nothing.

He was on the other side of the room. "You don't know her, but those two ladies did. That's the same Ruth. I saw the expression on your face."

"I don't know," Nora said. "It could be."

He stood there, thinking. He brought another cigarette out and lighted it. "Maybe it'll be this simple," he said. "Maybe she's got them—"

"I wouldn't know," she heard herself say.

"Yeah." He looked around at the walls. "Jack was a guy with secrets."

When the house was reasonably back in order, he went to the door and looked out. It was almost dark. There were no streetlamps or any house lights. The Bishop farm was dark. He shut off the lights and then hesitated.

"What?" she said.

"Nothing."

In the car, he made her put her head down again. She began counting to herself, thinking of trying to measure the miles in this fashion, but then he was talking, asking her questions.

"Who worked with Jack?"

"Nobody. He subcontracted."

"Real estate people?"

"Plumbers, electricians, drywallers."

"Did he know any real estate people?"

She sat up a little to look at him.

"Put your head down."

She did so.

"Did he know any real estate people?"

"He knew some, yes. You heard what the James sisters said."

"What're the chances this Ruth is the same one?"

"I already said I don't know," she said. "How would I possibly know that?"

"Well, think about it."

They were climbing now, the angle had changed, and he had slowed some. She felt a blast of the cold air; he had opened his window to throw the cigarette out. He shut it again.

"What about other people? Lawyers—did he know any lawyers?"

"Of course."

"Well?"

"I don't know."

"Think," he said. "Goddammit."

"He saw lawyers. He was thinking—we were thinking about declaring bankruptcy."

"Shit!"

The car jerked along a curve, and the wheels made a screeching sound.

"Get pulled over," she said. "That would be really smart."

"I'm gonna tell you something," Travis said. "We don't find the chips, and we might all end up dead. We gotta find some way to stall Reuther. If this piece of paper—this bank—if this is just it, then we ain't got any control."

She sat up. He was staring out.

"I don't understand."

He didn't answer. At some point he had lighted another cigarette. Ahead of them the road seemed to be narrowing in trees and high dirt banks with gnarled roots jutting from them. She did not recognize anything. She tried to see into the woods, to find some sign of other houses, but there was nothing—the shifting gray shapes of trees retreating into the darkness. But the road was inclining upward.

"What're you saying?" she asked him.

"I'm telling you the truth." His voice shook.

"He wouldn't hurt Jason," she said. "Tell me he wouldn't hurt my boy." Trembling, she looked out at the nightmarish twisting of the tree branches reaching into the fan of the headlights.

"You know how my brother is?" he said. "Well—"

"Oh, God," she said. "No."

"Look, we have to do some more looking. Hear me? What we do—we say we got interrupted by the cops—those—those women. If you want to survive. You understand? We say we have to go back to the house tomorrow and look through—that we didn't get to everything. I need to get those chips in *my* possession, or all kinds of bad stuff will happen."

"I thought you said you'd get them and we'd never see you again."

"If *I* get them." He spoke thinly, as if his throat were closing. Smoke ran out as he went on. "Just follow my lead," he said.

ALONE

Jason lay in the rags and newspapers of the upstairs, hazily aware of lapses of time, little blank intervals when the pain was less, the anguish not quite so sharp. Though it hurt to stay awake, he felt the need to fight sleep, and he kept losing the fight. Intermittently he jerked back to consciousness and then had to work to muffle his own cry of alarm.

He heard the car, saw the light at the window. There was activity downstairs. Travis's voice.

"Mom!" he called.

And her voice rose to him from the stairwell. "Jason? Son?"

There was a scuffling on the steps, then silence.

"Mom?"

Nothing. He tried to move. His arms and legs were almost without sensation, though his back and neck pulsed with sharp pain through each attempted motion. It seemed a long time. But then someone was coming up the stairs.

"Honey?" His mother's voice. She hurried to him, began working the knots over his wrists. He began to cry, soundlessly. "Are you all right?" she said.

"I'm okay." His own voice sounded far away to him.

"Come on." She stood and helped him toward the stairwell.

"Is it over?"

"No."

They went down into the kitchen. The three men were waiting there, Reuther sitting in the chair, Bags standing by the door, Travis perched on the counter, smoking another cigarette.

"We couldn't get to everything," Travis said. "We have to try it again."

Reuther said, "Why didn't you stay there until you did get to everything?"

"We got visited once by the cops. She said she was sick. I figured if the place was lit up all night, it might draw some more visitors. We'll go back early in the morning."

Jason put his arm around his mother's middle and held tight. He saw Bags staring at him with that look of complacent malice; Bags was confident that he would get to work his revenge.

"We have to talk to this—Ruth," Reuther said. He thought a moment. "Travis, you and the lady go back tonight. We'll keep the boy here."

"No," Jason's mother said. "You can't."

"I think so."

"Why?" Travis said.

"The police may come back through. I would, if I were the police. Wouldn't you? It's safer to have somebody there. And maybe leave the lights on. A lady staying in a house next to the murder house—scene of the terrible hate crime." He took Jason by the arm above the elbow and pulled him close. It was almost an embrace. Jason smelled something lemony and sour. Reuther was looking down at him, smiling.

"The man—the detective," Jason's mother said. "He—he knew someone else was—where the—at Mr. Bishop's house. He wanted to talk to my son."

"You've already been seen there," Reuther said to Travis.

"Yep. The two ladies saw me."

He let go of the boy and paced slowly. He stopped before Jason's mother. "Yes. I think you should go back there. And keep looking. The police are looking for a cult. The cult called the news media and claimed credit for the crime. The media is crazy with it."

Travis pushed off the counter. "Okay."

When the boy's mother and Travis had gone, Reuther took him upstairs and tied his hands and feet. Jason heard Bags whistling on the stairs, and he murmured to Reuther, "Please don't leave me alone with him."

"What?" Reuther spoke in a normal tone.

"Please."

"Please what?"

"He'll kill me."

Bags strolled into the room. Reuther said, without turning, "Go back downstairs, please."

"I'm comfortable here."

Reuther stood. "Oh?"

"Think I'll spend the night up here."

Reuther seemed to accede to this. He reached down and made one tightening pull on the cord that held the boy's hands, then stood again. "It's important to understand the consequences of one's decisions," he said.

"Yeah," said Bags.

Reuther sidled to the other side of the room. "Yes, I'd say it's crucial."

"Good for you."

He took the pistol out of his jacket and held it in the palm of his hand, still moving along the opposite wall. "I'd go back downstairs."

"Why don't you?" Bags said. "I'm gonna stay up here and have some fun."

Reuther put the pistol back and started for the stairwell. "All right," he said. "But remember he's no good to us dead."

"Yeah, I remember," the fat man said.

Reuther looked back at the boy. "Scary," he said. "Hmm?"

Then he descended the stairs.

Bags remained where he was for a long minute. He appeared to be listening. Jason could see him out of the corner of his eye, a blur, through tears. He said, "Please."

Bags came to him in three heavy leaps. With each one, the boy cried out. Bags leaned down, hands on his knees. "What have we got here, huh?"

"Don't," Jason said.

"It's gonna be a long night, boy. Some fun." Bags knelt, unzipped his pants, and reached in. Jason tried to turn his face away.

"Come here, cowboy."

"You can eat shit and die," the boy said.

"Ain't you tough?"

The heavy fingers closed on the hair at the crown of his head and turned him slowly. He fought to free himself, and the hand pulled; it felt as though his hair would be torn out at the roots. "No!" he screamed. He felt something warm and wet run down his neck. Somehow he kept his face turned away, flailing in his bonds, choking.

Bags said, "You're all wet, kid."

Jason closed his eyes tight, relaxed all his muscles, sliding toward blackness, and abruptly something changed in the room, a roiling. He looked up and saw Bags fall to one side. Reuther had bulled him to the floor and now kicked him where he'd opened his pants. Bags yelled and rolled away, his legs curling toward his heavy stomach. Reuther kicked at him and then stooped to slap his face, his ears, the top of his head. Bags held his groin and bellowed.

Jason saw the barrel of the pistol come down against the side of the fat man's head, a small, hard striking motion. Reuther held the gun on him. "Now, will we go downstairs like a good piggy?"

Bags whimpered something unintelligible and struggled away, not quite getting to his feet, still holding on to himself. When he was gone, Reuther put the pistol in his belt and turned to the boy.

"Did he hurt you?"

"Are you going to shoot him?" Jason got out. "Shoot him."

"I would like to. And if I have the chance, I will." Reuther shook his head, turning to the stairwell. "You are something. Your mother ought to hire you out to be a tough guy." He brought the pistol from his belt and started down the stairs.

The boy made an effort to hold his breath, to hear. A low muttering came to him and kept on, the same droning sound. It
might've been a radio, he couldn't tell. Finally, it gave over to something else, Reuther's voice, definite, full of malice, controlled. The
words weren't clear. Then the lower sound resumed; it was the sub-
dued drone of the fat man's higher-pitched voice. It went on. They
had apparently come to some arrangement. Finally, Jason thought
he heard the distant strains of music. It was a radio. He began to
doubt everything and thought he smelled smoke through the acrid,
ammonia-like fumes of what Bags had done. His bones were a
structure of torment. The cuts on his hand and ankle gave him back
his own heartbeat in stabs of discomfort.

He saw something move on the wall, the shadows shifting there,
and abruptly he was wide awake, hearing the heavy tread of the fat
man on the stairs. Jason shouted Reuther's name.

And Bags was in the doorway.

The boy tried to work up another shout, but his mouth was dry
now—his fright so complete—and with stunning quickness Bags
was on him, the full weight of the big knee in the middle of his
back. He coughed up something; it was on the floor in front of him.

"Show time," Bags said. He had opened the knife.

The nerves along the side of Jason's skull pounded with blood.
Everything spun. Bags leaned down, smelling of sausage and beer. "I
stuck Reuther," he said. "And now I'm gonna stick you."

The boy looked up into the heavy, round face and abruptly it
was shoved aside, gone, the weight on his back lifted; he could
breathe. The room thundered with footfalls, another struggle, loud
breathing, gasping, straining. He could see only the fat man's bulk,
the heavy legs pushing and bending, and then he saw Reuther,
swinging once, twice, into the bigger man's abdomen. Reuther
pushed him against the opposite wall, working at him. Bags yelled
and went down and crawled along the base of the wall. Reuther followed him, kicking his big side, kneeing him in the side of the head.
Then he had the knife, and he seemed to reach with it, like someone
stretching to pull something from under a bed, his shoulder low, the
hand with the knife in it disappearing into the darkness at the level

of the floor, where Bags was roiling and struggling. The fat man lay flat and was still, his wide-fingered hand lying open. Reuther moved twice more in that odd reaching way, and Bags gave forth a low, animal-coughing sound, a ragged, elephantine gasp of air, then was still.

Reuther stood back, dropped the knife, then kicked at it, missing, almost falling. He came and stood over the boy and seemed to falter again.

"Help me," Jason said.

"Fucking can't believe—" Reuther said. "Fucking stupid—"

Jason whimpered. "Untie me."

Reuther was out of breath. "Pig," he muttered. He took a step back and then toppled over.

The boy opened his mouth on a long, tearing, whispered shriek. Then he was crying, struggling with the knots that held him.

There was movement on the other side of the room.

Bags stirred. One boot heel scraped the floor. Bags opened his eyes and spit blood. Then he pushed himself to a sitting position against the wall. Blood poured from his mouth. His small green eyes fixed on Reuther. "Fuck with me," he said. The moronic little laugh came with blood and coughing. And now the pig eyes settled on the boy, who tried again to squirm out of the ropes. Bags tipped over onto his side and reached for the knife. There was blood everywhere. It ran out from where Reuther lay, and it kept coming from the fat man's mouth, but the fat man had stuck the end of the knife in the floor and was using it to pull himself along. The knife gave way, and he put his head down and gasped. The blood shone on his hands; it was in his hair. He lay there a moment, then stirred again, both hands out in front of him on the floor, the one hand still holding the knife. Bags inched forward, face up now, the lower half of it blotted out with blood, but with a brutal, blood-spattered glitter in the eyes, an almost childlike excitement, as if this were a game—not to let go, not to die of his wounds until he could get to the boy.

Jason watched him come. Almost no actual sound was issuing from his own open mouth—a thin hissing screech—as the fat man came closer, the hand with the knife in it reaching almost to his back. He closed his eyes. The whole world was stuttering to a stop. He breathed and felt the groping of the fat man, so near now, and it was happening, the hand came down in the middle of his back; he was being murdered.

But the fat man didn't move, and the hand with the knife in it was deadweight. There was a cut where the knife had glanced him, but everything was still now. He opened his eyes.

Bags was motionless. No breath. No movement. The hand with the knife lay across the boy's back. He couldn't stop shaking, lying there with the deadweight of the hand and arm across his back. The minutes stretched and died.

Finally, slowly, coming out of the reaches of panic, he sought, with his blistered and abraded and tied hands, the wet blade. He could just get his fingers on it. Carefully, he brought it along his palm to the handle, cutting himself on the sharp edge. He felt for the cord and dropped the knife. But he managed to roll over on his side and retrieve it. Once more, it cut him. But here, at last, was the tension of something across it; the cord, some part of the binding that held him. He cut. His feet came loose. He used this new freedom to scramble away from the shape of the fat man lying there, and now he was sitting up, the knife had cut him still again, but he was working it to the place where his hands were tied. He cut this, too, cut through, and was free. He dropped the knife, and then remembered to pick it up, backing away, falling and rising again, feeling the raw tissue of his voice as if it were torn, getting himself to the wall next to the door.

Reuther lay face up, eyes closed, mouth partly open. The fat man lay facedown, one arm out. The floor was all blood.

Jason retched dryly on the wall, then made his way to where Reuther was. He opened Reuther's coat, looking for the revolver. Reuther had no wounds on his front, but his body lay in a wide spreading lake of blood. Jason searched the coat, gasping and trying not to be ill again.

Reuther took hold of his wrist. The grip held him.

Jason tried to scream, to pull away. Reuther stared, dead-eyed, and seemed to be attempting to speak to him. His eyes reflected the dim light of the hall. He appeared to gape, mouth open wide, as if he wanted to release an enormous sound, but nothing came, and at last the pressure of his grasp lessened. He lay back and let go.

The boy staggered to the stairwell and down into the lighted kitchen. The windows were blackness. He found Reuther's gun on the floor near the kitchen counter. There were smears of blood, footprints, signs of a frantic moving back and forth. Reuther hadn't been able to find the gun, evidently, slipping and faltering in the room, in his spilled blood, trying to find it, and finally staggering away to the stairs and on up. Reuther had come, already dying, to kill Bags. Jason put the gun in the belt of his pants, then turned the light off. A wind was blowing outside. He opened the door and stumbled forward into the dark, toward the trees. He kept shaking, faltering, and he thought about how it would be to fall on the knife. He was too woozy to walk. He stopped and held on to the skinny trunk of a pine sapling and took the cold air into his hurting throat. It was too dark to run. He walked a few more steps, leaned on another tree. Beyond the shape of the hill in front of him was a soft glow. Light from some distance. He climbed the hill, still holding the knife. At the crest, he saw water, a large open expanse of it shimmering faintly in the reflection of distant light. Windows, or streetlamps—he couldn't tell. The cold stung him, and he grew dizzy, gripping the knife and leaning into the hard uneven surface of the base of the tree. The pain had somehow reached past itself; there was something weirdly exquisite about it now, though he had no words for this: he simply felt that he had gone inside it, to another level. It made him feel drunk, as he had felt that time, shortly after his father's death—one of the first times he had come home from school alone and had got into his father's whiskey, drinking it to lose himself, to lessen the anxiety and the hurt, as he had seen his father do, and it had made him so sick, dizzy and elated and desperately sick. Now he lay in the dark at the base of the tree, sick again, trying to move away from the small pools of spittle and stomach acid, still pulling and straining to rise. Time had stopped again. All the world around him was terribly still.

SHAW RESTED HIS HEAD ON HIS arms, sitting at his desk in the lamp light. Frank Bell had taken the chair on the other side of the desk. He looked through a manila folder—part of the report of the trace evidence team: the print in the blood was that of a boy's tennis shoe. Probably it was as they had surmised. The boy had stumbled into the scene, and run away in panic. There were two more prints out in the gravel drive and several more in the ground near the little stream; the distance from each other of the prints in the driveway indicated the long strides of flight, of someone running. But who and where was this boy? There was no logical choice, other than Jason Michaelson.

Shaw had spoken with three of the boy's teachers. Jason had not been in class for several days; his mother had been asked to seek counseling for him outside the jurisdiction of the school. The loss of the father had changed him: a bright, inquisitive, and rather witty boy who had become sullen and withdrawn, even unruly and disruptive.

All the adjectives, Shaw remembered, from his own grief.

Probably what Nora Michaelson had said was true: he had left the evening before, on a car journey south with his grandfather. But there had been a boy in the Bishop house; a boy had hidden in the bloody space behind the couch. Who?

Edward Bishop lived alone and saw no other boys in the area that anyone knew about. Everyone mentioned that he had been going over to the Michaelson house in the afternoons to check on Jason Michaelson.

And there were the hate messages warning him away, too.

All right. The boy had been getting into trouble. It stood to reason that this might be why a grandfather traveled east, to take him on a road trip south. There was no basis for questioning what Nora Michaelson had told him. But it was possible, wasn't it, that knowledge of the murder had frightened Nora Michaelson into putting the boy out of the way of questions?

Shaw thought of the shaken look on her face in the small opening of the front door of the house that had belonged to his grandfather.

"Two intruders," Frank Bell said. "As if we couldn't figure that from the way he was trussed up."

"Wait a minute." Shaw sat forward.

"One strong man could do it, I suppose."

"What if this has nothing to do with the Virginia Front?"

"I've been thinking that, too."

"What if it's somebody else?" Shaw said.

"Yeah?"

He picked up the phone and dialed David Ross at home. He got the machine. At the voice prompt, he said, "David, pick up if you're there."

The line opened. "Tell me."

"What if there's something else going on?"

"I just took a kid named Greg Cullen over to the psycho ward. He claims he's the Virginia Front."

Shaw waited.

"A mental defective, Phil. He didn't have squat. He had some printed stuff that looked promising—desktop publishing, you know. But nothing else. Kid produced some hate letters from his computer and tried to get us to arrest him. Whole thing was made up."

"Did you let him go?"

"He couldn't supply a single link to the crime scene. He's a persecution freak."

"Yeah, but he just might be the Virginia Front, too."

"I don't follow."

"What if this crime has nothing to do with hate?"

Ross was silent for a moment. "I still don't follow. We've got the printed messages, and we've got a public claim from a hate group that it's their killing. The phone guy knew about the messages, and he had crime scene stuff, too."

"Did you hold Greg Cullen?"

"I took him over to the mental health clinic, Phil."

Shaw thanked him and started to hang up.

"There'll be FBI types tomorrow," Ross said. "I got the call in my office this afternoon. Violation of Bishop's civil rights."

"I'll be glad to have their help," Shaw said.

Ross sighed on the other end. "We find the guy wearing those boots, and we find the so-called Virginia Front."

"I don't know," Shaw said. "It's too tidy."

"It was all over the news tonight. They're all so goddam excited. Especially that Susan Jones woman. I got the feeling she was going right out to pray for another murder, so she could *really* get into it."

After Shaw hung up, Frank Bell said, "I agree with you."

"I don't know."

"Imagine stumbling into a thing like that. You think a kid could manage not to yell, seeing it happen? Blood washing over his shoes that way?"

"He's the one who broke all the lights. I think he came in after it was done. I think he was alone in the house for a while, hiding."

"Lord," Frank Bell said. "I hope we don't find a boy's body somewhere out there." He only glanced in Shaw's direction. "Sorry."

"Go on home," Shaw told him. "There's nothing else we can do right now."

The other man stood and dropped the folder on the desk. He rubbed his eyes. "You holding up okay?"

"Some," Shaw said.

Bell walked over and put one hand on his shoulder. "Tough time of year."

"Yes."

The other stretched and yawned. "I don't think I'll sleep tonight. If you're up, give me a call. I'll come over and we'll play some blackjack or something."

Shaw said, "I'll be all right."

When he was alone, he looked through the folder again. There wasn't much there: they had found no fingerprints, no fibers, no signs of the struggle that must've taken place. A man doesn't simply lie down and wait for people to tie his hands to his feet. Whoever these men were, they had taken the trouble to wipe all the surfaces in the room and to put whatever had been disturbed back in place. And they had left the music playing.

The probability he had to face was that he would never know more than he knew at this moment, and if he didn't find another body—some boy's body?—or if he managed somehow to find whoever this boy was, and the boy was still alive and could be spoken to, the interview would yield only the fact that the boy had come upon the scene before Bishop's housekeeper did. And the shadowy Virginia Front, whoever they might be, were out there somewhere, with their retrograde derangement.

He closed the office door and went along the lighted hallway to the lobby, where two uniformed troopers stood talking.

It had grown even colder outside. The lights of the hospital were visible, the low buildings ranged across the top of the hill, with the flagpole shining in the light. He drove toward home. The moon went behind a thick wall of clouds ahead, and he thought of snow. As he pulled past the subdivision, he decided to stop in on Carol and Mary. His old house, he noticed, was also lighted, upstairs and down. Carol answered the door after peering out at him. She wore a bathrobe and slippers; her hair was up in curlers. "Well?" she said. "What is it? You scared me."

"I said I'd try to look in on you."

"It's late," she said.

He nodded. "I know."

"Did you—?"

"Nothing yet," he said.

She didn't move from the door. "Mary's upstairs asleep."

"Her light's on."

"We're keeping all the lights on."

"Can I come in a minute?"

She stepped aside. The sofa in the living room was piled with clothes and boxes and Mary's schoolwork. He saw through the kitchen hallway to the back entrance, where Carol had stacked tin cans against the door. On the counter, the chairs, and the table were other boxes stuffed with newspaper-wrapped dishes. Opposite the sink, on a microwave table, a small portable television flickered.

"I don't have any coffee made."

"I wouldn't want any." He walked through to the kitchen and looked out that window. "Have you been hearing noises?"

"Of course. We're both scared out of our minds." She clutched the robe about her chest. "I feel like everything's closing in on us."

"I know the feeling."

"It's the winter. The dark. I wish we were out of here."

"It gets dark in Richmond, too, Carol."

She did not respond to this. On the kitchen table were books she had been studying—a sociology course she was taking at the community college. The winter quarter was ending soon, and there were exams to study for.

"Can I go upstairs and kiss Mary?"

"She's asleep. Don't wake her."

"I won't wake her," he said.

Carol shrugged. He interpreted this as permission, and walked to the stairs and up, along a passage still adorned with photographs of his little family when it was still a little family. Carol could not bring herself to take them down, even now—photographs of Willy as a baby and a toddler, and a solid, square-shouldered boy unafraid of anything (all boy, Carol's mother had said about him).

Mary lay in a sprawl on top of her covers, an afghan pulled over her shoulders. Her legs were exposed. He got a blanket from the linen closet out in the hall and covered her, then bent down to kiss her gingerly on the cheek. He touched the top of her head, the soft richness of her dark hair. He wanted to lie down here and hold her, and he thought of the woman, Marjorie Powers, starting out on a bright winter morning, carrying her life and her assumptions that would be changed forever in the awful minute of discovering Edward Bishop's body. Mary sighed and turned. He kissed the side of her face, then backed out of the room.

Downstairs, Carol stood by the front door. Evidently, she wanted him to leave.

"Do you want to stay?" she said.

He paused.

"You can sleep on the couch."

"No," he told her, and some small part of him felt the stir of vindictiveness, that she only wanted the security of him in the house, and he could deny it to her. The thought went through him and then he was left with an unbidden sense of being wrong again—the knowledge that there were things about which neither of them had been very forgiving or understanding. He had an image of his girl upstairs, so sweetly asleep. He said, "If there was any danger at all, I would. But I think this business with Bishop was *about* something. I don't think it's random. And I don't think there's anything for you to be afraid of."

"Okay," she said. "But I'm afraid nonetheless."

He opened the door. Perhaps a month ago, she had paid a man to change all the locks. "Good night," he said.

She watched as he walked out to the car. Heavy, dark clouds were moving across the brightness of the moon. He got in, started the engine, looked out to see that she still stood in the light of the open door. There had been times when, leaving his house, he had paused to wave, and she had waited just like that, leaning on the frame, a sad shadow.

He waved now, and she backed off and closed the door.

Driving home, he remembered with an ache that Mary had won her spelling bee. There were people all around him who had solid families; the ground under their feet was shifting slower for them, changes were coming at a speed they could bear, that most of them never even noticed.

ONE INSTANT

HENRY SPENCER STARTED TO LEAD the way down into the basement. He had decided there wasn't any choice but to try something: this nervous man did indeed have it in him to kill, and in fact he was struggling with himself about that, and nothing else. Spencer had this impression and found in himself the curious, empty will to go through with everything—take him downstairs to the safe which could not be opened and try something, anything, to survive. There were things he might pick up and use in the basement.

Mostly, he was stalling for time to think.

"I think we'll use the duct tape again," Ricky said.

Gwendolyn breathed forth a small sound of alarm.

"No," Spencer said. "I don't think so."

"You don't have a choice, man."

"Oh, but I do have a choice. I won't tell you the combination of the safe if you tape us up again."

"Nor will I," Gwendolyn said.

Ricky paused to think. It had become quite clear to Spencer how vacant this man was. Ricky put the gun hand up to the side of his head and used the square end of the pistol to scratch there. He looked like a suicide whose attitude about the act he was about to commit was almost whimsical. Then he glared at Spencer. "You don't have the upper hand here, you know."

"Come on," Henry Spencer told him. "Don't you think I want you out of here? I'll give you what's in the goddam safe and you'll have it. It'll be all yours. I don't want it. I don't have the slightest use for it."

"I could make you give me the combination," Ricky said.

"I'm gonna open the safe for you," Spencer said. "What if the phone rings?" He was reaching, he knew. But the other seemed to have been affected by the thought.

"I have to answer the phone," Gwendolyn said.

Ricky scratched the same place on the side of his head, this time with the blunt handle end of the pistol. "Okay. We'll all go down."

"Let my wife stay up here," Spencer said.

The other seemed suspicious.

"The phone."

"Naw. She comes too," Ricky said, showing anger. "What do you think I am, man? You think I'm stupid or something? I'm not stupid."

"I didn't mean anything by it."

Ricky aimed the gun. "You go first."

Spencer opened the door to the basement and flicked the lights on. He started down.

"Slow," Ricky said.

He paused. Gwendolyn was directly behind him. If he faltered or took a false step, the other might get a round off, and Gwendolyn would be shot. He went very slowly to the last step. The safe was in the middle of the basement floor, surrounded by hanging laundry and dress forms and boxes. There was a counter on the left side crowded with tools and open parts of a computer Spencer had been working to upgrade. The shell was standing open, and two hard drives had been set on either side of it. On the wall above this, there were screwdrivers, wrenches, a hammer, pliers, a wood saw. On the other side of the room, the washer and dryer seemed hunched into the dim corners, and clothes baskets sat on top of them. There was a jar of nails and screws atop the safe, along with a pair of work gloves, a tape measure, part of a radio alarm clock Spencer had planned to fix, and a bottle of bleach.

Ricky came to the last step and pointed the pistol at Spencer. He indicated the safe. "That? That's not big enough."

"It's where I put what he sent me," Henry Spencer said. There was nothing else to say. He knelt down and turned the knob, which was stiff from the decades of disuse. It squeaked. The inner workings were rusted. He turned it halfway, then stopped and turned it back. It resisted.

"It's too small," Ricky said, with dismay.

Spencer could hear Gwendolyn breathing, standing near. Absurdly, he recalled talking with friends about this odd thing, this safe built into the floor of his basement that he could not use. It had been a conversation piece, a joke.

"Come on," Ricky said. "I'm telling you they couldn't be in that little thing."

"It's temperamental," said Gwendolyn in a trembling voice.

The knob had caught. Spencer couldn't get it to move either way. He was aware of the younger man behind him, at a distance, growing more agitated every second.

"Come *on*, man."

In that instant Gwendolyn moved, a sudden turn, her arm swinging, and a heavy thud was followed by a huge shattering fall. Spencer got painfully to his feet—the arthritis in his lower back and knees—and saw Ricky lying on the stairs, scrabbling to get up them, his gun hand back, the Glock firing now as if by reflex. Something hit Spencer in the scalp, at his hairline, tearing past him, knocking him back into the safe and onto the floor. The gun kept going off, over the sound of the other man still struggling with the stairs. Spencer made an attempt to sit up and couldn't. The area of light available to him closed down, grew smaller from the periphery inward, to a small pinpoint, and then that, too, began to diminish. He couldn't see Gwendolyn. He looked for her in the spreading dark. He tried to cry out, to make any kind of noise, and realized that sound, too, had thinned out, a narrow band of high-pitched shattering, something squalling, far away, in a distance. It faded, was lost. Then quite abruptly everything went away. He was in a stillness, under water, in a great, sunless sea. Floating. The borders of his being changed, then changed again. He was a boy, staring out a window at snow. 1932. People were crowding away out of a lighted room, and snow was at the windows, thick, windblown. Someone moved him, or moved at the perimeter of this silence, this blindness that was himself.

And he opened his eyes.

Gwendolyn was holding him, had lifted him onto her lap, whimpering, pressing a folded towel against his forehead.

"Honey?" he heard himself say.

"It cut you," she said. "I threw the jar of nails into him and he ran. He shot twice and dropped the gun and it went off again. Oh, Henry, you're all right." She ran the towel over the burning spot on his scalp.

"I'm shot," Spencer told her.

"It cut you," his wife cried. "It's a cut. It went into the wall behind you, Henry. Oh, Henry, are you all right? Can you see me? You were knocked out. Tell me you're all right."

He lost consciousness again. The edges blurred, and came back. "Where—" he said. "Where's the gun?"

She had it in a fold of her skirt. She brought it out and showed it to him. Then she began to sob. Her eyes were hysterical, brighter than he could believe. "I hit him with the jar of nails. It bounced off his chest and he panicked. He's sitting up in the living room crying like a little boy."

Spencer started to get up, but couldn't. She lifted, and he used the corner of the iron safe for support.

"I'm afraid to call the police," she said. "I'm afraid what might happen in Virginia." They tottered to the stairs, and he took the gun from her.

In the living room, Ricky sat on the sofa, elbows resting on knees, hands to his face.

"I'm not a murderer," he muttered. "I never killed anybody. I'm three thousand miles away. They can't say I had anything to do with it."

Spencer took a step toward him, but felt abruptly light-headed and hung back. His wife leaned into him, holding him up. He made his way to the chair opposite and leaned on the back of it, still standing.

Ricky looked at him. "Oh, Jesus—call an ambulance."

Spencer's shirt was covered with blood. Gwendolyn still held a piece of cloth to his head, standing next to him, staring at him with that brilliant-eyed hysteria. Spencer aimed the gun at the abject figure on the couch.

"Don't shoot," Ricky said pitifully. It was clear that the fight and the menace were gone out of him. When he spoke again, it was with exhaustion. "It's over, man."

Spencer relaxed his aim. "How many of you are there," he said without inflection.

"Four."

"Here?"

"I'm the only one here. The other three are in Virginia. Look, I didn't hurt anything. I'm not a murderer. I thought the gun went off and killed you."

Spencer was silent. He had begun to feel as though he might pass out. "I need to help my daughter and her son live," he said.

Gwendolyn sat down on the piano bench, the bloody cloth in her lap, and set her frightened gaze on the young man. "Will you please help us?"

THIRST

Shaw walked into his apartment and felt for the first time as though he might cave in. All the nerves of his mind were jumping. He wanted a drink. The room was a mess—clothes strewn on every surface, newspapers, books and magazines piling up, dishes stacked in the small sink. He thought of Edward Bishop, living alone in that big old farmhouse. Bishop going through the last day of his life, putting music on, perhaps fussing in the kitchen or tidying up—being the only sound in his house—or looking at his deck of pornographic playing cards, the private little peccadillo of a lonely middle-aged man.

Shaw believed that he himself probably deserved to be alone. But these were thoughts that made for sleeplessness, or worse.

On his answering machine was a message, forwarded to him from the dispatcher at work, from Susan Jones requesting an exclusive interview with him in the morning, before he made his standard report to the gathered media about the latest development in the case: they had all got wind of the young man who tried to claim responsibility for the murder. Susan Jones wanted to know if Shaw could arrange for her to photograph Greg Cullen, or perhaps even speak to him. Would Cullen be indicted? She had it, on good authority, that Cullen knew who else was involved and had given names. In any case, she hoped Shaw would call her in the morning. There was also a rather terse communication from Mr. Lombard. Had it been the perpetrator of the Bishop murder who slaughtered his cattle? And while Mr. Lombard realized the relative insignificance of his cattle when put next to a murder, would there be any compensation for him if and when the guilty parties were brought in? He wished for better and more frequent information from the police about the progress of things.

Shaw turned the machine off and sat at the kitchen table drinking a big glass of ice water. He put the glass in the sink and began putting things away. But he lacked the will for it now. He dialed Eloise's number, and she answered sleepily. "I'm sorry, I guess it's pretty late," he said.

"Not really," she said. "You know me. I never go to bed early."

He could think of nothing whatever to say. He was alone and didn't want to be, and there wasn't an answer for it.

"Dad went out somewhere. God, I don't think he's back yet."

"Where'd he go?"

"I don't know."

"Isn't it a little late, and cold?"

"What time is it?"

"It's almost eleven."

She said nothing for a moment. "Aw, Jesus, Phil."

"You want me to come over there?" Shaw asked.

She was silent.

"Well?"

"He walks down to the lake and sits and watches the moon. It's so cold out. He did this last night and came back and couldn't understand why I was upset."

"I'll be up there in a while," he told her.

In the cabinet over the small sink was a bottle of blue curaçao that he had once used to make martinis back in the days when he and Carol were both drinking in the evenings, after Mary was in bed.

He wanted a drink very badly.

He went to the cabinet and brought out the bottle of curaçao and poured a little into a shot glass. He sat at the kitchen table and stared into its ocean-colored depths, turning the glass. Eleven years since the boy's death. Eleven years and nine and a half hours.

He brought the glass to his lips, and the odor searched up through his nasal passages. It made him weak. He set the drink down and put his hands flat on either side of the glass. The blue martinis, a tablespoon of curaçao with equal parts vodka and gin, had been Carol's special drink, at first. He had drunk mostly whiskeys—Irish, Scotch, and bourbon. The occasional Canadian, for its flavor of rye. He had been one of those drinkers who liked the taste of the various kinds of liquor. He had not had much taste for vodka or gin. Except putting them together with the curaçao. Only toward the end, when it had ceased to matter what he took—when he was seeking, always, and as quickly as possible, the effect.

As in the present circumstance.

He took hold of the glass again, then put it down without taking his hand from it. He waited. How long had it been since he had drunk anything? Two years, two months, three days, two hours. No. He went to the sink, poured it down the drain, closed the bottle, and put it back in the cabinet. Blue curaçao, no. He would not fall off the wagon with something Carol might use.

He went out into the cold. The night was clouded over. The faintest glow of the moon was visible in a thinness of cloud, almost directly above the line of trees bordering the apartment house. He drove into town to the county mental health clinic. As he crossed the asphalt lot, he had an image of himself asking someone, anyone in there, for help. He showed his badge to the young man sitting behind the desk and requested to see Greg Cullen. The young man had unhealthy-looking skin and long, stringy hair. "Visiting hours were over at nine o'clock, sir."

Shaw showed his badge. "Would he be asleep?"

"I don't think he is, no."

"Well?"

The other seemed doubtful.

"You want to call the commonwealth attorney? This is not a visit, as in family calls, you see. If he's awake, I need to talk to him."

"All right."

Greg Cullen was sitting on the bottom bunk in a small room with cinder-block walls and aluminum-framed windows. The top bunk was bare mattress. There were eyeglasses, a small stack of paper cups, and a plastic pitcher of water on the nightstand. This looked like any hospital room.

Cullen was apparently medicated, sitting vacantly with his hands folded on one thigh watching television—some cartoon sitcom. He was just a kid. Shaw looked into the dull eyes.

"Do you mind having a visitor?" the young attendant said.

Cullen stared. "No," he said. "I don't mind."

The attendant left the room, and Shaw took the empty chair next to the bed. He said nothing for a moment.

Cullen watched television. When a commercial came on, he turned to Shaw. His eyes were almost colorless. "Well?" he said.

"I wanted to talk to you about Edward Bishop."

"I killed him," Cullen said.

"Tell me about it."

"Nothing to tell."

"I'd like to hear it anyway."

"The other guy took what I had to say."

"He did—you weren't ever in the house."

Cullen didn't answer this.

"Son?"

"I killed him," Cullen said.

"How?"

The cartoon show had come on again, and he watched it, his face blank, the stare of someone far away.

"Hey, buddy," Shaw said. "Come on, give me something here."

"What do you want?"

"I want the truth."

The other's eyes welled up. "I've been sitting here thinking about it. All day. I've been sitting here going over it in my mind."

Shaw leaned forward. "Going over what?"

"I might as well have killed him."

Shaw stood. "You're the sender. The Virginia Front—all that."

"I never thought anyone would get hurt."

"You did it all alone."

"I'm sorry." Cullen started to weep. "I should be punished. I killed him."

"You never got any closer to him than his mailbox," Shaw said.

Cullen looked at him. "I don't know how these others—the ones who called—" He halted, sniffling. "I don't know."

"Who are they?"

"I don't *know*," Cullen said. "That's the thing. It was just me. I was making the letters and going around putting them in the mailboxes. I didn't tell anybody else. I know Mrs. Michaelson at the school, and I heard some of the teachers talking about her friend. I had been sending all the others—the other letters, and she—she was such an ice queen with me. That was all. I just wanted to scare them. I don't know who these others are—but I started it all. I'm the one that got it started. I don't even really feel that way—you know, about them. The blacks and the Jews and Catholics. I thought I could just use it to make them notice. It was just to make them notice—"

"What did you want them to notice, son?"

The other sobbed. "Me."

Shaw took a tissue from the box of them on the bedside and handed it to him. Cullen wiped his whole face.

"I'm sorry," he said.

Shaw left him there and went out into the cold. There were bitter, needlelike crystals of ice in the air; the sky was disappearing fast behind a moving continent of thick clouds, a storm coming. On a summer day, you would look for lightning forking out of clouds like that. He got in his car, picked up his radio mike, then put it back. He would wait until he knew more.

On an impulse, he drove to Steel Run, past the Bishop farm, and stopped in the road across from the Michaelson house. There were lights on upstairs and down. He turned the engine off, got out, and stood leaning on the car door, listening. There was no hint of movement. It was possible that she needed to keep all the house lights burning. He wanted to go knock on her door, ask if he could come in and talk. A light in the upstairs went out. He kept watching. Nothing else moved or changed. The wind had lessened, momentarily, and even so the night seemed to be folding into ice. He watched the other windows wink out, one by one.

PART FOUR

RAGE

Travis wanted her to keep away from the windows. She had gone through the rooms, turning the lights on, and he had followed. Irrationally—and she knew this—it seemed to her that she might get through this night if there were lights. But in the car, on the way here, she had remembered his overtures earlier in the day. Everything was in question now—and the fact that he had kept from Reuther what they had found frightened her all the more. Reuther still had Jason. She was beginning to believe that if they could find the chips, Travis would take them and leave her alone to deal with Reuther. Except that Travis's brother was still back there. Perhaps Travis thought that if he could get the chips, he could bargain with Reuther. But why, then, had Reuther trusted him at all?

She had to stop thinking in these paranoiac circles.

Travis called to her from the master bedroom. "Come here."

She stood still. She was in the hallway and had thought he was still behind her.

"Look at this," he said.

She stepped to the doorway and saw that he was standing by the closet door, pushing it into the jamb and letting it come back open. It seemed to bend and then let go, opening slowly as if the slant of the house were pulling it. He flicked the switch on the wall and nothing happened.

"That light in there hasn't worked for years," she told him.

He closed the door again and watched it come open. Then he reached up to the top of the frame and ran his hand along it, toward the top hinge. He brought his hand down. His fingers were black. "You don't do much housework, do you?"

She did not respond.

He stepped into the space just inside the closet and moved the door, running his hands along the inside frame of it. "Lookie lookie, sugar cookie," he said and ripped something, a small sandwich bag–sized strip of adhesive, to which was attached a tag and a key. He held it out to her. "What's this?"

"I don't know."

He held the tag out. "Bryce Mountain Storage."

"When we first moved here, we stored some things there."

"You know what this is?" he said. He came toward her, brandishing it. "This is it. I'll bet anything."

She was silent.

He put the tag and the key in his shirt pocket. "Damn straight," he said. Then he pushed past her, grabbing her by the wrist and pulling her down the stairs into the living room. "You know this is it. He gouged out the damn frame and stuffed it in and taped it right where the hinge attaches."

"I don't know," she said. "And even if it is, we still need the contract. Whatever he signed."

"I got the key," he said. "And the tag, with a number on it."

"You'll still need me. They won't let you near the storage pallet, key or no key. You can't just walk in there and use it. I'm Jack's wife, remember?"

"You knew where they were all along, didn't you?"

"No," she said. "I didn't." She paused. "We used the place years ago to store furniture. We kept it there for a month—I haven't been back there since. It isn't a place that leapt to mind while I worried about my family being murdered by thugs for something I had no knowledge of."

"You should've thought of it in the first minute. You might've saved all of us a whole lot of trouble."

She made no answer to this.

"Yeah," he said. "Well—we've got it. That's the important thing. This is it, lady doll. This is salvation."

Now he sat in the living room, his legs stretched out before him, watching television. There was about him the attitude of a man who believes he has the time to plan his course of action. He had clasped his hands behind his head. His foot agitated, a nervous tic. She sat on the other side of the room, out of the line of the television screen. It was a movie about detectives, and there were car chases. Shouts and gunfire. She had a woozy, sickening sense that this was her life now; this would only change with her death.

"Every one of these cop shows is a fucking cartoon," he said bitterly.

She said, "What happens when we get the chips?"

He said, "Listen."

She waited. The voices went on in the movie. Squealing brakes, more shouts, more shots. "I need to know," she said.

He seemed not to have heard.

"My parents—my son. Me. Tell me."

"Shut up, will you?"

"What will Reuther do?"

"Will you listen?"

She hesitated a moment, then stood. "I'm going into the kitchen."

"Just remember where your boy is."

The little saw blade in her shoe had formed a bad blister. It was hard to walk without limping. In the kitchen, she opened the cabinet and brought out a loaf of bread. She knew she should eat, though she felt no hunger at all. She buttered a slice and tried to chew it, but it wouldn't go down. She washed her mouth out. Her foot was bleeding, she was sure of it now. She bent down and put a finger into her shoe, trying to move the little blade.

"Got a stone in your shoe?" He was in the doorway.

She straightened quickly. "No. An itch."

"You limped."

"No."

"You ain't had a bath today, huh." Behind him, the TV still played. Music, now. Some commercial about stocks and investments.

"If the cartons—the chips—are at this storage place—" she began.

"We take them back to Reuther and Bags."

"Then what?"

"I think me and Bags might have to deal with Reuther."

She waited for him to continue.

"Bags fucked up bad with that business next door. There's no doubt about it. He's crazy as they come and getting worse all the time. And things've changed with Reuther. I've been noticing—I think he's pretty much arrived at the conclusion that since he's here now, he won't need two partners once he knows where to get his hands on the merchandise. Anyway, that's what I'd be thinking."

"He won't—" She stopped. She couldn't say it. The terror went through the marrow of her bones.

"Well," Travis said. "Let's just put it this way. Bags kills stupid. You know? And Reuther—well, Reuther kills smart."

She interrupted him. She couldn't help herself, anger climbing up through the panic-stricken center of her. "And you, Travis. How do *you* kill?"

His expression was passive. He simply took her in. But when he spoke, there was an edge of regret in his voice. "To tell the truth, I'm a little worried about Reuther."

She took a step away from him and felt the blade cutting the skin of her foot. The nerves of her legs shook, forking currents of shock into her hips and on up her spine. She put her hands on the counter.

"Tell me the truth," he said, behind her. "Haven't you come around to liking me just a little bit?"

This pure misreading of her, the unbelievable irrelevance of it, brought her close to a kind of insane hilarity: she almost laughed in his face. "Please," she said. "I'm sick. I'm going to be sick."

"That's what your boy said, and he slithered right out of the house."

"I mean it."

He hadn't moved from where he was, standing there in the entrance of the room. He watched her.

"The one in Seattle—he's—he's—is he with Reuther?" she managed.

"Oh." Travis smiled. "It looks like we're all with Reuther."

"You know what I mean, goddammit."

"Rickerts was an army buddy of mine. And Jack's. Remember? Don't cuss like that."

"Fuck you," she said.

He sighed, but stayed where he was.

"What will he do?" she got out. "Your friend in Seattle."

"He'll do what I say, I think."

She took a step toward him. "Will you tell him to leave my parents alone?"

He had stopped smiling. "Not now, I won't. They're my trump card."

"You already have my cooperation," she said. "I don't care about anything else. I just want my boy safe. My family back. I'll do anything. *Anything.* Do you understand me?"

He said, "Did you just have this thought?"

"Do you understand me?" she said.

He pondered this, staring. Then he nodded slowly. "Yeah," he said. "I do understand. But—well. There's still Reuther to consider."

"Oh, come *on,*" she said. "For Christ's sake. You know what I'm talking about. Will I have your help?"

After a pause, he said, "This exchange is what I think it is?"

"Have you been listening to me?"

"We're not just talking about the chips?" There was a lubricious leer on his face now.

"You're as dense as your brother," she said through a shiver. She was thinking that she would actually go through with it.

He was looking at her body. "We'll have some fun," he murmured. "Your call."

She turned to the sink, ran the tap, and laved the cold water over her face. He waited in the doorway, with that look of unappeased appetite playing in his features.

When the telephone rang in the hall, she cried out and saw that he had jumped. The two of them moved to the telephone table, and he picked up the handset and gave it to her. She hesitated, said, "Yes?" And she heard the murmur of words rushing at her. "I'm with your parents and they're safe. I gave them the gun. I never wanted anybody to get hurt."

"Who is it?" Travis hissed, trying to get close enough to hear.

She took a step away, turning. "This is Nora Michaelson."

Her mother's voice came from the other end. "Nora?"

"Yes," Nora said.

"It's true, baby."

Travis was trying gingerly, without sound, to pull the receiver from her ear, so he could listen. She gripped it tightly with both hands. "I can't talk right now, officer."

The connection was broken immediately.

She spoke into the dial tone. "I know, but it's late. I don't have anything else to tell you. Good-bye."

Travis took hold of her neck from the back and pulled the handset from her. He put it to his ear. Then he hung it up and took hold of her arm above the elbow. "Who was that?"

"It was that detective," she said. "He wanted to ask me some more questions."

"You think I'm some kind of idiot?" Travis pulled her to him. "You asked me about how *I* killed? I'll tell you. I kill *expedient.* You understand? Now who was that?"

"I just *said* who it was."

"I might just kill you right now," he said.

He was choking her. She felt her legs go, and he was holding her up. Her feet had left the floor. Then she was standing again.

He'd let go.

She gasped. "Oh, God—"

He dragged her along the hallway into the little downstairs bedroom with its clutter of hastily reassembled furniture, its shards of mattress stuffing. She did not try to resist and still it became a struggle; her knees hit the floor hard. The muscles of her upper arm, where he still gripped her, felt as if they might pull away from the bone. He let go. They were just inside the doorway of the room. Then he reached down and took her feet, pulled at the shoes, turned himself around, holding her foot tightly between his legs, and worked on her until he had pulled the shoe off and was holding the blade of the hacksaw, turning to wave it at her in a kind of demented triumph.

"Well," he said. "What's this? Hmm?" He was doing Reuther, imitating the accent, the mannerisms. "What have we here, hmm?"

"I don't care," she said, gasping through the pain. "I don't care anymore. I don't care. If you do anything to me, if you hurt me or let those pigs hurt my boy, I won't help you."

He shouted, "Just tell me who was on the fucking phone!"

"I told you who it was. Why don't you believe me? You want me to make something up? It was my husband, back from the dead. He wanted to apologize for everything."

Travis reached down and put his arm around her neck, holding the little blade to her face just at the chin. "You never called that guy 'officer' today. Why'd you do it this time?"

She couldn't speak until he let go. When he did, she coughed for a few seconds, aware of him standing over her. "When all this is over," she said, "maybe I'll have some ideas about why my behavior was so fucking inconsistent. Jesus *Christ*."

A few seconds later, she said, "I don't give a fuck whether you believe me or not anymore."

He stepped past her, out along the hall. "Give me your parents' number again."

"Why?"

"Just do it."

She did so. He pushed the buttons angrily and waited.

"I won't help you, if you don't help me," she said.

He waited for the connection to go through. He had turned partly away from her, though she understood that if she moved, he would see it out of the corner of his eye.

"I don't care," she said to him.

"Well, we'll just go back and get your little boy and we'll see who doesn't care." He waited. She thought she heard him say "come on" under his breath.

"Please," she said. She had put both hands to the floor, supporting herself. "Can't you just leave me alone. If you leave me alone, and let my son go, I'll help you get what you came for."

He spoke into the line. "Let me speak to Ricky." He waited a second. "This is somebody who wants to speak to Ricky, goddammit." A moment later, he said, "Is everything all right there? What do you mean, what do I mean? I asked if everything is all right there. Oh, well great. I'm glad to hear the fucking rain stopped, Ricky. That's the best news I've heard all day. Just remember it's a murder rap if you fuck it up. Understand me? Keep that the fuck uppermost in your mind."

He slammed the phone down. "Fuck," he said. "Something's fucked. I can feel it."

She got to her feet. The saw blade had cut her—she was bleeding into her sock.

He came quickly to her and grasped her again by the already bruised, sore part of her upper arm. He pulled her into the living room and sat down on the sofa, forcing her to sit next to him. For a minute he flicked through the television channels madly. His action seemed to have no relation to anything. He turned the TV off. "Come on," he said. "We're gonna turn off the lights."

She said, "I don't think so."

He smiled. A cold, fleeting gesture that involved no other part of his countenance—just the parted, thin lips, showing teeth. "You've got opinions now."

"I'm not cooperating anymore until my son—and—until my family is let go. You tell that to Reuther. We'll go to the place, I'll get the chips and give them to you and Reuther, and you'll both disappear for fucking ever. But not until my child and my mother and father are let go."

His smile went away. "I told you, we can't trust Reuther. We can't bring the fucking chips to the lake."

She was quiet.

He stared. He seemed to be trying to gauge what she might have been able to glean from what he had said about a lake. She strove to keep her face as expressionless as possible.

"Shit," he said abruptly. "We can't stay here. I don't like the way this feels. I've got the key. I know where the shit is."

"It's past eleven o'clock," she said.

He took hold of her once more. "We're gonna get these lights turned out." She did not resist. They went upstairs, retracing her path through the house, putting it back in darkness. There was no other sound now except their clumsy movement along the wood floors, her small gasps of pain from the cut sole of her foot and from the bruising of her upper arm, where he still grasped it tightly. She wanted to be still, to catch her breath, but he pulled her along with him. The sense of herself as being controlled, helpless against him, filled her with a tidal anger and loathing. She understood that she would gladly shed his blood, would cheerfully kill him, slowly and with pain. They almost fell on the stairs. He had turned everything off except one lamp in the living room, where he sank down on the sofa, still gripping her arm, and forced her to sit as well. She saw that she had left a trail of blood drops on the carpet.

"I'm bleeding," she said.

"Where's your shoe?"

"I don't know."

He stood. "Shit."

"I'm going to kill you," she told him. "I'll find a way."

He sat down and took her face into his hands. "What'll happen to your little boy?" He let her go, pushed her a little, then sat forward—it was as if something had occurred to him. He had one hand up, a warning for her to keep still.

She breathed a long, blood-weary sigh. "What?"

"Listen," he said.

She heard it now, too. A footfall on the porch. Someone out there. Travis sprung across the room soundlessly, ducking into the hallway. He waved at her with the hand that held the pistol. "Answer it."

She limped to the door and opened it the thinnest sliver, feeling the cold on her face.

"Sorry," Shaw said. "I hope I didn't frighten you."

She felt a surge of nearly uncontrollable frustration and anger. "I'm fine," she muttered.

"May I—come in?"

"What're you doing here, anyway? I told you everything I know."

He waited a moment. "Mrs. Michaelson, are you all right?"

"I'm sick," she said. "Remember?"

"I'm sorry."

"Now, please."

"Will you call me, Mrs. Michaelson, the minute you hear from your son?"

"Yes." She had opened the door a little more, and he shifted, half-turning. She saw that he was shivering. "I'm cold," she said. "Okay?"

"Yes, ma'am. I was in the area and saw your lights. When you started turning them off, I knew you were up, and I did say I'd check in."

"I'm going to bed now," she told him, narrowly managing to keep the tremor of fury out of her voice.

"Well, good night," he said.

She closed the door on him and limped back to the sofa.

Travis remained in the hall, in that pose of wariness, listening. They heard the car pulling away. He put the gun in his belt and walked across the small space to where she sat on the couch. "It's time for bed."

She said nothing.

"Well?"

"Why don't you say what you want me to do," she told him.

"Really? What if I said I liked the offer you made earlier and that I've decided to accept it."

She waited a few seconds. Then: "You can't be serious."

"I wouldn't joke about a thing like that."

"No," she said. "You need me to get into that storage company for you."

"You've been lonely," he said.

"Fuck you."

He slapped her.

She said it again.

And again, he struck. Then he leaned in, all power, coiled to unleash. "You made the offer," he said.

Exhausted, she simply returned his gaze. She had gone over some line in herself, some border beyond hope or care for herself.

"I like the trade," he said. "And I will get your boy back for you."

"No," she said. "You won't."

He leered at her. He had taken the exhaustion in her voice as desire. She knew this somewhere in the pit of herself, the moment that he grabbed her. He pulled so that she was standing. He put his mouth on her neck, gripping her upper arms. She went deeper into the almost catatonic space she had entered, watching it happen. His arm came around her, tightening at her waist, and he put his face on her chest, the other hand pulling at her blouse, tearing it. She had no weight, had been pushed back against the sofa and down. She couldn't get any leverage. He had torn the blouse and was working at her abdomen, slobbering, moving down, pushing her legs apart. She lay back, looked up into the dark, giving way inside, sinking even deeper into the abyss that had opened in her soul. But then, as his hands fumbled with the top of her jeans, the physical reality of it brought her back as if out of a sleep, and she began working toward the surface, a drowning someone swimming toward light. She could calculate now. She put one hand in his hair and caressed, as he moved still lower, tearing at her, and she heard him murmur something, some phrase of his assumed power over her, his knowledge, all the time, that she wanted him. On the coffee table was the small statuette atop its wooden base. A smooth, delicately carved cherub, sitting languidly on a small marble pedestal. The thought occurred to her that it could do no real damage, wasn't heavy enough, but she reached for it anyway, as he pushed in with his tongue, slavering over her, his hands on her thighs. The cherub was too far away. She moved her hips, moaned. "Let me." He pulled back, was undoing his belt buckle. "Don't stop yet," she said to him, shifting her weight, allowing him to move down on her again, and now she took the cherub in her palm, held it up, looking along her body at the crown of his head where he licked and sucked, and with all the strength she could muster she brought it down. It left her hand, and while he dropped to the floor and screamed she frantically sought it out in the weirdly displaced cushions; he was roiling, swinging at her, and she got hold of the statue; it was in her fist as she swung it downward at the white shouting face. She struck. He sat down on the floor, and she got to her knees on the sofa and struck again, across the side of his head. He cursed and rolled over, and she stood, half in, half out of her jeans. She tried to run and fell, and his hand took her wrist. She swung again, flailed at the shape of him, hit bone, and the cherub went flying across the room. He let go. She crawled crying and gasping to the other side of the room and picked up the statue. Scrambling to her feet, she leaned against the wall and pulled her jeans back on. He was still, but she could hear his tattered breath, knew he was fighting back to consciousness. She looked around the room for something else to hit him with, but it was all a blur of shadow-casting objects and angles. He had risen to all fours, his head down; he was bleeding into the carpet. She took a step toward him, and threw the statue.

It hit him in the forehead and he went down again and lay still.

She heard herself, the desperate groaning sound she made, the only sound in the rooms now. She gasped for air, terrified that she might pass out. She made it into the kitchen, opened the utility drawer, rattling the knives and eating utensils there. It was a confusion of metals and plastics and gadgets. She pulled out a pasta fork, a spatula, a corkscrew. She found a paring knife, too small. She threw it and reached in again, stirring everything, and at last she had a butcher knife. Behind her, it was quiet. Nothing seemed to be moving—but she had made a lot of noise in here, and in the interval he could have come to. She held the knife with both hands and started back to the living room. It was dark. This came to her in a white-hot rush. The living room was dark. She got to the entrance of the kitchen and, gripping the handle of the knife, crept to the hallway wall and flattened herself against it. Silence: her breathing, the uncontrollable sobbing. The place where he had lain was empty. She saw the blood-spattered floor there.

Something broke in the bedroom behind her. She ran to the door, feeling the sting of the wound in her foot. For a terrible few seconds she fumbled with the knob. The blood on her hands made it slippery; it wouldn't turn. He was coming. She heard him in the hall, groaning, muttering, and then abruptly he was nowhere, everywhere.

She waited, perfectly still, listening. There was nothing. She started for the stairs, and he leapt out of the darkness of the hall, knocking her to the floor. She had dropped the knife; it went clattering off in the dark. She got up and limped after it, reached the bottom of the stairs before he had her again. He'd got hold of her foot.

"Gonna hurt you now," he said. It came to her in a ragged whisper.

She lay on her side, reaching through the bars of the stair railing for the knife, which was visible, lying on the floor out of reach: her shoulder stopped her. She stretched, screaming. He had hauled himself forward, head drooping, still holding on to her foot. When she looked down at him she couldn't make out his face for the blood. He lay his head on the side of her leg—it hit her like a falling stone—and a cough issued forth from him. His other hand went against the wall for support. Then she saw he was reaching for the gun. It went off once, the flame-end blasting out from his belt, the bullet shattering the window. She kicked at him with her hurt foot, hit something, shrieking, and now he was pulling her away from the stairs. He had got to his feet and was dragging her across the floor. She made one hopeless thrashing try with both hands for the knife and watched it glide away as the stairs receded. But something caught at her side, and she realized, just in time to catch it, that it was the little statuette. Still being dragged across the floor, she had it locked in her fist, and when he let go of her, turning to face her, mouth agape, gasping for air, his face covered in blood, she got up to her knees and struck him in the groin so that he dropped, squalling. His face was before her for another instant, and she struck again, with everything. The statuette went flying from her hand, and she began crawling toward the knife, in the shiny distance, on the floor next to the stairs. She felt her strength leaving her. But she made it to the knife, picked it up, turned herself, and sat against the bottom step.

Travis lay in a heap on the floor.

She tried to stand, but her legs wouldn't work. The substance of things around her had thinned out. The room was in shadow, colors fading into colors, sounds blending into the one sound of her sobbing. She held the knife and heard glass breaking. It seemed to come from a distance. Travis was still. She watched him, then thought of rising, getting the gun from him. But someone else was in the room now, a shadow on the wall, not Travis. She gathered herself, keeping the knife ready.

"Mrs. Michaelson."

She flailed with the knife, screamed.

"Mrs. Michaelson, it's me, Phil Shaw."

By slow, wary stages, she relaxed her grip on the knife, crying, breaking down. He had knelt beside her and put his hand gently but firmly on her wrist.

"It's all right," he said. "It's over."

But the words drifted to her from far away. She was trying to tell him about Jason. She was telling it, everything, but the phrases flew off like thoughts, and the field of her vision was opening out, including too many images, all tilting and circling. Faces, unreal, elongated, curious and intent, watching her trying to speak, trying to shout through the exhaustion and the loss of blood and the shock. From someplace, from her failing consciousness, she hurled one last scream, one last helpless word, then lapsed back into the silent dark.

LOST

Jason skirted the lake in slow stages. At times it was as if he were treading helplessly without moving. He pushed through the dry, tall grass at the edge of the partly frozen water. The light he was moving toward receded before him, and he began not to believe in it anymore. He understood, without words, that he must not lie down. The cold whipped at him, and the greatest urge was to get away from it, out of the encasing sting of it. At one point he fell. He looked along the uneven, grassy line of the ground to where the light seemed to fade. Someone was walking there, along the edge. He saw the thin shadow cross the diminished border of light.

He got to his feet, unable to decide about being quiet or calling out. The night sky reeled; the ground tilted. He dropped to his knees again. The light was lost. Shapes moved in the darkness, prodigious folds of something shifting, and abruptly he recognized the moon, a faint shimmer spreading widely beyond the massive snarls of drifting cloud. He was lying on his back. Something touched his face, a chilly point of sensation, and another, and then another. He sat up, gasping, afraid of sleep. It had begun to snow. The snow came fast, seemed thrown out of the area of sky where the moon had intricately broken through. But then the moon was gone, and there was the steady fall, the silence, no wind stirring. The ground had already begun to whiten.

Jason struggled over onto all fours, then with great effort rose to one knee, straining inside himself, straightening, coming to stand. The snow lay in tufts on the grass; it had already covered the ground. He looked back through the trees, confused, frightened of heading the wrong way. Before him, the water had taken on a deeper blackness, and the light he had been trying to reach shone again, far beyond the swirl of flakes. He took a step toward it, remembering the shadow, holding the knife still, surprised to find it in his hand, crying again, thinking of his mother. He must find a way to get home. He would know what to do when he got there, though he did not know what he should do now. He put his hand down to where the gun had been and realized, to his horror, that it was gone. Carefully, he made an attempt to retrace his steps, looking for it. He was freezing. The cold would kill him before he found the gun or wended his way into the light. The gun was gone. He turned and kept on, keeping the light before him, and then slowly he realized that he wasn't moving, that he was lying on his back again, being buried by the snow, in the utter dark. He tried to raise his head, to find the black circumference of the lake. The lake was small in the distance, but it dissolved, and elongated, and came toward him. It walked up out of the vast, rapidly settling whiteness and loomed above him. Jason held the knife tightly, but he couldn't lift his hand. He thought of Travis.

A voice spoke. "Hey."

He tried to move. The tall blackness of the lake bent down and became the face of a man.

"What're you doing here?"

"Help," Jason said, or thought he said. "Don't hurt me."

"Hurt you?"

He opened his eyes wide into the heavy turmoil of snow, and the figure before him came close. The face of someone old, a lined, calm face. "Help," Jason said. "Please."

"You're lost, too," the face said.

"Lost?"

"I've been walking around here for a couple hours, feels like."

The boy believed now that he was dreaming.

The other seemed to sniffle, then ran his forearm across his nose. "You hurt?"

"Yes."

"Where's your coat?"

"I left it," Jason said.

"Well, here." The man reached in and lifted him, opened his heavy coat and wrapped him in it. "That better?"

The boy began to cry again. In his mind he had begun to tell it all, he was saying it all out, everything. But the other did nothing, and Jason searched for the sound of his own voice. Nothing would come.

"Cold," said the old man from somewhere above him.

Jason shivered and wanted to nestle into the warmth. The urge to sleep came back, almost too strong to resist.

"I don't think I can carry you." The voice broke in on him.

"I can walk," Jason said, or tried to say.

"You know where you're going?"

Then he *had* managed to speak. He tried again: "No."

"That makes two of us."

He put his face down in the fold of the coat and breathed his own warmth back.

"I knew a couple of hours ago," the other said. "I think. Just can't—can't seem to decide which way's best. You know? That ever happen to you?"

"No."

"Guess not."

"Someone tried to hurt me." Jason stumbled over this. The urgency of getting to his mother before the night ended caused him to push away and try to stand.

"You got an idea?" the old man said.

The boy held on to him. His ankle felt broken. The cuts on his hand and lower leg had frozen and were tingling. A numbness was leaking into his bones, and it filled him with dread. "Help me," he said. "Please."

"Hey, you cut yourself?"

"Help me," Jason said. He had got to his feet.

"I'll try," said the old man, reaching to put the coat around him again. "I don't really know where . . ." The two of them stood there in the wind-driven snow.

MIDNIGHT

Ɪᴛ ʟᴏᴏᴋᴇᴅ, Sʜᴀᴡ ᴛʜᴏᴜɢʜᴛ, ʟɪᴋᴇ one of those squalls that sometimes broke over the hills from the north, a lightning shower of snow that could leave four inches of wet, heavy flakes in less then twenty minutes. Twice in his life he had actually seen lightning and heard thunder in such storms. Now he drove through it, heading up into the foothills of the Shenandoah, to Darkness Falls. The snow would be worse at altitude. He kept a slow, steady pace. His was the only car, the only light. He put the roof lights on, anyway. The road was quickly disappearing in the whiteness.

He had helped put Nora Michaelson into the ambulance and had got from her, in her murmured hysterical speech, something about her son and the lake. She said it over and over, in a kind of whispered scream, like the sound people make while tossing in a nightmare. Well, and this was all of that, wasn't it?

The man on the floor of her house had suffered serious head trauma and had been taken away in another wagon. There were gunpowder burns on his hip and lower back, where the unregistered pistol he had been carrying in the belt of his jeans had gone off. Shaw decided that he would drive up to Darkness Falls and see what he could find. The whole picture of these events still eluded him—but he was certain that Ed Bishop's murder was at the heart of it.

He decided to stop in on Eloise, remembering that she had been worried about the old man. If he wasn't home now, he could be in real trouble in such a storm.

Eloise had the floodlights on. Her shadow was in the window of the front door, and before he got out of the car she had come along the walk, bundled in her coat, arms clasped tightly about herself. "He isn't back yet, Phil."

He looked into the flying storm.

"I'm afraid he's fallen into the lake."

Shaw turned his spotlight toward where the ground slowly descended to the lake edge. He crossed that space, carrying his flashlight. The snow was already ankle deep. Eloise walked with him, calling her father by name. "Aaron? Aaron? Can you hear me?" There were tall trees around much of the circumference of the water. Here the grass grew tall and whiplike, standing up out of the collected snow. They moved along to the right, searching for footprints. The trees closed the light off from the street, and they had to depend on his flashlight. They found animal tracks. Eloise had taken hold of his arm for support and kept calling the old man's name. The wind rushed at them in blustery gusts from the west, hurling the snow. It came flying at them out of the dark, sparkling in the beam of the flashlight, speeding toward them so thickly they couldn't see more than a few feet.

"Daddy!" Eloise called.

They kept going, until the grass and weeds turned to briars, where no one could walk. Then they turned and retraced their path back to the wide area of illumination and blindness under the spotlight. The animal tracks were gone.

They crossed to the other curving away of the lake edge and into the trees there. The snow blasted at them. They were making their way around toward the cleared area of the beach. The ground dipped and rose, and the wind whipped at them. The flashlight went out. Shaw stopped and slapped it against his thigh.

Eloise called out, forging ahead of him in the fiercely onrushing whiteness. There was thunder. It cracked right overhead, an explosion. She cried out, "Jesus God." Shaw kept following, the flashlight blinking. He hit it against the palm of his hand, and it came back on, showing a moving wall of glittering turbulence. He pushed through, trained the beam on the ground before him. Eloise's tracks had nearly filled already. He had lost her. "Eloise," he said.

Her voice came from a surprising distance. "Over here."

He went toward it. The ground tripped him up, and he stumbled forward. One foot stepped down in water, and he realized he had come close to the lake's edge. The cold of it felt like a burn through the skin of his foot. He worked his way back upward, the flashlight blinking again.

"Hurry," Eloise said.

She was nearer. He pointed the light. The flakes were showering down too thickly; they gave the light back. He felt blind, helpless, pitching toward the sound of her voice. The light flickered out again, and he had almost fallen over her, where she knelt in the lee of a big fir tree. Before her was the old man, also kneeling, and between them, the shape of something else.

"What is it?" Shaw said, trying to get the light to work.

"Dad," Eloise was saying to the old man. "Can you walk? What happened here?"

"Hello," the old man said. "My little friend here is hurt."

"It's a boy," Eloise said. "My God, Philip."

He fell to his knees, and the flashlight flickered.

"We just met up out here," Aaron said.

"I don't think he's breathing," said Eloise. "He's not breathing, Phil." She pulled at the shape there between her father and herself. Shaw put his hands on the solid form. He felt bone, a stillness. Eloise commenced working at the snow-frozen clothing.

"He's asleep," the old man said. Evidently, he did not understand what had happened.

Shaw worked on the boy. Put his two hands down on the chest.

Eloise had helped her father to stand, and they loomed over him. They were taking the air away.

"Get out of here," Shaw heard himself say through his striving. "Get back, leave us alone."

They went off into the screen of flakes.

The snow was coming horizontally now, in a hoarsely moaning wind. The boy was still, eyes open, mouth partially filled with the snow. Shaw cleared the mouth and began working to get the lungs to accept air. The flashlight lay at his side, still flickering, and he cursed low, pushing gently on the boy's chest. The eyes, in that eerie light, seemed to move, but when he paused, there was nothing. He began working again, brushing the snow away from the neck.

"Come on, son," he heard himself say. "Come on, boy."

The eyes were clouding with snow.

"Oh, Christ," Shaw said. He stopped, looked up into the flying tumult of the sky, and screamed, "God!"

His hands were down in the snow, on either side of the boy's head. He lifted them out of the cold, lay them against the chest, and pushed once more, and again, and still again, then put his mouth on the boy's cold mouth and blew. The light went out, was gone. He was being buried in the storm, wind sweeping at him as if it had been dragged all the way here across arctic canyons. He would stay, even if it covered him. He would freeze here in an attitude of furious refusal to give in. He kept working. Somewhere nearby, he heard Eloise and her father. They might as well have been static on a radio. Their voices went away, and he brought the boy up into his arms.

"Please," he said. "Come on, son. Please." He lay the body down and pushed on the chest again, breathed into the mouth, stopped.

And heard the smallest high-pitched sound of supplication.

The boy was only a dark outline, fading before him. But there had been the sound. He put his ear down to the mouth and felt the softest current of motion that was not the wind. It was not the wind, and another sound came—a cough. The boy coughed deeply and began to cry. Then he kicked, trying to scramble to his feet. In one hand, Shaw saw a knife. He had to pry it from the fingers.

"It's okay, son," he said.

The boy struggled, and Shaw held him, put his hands under the wiry body and lifted, standing in the blast of the storm. Eloise and her father were a few yards away. He could hear them. "It's okay," he called out. "He's all right."

He held the vital, breathing, moving body in his arms and made his way toward the brightness, toward those other voices from the world of his old heartbreak, and he held tight, feeling against the side of his face the bony cheek, the wet hair, of this other boy—this saved, solid boy in his arms—and he said softly, so as not to frighten him further, that everything was all right now. It was going to be fine. Fine.

The boy held on to his neck, breathing better now, crying and trying to speak.

At the house, Eloise took her father into the bathroom and got the bathwater running. Shaw carried the boy into her bedroom and wrapped him in blankets from her bed. There were cuts on his hand and on his ankle. He was bruised and dehydrated and still only half-conscious. Shaw said, "Son, is your name Michaelson?"

There wasn't any response.

"You don't have to talk," Shaw told him. He touched the side of the face, put his hand gingerly down on the chest.

"Dad?"

Shaw said, gently, "It's okay, son."

Eloise was working with the old man in the bathroom, and their voices, echoing in the sound of rushing water, seemed to frighten the boy further. He was attempting to talk. Shaw made efforts to calm him, to give him time to realize that he was safe at last, but it was apparent that something kept forcing a pressure to speak. His eyes were wild. He said something about his mother.

"Yes," Shaw said. "She's safe."

"Travis," the boy got out.

"Travis. Well, he's got head trauma. He's in the hospital. Your mom is fine."

The boy shook his head, lay back on the pillow, and tears dropped from the corners of his eyes down the sides of his face.

Shaw said, "It's over, son."

"My mother," the boy sobbed. "He's still got her."

"We took take care of him," Shaw said. "No, *she* took care of him. She's safe."

The boy slipped into unconsciousness again. He had both hands over Shaw's hand where it lay on his chest.

THE ATTIC

IN EARLY SUMMER, ED BISHOP'S sister came to sell his house and everything in it—all that she herself did not want. She kept his books and a few personal things. She was an officious, rather imposing woman, Nora thought. There was something a bit standoffish about her. Even so, because the two women worked together dispensing with the contents of the house, a friendship began to form. Jason noticed it and remarked on it one evening as he and his grandfather sat side by side on the porch of the Michaelson house, which Nora had decided to keep, no matter what. They would spend a few weeks in Seattle, with her parents, but this house, which she had fought for, was going to be her house. She had settled this with her father while she was still in the hospital suffering from varieties of exhaustion and shock.

There had been emotional troubles, too.

One did not walk away from these things. Jason was on medicine to help him sleep. His mother had been in and out of the hospital and still didn't have much of an appetite.

Her parents had come from Seattle. Nora's mother had spent at least some time nursing all of them, though Henry Spencer was an old military man, and when the wound to his scalp healed, he wanted no more talk about any of it. Whatever he was feeling he kept mostly to himself; he expected the others to follow suit. Jason had decided that he disliked him, a little, without really feeling much animosity or bitterness. It was an aversion, really, a wish to be away from him when they were together.

As they were together now.

It was getting near twilight, a violet haze in the sky. The old man had a newspaper folded on his lap and was smoking a cigar. Jason breathed in the strong smell of it. Out on the lawn, his mother and grandmother were weeding the garden they'd planted. Ed Bishop's sister had pulled into the driveway in her Chrysler, having used the pretext of a question about the sale of the unused farm equipment to come over. Jason watched the women. Each day he lived by the little passing minutes, each minute, dreading nightfall and the silence of the sleeping house. Dark. The borders of the light that always burned now in his room.

"You okay?" the old man asked him.

This was the question they all asked of one another, many times, every day. "I'm fine," Jason told him.

The women laughed at something. Their soft voices came to the boy on the humid evening air.

They could laugh. It occurred to the boy that something resilient in them made it possible to laugh, made it so that they were not cringing in the corner of a wall somewhere, waiting. He understood this without words, and in the next moment he tried, unsuccessfully, to find some way to express it to himself.

The worst thing was the knowledge of the attic, that space above him in the house. It had come to mean all the bad things he had been through—and when he could sleep he was often awakened by an image of Travis Buford Lawrence Baker standing out in the brown grass staring up at him. Sometimes he dreamed that he walked up there and, against every nerve in his mind—forced by the illogical pattern of the dream—peered out to see Travis standing below, one hand visored over his eyes, staring. It tore him out of sleep each time with a thudding of his heart. And there was no returning to sleep afterward.

Travis had survived his beating and was awaiting trial. He was confined to a wheelchair. Of his three partners, two were dead, and another was in custody in the state of Washington.

Jason lay in bed at night reciting all this to himself. It helped a little, but only a little.

Sometimes, the county investigator, Shaw, came by. There was something oddly tentative about him with Jason, a sadness the boy sensed and once more failed to find some way to express for himself.

Shaw had brought some paperwork for the boy's mother to fill out, and there were matters of the court that he had handled. He made gentle, self-deprecating jokes about his first-rate police work, telling Henry Spencer that he had stumbled through the whole affair from beginning to end. Jason's grandfather spoke of being grateful for the outcome. Jason sought excuses to make Shaw stay, fantasizing that the policeman and his mother might discover an affection for each other. Nothing had come of it, though. Shaw had visited once, bringing his daughter along—the daughter was visiting from Richmond—but he'd had his friend Eloise with him.

They seemed happy.

Now the boy's grandfather put out the cigar, removed the ash, and stored the cigar in his shirt pocket. "What're you thinking about?" he asked.

"Nothing," Jason told him.

"You know what I'm thinking?"

The boy waited.

"I'm thinking about moving back here for good."

"Where would you stay?" Jason asked him, hoping to hear that he was thinking of moving into the house.

The old man took this the wrong way. "Don't worry," he said with a smile. "We'll find a place of our own."

"No," Jason said.

There was another laugh from the lawn, and now all three women crossed the expanse of grass to the porch.

"Eugenia has asked us to dinner," Nora said.

"Why, that'd be just lovely," said the old man.

"Jason?"

"I'm not hungry."

"Sure you are, honey. You just don't know it yet."

"I better get back and start," Eugenia said. "I'm still not used to that kitchen."

"Would you like some help?" Jason's grandmother asked.

"I'll be fine." Edward Bishop's sister walked off and got in her car. They watched her pull out and head down to the other house.

"She's sweet," Gwendolyn Spencer said. "But she's so held-in. I'm surprised she invited us."

Nora said, "Her brother was my friend. A splendid friend. And he paid for that generosity with his life." Her eyes welled up.

"I'm sorry, honey," Jason's grandmother said. "I didn't mean anything."

The old man brought the cigar out of his pocket and lighted it. "Guess I will finish this," he said.

"Henry," said his wife. She reached out and touched the small place, a discoloration, where the tear in his skin had been, the bullet that might have killed him. Jason looked out at the trees, where a pair of starlings were sailing and diving at a crow. The world was all violence; even the flat, spun shapes in the sky were taking on the shades of blood. One day in the spring his mother had gone with Shaw and an officer of the court to Bryce Mountain Storage and requested access to pallet 9. In it were several boxes of canceled checks (years' worth of them, the whole history of the failed business, all tightly bound in rubber bands), some deeds and contracts, a few tools, and four cartons containing more than two million dollars' worth of stolen computer chips. These were turned over to the police, and it was in all the newspapers. Jason's mother told him that everyone could plainly see now that the Michaelsons were without anything anyone could possibly want.

Now she stepped forward and put her hand on his cheek.

"I'm thinking of Dad," he said.

"You all right?"

"Yes," he said. "I wish we'd all stop asking that question."

"That's gonna take a while," she said.

For a time, they all watched the colors fade in the sky.

"I told Jason I was thinking of moving back to Virginia," Grandfather Spencer said.

The others simply took this in.

"He seemed a little worried that we'd move in here."

"No I wasn't," Jason said and felt abruptly as though he might have to fight back tears. He stood and went into the house. His mother followed him into the kitchen, where some of the vegetables she had harvested from the garden lay untrimmed—carrots mostly, and a few tomatoes.

"He didn't mean anything by it," she told him.

"It's not that," Jason said. "I'd *like* them to move in here."

She hesitated a moment, then put her hands on his shoulders.

It seemed impossible to imagine that people might go for years without any bad trouble, that he himself might go the rest of his life, as Shaw had told him, without ever seeing another criminal face-to-face. He thought of Travis and of the others and immediately felt weak, terrifyingly susceptible.

"We'll make friends with it," she told him. "Won't we, honey? We'll have to. Other people have managed to get on with things. We can do this, Jason. You and me." Her voice shook. "You'll see."

He put his head against her chest. He was thinking that soon, tonight if he could manage it, he would go up into the attic and straight to that window and stare full in the frame of it, looking out at what he could see of the world. He would stand there until the shaking in his bones stopped. He would make himself perform this ritual of exorcism, which he had no words for, but nevertheless understood. He would find some way to outlive this particular fear. For a second he believed this, but then it all dissolved in doubt—a hard, clutching feeling at the pit of his stomach.

LIGHT

Nora woke to the sound of him tossing in the other room, mumbling his distress, having the nightmare again. Living it all over again. She had experienced a bad few minutes in the night herself. She willed herself to a sitting position on the bed, heard him wake, gasping. She waited a moment. Perhaps he would go back to sleep, or call her. She didn't want to appear to be too watchful of him. A moment later, he got out of his bed and made his way to the hall. She put her robe on, being quiet. She saw him go by her door, and on, and she went there to look out. In another room, Henry was snoring.

Henry had decided, last evening, that Seattle no longer quite suited him. Her parents were coming home.

She had dreamed last night about Jack. Jack came to her in a blurry glow and asked if she wanted track lighting in the basement, whenever he got around to fixing it up as it should be. An absurd dream, and she had come awake with a start and lay trembling for an hour, while all the horrors of the winter played back. She wept, silently, and resisted the urge to get up and check the windows and doors. Shaw had told her that over time she would learn to believe in her own safety again; it was a normal reaction, this fear. It felt per-

manent, the rest of her life. For a little while, she had been depen-
dent on him, but she came to understand it as a function of her
recovery. He was a good man whose life turned on regret, and she
could offer him friendship—as his own young daughter and Eloise
could offer him love. Nora had said as much to him during his last
visit. They had been talking quietly about Jason and the aftershocks
of sleeplessness and lethargy, the doctors, the medicines, and Shaw
said to her, "I have to tell you, I lost a son not much younger than
Jason eleven years ago." He said this in an even, tight voice, not
looking at her. "Something happened, that I—I should've avoided.
You know?"

"Yes," she said, deciding to let him take this where he wanted to.

"I hope you don't mind my stopping by now and then."

She said, "If I can learn to make friends with my fear, maybe you
can learn to make friends with your regret. Those two girls love
you."

"I'd like to find some other line of work," Shaw said.

Nora smiled at him. "I know exactly how you feel."

Now she padded out into the hall, and here was Jason, with one
hand on the cord that pulled the attic steps down. She hadn't meant
to, but she startled him.

"I couldn't sleep," she said, hoping to deflect him from supposing that she had spied on him. "I was going down to the kitchen to
make some warm milk."

He was silent. His eyes shone.

"Jason?"

"I'm tired," he said.

"Me too."

"It's not fair."

"No," she said. "I know."

"I keep telling myself if I let it get me, they win."

Her heart ached for him, but she kept still. It could do no good
to talk at him now, while he was so bravely learning to express his
own sense of what they had suffered.

"Maybe they win anyway," he said.

Now she had to speak. "No. Travis Baker is in a wheelchair for life. The other two are dead. They'll never see the sun come up again."

"They didn't give a damn about the sun."

"I know."

Tears ran from his eyes, but he made no sound, nor did he take his eyes from her.

"Jason," she said.

He pulled the steps down slowly. The wood protested; the hinge squeaked. She approached him, then stopped. With what was apparently an effort, he took the first step, gazing up into the dark.

She said, "Do you mind if I come, too?"

"If you want to, after I'm up there."

She waited, as he made the climb in stages, a step at a time, hesitating on each one, twice making as if to turn around and come back. At the top, he looked down at her. "I feel sick."

"Can you come down?"

He didn't answer, but went on, and after a moment she followed. She found him crouched by the window overlooking the back field. The window was a pale square in the darkness. Signs of the searching she had done with Travis were still evident—displaced boxes, debris scattered about, insulation hanging from the walls. She would have to put all this back together; she would have to put everything back together. The thought of it sent a wave of lassitude through her. She wended her way through the debris to her son's side and then remained quite still, waiting for him to speak.

"It isn't ever going to go away, is it?"

"No," she said. She would not lie. "I can't believe it will. Not completely."

"We can't ever be like we were before."

"No."

He was quiet, looking out. The silence of the house took on an expectant quality, as though they were both listening for something.

She put her hand on his shoulder.

"What will we do?" he said.

"Love each other as best we can, and go on."

"Then they lose."

"Yes," she said, feeling the tears come.

Presently, he said, "I did it. I came up here and looked out."

"What did you see?" she asked him.

"Nothing. The field."

She knelt and put her arms around him. "Look again, sweetie," she said. "See?" She indicated the faintly rose-colored horizon. "See it, darling?"

"Yes."

"What do you see?"

"Dawn," he said.